Also by Eric Brown

Novels

Xenopath

Necropath

Cosmopath

Kéthani

Helix

New York Dreams

New York Blues

New York Nights

Penumbra

Engineman

Meridian Da

Guardians of the

Novellas

Starship Fa

Starship Summer

Revenge

The Extraordinary Voyage of Jules Verne

Approaching Omega

A Writer's Life

Collections

Threshold Shift

The Fall of Tartarus

Deep Future

Parallax View (with Keith Brooke)

Blue Shifting

The Time-Lapsed Man

As Editor

The Mammoth Book of New Jules Verne Adventures (with Mike Ashley)

First published 2011 by Solaris
an imprint of Rebellion Publishing Ltd,
Riverside House, Osney Mead,
Oxford, OX2 0ES, UK

www.solarisbooks.com

ISBN: 978 1 907519 71 0

10 9 8 7 6 5 4 3 2 1

A CIP catalogue record for this book is available from the British Library.

Designed & typeset by Rebellion Publishing

Printed in the UK

ERIC BROWN

THE KINGS OF ETERNITY

SOLARIS

To
M.E.
for all the hard work

Summer in Kallithéa

CHAPTER ONE

Kallithéa, July, 1999

THAT NIGHT, DANIEL Langham dreamed. He had a nightmare about an alien being that came to Earth through an oval of brilliant blue light to assassinate him and his friends. The beast was reptilian and stood upright on two legs, fast and darting and vicious. It carried a rifle that spat liquid fire and annihilated its victims in seconds. In the nightmare, Langham was running, and getting nowhere, and the alien was bearing down on him.

He came awake in the early hours and sat upright, crying out loud in panic. He was sweating, his heart pounding. He calmed himself and stared around at his familiar bedroom.

He wondered if the dream was a warning for him to be even more vigilant. He climbed quickly from bed and dressed. From beneath his pillow he took the oval, amber mereth and slipped it into the pocket of his trousers, which he had done habitually for the past twenty-five years.

Then he left his villa and hurried along the path through the pine trees.

The moon was out, silvering his way, and the night was absolutely silent. Through the trees he could see the sea, twinkling.

He strode out over the uneven ground until he came to the shape of the villa on the hillside to his left. It was beautiful stone-built building constructed on two levels, with a spectacular view over the sea.

Yesterday, according to Georgiou at the taverna, an English woman had moved into the villa. Langham wondered if it was this that had provoked the nightmare.

He walked up the sloping drive and around to the rear of the building. He came to where he knew the bedroom to be. Eight years ago, when old Helmut had moved into the property, Langham had performed the very same... vetting operation, he had called it then.

Now he paused outside the open bedroom window and slipped the mereth from his pocket. He held it out towards the window, his breathing uneven, ragged, lest the mereth tingle painfully on his palm.

It did not tingle: it thrummed healthily, as if a tiny engine were embedded within its polished amber shape.

The English woman was, then, what she claimed to be.

Feeling light-headed with relief, Langham hurried from the villa and retraced his footsteps home.

For the rest of the night, he slept well.

THE FOLLOWING MORNING, in common with every other morning for the past ten years, Langham sat in the shade of the vine-covered patio and wrote his customary four pages.

It usually took him three hours to complete his quota, from nine until twelve, but today he finished an hour ahead of schedule. The characters had taken over and chatted amongst themselves for the entire scene. All Langham had had to do was listen and take down what they said.

Over the years his writing routine had made him a creature of habit. He would no sooner dream of taking a morning off than he would of jumping into the sea from the rocky headland outside his villa. It helped, of course, that he was a recluse, and never left the island.

The trouble with being a respected writer, and trying to keep a low profile, was that his insistence on shunning the limelight itself became an issue of intense debate in the middle-brow press and the review sections of the Sunday papers. The more privacy he wanted, the less he got.

Perhaps, he mused as he slipped his manuscript book and pen into the drawer of his rickety writing table, it was time to move on again.

He took his sun hat from the hook on the whitewashed wall of his villa and stepped from the patio. Last year his editor, on one of his rare visits, had expressed shock and concern with Langham's habit of leaving his novel in progress in the drawer of the table, where any Tom, Dick or Harry – or even, Langham had corrected him playfully, Spiros, Kostas or Yannis – could get their thieving hands on it. Langham said that he'd left his manuscript books in the same place for ten years, and they had never come to any harm.

"But what would you do if some light-fingered Kostas *did* run off with a work in progress?"

He'd thought about that for a while, and then replied, "Start again, I suppose. After all, I have plenty of time."

He left the villa and walked up the track that climbed the ridge of the headland and led, a mile further on, to the village of Sarakina. Cicadas strummed their incessant, two note thrum, sounding more like some faulty electric appliance than insects. They fell silent as he passed, only to start up again in his wake; like this, he felt himself to be walking in a globe of temporarily reduced sound. It reminded him of the few times he'd ventured into the island's capital, Xanthos; he felt sure that islanders and tourists alike were commenting on his passing among them: "Look, that's the hermit novelist, Daniel Langham. Shh, here he comes!" How paranoid, he thought!

The Ionian sea must be, he thought for perhaps the thousandth time, the most beautiful sight in the world. It was something to do with its unruffled cerulean calm, its dignity in agreeing to make hardly the slightest wave as it came ashore. Its grace was always enhanced by the presence of a boat upon its surface. A fishing boat, drawing a feathered wake, puttered from the harbour far below and headed for the fishing grounds on a lazy curve, and the sight of the vessel riding upon its back gave the sea a sudden dimension of vastness.

He continued walking, passing through pines fragrant with resin, and occasional fig trees, which had dropped their fruit like sticky bombs all along the track.

Ahead was the villa that belonged to the English woman, and outside it, seated upon a wooden packing case outside the gate to the villa, was the woman herself.

He slipped his hand into his trouser pocket and caressed the mereth, as if last night's test had been a dream... The device thrummed, reassuring him.

The woman stood and waved when she saw him. She was perhaps thirty-five, small and broad-hipped, with bobbed black hair and pale face. When he came closer, he saw that her hair was flecked with grey, and that crow's feet wrinkles at the corners of her eyes made her appear older than his first estimation. But she had an attractive face, especially when she smiled.

"Don't tell me," he said, gesturing at the case, "Christos and that useless mule of his dropped it there and you need to get it inside?"

"You obviously know him well," she laughed. "When I came out this morning, here it was. He didn't even tell me."

"He's not being rude. That's how things work on the island. No-one would run away with it."

She gave it a kick with a plimsolled foot. "They wouldn't be able to pick it up!"

"Perhaps between us...?"

"Would you mind? That would be lovely."

It was more awkward than heavy, and one person would have struggled with it. Between them they managed to manoeuvre it through the gate and into a stone building next to the villa. "Just here. That's fantastic."

He straightened up and looked around. "A studio. You paint?"

Gorgeous oils of abundant flower gardens, bright still lifes, and Greek seascapes adorned the walls; other paintings, in various stages of production, sat upon easels. Two big Velux windows in the south-facing sloping roof provided ample light.

"Would you like one?"

He was taken aback. "I couldn't. You must sell them for small fortunes."

"Please. I insist."

"No, really." He indicated the crate. "It was nothing. I wouldn't want you to feel beholden."

She smiled. "Anyway, it's nice to meet you." She held out a hand. "Caroline. Caroline Platt."

"Daniel Langham. We're neighbours. I have the place on the headland." He noticed her hands, then. They were perhaps the most beautiful hands he had ever seen; there was something about the grace and articulation of the fingers, the oval perfection of the nails, that took his breath away. His reaction disturbed him.

She was nodding. "I've seen it. You have a wonderful view."

He was gratified that, if she did know he was Daniel Langham, the novelist, she did not say so.

"At least let me get you a drink, then."

"Actually, I'm late as it is. I hope you don't think me rude."

She was smiling. "Not at all. Drop round any time. Any excuse not to work..."

As he raised his hand in a wave and retreated from the studio, he hoped that her invitation had been nothing more than a courtesy which he could ignore.

He made his way down the winding path towards the village and found himself recalling the beauty of her hands, and something else. Despite her smile and her affable nature, she possessed an air of sadness that he found hard to define. He was troubled that the novelist in him, usually so observant, could not pin down exactly what it was about her that suggested a faint air of melancholy. He wondered, briefly, if she had been recently bereaved, and he was subconsciously picking up on the fact.

He came into the village and sat at his usual table beneath the red and white striped awning of the taverna, and let thoughts of Caroline Platt slip from his mind.

He would spend an hour eating his meal, and later sip Greek coffee and stare out across the harbour. He would concentrate on his latest novel, the chapter he was working on, allowing scenes and characters to drift across the stage of his mind. Most people would call it day-dreaming; Langham insisted that it was work.

He ordered Greek salad and freshly-caught catfish, with a glass of rough local retsina, and ate slowly.

As he ate, another customer seated himself beneath the awning and ordered a meal. Instantly upon seeing the man, Langham felt for the mereth. It thrummed, signalling that he was safe. He was, he realised, a slave of the device... but how could he be otherwise, after the events of '75?

The man was fat and wore a tight, fawn-coloured polyester suit. The man's weight, his entire bearing, was clearly not suited to such temperatures: he had the look of someone enduring a penance. He was reading an English newspaper – the *Daily Mail* – which *was* a penance that Langham did not envy.

The man lowered his paper once and gave him a quick glance, and Langham wondered if he was being stalked by a journalist yet again. But the fat man drank his bottle of Amstel and did not approach and ask for an interview, and Langham relaxed.

He scanned the headlines on the front page of the tourist's paper, and their blaring banality reassured him in his resolution never to read newspapers. That was another aspect of Langham's life that his editor found strange, his repudiation of the modern world: no papers, no TV, not even a radio, still less a computer. "How on Earth do you keep up with things, Daniel?"

His answer was simple. "I don't."

At two he climbed to his feet, entered the taverna to pay Georgiou, and walked back to his villa. The fat man did not follow him, and Georgiou had been primed to say nothing to strangers who asked where the English Writer lived.

At three he began work again, cutting and correcting what he had written that morning. He finished at six. It was, he thought, another day spent satisfactorily.

At nine o'clock that evening he was enjoying a beer on the patio, and watching the sun extinguish itself in the sea, when he heard a noise on the path outside the villa.

He expected the man to come waddling around the corner, perhaps bearing a bottle as a gift. He was about to slip quickly inside and lock the door when he saw that his visitor was not the fat Englishman.

"I hope you don't mind," she said, "but after what you did for me today..."

He was standing before the door, his hand actually stalled in the process of pushing it open. Some instinct told him to continue the movement, step inside and ignore the woman. He was famed on the island for his churlishness; it would be entirely in character.

She had stopped at the foot of the short flight of steps to the patio. She smiled again, and held something out in her left hand. "I know it's rather late, but I saw the patio light and I thought..."

It was the sight of her left hand that did it, its grace and elegance.

"That's perfectly alright. In fact I was just going inside for another beer. If you'd care to join me..." He gestured across the patio to where the ancient, overstuffed sofa was positioned before the view of the sunset.

She picked her way up the steps in her dusty plimsolls and smiled at him again.

He moved into the kitchen, retrieved two bottles of beer from his old fridge, and returned to the patio. Caroline was sitting on the very edge of the sofa, knees together, beautiful hands clasped on her lap.

On the table before the sofa she had placed the package she had been carrying: something rectangular and flat, in gift wrapping.

He sat beside her, maintaining a respectable distance, and poured the beer.

"I began work shortly after you left," she said, "and was hard at it for the next few hours. I don't know if you ever find that. Sometimes your work just carries you away and you lose all track of time."

So she must be aware that he was a writer. He smiled and murmured some affirmative reply. He wondered if she was another journalist, and the whole artist thing was a clever charade to catch him off guard and win him over. The trouble with attempting to maintain one's privacy was not only the danger of paranoia, he thought, but the pitfall of solipsism.

"How long have you been painting?" he asked, watching her left hand as she reached out and picked up the glass. The nail of her little finger was long and oval and breathtakingly perfect, like an opal.

"Oh, ever since I was this high," she said, holding her right hand two feet off the ground. "My mother was an amateur artist and encouraged me. It was always something I did."

"Because you needed to, or because you could do it?"

She regarded him; she had expressive lips, which she screwed now into a crushed rosebud of intense thought. "Good question. I honestly think because I needed to do it. I mean, there were weeks when I couldn't paint or draw – when I was thirteen I fell off my bike and broke my left arm. The next few weeks were absolute torture! Painting... I don't know, it's elemental. It expresses something I think or feel that no other endeavour can quite achieve. Your writing must be the same?"

She took a sip of beer, looking away, and Langham felt something open in the pit of his stomach; he experienced an abyssal disappointment that her visit, her friendliness, was nothing but a pretence for an interview.

He smiled. "I find it hard to talk about my work," he said.

He took heart from the fact that she nodded, seemingly not at all put out by his reply. "Oh, I nearly forgot. This is for you. In thanks. And please don't refuse it – it's just something I did in a spare hour the other day."

She passed him the gift-wrapped package and he opened it on his lap. "This is exciting, like Christmas come early."

He pulled out the painting, perhaps eighteen inches by ten, and held it to the light.

It was a simple still life, a bowl of oranges, but the fruit seemed to glow with radiance, as if throwing back to the viewer all the sunlight the real things had soaked up in the process of growing.

"It's absolutely beautiful," he said, and his reaction was genuine. "It really is. It generates life, vitality. It's hard to believe it's just oils, and not the real thing."

She laughed. "Well, it's acrylic, but I won't split hairs. I'm delighted you like it."

He laughed. "Oils, acrylic... Some art critic I'd make!"

He propped it on the coffee table, against the railings, the better to admire it. Perhaps, he thought, she was not a journalist after all, but a genuine artist with a genuine, friendly interest in her creative neighbour.

"Have you had many exhibitions?" he asked, which he supposed was a diplomatic way of enquiring as to whether she made a living from her art.

"Dozens back home," she said. "A small gallery in London sells my work. I got the big breakthrough about ten years ago. Before then it was always small shows and local galleries in the north. I scraped a living. But once London became interested..."

"You're from... let me guess. The accent..."

"I have an accent?" she laughed.

"Beneath the Queen's English I detect an undercurrent of Yorkshire, am I right? Maybe even Lancashire?" He smiled. "I suppose that covers most of the north of England."

"Right first time. Yorkshire. I was born and lived in Harrogate for twenty years, then moved into a village not far from Leeds when I married."

"What does your husband do?" He wondered, later, if he were fishing.

"Did. He was a landscape gardener. We divorced ten years ago."

"Just when your career took off? You saw the bright lights of London and decided to ditch your poor gardener?"

She picked up on the playfulness in his voice, and laughed. "How dare you! Not at all! In fact, I realised I'd made a mistake. A big mistake. He was domineering and small-minded. A woman's place, etc. It was a miracle I painted at all, what with looking after him and the boys."

"How old are they?"

"Twenty and eighteen, and both at university. Anyway, I ditched my gardener, as you say, and suddenly the work improved. I began to get commissions, and then the London gallery took interest."

"And it's been plain sailing ever since?"

Her smile faltered. "Something like that."

And there it was again, that undercurrent of sadness and melancholy he'd noticed that morning. It was almost a shadow in her eyes, a secret she was harbouring and could not divulge. He told himself that it was the novelist in him that was interested, and no more.

She brightened. "And talking about exhibitions, I have one on the island next week. You will come?"

He never went out on an evening while working on a novel; but now, inexplicably, he found himself nodding. "Yes, why not? I'd like that. But don't expect any insightful critical comment."

"I won't. As long a you have a good time."

A private showing, he thought. People, crowds of people, all murmuring platitudes that failed to say what they were really thinking. A kind of polite gentility that would stick in his craw. He would hate it.

"And what brought you to Greece?" he asked.

"Always loved the place. It's a cliché, I know, but the quality of the light is quite miraculous. There's something about the sunlight around mid-afternoon. It's an ambition of mine to capture it before..."

"Before?"

She smiled. "Before my talents run out, or I become old and grey and blind."

"You've a way to go yet," he said.

"Why, thank you, Mr Langham."

He raised his glass, uneasy with the course of the badinage. He was well out of practice in the art of talking to attractive women.

"What brought you to Kallithéa, Daniel?"

There it was again, the not so subtle shift away from herself as the topic of conversation, to him.

He shrugged. "Hate publicity, the modern world. The West, or rather the trappings of the West. I know this is the West, and becoming increasingly more so, but it's easy to close yourself off from all the commerce and advertisement." It was more than he'd meant to say, and came out in a spurt, but it was no more than he was on record as saying in the past. It was no scoop.

But she didn't pursue the matter, which heartened him. He drained his glass and picked up the painting. "I think I know just the place for this," he said, moving from the sofa.

He stepped into the villa and Caroline followed. She looked around the small lounge, examining the pictures on the walls: pen and ink sketches of Tangier, street scenes, Moorish buildings and local characters.

He crossed to where an old wood-burning stove stood in a recessed hearth. He placed the painting against the raw brickwork. "There? What do you think?"

"Down a little. Perfect. I think it'll look lovely there."

"Certainly brighten up the room."

She was looking at a photograph on the mantelshelf. "Do you mind?" She indicated the picture.

He gestured, and she took the photograph from where it had stood for years. It was black and white, and dusty, and showed three men standing on the steps of a big, old country house. They were wrapped in overcoats and caps, giving the impression that the picture was taken in the middle of winter.

"The man on the right. Your father?"

He took the picture and stared at the three figures. It was a long time since he'd examined the photograph. The man on the right was of medium height, smiling, fair-haired and rather boyish looking.

"My grandfather, Jonathon Langham. Oddly enough, he was a writer, too."

"That's obviously who you inherited it from. You do look very much alike." She glanced at the carriage clock on a nearby bookshelf and exclaimed. "Heavens! Nearly eleven! I didn't realise it was that late."

He saw her out to the patio. "Thank you for the painting. It's wonderful."

She smiled up at him. "Thank you for a lovely evening. You'll have to stop by sometime, and I'll return the favour. Oh, and I'll drop an invite around for the private show next week."

He lifted a hand in farewell and watched her pick her way down the steps of the patio and around the side of the villa.

He returned to the lounge and took the photograph from its place on the mantelshelf. He wondered if it had been last night's dream which had made him so edgy today. Whatever, he should not have kept the photograph in so prominent a position. He was becoming complacent.

He moved to his study. He unlocked the top drawer of his big oak desk and slipped the picture inside. He saw the pile of yellowing, hand-written papers within the drawer, then hesitated before lifting them out.

He carried the manuscript out to the patio, switched on the light and sat down on the sofa. He stared up at the mass of stars above the sea for a long time, his thoughts far away.

Then he began reading.

CHAPTER TWO

London, February, 1935

It never ceases to amaze me how I have managed to accommodate myself to the fantastic series of events which transpired during the freezing winter of 1935, just one year ago as I write this. More amazing still, perhaps, is that I have come to accept the personal, I might even say psychological, changes that the series of events brought about in me. We are adaptable creatures; we quickly learn to accept changing conditions, however unexpected those changes might be.

It was the February of '35, that drear month at the very heart of winter, with the festivities of Christmas and New Year a fading memory and the delights of spring a distant promise. An arctic chill held the country in its grip; London was spared the worst of the inclemency – but not the penetrating, bone-aching cold. It was weather appropriate to my frame of mind.

I was thirty-five – as old as the century – a struggling writer with three published, but unsuccessful, novels behind me. My father, with whom I had a close and cordial relationship, that month informed me that he was ill and would not recover. At the same time, as if this were not enough, I was involved in a love affair which, if the woman or the circumstances had been different, might have brought me some measure of relief, but which did nothing of the kind. It was one of those doomed liaisons between two mismatched souls who have been together longer than is healthy for either party. I was at that self-deluding stage of telling myself that I loved the woman, with the hope that, one day, I might actually, magically, experience that desired state. Carla, for her part, treated our affair with an informal and casual off-handedness which infuriated me, and often caused me severe emotional grief. I should have been stronger much earlier in our relationship, and put an end to it there and then – but the fear of loneliness, and the hope that some day Carla might return my affection, had stayed my hand. The fact was that Carla DeFries was my very first lover, and I was immature and uncertain in the treacherous matters of the heart.

The passing year has done nothing to dull my memory of that fateful month. There occurred, on the very first day of February, three significant incidents. My father issued a summons to visit him; I had a less than satisfactory outing with Carla; and at midnight I received the phone call from the editor Jasper Carnegie which was to change my life for ever.

On the proceeds of an advance from my publisher for my third novel, I had taken a year's lease on a roomy flat in Battersea: it was a short walk from where Carla lived in more fashionable Belgravia, and overlooked the park where I was in the habit of taking an extended morning stroll.

My mornings always began with good intentions: I would rise at seven, breakfast, attend to any post that might have arrived, and then take a turn around the park. I told myself, and friends, that my morning constitutional was a necessary part of the creative process.

That morning, as I tramped through frosted grass towards the stand of ghostly oak which marked the mid-point of my walk, I could not concentrate on the novel I was plotting. Instead my head was full of Carla, as ever. At the weekend we had dined at a restaurant in Belgravia which might have been within the means of a successful actress – which Carla was – but put severe strains on my meagre author's pocket. Fortunately, Carla always insisted on paying her share of the bill.

At one point she had slipped a theatre ticket from her purse and slid it across the table, face down, like a blackjack dealer.

She was appearing in a stage version of James Hilton's novel *Lost Horizons*, due to open that week at the Curzon on

Shaftesbury Avenue. The complementary ticket was for the opening night and she wanted me to attend.

We had argued. I told her that the last thing I wanted to do when I was mid-way through a tricky chapter was to sit through some tawdry adaptation of a bad novel. My selfishness was prompted, I might add, though this is no defence at all, by Carla's behaviour on the last occasion we had met: she had ignored me throughout a dinner party given by mutual friends, and then decided – contrary to what we had agreed – to return to her flat rather than come back to mine.

That morning, as I strolled through the freezing fog, I decided to ring Carla and apologise, tell her that I'd love to go to the play.

Resolve hastening my pace, I hurried back to the flat and put a call through to Carla. To my disappointment, she was out.

I moved to my desk, stared at the page of notes I had scrawled the night before, and tried to inspire myself to write. Minutes later a knock sounded at the door.

My father had an aversion to the telephone; in fact he disliked all things that smacked to him of modernism: he mourned the passing of the Hansom cab, and would take a taxi only with a grudging reluctance born of necessity.

In consequence he never phoned me; he sometimes wrote – how quaint to receive a hand-written note inviting me to dinner – or, if the matter was more urgent, paid a boy sixpence to deliver a message.

I opened the door to the beaming face of a tousle-haired youth, who thrust a manila envelope into my hand and scooted off.

I returned to the fire and read the stilted message in his meticulous copper-plate hand:

My Dear Jonathon, I have a matter of most urgent import to discuss with you. I apologise if this interrupts your work.

If you could join me for lunch at one o'clock, I would be most grateful.

It was signed, with a grandiose flourish – the only excess that he ever exhibited – *Harold.*

I spent the duration of the 'bus journey in contemplation of the 'most urgent matter' which my father wished to discuss with me. A similar summons before Christmas had transpired to be about nothing more than his concern over my parlous financial situation. A long working life spent in the retail trade – he had over the years built up a profitable chain of haberdashery stores in London and the Home Counties – had narrowed his view of what was important in life: fiscal security was to him a requisite attainment, but it was not a God to which I paid any obeisance. On our last meeting, a fortnight before, I had let slip that my last novel was not selling well. No doubt this fact had vexed him sorely, and he now wished to advise me upon matters of investment.

I would weather his well-meant words with a weary smile; he seemed to be under the mistaken impression that I had money to invest. The advance on my third novel might have covered the lease of the flat for a year, but to fund my day to day necessities I was reliant upon finding the occasional odd job in Grubb Street: book and theatre reviews, pseudonymous articles at two guineas a time on subjects as diverse as archery and the breeding habits of the Indian elephant.

I alighted on Kings Road and hurried through the mist to Templeton Mews. My father employed a housekeeper to cook and clean during the week (at weekends he dined at his club), and it was Mrs Johnson who opened the door and showed me into the lounge.

My father was seated in his high backed armchair at the far end of the long room, overlooking the street.

He must have heard my entry, but made no move to get up.

I pulled a chair alongside his and sat down.

He turned his head to regard me. "Jonathon, how's Carla these days? Haven't seen her for months!"

"She's keeping well. Busy as always. She's in a new play in the West End. Opens tonight."

He looked grey, and much older than his sixty-three years. He was a small, thin man, with a refined, aquiline face, steely grey eyes and a moustache at once military and severe. His somewhat martial aspect was a throwback to his beloved Victorian era, as was so much about his character. He was a Tory of the old school, a devoted champion of Baldwin. We had argued politics, briefly and heatedly, in my early twenties, and then steered away from the subject.

Although I found his views anathema, he was a kind and loving father. We had in common a passion of chess, and it was from him that I had gained my love of books: he was a voracious if undiscerning reader – during my teens, shortly after my mother's death, together we had escaped into the worlds created by the likes of Haggard and Buchan, Doyle and Stevenson.

Now we chatted about Carla. I described the play she was rehearsing at this very minute, and promised to get him tickets.

In the early days of my relationship with Carla, when I had been madly in love, my father had taken a dim view of the woman. Perhaps it was the fact that she was both an actress and half-French – and sometimes played up the Gallic side of her nature – that had so bothered him. She was not a lady, and certainly not an English lady.

Paradoxically, when my relationship with Carla was at its stormiest, my father let it be known that he had quite taken to the girl. Carla was an accomplished actress, and her practised display of daughterly devotion had won him over. More than once he had hinted that she would make a good wife.

"And how's the book coming along? Sorry to interrupt the writing, and all that. Time's money, as they say."

I made some dismissive gesture. "I'm between chapters," I lied. "It's progressing."

He brought both hands down on the arms of his chair, a habitual gesture denoting imminent movement. "Peckish? Fancy a spot of lunch? Mrs Johnson's prepared a feast. Let's get to it."

He waved me on ahead, so that I would not see him struggle from his chair. His gnarled fingers curled like broken cheroots around his silver-topped walking stick, but even with its aid he was breathless by the time he had hauled himself to his feet.

He had always had an upright, ramrod posture, but now he was markedly stooped, hunched around his hollowed chest.

In the dining room we occupied the small table by the window and enjoyed a cold ham salad and an excellent claret. My father kept the conversation light and inconsequential, much to my exasperation. More than once I found myself on the verge of asking him why he wished to see me.

He changed the conversation and began discussing my books, and I knew that he was manoeuvring towards the delicate matter of my finances.

"Halfway through your latest, my boy." He pointed across the room, to where my novel, *Summer in Kallithéa*, lay open upon an occasional table.

"Enjoying it immensely, of course. Brilliant evocation of Greece."

I murmured my thanks. He took a genuine pride in the fact that I was a published author: my novels and the anthologies to which I had sold short stories were prominently displayed, and he was forever mentioning me to friends. He often told me that he was anguished – and mystified – as to why I had never succeeded in having a best-seller.

"I'm getting through it rather slowly, of course." He tapped his temple. "The old brain, you know. I find I can read only for an hour before the concentration lapses."

"Have you thought of getting away for a while? Somewhere warm, away from this damnable weather. It'd do you the world of good."

He snorted. "I don't need the sun, Jonathon. I've everything I need here in London. About your books..." He dabbed at his lips with a napkin. "The other day you said you could be doing better. I know you must be worried about that side of things. I just want to reassure you..."

I raised a hand. I had managed to hold body and soul together without going cap in hand to my father: I didn't resent his offers, but it was a matter of pride that I could survive from the proceeds of my pen alone.

"I'm doing quite satisfactorily."

Something in his steely gaze stopped me. "Jonathon–" and he reached across the table and took my hand in a grip surprisingly strong, and cold. "Jonathon, you have no need to bluster. I know how hard it must be. I just want to reassure you that I've made adequate provisions in my will."

"Good God," I laughed. "There's no need to be so morbid."

His gaze held mine, and he said, "Jonathon, there is every need."

He obviously found it hard to tell me; he was a man unused to showing emotions. I could see the battle raging in his eyes. He wanted to tell me, but at the same time wanted neither to hurt me nor elicit my sympathy.

My heart began a steady, laboured beating.

"I have been ill for a number of months, Jonathon. Little things. Lapses of memory, periods of confusion, lack of concentration. Two weeks ago I suffered what I thought at the time was an epileptic fit. Old Harvey examined me, said it was more than likely a minor stroke, but that they'd conduct a few routine tests." He fell silent, something stricken in his grey eyes.

"And?" I asked.

A stroke, I thought. Please let it be no more than a stroke. One could recover from a stoke, with care and attention, regain one's former faculties...

He could not bring himself to look up. His eyes regarded the sugar bowl. "They discovered a tumour," he said, "lodged deep in the temporal lobe, apparently. Been there for some time. Malignant and inoperable."

I heard the words, and swiftly thereafter experienced their physiological effect: I was drenched in a cold sweat, then I felt suddenly hot. I found speech impossible.

"Specialists?" I managed at last.

He shook his head. "Been to three or four of the best, my boy. There's no benefit trying to deny destiny. I've had a good stretch."

I felt, then, a sudden anger. His attempt to mitigate the fact of his illness in banal platitudes made me want to shout out loud.

Our glasses were empty. I managed to steady my shaking hand long enough to pour two generous measures.

I wanted to ask him how long the doctors had given him, and it was as if he discerned the question in my stricken look.

"Harvey said I have about a month or two," he said.

A part of me wanted to reach out and take my father in my arms, but a life-time of emotional reserve between us would not allow me this option. Also, I received the impression that he would be unable to cope with any expression of sympathy, as if pity might make the fact of his imminent demise all the more real.

"Dessert, Jonathon? Mrs Johnson's prepared a heavenly crumble."

He rang the bell before I could protest, and a minute later Mrs Johnson, eyes downcast, delivered the dessert on a tray.

We ate in silence. I had no appetite, but forced down the food nevertheless. The wine helped; we finished the bottle and opened another.

Amazingly, my father managed somehow to steer the conversation back to the banalities of the everyday. He told me of the latest Christie he had read last week, and a film he had seen at the local Odeon.

I forced myself to respond as I normally would, all the while wanting to break through the artifice of our conduct and communicate something of my pain and sympathy.

We finished the last of the wine, and my father consulted his fob watch. “Lord, is that the time? Said I’d meet Donaldson at the club at two.”

“I’ll get my coat,” I murmured.

He saw me to the door, then stopped me with a hand on my arm. “About the play your girl’s in,” he said. “If you could get a couple of tickets, I’d be delighted.”

I smiled. “I’ll do that, “ I said. “I’ll call in to see you tomorrow.”

“Donaldson’s invited me down to Kent for a few days,” my father said. “I’m leaving in the morning, but I’ll drop you a line when I return.”

I was about to embrace him, but he forestalled the gesture by holding out his hand, and I shook it and hurried down the steps and into the street without looking back.

I walked. I have found that, in times of emotional stress, the act of physical exercise works as a catharsis, burning off emotional energy. I strode through the fog-shrouded streets of London, taking little heed of where my steps were propelling me, glad of the anonymity afforded by the crowds of strangers who passed back and forth unseen by my gaze.

The fact was that in one month, perhaps two, my father would be no more. The person whose presence I had taken for granted for so long would be erased from my life. I would be unable to rely on the reassuring fact of his being available: I would miss him in a hundred small, often trivial, ways. More tragic yet – setting aside my own personal loss – was the fact that his consciousness, his one and only experience of this vast and complex world, would soon be no more, would gutter like a spent candle. After his death, life would go on, the sun would rise and fall, and he would no longer be around to witness the miracle of existence.

This thought brought tears to my eyes. I walked through the streets in a blind daze: I realised that I needed to talk, to confide in someone.

Perhaps it was my subconscious that propelled me in the direction of Shaftesbury Avenue, and thence to the stage door of the Curzon.

I pushed through, into a narrow dusty corridor. An assistant stage manager of my acquaintance was passing by. "Jonathon. Looking for Carla? They're going through a final run of the first scene."

"I'll wait here," I said.

"Go through and watch from the wings. They won't mind. This way."

He led me through an obstacle course of pulleys and discarded stage props, flats and enormous wicker baskets. The evocative aroma of grease paint, of dust frying in the footlights, permeated the air.

After the gloom of the backstage, the stage itself was a dazzling, other-worldly vision. I stood in the wings and stared.

The illusory miracle of the theatre casts a spell like no other art-form. Conjured before one's eyes are scenes and visions that mundane reality can rarely match. I stared in wonder at the recreation of a magical Himalayan paradise, the snow-glittering peaks and slopes of Shangri-La, the fuselage of a crashed air-liner, and the incongruous sight of a group of Westerners standing around the wreckage.

Carla was centre stage, exhorting the group not to lose faith. It was Carla, and yet not Carla, the woman I knew: I marvelled, as I did every time I saw her upon the stage, at the new identity she could assume with the help of a little make-up, a change of attire, and consummate acting skill. The sight of her made me wonder, not for the first time, if I truly knew the real Carla DeFries, if the persona she adopted in my company was merely another guise which she assumed to play a part.

Then I saw Alastair Ticehurst, a young man dressed inappropriately in plus-fours. He was kicking his heels in the snow, from time to time contributing a line.

I stepped further back into the wings, wanting neither Carla nor Ticehurst to see me there.

Alastair Ticehurst was a rapidly rising star on the West End theatre circuit, a young, ridiculously handsome Don Juan towards whom I had good reason, I thought, to feel jealous. Two years ago he and Carla had conducted a brief affair, passionately romantic if the newspapers were to be believed. Carla had said very little about him to me – though she had told me more about her other lovers – and I had guessed that she still felt something for her old flame, discarded but evidently not extinguished.

Perhaps it was the emotional state I then found myself in, or the fact that I interpreted Ticehurst's gaze as covetous of Carla. At any rate, I was overcome by the irrational, stomach-churning sickness of jealousy. I turned on my heel and fled from the stage, managing in my haste to trip up twice on the way out.

After the heat of the footlights, the chill of the rapidly descending twilight hit me like a refreshing shower. I all but ran from the side-street, taking in great drafts of cold air. An omnibus drew up to a stop not five yards ahead, and I needed no further invitation. Within fifteen minutes I was home.

I built a fire and brewed a pot of tea. I sat before the blaze, holding the steaming mug in both hands and staring into the flames. My thoughts were confused: they cavorted alternately between the plight of my father, and Carla... By turns I convinced myself that she was conducting an affair with Ticehurst, and then, the very next second, told myself that I was suffering nothing more than a lover's insane paranoia. Whereupon, the image of my father would swim into my mind's eye, and I immediately experienced guilt at the selfishness of my thoughts.

I was hauled from my reverie by the insistent summons of the telephone: I ignored it. I was in no mood to share my feelings with anyone, least of all Carla, should she be ringing in a bid to tempt me to that night's opening performance.

The ringing ceased and I lost all sense of time. I think I dozed, but for how long I had no idea.

I had been listening to the knocking upon the door for at least a minute, without realising quite what it was, before sense returned and I moved myself from the lounge and into the hall.

"Jonathon! What have you been doing? I've been knocking for absolutely ages, and before that I rang!"

She pecked me on the cheek and hurried past. When I followed her into the lounge, she was bending before the fire and toasting her fingers.

"Oh! So cold out there!"

I was constantly amazed at how, once off stage, she reverted to speaking with a pronounced French intonation. I could not deny that I found it attractive.

"I have one hour before I must get back to the Curzon, Jonathon," she said, turning and wiggling her bottom at the flames. "I have come around to see if you would like to come tonight."

She pulled a pained face in anticipation of my refusal. "Oh, Jonathon, please say you will! For me!"

She was tall and slim, with a pale beautiful face and dark hair cut in a page boy style. She wore a tight-fitting red dress, silk stockings, and a tiara in her hair. My heart melted at the very sight of her, fool that I was.

I wanted to tell her about my father, and at the same time did not want to spoil her opening night. She was over-excited from the dress-rehearsal, like a child anticipating Christmas day.

"Do say you'll come, Jonathon!"

I stared at her. "Do you love me, Carla?"

She came to me, her lips forming a hurt *moue*. She lay her head on my chest and said, "You're the only man in my life, Jonathon," which was not quite the answer I was hoping for.

She was thirty, and divorced, and had had a string of lovers over the course of the years, and I often found myself feeling inadequate in the light of her amorous experience, and not a little jealous of her past lovers.

I held her and kissed the top of her head. "Leave the ticket. I'll try to make it. I've had a tiring day."

She looked up through lashes like curled wire. "How is the novel coming along?"

I smiled. "Slowly, as ever. Little by little."

"Little by little." She often repeated my habitual phrases, an affectation I found delightful. It somehow convinced me that she was mine.

"Jonathon, are you alright? You seem distracted."

"I'm still living the novel," I said. "I'm fine."

Thus reassured, she pulled away and resumed her coat. She fished in her purse for the ticket and passed it to me.

"Please do come, for me, *oui*?" She smiled, mischievous. "And later, after the show, come back to my place, yes?"

And, with another swift peck on my cheek, she was gone.

I stood before the fire, contemplating feeding the ticket to the flames. Something stopped me, perhaps her invitation, the promise of her body that night. I thought of my father, and Alastair Ticehurst, and moved to the bedroom to change for the play.

Two hours later, as I approached on the 'bus, the Curzon hove into sight through the gloom like an illuminated cruise liner. Picked out above the entrance of the theatre in a pointillism of glowing bulbs was the title of the play, its author and, I was gratified to see, the name of the leading lady, Carla DeFries, alongside that of the leading actor. I was pleased to find that the name of Alastair Ticehurst was relegated to a poster beside the entrance.

I joined the well-dressed crowd that filed into the foyer, submitted my ticket and slipped into the auditorium. Carla had provided me with a good seat in the centre of the stalls. I scanned the programme, reading the biographical details of the leading lady and marvelling, not for the first time, at the fact of our intimacy.

The lights dimmed and the murmurous audience fell silent; the curtain parted to reveal the pristine Himalayan scene, even more remarkable when viewed head on, without the apparatus of the wings to mar the verisimilitude.

Survivors scrambled from the wreckage of the plane, at the forefront of which was Carla. For the duration, I forgot myself, my father's illness and my stalled novel – even my troubled affair with the beautiful woman who held the audience spell-bound. Like them, I was captivated.

As I watched her upon the stage, playing the part of an English lady with the poise and grace of someone to the manor born, I looked back to the time before our affair. It is a fault of the human psyche that we are forever dissatisfied: before Carla I had been lonely, and craved amorous affairs with beautiful women – but yet my heart did not know the turbulent emotions that love would bring. Now, there were occasions when I hankered after the emotional simplicity of the time before I'd met Carla.

But intimacy with another, I reminded myself, brings a greater understanding of oneself – even if what one discovers is not always pleasant. Surely, I reasoned, self-knowledge is what all of us, especially those of us attempting to make sense of existence through the medium of art or literature, are striving to attain?

So I sat and stared at the story unfolding on the stage before me, my mind often wandering, at times absorbed by the production, at others merely in awe of Carla's presence, only to be brought up short from time to time by the jolting reminder of my father's illness.

I recalled that he had asked me to obtain tickets for the play, and wondered now if that would be such a good idea. In the play, a group of travellers crash-land in the sequestered mountain Kingdom of Shangri-La, and find immortality in this magical realm for the duration that they might remain there: to stray beyond the environs of Shangri-La meant the onset of rapid and irrevocable ageing.

I could hardly subject my father to such a crass reminder of his condition. I determined to seek out another play that might interest him instead.

The story played itself out, the finale predictably romantic and satisfactory. The curtain came down to enthusiastic applause; the cast took five curtain calls.

Released from the visual spell of the production, I became critical. The writing was loose and inaccurate, the characterisation shallow; the play was unbalanced and a trifle absurd... I resolved not to apprise Carla of my opinion, at least not immediately after the show when she would be charged with adrenalin and in need only of praise and support.

As the auditorium emptied, I moved backstage; I made myself known to a member of staff at the door and was duly admitted into a noisy and crowded bar.

I knew the routine. I bought myself a half of stout and stood at the bar, surveying the great and the good of the London theatre scene. I recognised one or two faces; agents and entrepreneurs, but avoided falling into conversation: I disliked the compulsory approbation that permeated the air of a backstage bar in the immediate aftermath of a production. As a reviewer, I often had to lay my critical facilities aside for the interim, until the cold light of the following day permitted me to dip my quill in spleen.

The door from the dressing rooms opened from time to time, and heads turned *en masse* to greet the conquering heroes. When Carla finally emerged, she was met with a flurry of waves and smiles.

She dodged through the gathering in a sinuous series of side-steps, snared here and there by affected kisses and the laying on of hands. Once or twice she saw me, as I waited patiently at the bar, and made a big-eyed face of forbearance – but I could tell that she was revelling in the sycophantic attention.

She reached me at last, by which time I'd ordered her a double gin and tonic. She reached up to kiss me.

"Jonathon, you came! Wasn't it wonderful? Five curtain calls! Five!"

"You were marvellous." Over her head, I scanned the gathering for any sign of Alastair Ticehurst.

"What did you think of the first scene in the second act? That line, 'Where all the birds fly to at night.' Isn't it just too obvious, darling? I wanted to change it, but the director wouldn't hear of it. I mean, he's such a dear most of the time, but he does dig his heels in occasionally. I should introduce you to the writer who adapted the book. He's around here somewhere. Sweet man..."

She was off, an unstoppable flow of adrenalin-induced prattle that I found at once endearing and infuriating.

She finished her drink, and I had another one ready. She tipped it back. "Jonathon, you did like the play, didn't you? I know it's only an entertainment, but it does say *something*, doesn't it?"

I smiled at her. "As an entertainment, it's very enjoyable," I offered, hoping this might suffice.

The feel of her in my arms made me want to leave the place there and then, whisk her off to her flat for a night of intimacy, the worries of the world forgotten. But these gatherings were wont to drag on for hours, moving on to a nearby pub, and then continuing to a night club, until the post-production energy had dissipated into hangovers and depression.

Carla waved and danced across the room. She returned a minute later with none other than Alastair Ticehurst. He was a short, clean-faced handsome man in his late twenties, with blonde curls and a look, I swear, of insufferable arrogance.

Carla introduced me. "Jonathon, this is Al." I wondered if she was playing a game, or merely drunk. She was downing her third gin and tonic with an abandon that bordered on the obscene.

I shook hands with Ticehurst and exchanged a few strained pleasantries. To my annoyance, he insisted on asking me what I 'did'.

Carla was still hanging on his arm. "Jonathon's a novelist, Al. I told you."

The prig swirled his brandy with a practised air of condescension and stared up at me. "A novelist? Are you published?"

I'd had this response before, and it has always struck me as asinine. If one introduced oneself as an air-line pilot, would the other person then ask, "Have you ever flown a plane?"

I drained my glass. In the crush of people jostling us, I found it easy to ignore him. I squeezed from the press and bought myself another drink, a pint this time, and remained at the bar for the next hour.

Towards eleven, Alastair Ticehurst sought me out. He was more than a little tipsy by now, and I was in no mood to suffer fools.

"You're a ler-lucky man," he slurred.

"How's that?"

He gestured with his brandy glass, sloshing the contents, towards Carla, who was laughing uproariously among a group surrounding the play's director. "God, what a beautiful woman." His eyes devoured her, and it was all I could do to stop myself from punching the fool.

He focused on me. "Did she tell you that me and her–" he hiccupped – "me and her, once upon a time..."

I lowered my head and whispered into his ear. "She did tell me that you were an insufferable prig," I began.

Rather than bridle at this, he laughed. "That's interesting, be-because she, she told me that you're insanely jealous."

I decided that, rather than continue the insults, I would get myself another pint – but he was like a dog with a bone. He sidled up to me. "Langham, I remember now. Jonathon Langham. Of course, now I come to think about it... I have read one of your novels. *Summer in Kallithéa*, ser-something like that."

I tried to ignore him, eased myself through the bodies to Carla. She wrinkled her nose. I sought her hand, but she pulled it away.

Ticehurst was right behind me. "To be perfectly honest, I didn't much like it. Very shallow, unbelievable."

"Very much like you performance tonight," I said. "And I noticed you fluffed a line in the first act."

I had the bad luck to state this during a lull in the conversation, and everyone heard.

Carla turned to me, wide-eyed. "Jonathon." She swayed. "I think you owe Al an apology."

"I was merely stating a fact, darling. Or can't you people take criticism?"

Carla reached out and linked arms with Ticehurst. There was something at once malicious and calculating in her gaze as she stared at me. Pointedly, she mock-whispered to Ticehurst, "Take no notice of Jonathon, dear. He can be an awful stuffed-shirt at times."

I heard a round of stifled giggles as the carousing continued. I escaped to the bar, contemplated yet another beer, then thought better of it.

I pushed through the crowd towards the exit, hoping that I had departed unseen. I was drunk, and the drunkenness exacerbated my rage. I was angry at Carla and Ticehurst, quite naturally, but also at myself for so crassly losing my temper. I should have treated the creep with the contempt he deserved, and cut him dead. Instead, I had given Carla more ammunition to use against me.

It was almost midnight by the time I arrived home. By some miracle, the fire was still glowing. I added more coal and brewed myself a tea – the universal panacea. I pulled up the armchair and sat in the warmth of the fire, going over and over the events in the bar and resolving that I should do the wise thing and end my relationship with Carla.

But I had made the same resolution more than once in the past, to no avail. Always the fear of being alone had stilled my tongue, and for a time afterwards the intimacy I shared with Carla would make it seem worthwhile... until the occasion of our next tiff, or the inevitable bout of blind jealousy on my part.

The phone shrilled. I snatched it up, fully expecting Carla to start haranguing me for my behaviour.

It was a man's voice, and it was a little while before I could gather my senses and identify it.

"Hello, is that Langham? Jonathon Langham?"

"Langham here. Who?–"

"Thank God," said the voice, deep and rumbling. It came to me that it was a friend of my father's, ringing with bad news.

"It's Carnegie. Been trying to reach you all night."

"Jasper? How can I help...?"

Jasper Carnegie was the editor and publisher of a small literary magazine called *The Monthly Scribe*. He'd often called me with the commission for an article or short story, but never at midnight.

"Jasper?"

"Can you get away for a few days, Langham? Come down to the Grange?"

"Ah..." I began. I had been at university with Carnegie, and I had seen more of him since he'd founded his magazine a couple of years ago. He had never before invited me to the Grange – but why now, I wondered, and why at this ungodly hour? "Did you hear me, Langham? Can you see yourself free for a few days?"

My father would not be in town for a while, and the novel was going nowhere. Also, it would be the perfect opportunity to get away from Carla. I would go without informing her of my destination; perhaps it might be the precursor of the ultimate break that I knew, in my heart, I needed to make.

"Yes, yes of course."

"Excellent, Langham. Y'see, there's been some strange goings on down here. I'd like you to help me investigate."

I almost laughed aloud. It was like something from a penny dreadful.

"Edward Vaughan's coming too. In fact, he can pick you up. Ten in the morning, Langham, outside Waterloo station."

"Carnegie," I interrupted. "Investigate what, exactly?"

"Plenty of time for all that tomorrow, Langham."

The line went dead.

I had met the novelist Edward Vaughan a couple of times. He too wrote for Carnegie's magazine, but unlike me he was wealthy and respected. I had always been in awe of the man – I considered his novels of the highest standard – and I looked forward to meeting him again with anticipation and not a little nervousness.

I retired to bed, my head swirling with the events of the day. As I lay staring up at the darkened ceiling, I went over and over my conversation with Jasper Carnegie.

Strange goings on at the Grange...

CHAPTER THREE

Kallithéa, July, 1999

ONE WEEK AFTER he first met Caroline Platt, Langham received an invitation to the private showing of her exhibition. He had seen nothing of her that week, which reassured him that she was not an undercover investigative journalist stalking him for an interview.

He found himself looking back to the evening they had spent chatting on his patio, and he realised that he'd enjoyed her company. Oddly, he was disappointed that she had not been in touch since then. Caroline Platt was friendly and intelligent and strong – she had her own opinions, and could articulate them. It was the first time for years he had engaged in extended conversation with anyone other than his editor, and it had not been as painful as he'd feared.

At eight he made his way out to the patio with his customary breakfast of black tea, plain yoghurt and honey. He found the envelope containing the invitation propped against an empty bottle of wine on the table.

He considered attending the private showing that evening. It was a long time since he had been to anything vaguely formal on the island, and only the thought that he would have the opportunity to meet and talk to Caroline again persuaded him to go.

He reached into his trouser pocket and held the mereth, reassuring himself.

At nine he began writing. He was working on a novel set in Cairo in the late sixties. It was a follow up to his most critically acclaimed novel *Tangier*, and while he usually shied away from committing follow-ups or sequels, the female protagonist of

Tangier had demanded that he write about her further exploits in Egypt in the summer of '72. While he found it painful to write about Sam, who had existed as a real person, once upon a time, it was also an act of catharsis to extend in fiction a life that had been cut tragically short in reality.

He arrived at the end of the scene just before midday, put away his manuscript book and pen, and walked into Sarakina for lunch.

He passed Caroline's villa on the way into the village, but saw no sign of her; no doubt she was over in Xanthos, making last minute preparations for the exhibition.

The writing had gone well that morning, and he was in good spirits as he strolled towards the taverna. But the sight of the fat Englishman, wrestling with a newspaper in the slight sea breeze, put a damper on the prospect of a quiet lunch.

He took his usual table beneath the awning. At least from here, close to the entrance of the taverna, he had a view of the Englishman, and not vice versa. To have eaten his lunch under threat of scrutiny would have been unbearable.

He ordered squid, with salad, and his usual glass of local retsina.

The Englishman had chosen a table in the shade when he had arrived, but he had reckoned without the movement of the sun. Now he was in its direct light, and it was basting him like a wild boar on a spit. The simile, Langham thought as he ate, was not inappropriate. The man was porcine in more than just his surplus of blubber; he had a turned up nose and rheumy eyes, and ginger bristles instead of real hair. Langham decided to use his physical aspect in the next scene of his novel. His heroine was due a run in with a particularly vile military policeman. The Englishman would suffice as a template.

He wondered if, his suspicion constantly primed, he had taken against an innocent tourist. He had first seen the man a week ago, when he'd convinced himself, on flimsy evidence, that he was a grubby journalist.

Langham chastised himself for being so uncharitable – and then he saw the man produce a book from an overstuffed hold-all beside his chair, and he knew that his initial assumption, and subsequent irritation, was fully justified.

The book was a hardback first edition of Langham's third novel, *In Khartoum*.

There was something almost arrogant in the way the man pulled it from his hold-all, thumbed through it negligently, and began reading the book at arm's length. A minute later he decided it was too hot in the sun. He moved into the shade, and consequently closer to Langham's table. Langham knew it to be a ploy. Soon the man would find some pretext with which to start a conversation.

But not if I can help it, he thought, and quickly finished his squid and gulped down the wine. He hurried into the taverna and paid Georgiou, then slipped out again behind the broad, sweating back of the journalist and escaped up the road leading from the harbour.

In the shade of the pine trees, put out at having his usually leisurely lunch curtailed, he wondered if he was being paranoid. Perhaps the Englishman was not a journalist at all, but some innocent tourist who enjoyed the novels of Daniel Langham.

But he had Fleet Street stamped all over him, and Langham knew he had not seen the last of the man. Battle lines had been drawn. He was content in the knowledge that he would vanquish his foe, as he had in the past. They might come after him, but he would retreat into silence and wait out the journalistic onslaught. Their papers had limited staff – the hack would be needed on other stories when this one drew a blank.

He showered when he arrived home, and at three rewrote that morning's work, cutting and tidying up. At six he made himself a simple Spanish omelette, ate it with a beer while gazing out over the calm blue sea, and at seven walked back into the village and hailed one of Sarakina's three taxis.

There was no sign of the Englishman at the taverna. Langham wondered when the approach might be made, and from what quarter. A letter, requesting an interview, a brazen demand one morning at the taverna, a visit at his villa one afternoon? Whichever, Langham would be ready.

As he rode in the back of the taxi from Sarakina, on the old road high over the hills, he put the journalist from his mind and thought about Caroline and the evening ahead.

The private showing was taking place in the town hall at Xanthos, a quietly impressive building overlooking the main square. As the taxi drew up outside the sweeping steps of the building, Langham made out a parade of the island's dignitaries making their way across the square.

He climbed the steps and entered the main exhibition hall, his hand instinctively reaching for the mereth. Activated by the presence of sentient beings, it thrummed reassuringly.

As Langham stood and stared about him, he realised that the work he had seen in the studio had done nothing to prepare him for the exhibition.

It was more than just the colour of the paintings, he realised as he joined the widdershins procession around the room, but the effect of the vibrancy she somehow achieved, that tricked the eye into thinking that the shapes portrayed had a pulsing, rhythmic life of their own.

I'll have to ask her how she does it, he thought, before realising that it was perhaps a crass question: it was no doubt not so much a conscious technical effect, but something that emanated from the soul of the woman, something inherent in the essence of her personality. Viewing the paintings, he liked Caroline Platt even more.

One picture in particular took his breath away with its beauty and vitality. He remained standing before it, a rock in the stream of people passing around him.

The canvas showed three figures in a sunlit landscape; they were in the foreground, but small, reduced by the immensity of the plain or desert before them. The sun was setting, and high above in the sky the first stars were beginning to glimmer. Langham found himself choked by it, near to tears. There was something elemental and yet original in its portrayal of humanity in a landscape. It spoke of optimism and eternity.

He squinted at the tiny note beside the painting. It said simply: *Contemplating the Future*, acrylic on canvas, May 1999. Very recent, then.

"Do you like it?"

He turned. It was Caroline. She passed him a glass of wine. "I'm delighted you could come, Daniel. I've been talking to a few people, and they said they didn't think you'd make it. Did you know you have a reputation as a recluse?"

He laughed. "Is that all? Recluse, misanthrope, all round miserable churl."

She clapped her hands, delighted at his ironic self-appraisal.

Despite her animation, she looked drained. Her face was pale, her eyes tired. No doubt all the arrangement, the stress of the exhibition, had taken its toll.

She took his arm and escorted him around the show. "So, Mr Recluse, having you here is something of a coup."

He laughed, again, and he couldn't recall laughing twice in as many minutes for a long time. "I'm that much of a draw, am I?"

"Sequestering yourself away has increased public interest."

"Something like the last dodo on Mauritius, hmm?"

"Now, I never said you were a dodo."

"Feel like one sometimes," he said, pausing to admire another vivid landscape.

"I do hope you like them."

He turned to her. "Isn't it wonderful when you come across work by a colleague, a fellow writer, artist, whatever, which you can be wholly enthusiastic about?" He gestured around the exhibition. "They're not only beautiful and technically accomplished, they contain a life and an optimism that touches something in here," he touched his chest. "They're truly staggering."

"I'm blushing."

He smiled. "Sometimes, you come across accomplished work by someone in another field. You wish that you had their skill. It's as if... you know your own discipline so well, its tricks and short-cuts, that you just want to start again in a field you know nothing about, so that you can perhaps achieve an innocence of vision... I'm babbling."

"No, no," she said, dragging on his arm. "I know what you mean. I felt like that when I discovered your books."

He stopped walking and looked at her. "You never said you'd read them."

"Well, you never asked."

They had come full circle, and in a bid to change the subject, he gestured at the painting entitled, *Contemplating the Future*. "My favourite."

She was silent, regarding it, and when he looked at her he saw that her eyes were brimming with tears.

Someone called her name from across the hall, and she turned and replied in fluent Greek. "Damn, Daniel. I'm wanted. What are you doing later? Say, in an hour?"

"In an hour? Nothing planned."

"Then I'll meet you outside on the steps, okay? There's a lovely, quiet bar by the harbour. We'll have a sedate night-cap."

"Sounds wonderful."

She squeezed his arm and hurried away.

He watched her go, aware of the beating of his damnable, maddening heart, and then returned his attention to the paintings.

He picked up a pamphlet about the artist and her work, in both Greek and English. It told him little more than she had told him during their first meeting, but he did learn that she was born in 1960, had attended art college in Leeds, and had had an exhibition in New York. He would have to ask her about that.

So he could relax and take Caroline Platt at face value; she was not, it seemed, an investigative journalist – or anything else, for that matter. He wondered how he could have suspected her of being anything other than an attractive, warm-hearted human being?

He took another turn around the exhibition, finding new things to see in each painting. He would have to come here with Caroline when it was quieter, and she could talk him through the paintings at her leisure.

He saw the fat Englishman before he actually noticed him; the man was an awkward blur of beige in the periphery of his vision, somehow spoiling the composition of the exhibition like a fly trapped in the tesserae of a kaleidoscope.

He caught another glance of the man, and at that second his brain registered his presence and alerted him.

Langham felt at once angry at the man and annoyed at himself for feeling this unwarranted anger. The man was dogging his steps, and he had no right to invade this private showing. He would have to ask Caroline if she had invited him.

Worse, the creep was not taking much notice of the paintings, but talking to people: no harm in that, except that he was less talking to them than questioning them. He was clutching a spiral-bound note-book and taking down what they said in the rapid shorthand of a seasoned reporter.

The man did not make the mistake of glancing at Langham – but the couple he was interviewing, with no need for duplicity, looked across at him and nodded at something the Englishman was saying. Langham knew the couple: they owned the hotel in town where he had stayed on arriving on the island. The bastard was scraping the bottom of the barrel for copy about the famous writer. Let him try!

The Englishman moved on, introducing himself and engaging locals in conversation. His Greek seemed to be up to the task.

Langham manoeuvred himself through the crowd and caught the eye of Alexis, the hotelier.

"Mr Langham," Alexis said, beaming, "what brings you out?"

"I know the artist," Langham said shortly. "What was the Englishman asking about me?"

"Oh, to be famous! He said he was writing a book about you, a – what do they call them? A biographical book?"

"A biography? About me?"

"That's what he said, Mr Langham. He also said that you knew about it."

"Well, the bastard was lying. Excuse my English. I've authorised nothing of the kind."

Alexis touched his arm. "Don't worry, Mr Langham, we reported no scandal or gossip about you!"

"Much appreciated. Excuse me, I must see about this..." He left Alexis with a nod, then looked across to where he'd last seen the journalist. He turned in a circle, but the Englishman seemed to have vanished into thin air. He hurried to the exit and pushed through the double doors. A gaggle of children obscured his view of the square, and by the time he pushed through them the fat Englishman was squeezing himself into a tiny taxi – like a genie being sucked back into a magic lamp. Langham hurried down the steps, but the taxi was accelerating with its load away from the square.

He stood in the mellowing evening sunlight and fumed.

"Daniel? What's the...? Is something wrong?"

It was Caroline, hurrying down the steps and across the cobbles towards him.

"I don't believe it."

"Daniel? Don't tell me" – she was smiling – "has someone tried to steal a painting?"

He shook his head. "No, someone is trying to steal my life."

She touched his arm and peered at him. "You're shaking. Are you okay?"

"I'll be fine. No thanks to..."

"Look, let's go and get that drink, and then you can tell me all about it."

She linked arms with him and they walked across the square to the harbour. "I'm sorry," he was saying. "I noticed this fellow loitering around the village a week ago."

"What fellow?"

"From time to time I've had journalists come and try to interview me. They know I don't give interviews, but that doesn't seem to stop them."

They came to the waterfront and a café bar called, appropriately enough, the *Oasis*. "Inside, or out here?" Caroline asked.

"Ah... why not outside, it's a beautiful night, and soon the stars will be out." He smiled. "They always seem to have a calming effect."

They sat down at a table overlooking the water and ordered drinks, a beer and an orange juice.

From here he could see the entire majestic sweep of the coastline and, in the distance, hazed in the diffuse light of the setting sun, the peninsula on which his villa was a tiny white chalk mark in the olive groves.

All he could think about was the bastard racing away in the taxi; he wouldn't put it past the man to break into his villa while he was away and rifle though his personal effects for scandalous information.

He was relieved that everything, scandalous or otherwise, was safely locked away.

"So tell me about the journalist," Caroline said.

He took a long swallow of refreshing beer. "Do you know what he was doing at the exhibition? He had the cheek to go around quizzing the locals about me. It turns out that he isn't just a journalist, oh no – something far worse."

She peered at him, mock-shocked. "You mean, there's something even worse than a journalist?"

"The bastard – I'm sorry – told Alexis that he was my official biographer, and that I'd authorised the book."

"And did you?"

"What do you think?"

She laughed, reached out and squeezed his arm. "I know, I know. I'm joking!"

"A biographer! Can you imagine what pile of lies a man like that would write about me?"

"A man like what, Daniel? You don't even know him."

"A man," he said patiently, "who would sneak behind my back asking people about me and lying that he was doing it with my permission. That kind of man."

She was watching him. "I'm seeing a different side to you from the side I saw last week. You struck me as Zen calm, unflappable."

"I'm sorry. It's just that for years... Look, I hate publicity. I hate the lies they write about you. Modern journalism is shallow and reductionist. Two million people read the *Daily Mail*. Isn't that a national tragedy?"

She took a long drink of her orange juice, watching him over the miniature parasol. She said, "Do you mind if I ask you why you've locked yourself away on the island?"

"I thought I'd explained. I detest publicity. I don't want fame. Or the meretricious lifestyle that goes with it. I–"

"If you'll let me finish, Daniel. I was about to say, I understand why you might shun publicity, but why do you shun people as well?"

That brought him up short. He retreated into his beer, wondering how to respond. He fondled the mereth in his pocket, and the gesture calmed him.

At last he said, "I'm a novelist. I need peace and quiet in order to work. I find that company spoils my concentration."

She leaned forward, almost playfully. "I spot a contradiction. I thought novelists needed company, emotional involvement. Isn't that the compost in which ideas take root and grow?"

"Very well put. Where did you get that from? Forster's *Aspects of the Novel* or a gardening manual?"

She pouted, mock-disappointed at him. "You're avoiding the

issue. I can understand you wanting peace and quiet, but to shut yourself away like a monk for ten years, seeing no-one, hardly speaking to anyone..."

"Listen, I've had enough involvement in the past to last a lifetime or more. Now I'm writing about it."

She was shaking her head. "It just seems a little strange." She paused for a long time, watching him. "I read *Tangier*."

He thought she had let him off the hook, and was relieved at the change of subject. "What did you think?"

"What's the back cover quote from the *TLS*? 'A beautifully written work of art possessing human insight matched only by its artistic integrity.' I thought it enchanting, deep, moving, unputdownable, all the clichés. I marvelled at the way you made the characters so believable. They live with me still, Daniel. That's a fantastic achievement."

He nodded, murmured, "Thanks."

"That's what I meant when I said I knew what you were talking about back there. When I read *Tangier* and the *Penang Quartet*, I wanted to have that magical ability to wholly captivate and convince the audience."

"I think you do it with your paintings."

She ignored the compliment. "I read somewhere that you based your characters on real people."

"Don't all novelists, worth their salt? They're mainly based on me."

"What about the female characters?"

She was getting too close to home again. "Some were based on real people. Others were pure invention."

"The male characters always seem unlucky in love."

He said, "It's a device of technique. Unrequited love drives conflict. Happy endings are anathema."

"Don't demean your art," she said. "'A device of technique', indeed! Your books are written from the heart, with integrity. You've been through what you put your characters through, which is why your books are so convincingly truthful."

She stopped. He thought that she was about to ask him to tell her about the loves of his life, his losses, and he was thankful that she had the sense, or the compassion, to desist.

She laughed. "Aren't we getting awfully deep!" she said, and the awkward moment was broken. "What did you think of the exhibition, Daniel? I'd like to talk you through it at some point."

He was sweating with relief that the interrogation was over, and that he could enjoy this strange woman's company without fear or threat. "I was actually thinking that myself. I'd like to ask you about one particular painting. But first–" He indicated her empty glass. "Another?"

"If you're having one."

"Same again?"

She nodded. He signalled the waiter and ordered the drinks. The sun was going down over the bow of the distant horizon, and the breeze was a delight after the heat of the day.

"*Contemplating the Future*," he said. "Tell me about it. When, where? What does it mean to you? Or do you think that doesn't matter? Is what matters the viewer's interpretation?"

"You're right. A painting might mean something different to everyone, and what I think about it is no more valid than what anyone else thinks. Tell me, what does it mean to you?"

"It's an incredibly optimistic piece of work," he said. "I see three figures facing a beautiful landscape, maybe a desert, and night is bringing out the stars. It's full of hope for the future."

She was watching him, twirling the miniature parasol between thumb and forefinger. "So the night, for you, is a symbol of optimism?" she asked.

"Not necessarily," he said, "but the stars are." He paused, watching her. "What does it mean to you? Do you see the night, rather than the stars?"

She shook her head. "I'm not telling. Maybe at some time in the future, okay? I'll tell you then, perhaps." So much of her conversation was playful, and it delighted him. He wondered, though, at the accuracy of his interpretation. What had she said? That everyone's individual interpretation was valid? And her own? Was *Contemplating the Future* pessimistic, in her opinion?

She was nipping the brow of her nose, eyes screwed shut. "Damn. I think I'm coming down with a migraine. Exhibitions always bring them on. Do you think you could call a taxi?"

"Of course. Can I get you something?"

"I have pills at home. I should have brought them with me."

Five minutes later they were riding home. Darkness was falling, and the massed stars were appearing overhead like a benison.

The taxi dropped them at the end of the track, and they were forced to walk the rest of the way over the uneven terrain. He was practised from many such treks back from the village, but she stumbled, stymied by migraine and unfamiliarity. At one point he took her hand to guide her, and it came to him how soft and warm human flesh seemed, after so long without touching any but his own.

Outside her villa, she squeezed his hand farewell. "And remember, Daniel, do call around at some point. Don't leave all the socialising to me."

He promised to call one afternoon, and made his way home in a daze.

He fetched a beer from the fridge, sat on the sofa and watched the stars for a long, long time.

They seemed incredibly bright tonight.

CHAPTER FOUR

Cranley Grange, February, 1935

EDWARD VAUGHAN WAS a tall, broad man, whose choice of dress ran to rough and ready tweeds, and he was never without a lighted pipe. His hair was grey and swept back in leonine profusion, his face craggy and weathered, fissured like some outcropping open to the depredation of the elements. It was an apt metaphor: although quiet and private, he had let slip, late one night after a succession of double malts had loosened his tongue, that he had known tragedy in his life. He had lost a brother in the Great War, and three years ago his wife had succumbed to cancer.

He was introspective, but amiable: on our first meeting he had praised a short story of mine published by Jasper Carnegie in *The Monthly Scribe*. In company he was thoughtful and somewhat reserved – though his reserve suggested not the suspicion that some taciturn men emanate, but a wealth of quiet understanding of the ways of the world.

He was standing beside his Austin 16 when I hurried along the pavement with my overnight bag, somewhat out of breath.

"Mr Vaughan!" I panted. "Forgive me. Late as ever! The 'buses–"

He smiled around the stem of his pipe. "What's five minutes, Jonathon? And please, call me Edward."

He took my bag and stowed it in the back of the car, and I climbed into the passenger seat beside him. He pulled into the street and proceeded to drive through the city with a quiet attention and thoroughness I came to view as characteristic.

"What are you working on at the moment?" he asked, glancing my way.

I said that I was stalled on the latest novel and he smiled, nodding. "I know the feeling well," he sympathised.

He puffed his pipe, and soon a pungent fug filled the car. He opened the quarter-light, murmuring apologies, and I breathed freely again.

Vaughan published his first novel in 1925, at the age of forty. It was much publicised at the time as being in the tradition of H.G. Wells – a Scientific Romance set thousands of years into the future of planet Earth. It was an odd choice of subject matter for a beginning novelist to pursue, and a practitioner with less literary skill and intelligence might have failed miserably. The book was an instant success, however, earning the plaudits of the crusty literary establishment for its undoubted stylistic merit and the breadth of its imaginative daring. He proceeded to write one book a year for the next ten years, all of them eschewing the more mundane subject matter of contemporary society and its manners and focusing instead on matters bizarre and frankly extraordinary. My favourite of his books, *Solar Equatorial*, posited a time in the distant future when the descendants of humankind possessed the technological wherewithal to construct great artificial habitats girdling the circumference of our fiery primary. His other books considered the possibility of life on other planets, of great civilisations that might have existed in our distant history. It was all heady stuff, and perhaps easily dismissed but for the literary quality he brought to bear on his subject matter, the depth of his characterisation, and the merit of his prose.

I ventured to ask what he was writing now, and he told me that he had just finished, and submitted to his editor, his latest novel.

For the next thirty minutes, as we drove though the mean environs of outer London, the steady drizzle turning to snow as we went, he told me about the book.

He detailed the plot, then described the characters, ideas and themes. He spoke with quiet conviction, and held me spellbound.

"You see, Jonathon, I'm not much interested in the here and now. I cannot merely limit myself to the contemporary. The novelist owes his reader more than the mere documenting of the world already known and written about by a thousand other writers. I try to offer alternative visions, views that perhaps no-one has quite broached in the same way before. But don't get me wrong, I'm interested in human beings, in the constancy of human motivation and reaction – you'll find these in my novels, as well."

"The problem that most of us have," I ventured, "is finding suitable subject matter, a subject that's both interesting to the author and engaging to the reader. It's all I can do to write about contemporary society. I've no idea how you come up with some of your ideas."

He smiled. "I stare at the ceiling, empty my mind, and dream."

Like this we whiled away the time as we left London in our wake and motored along the rolling roads of Berkshire.

For miles and miles in every direction, snow bequeathed the land the appearance of uniformity and innocence; not a soul was to be seen, and ours was the only automobile upon the road. I truly felt as though I were embarking upon some fantastical adventure... and my mood of questing levity was broken only by thoughts of Carla and my father.

Inevitably, perhaps, the conversation found its way on to the subject of Jasper Carnegie.

"Have you been to the Grange before?" Vaughan asked.

"Never. This will be the first time. I usually meet Carnegie at the office in London."

"You've known him long?"

"He was in the year above me at Cambridge," I said. "So, what, over fifteen years?" I smiled. "He was editing a magazine, even then. Inevitable that that's what he'd do out here in the real world."

"He was a friend at Cambridge?"

"I'd hesitate to call him a friend. More of an acquaintance. I've actually come to know him better over the past two or three years, since he started the *Scribe*."

Vaughan glanced at me. "So, what do you make of him?"

I thought about it. "He was always the nervous, excitable sort. He always had a dozen literary projects on the go, without quite being able to settle on one and see it through. Since his father passed on and he inherited the Grange, he's had more time and money to put into the magazine." I fell silent, having realised, as I spoke, that I really knew very little about the editor of *The Monthly Scribe*.

Vaughan was silent for a while, then said, "In your opinion, is Carnegie of sound mind?"

The question surprised me. "Well... I've never had reason to question his sanity, if that's what you mean."

He gripped the apex of the steering wheel and glanced at me. "What did you make of his phone call?"

"It was somewhat surprising, to say the least."

"What did he tell you?"

"Not a lot, and to be honest I'd had a little too much to drink at the time. He invited me down to the Grange, said something about wanting you and me to help him investigate something."

"But he didn't say what?"

I shook my head. "No, nothing at all. Just a second – he did mention something about some strange goings on."

"He said much the same to me. When I tried to question him, he clammed up. Very odd, if you ask me. And all the more so because he hardly knows me. I've met him, what, on three or four occasions, when he's bought pieces from me for the *Scribe*. I was the last person I thought he'd summon when he was in need of help."

I glanced across at him. "You thought that that's what he wanted?"

Vaughan frowned. "He sounded agitated, disturbed. More than once he mentioned an investigation, and odd happenings which he thought might interest me. But as I say, I hardly know the chap."

"He always was a loner," I offered. "He never made friends easily. Apparently he's become a bit of a recluse at the Grange, only venturing out to oversee the office in London."

"Curiouser and curiouser," Vaughan murmured to himself.

In due course, as a swollen, ruddy sun was extinguishing itself over the low folds of the horizon, we drove through a snow-bound Aylesbury and followed a signpost to the village of Fairweather Cranley, ten miles to the south.

Forty minutes later Cranley Grange, to give Carnegie's ancestral home its full title, appeared as we crested a rise in the lane; it stood between beech woods in the lee of the Chiltern hills, an imposing, foursquare pile with the folly-like addition of gothic towers or belvederes at each corner. Its dour façade appeared all the more eldritch between a roof upholstered in snow and the dazzling white mantle which covered the entirety of the surrounding countryside.

Vaughan halted the car in the lane, the better to view the Grange as the setting sun, behind us, blazed in the building's serried windows.

"He lives there alone?" I enquired.

"Apparently. He has a brother, but I rather think he's in India."

"Charles. He's a doctor in Bombay," I said. "He was in the same year as me at Cambridge. A greater contrast to Jasper you couldn't meet. Chalk and cheese."

Vaughan ground the gears and we skidded down the gentle incline of the hill and turned into the drive-way. The snow had not been cleared, and progress was slow. Eventually we arrived before the rise of steps that gave access to the double doors. I climbed out, retrieved my bag, and accompanied Vaughan towards the house.

He manhandled the bell-pull, and seconds later we heard its sepulchral tolling deep within the house. We waited for what must have been five minutes, stamping our feet against the chill.

I stepped back from the door and stared up at the windows: there was not a light to be seen. We moved around the house, crunching through the thick fall of snow. I paused once to peer in through a high window; the room was in darkness, but I could just make out the shadowy shapes of what appeared to be cameras mounted upon tripods, spindly arc-lights, and other apparatus I was unable to name.

We came to the rear of the Grange and beheld the rectangle of a lighted window, and beside it the postern door.

I knocked, and a second later an old woman in a pinafore pulled open the door and ushered us inside. We stepped into a hot kitchen fragrant with the aroma of cooking meat.

"Mr Jasper's expecting you, sirs," said the cook. "Pleased to see he warned you not to use the front door. He often forgets to tell visitors, not that we get that many."

Vaughan smiled at me, and refrained from mentioning Carnegie's lapse.

The cook was saying, "If you'll step this way." We followed her into a darkened corridor, where we were instructed to leave our bags, and followed her along a lighted passage towards a large room within which, I saw, blazed a fire in a hearth the size of my lounge.

"Make yourselves comfortable, sirs, and I'll just go and fetch Mr Jasper."

This was evidently the library, for shelf upon shelf of leather-bound volumes spanned the walls. A desk in one corner overflowed with paperwork; it was much like his London office in its appearance of organised disarray.

Vaughan planted himself with his back to the log fire, while I inspected the books ranged along the west wall. Most of them appeared to be volumes of traveller's tales dating from the last century, along with a good number of atlases and bound maps.

"Gentlemen! Vaughan, Langham... you don't know how delighted I am that you could make it."

I turned. Jasper Carnegie stood framed in the doorway, a short, rubicund figure in moleskin breeches and a faded scarlet waist-coat. He was balding, with a well-fed face, and he appeared far older than his thirty-six years; indeed, it was hard to believe that he and I were almost the same age.

"Do let me get you a drink. Whisky, brandy? Something to take the chill from your bones!"

We both chose brandy and Carnegie rubbed his hands and beamed, delighted. "Brandy it is, and I think I'll join you."

He poured three stiff measures from a bottle on a well-stocked table in the corner. As Carnegie passed the drinks and joined us before the hearth, I was struck by the resemblance between the editor's physique and the glass he nursed in the palm of his hand.

I also noticed, as he raised the glass to his lips, that his hand trembled, ever so slightly.

He enquired as to how our respective writing projects were faring, and for a while we traded business talk. He informed us that the latest issue of the *Scribe* was with the printers, and launched into a diatribe aimed at that beleaguered profession.

I wanted nothing more than to ask him why he had summoned us here, but thought it diplomatic not to interrupt.

He recharged our glasses and I admired his library.

This provided a further ten minutes of conversation. I was about to ask what, exactly, Carnegie had meant by the 'strange goings on' that he wished us to investigate, when he said, "I'll show you to your rooms, and after you've changed we'll dine. How's that sound?"

My room was on the ground floor, next door to the room in which I had seen the photographic equipment. A fire blazed in the grate, and a majestic four-poster stood with its sheets drawn back; on a chest of drawers before the window was a bowl and pitcher of steaming water.

I washed and changed, then joined the others in the library, where we were to dine.

The dinner, I was somewhat surprised to find, was superb: a haunch of venison, roast vegetables, and numerous bottles of the finest wine I had sampled in ages. We ate and drank for over two hours in the flickering light of the fire, and after the initial uneasiness of our arrival, we fell into conversation as if we were old friends reunited.

Carnegie and I recounted our Cambridge days, while Vaughan spoke of his time at Oxford. I asked after Carnegie's brother, Charles. As I thought, he was in India, working as a doctor.

"But," said Carnegie, waving his glass – by this time we were all somewhat the worse for the grape – "You'll be delighted to learn that he'll be back next week. You'll have to come over. What a reunion that will be!"

Vaughan regarded his glass. "If you don't mind my asking, Carnegie, you mentioned on the phone–"

"There's plenty of time for that tomorrow, my dear Vaughan."

"You can't even give us some hint?" I ventured.

He lowered his glass and leaned forward slightly, both palms flattened on the table to either side of his empty dessert bowl. "Gentlemen," he said, regarding us in turn, "I rather think that, if I were to recount the reason for your presence here, you would in your current state of inebriation take me for a madman, and in the morning believe not a word of what you'd heard."

"You are nothing if not intriguing," Vaughan said, smiling.

Carnegie changed the subject. He stared at me with pop-eyes. "What do you think of the world, Langham?"

"The world?" I asked, surprised. "Well, that's rather a big question after so much excellent claret."

"I'll be more precise. I mean, the modern world, society. Commerce, popular culture..." He waved, as if to encompass all the other aspects of the world he had omitted to mention.

"Well," I began. "I think the great evil is the fact that popular culture is driven by commerce. People in power, with vested interests, are force-feeding a populace what they think it wants..."

Carnegie was nodding. "That's why I like your novels, Langham. They seem not of this time. Your characters are paradigms for the universal aspects of the human psyche. Perhaps I'm not making myself clear..."

He refilled his glass, tipsily. I glanced across at Vaughan, who was smiling quietly to himself.

"And you, Vaughan," Carnegie went on, "your visions... D'you know something, Vaughan? To be perfectly honest I'm sick and tired of the world I find myself inhabiting – I might even say, find myself imprisoned in. That's why I find your visions so liberating. They speak to me of something beyond the mundane, the petty concerns of humankind."

"That's what I'm trying to get at," Vaughan said. "I want to show the reader that there are more things in heaven..."

Carnegie reached across the table and gripped the cuff of Vaughan's tweed jacket. "Do you really think so, my friend? Do you think that out there, or somewhere maybe in the future, there exist races and civilisations of which we with our puny intelligence can but dream?"

His eyes burned, and something about the intensity of his sentiment sent a shiver down my spine.

Vaughan smiled and filled his pipe. "Carnegie, I don't just think there is more to the universe than we have ever imagined, I'm certain of it."

Carnegie nodded. "Good man! Excellent." He raised his glass. "To the mysterious universe," he declared, "and all who live in it!"

We raised our glasses. "... to all who live in it," we echoed.

"And tomorrow," Carnegie went on, "I want to show you... *something*. Be prepared for a hike, my friends."

This was his last coherent sentence, as shortly thereafter he slipped into unconsciousness. We eased him onto the chesterfield before the fire and retired to our respective rooms, I for my part intrigued by Carnegie's singular pronouncement.

I passed a surprisingly peaceful night, troubled by dreams of neither Carla nor my father – but woke at eight with the realisation of my father's illness pressing upon my consciousness. For a while, last night, inspired by drink, I had managed to push such thoughts to the back of my mind. Now they returned to haunt me. I tried to sleep a little more, but unsuccessfully.

We breakfasted in the library, Carnegie seemingly none the worse for his excess of the night before.

As Vaughan and I helped ourselves to kippers, Carnegie excused himself and told us that he would be back presently with something we might find of interest.

When he had departed, I asked, "What did you make of all that talk of other worlds and times last night?"

Vaughan smiled. "I could say that he's been reading too much Wells and Vaughan," he said. "But, coming as it does on top of whatever he's brought us here to look into..." He gestured with a corner of toast. "We'll no doubt find out in due course."

Two minutes later Carnegie returned with what looked like a portfolio tucked beneath his right arm. He cleared a space on the table and laid it before us.

"I would like you to take a look at some photographs, gentlemen, and see what you make of them."

Intrigued, we leaned forward as he opened the cover of the portfolio like some vast trapdoor to a magical underground kingdom.

He shuffled through a pile of perhaps a dozen large, glossy photographs, then handed us one each. I stared at mine, attempting to make sense of the image. I passed it to Vaughan, raising my eyebrows in mystification. Vaughan gave me the photograph that he had been studying, evidently with the same perplexity as I felt myself.

The first picture showed what appeared to be a flash of light, surrounded by darkness; the second displayed much the same, though in this one vague shapes in the surrounding darkness could be discerned.

We considered each of the dozen pictures; they were very much alike, all showing the ubiquitous light upon a dark field, with the light varying in intensity from one photograph to the next.

"Well," Carnegie said, glancing from Vaughan to myself. "What do you think?"

I exchanged a quick look with my fellow novelist. "Hm," I began. "Interesting, but what are they?"

Carnegie beamed. "That, my friends, is what I too would like to know."

Vaughan leaned over the photographs now spread upon the table-top. He pointed to one or two. "In the darkness here, and here, I can make out shapes – they almost look like branches. Trees."

Carnegie was nodding. "They were taken at night in Hopton Wood," he offered.

"And the light?" I asked.

"Look more closely at the light, especially in these two photographs." He pushed two images across the table towards us, and Vaughan and I bent to inspect them.

"Can you make out shapes, outlines? There, and there..."

Now that he mentioned it, I could discern the very vaguest of patterns upon the print. In the bright explosion of light upon each photograph was the faintest shadow.

"Do the shapes suggest anything to you, gentlemen?"

I frowned, and glanced at Vaughan; his perplexed expression must have mirrored my own. He shook his head. "I suppose, if one stretches one's imagination... one might almost convince oneself that they could be faces. But, then again, they might be many things."

If I squinted, and employed sufficient imagination, I could almost make out nebulous, ghostly visages.

"Faces," Carnegie declared. "Exactly. That's exactly what I thought!"

"I take it you took these photographs yourself?" Vaughan asked.

Carnegie tucked his thumbs into the pockets of his waist-coat and leaned back in his seat. "I set up the equipment to take these photographs, but I was not in Hopton Wood at the time they were actually taken." He gathered the pictures together and closed the portfolio.

"If you would care to explain..." Vaughan began.

"That walk I mentioned last night – after breakfast we'll take a stroll over to Hopton Wood. There is something there that I think you might find of interest. Stout boots will be in order."

Vaughan had brought a pair, but I had not. Carnegie furnished me with a pair of hob-nails belonging to his brother, which were a comfortable enough fit.

We set out at eleven, my curiosity more than a little piqued. I considered Carnegie's claim, that the shapes in the photographs were faces, far-fetched to say the least. But the fact was that something in the wood had prompted him to haul a good amount of heavy photographic equipment all the way from the Grange, and I could not hazard a guess as to what that might be. There was always the possibility, of course, that Jasper Carnegie was mad.

There can be few more beautiful landscapes than the English countryside when adorned with a fresh fall of snow. A bright winter sun was shining, and the effect upon the brilliant white mantle was almost blinding. When my eyes adjusted to the glare, I made out, stretching out before me, hills and vales softened by snowfall for as far as the eye could see: not a blemish marred the pristine perfection. The only contrast was provided by the vertical trunks of distant trees, dark strokes against the untouched canvas of the snow-covered land. It seemed like desecration to mark the fall with our footsteps.

Carnegie led the way, and I had to admit that he cut a somewhat comical figure in his ankle-length waxed coat and deerstalker. Vaughan and I followed, he striding out with his hands in the pockets of his tweed jacket and his pipe thrust resolutely before him.

Carnegie had packed a haversack with a thermos of coffee and, for good measure, a bottle of brandy. I felt like a schoolboy again, embarking upon some adventurous holiday outing.

Cranley Grange stood amid the rolling slopes of the Chilterns, with extensive beech woods covering the crests of the surrounding hills. We climbed for a time towards the distant trees, our steps compacting the snow in a series of high, musical notes. There was not a breath of wind in the air and the sunlight upon our heads was unseasonably warm.

After perhaps thirty minutes we paused to take in the view. I turned and stared down the incline at the Grange, reduced by perspective to the size of an architect's scale model. I was impressed by the absolute stillness of the scene, the air of calm and solitude. The cares and concerns of London seemed a million miles away.

The occasional, muffled call of a hidden wood pigeon made the silence all the more profound. I could make out not one living thing at any quarter of the vast panorama; even the cloudless blue sky was innocent of birds.

We resumed our trek, Carnegie pointing the way with his shooting stick and panting as he climbed the hill.

As I followed, I reasoned that even if Carnegie's quest proved to be nothing more than a wild goose chase, then at least I had enjoyed the outing and a break from the routine of city life.

"Ancient woodland," Carnegie panted, gesturing up ahead with his stick. "It's seen the history of England played out before it. If only trees could talk!"

I could see Vaughan contemplating this as he strode along. "Interesting idea, Carnegie. Intelligent trees, living long after humankind has quit the scene..." He fell quiet, contemplating the idea.

We came to the tree-line on the side of the hill and Carnegie paused. "Hopton Wood," he said, pointing. "Not far now, perhaps a mile, and the going will be easier under cover of the trees."

We entered the wood, passing single file down a narrow track between short ferns and tall beech trees. For the most part the snow had not penetrated the tree cover, and the effect was as if we had stepped from one world to the next, or from one season to another: we had left winter behind us, and were approaching spring.

The air was musty, something almost tobacco-like in the aroma of humus and dead wood. Sunlight slanted through the denuded branches, falling in columns and illuminating dust motes like swirls of smoke. The effect was almost fairy-tale.

Carnegie paused. Ahead of us, the path forked. "As children Charles and I haunted these woods," he said. "Can you think of a more ideal place to play?" He smiled. "We'd be away for hours, and often got lost... father had to come hunting us." I thought I detected sadness in his tone as he recollected those far-off days. He looked at us. "Do you know something, I was happier then than I've ever been since. The world seemed a limitless place, full of possibilities and opportunities, full of wonder. But we grow up, become mired in the petty concerns of the adult world, and somehow our horizons become narrowed."

He waved his stick. "This way!"

Exchanging a glance with Vaughan, I followed.

We took the path to the right, which climbed a slight incline past a tangle of tree roots that had obtruded through the surface of the earth and become weathered and smoothed over the years. I imagined Carnegie and his brother sporting here as children. As I watched him now, striding ahead with his stick and deerstalker, it seemed that he might hardly have grown up.

We came to a clearing in the trees, a circular area perhaps thirty feet across. I knew, then, that there was something... *peculiar* about the place, but at the time I could not quite define what made me think this. Only later, in conversation with Vaughan back at the Grange, did it come to me: despite the lack of tree cover, not a flake of snow had fallen upon the clearing.

"This is it, gentlemen," Carnegie declared. "This is where it happened."

We were silent for a time, and then Vaughan asked, "Where *what* happened, Carnegie?"

He did not immediately reply. As if in a daze, he wandered off into the middle of the clearing and gazed about him, first looking up into the sky, and then around at the enclosing trees. At last he regarded the ground at his feet, and nodded to himself. He poked his stick into the soil, as if having satisfied himself upon some point.

I glanced at Vaughan and shrugged.

Carnegie looked up, staring at us.

"Step forward," he commanded.

We did so, and he said, "Do you feel it?"

I said, "Feel what, Carnegie?"

"The change, the subtle shift."

I concentrated. Undoubtedly it was warmer in the clearing, but this was accounted for by the fact that we were now standing directly beneath the midday sun.

"There's a charge in the air," Carnegie was saying. "Something almost... I don't know... electric. Look at the hairs on the back of your hands."

Feeling ludicrous, I did so. I noticed that Vaughan was also inspecting his hand.

I started as I realised that, improbably, Carnegie was right: the hairs on the back of my hand and wrist were standing to attention. At the same time I convinced myself that I felt a frisson, almost a shiver, pass across my flesh.

I stepped back into the shade of the trees and again inspected my hand. No longer were the hairs standing upright. Vaughan conducted the same experiment and frowned at me. "Very strange," he murmured.

I stepped forward into the clearing, and this time I told myself that I did feel something, a charge in the air, a certain heat that could not be accounted for by the presence of the sunlight alone.

"Would you mind telling us what's going on?" I asked.

Carnegie paced to the far side of the clearing and stood with his back to us for a time, apparently lost in thought. At last he turned and said, "It's a strange tale, gentlemen, and to be honest I don't rightly know what to make of it myself. I can but describe the events as they occurred, and see what you think." He paused. "I'll begin at the beginning, or the beginning as far as I can tell."

I sat down with my back against the broad bole of a tree, and Vaughan joined me. Before us, Carnegie paced back and forth like an actor upon a stage, which in effect was what he was.

"I first noticed the phenomenon twenty-four days ago," he said, "though I dare say it had been occurring long before that. I'm in the habit of walking late at night – there are times when sleep does not come easily, and I find that a turn around the countryside for an hour or two tires me sufficiently so that I can get a good night's rest. On this particular occasion I had retired around ten, but could not sleep. I rose, dressed, and set off towards Hopton Wood. It was a clear night, and the moon was almost full. There was no snow, and thus the going was relatively easy. I was perhaps half a mile from the wood when I noticed the light."

"The light?" Vaughan echoed.

"It was a brilliant blue radiance that seemed to emanate from the very heart of the wood. It appeared as a great fan-like aurora above the tree-tops, pulsing in a slow, regular rhythm. As I approached, I could see that the light was at its most intense at ground level, as it shone brilliantly through the trees, silhouetting their trunks."

"Did you have any idea what it might have been?" I enquired. "Weren't you apprehensive?"

He shook his head. "No, to both questions. I had not the slightest idea as to what might be causing the light, but I did not feel the least concern. Rather, I was intrigued, excited by the possibilities." He smiled to himself. "Indeed, I recall hoping that the light might not have some mundane explanation – some campers or revellers or whatever."

"It occurred to you that this might be the explanation?" Vaughan asked.

"I'll try to apprise you of exactly my frame of mind as I stepped into the woods," Carnegie said. "Though the light was of such a nature as I had never beheld before, yet I feared a simple explanation. I was in two minds – a part of me wanted to discover the fantastical, while the more rational side of my being knew that I would be disappointed when I discovered the simple truth."

As I listened to him I realised that, from what he had told us thus far, there had been no simple explanation for what he had seen that night: our very presence here testified to the fact that he wanted us to investigate whatever it was that had occasioned the light...

"I hurried through the trees, following the glowing light. By the time I arrived at the clearing, I was exhausted, and realised I had run the last few hundred yards."

"What did you see?" Vaughan asked.

Carnegie smiled and shook his head. "At the very second I approached the clearing, the light ceased, vanished as if it had never existed. The clearing was in darkness, but for the light of the moon. I searched for any sign of the device that might have been responsible, but of course found nothing. However, I did become aware of the atmosphere in the clearing. The air was charged, more so than it is now, and there was a certain aroma – almost a burning scent. Have you ever turned on an electric fire which has stood unused for a time? The reek of singed dust which arises then is something similar to the scent that pervaded the air that night."

"Mysterious indeed," Vaughan murmured. "Did you investigate the clearing by the light of day?"

Carnegie smiled. "I returned home – though I could hardly sleep for excitement. At first light next morning I set off again..." He paused, staring around the clearing as if recollecting what he had discovered that day.

"And?" Vaughan prompted. "What did you find?"

"At first, upon arriving here, I noticed nothing untoward. There was still a certain charge to the air, and the singed aroma persisted, but that was all. Or so I thought. Closer inspection revealed a number of dead animals: an owl, a few moles and voles – and a fox. They seemed in good condition: that is, not subject to the attack of other beasts. They lay upon the ground as if in sleep. I know that the discovery of dead animals in a wood is to be expected from time to time, but the fact that I had happened upon so many in the same area, where the night before a singular light had manifested itself, struck me as significant."

"Did you by any chance recover the remains of these animals?" Vaughan asked.

"Of course – I returned with a sack and transported them up to a veterinary surgeon in Aylesbury. I explained that I had found them on my land, but of course refrained from recounting the exact circumstances surrounding their discovery, and requested that he attempt to find out what had caused their deaths."

"And he did?" I asked.

Carnegie frowned. He was standing before us with his hands in the pockets of his ankle-length coat, his deerstalker pushed back on his head to reveal his sweat-soaked forehead. "He reported that he was mystified. The animals seemed to be in perfect health – at least, they were free from any disease which might have caused their deaths. I could see that he was intrigued: he questioned me about where and when I had discovered them, but I merely repeated my story about having found them on my land."

"Stranger and stranger," Vaughan said, abstracted. He was slowly filling his pipe with Old Holborn, tamping the tobacco down with his thumb.

"Like something from one of your books," Carnegie smiled. "Now do you understand why I had to bring you here?"

I recalled the photographs he had shown us back at the Grange. "When did you set up the photographic equipment?" I asked.

"It didn't immediately occur to me that I might make a photographic record of the phenomenon," he said. "Every night for the next week I returned to the clearing and lay in wait. I was about to give up my nightly vigil – thinking that the light had been a unique event – when it occurred for a second time, or at least for a second time to my knowledge. It was midnight, around the same time that I'd noticed the light on the first occasion. I was on the very margin of the clearing, in a bed-roll I had brought along against the cold, when I heard a high whining sound in the air. I climbed to my feet, and at that second experienced an almighty explosion which knocked me to the ground and rendered me unconscious."

"You were injured?" I exclaimed.

He shook his head. "When I awoke, it was daylight. Hours had elapsed. I examined myself, but seemed to be in one piece, though I did feel nauseous and dizzy. I examined the clearing, discovering a few dead animals, mice and a vole or two."

Vaughan removed his pipe and used it to point at Carnegie. "The blast must have killed them," he said. "And I venture that if you'd been any closer, it would have accounted for you, too."

Carnegie nodded grimly. "I dare say you're right. The same thought occurred to me at the time."

I said, "So you decided to keep away from the clearing at midnight, and install the cameras instead?"

"I kept my distance from then on. I returned nightly, but nothing further occurred. Then it struck me that, perhaps, for some reason the light might keep to a regular rhythm. That is, it might appear a third time eight days after its second appearance, which was eight days after I first noticed it. Rather than risk life and limb again, I had the idea of setting up the cameras. I rigged up a device to take a photograph every few minutes, then retreated to the perimeter of the wood and pitched camp. Sure enough, the light manifested itself that night, eight days after the last occasion. I watched from a distance, afraid to venture any closer. The light lasted perhaps twenty minutes, after which I retrieved the cameras, and you have seen the resulting photographs."

Carnegie stopped there, and we contemplated his words in the eerie silence of the clearing.

It was Vaughan who spoke first. "Corposants," he declared. "Will-o'-the-wisps. Ball lightning. Something of that nature."

"But," I said, "then how do you account for the eight-day cycle, and the dead animals?"

Vaughan pulled on his pipe, industriously surrounding himself in a pungent fug of smoke which coiled, blue, in the sunlight. "No doubt natural phenomena, such as ball lightning, might account for small creatures," he said. "But I am perplexed by the eight-day cycle. There must, by necessity, be a logical, scientific explanation for what occurred here. First, we need to exhaust the probabilities known to the rational, natural world. Only when we have discounted these can we move on to more bizarre hypotheses, which our understanding of science has yet to embrace."

"There is a little more to add," Carnegie went on. "A couple of days following the first incident, I wired Charles in Bombay with a brief account of the event. He was sufficiently intrigued to bring forward his annual leave, and should arrive here next week."

We chatted for a while longer, over mugs of coffee laced with brandy, and then Carnegie suggested we make our way back to the Grange. He took us on a roundabout route, passing through Fairweather Cranley and Lower Cranley. The villages were tucked into a vale between forested hills, each a collection of some two dozen cottages, a church and a post office, as picturesque and silent as scenes from a Christmas card. We might have been the only beings on the road that day, judging by the unmarked fleece that covered the camber. The air of rural tranquillity contrasted with the feverish imaginings that swirled within my head.

As I walked, I thought back to what Carnegie had told us.

I made a rapid calculation, and then cleared my throat. "If the light does indeed manifest itself on an eight-day cycle," I said, "and it first appeared, as far as you're aware, twenty-four days ago... then it should be due to reappear tonight."

The thought, as I spoke, filled me with a strange sense of anticipation together with, I admit, not a little apprehension.

Carnegie was smiling. "Why do you think I invited you down here yesterday?" he asked.

"Are you suggesting that we venture into the wood tonight?" I began.

Carnegie beamed. "If you're game, my friends."

"Well," I said, hesitant. "Wouldn't it be a bit rash to get too close...?"

"We could always set up camp a safe distance from the clearing itself," Vaughan said. "We could take cameras along and erect them up in the clearing."

"If the light does appear," Carnegie said, "then it really would be too great an opportunity to miss." He indicated a cutting in the hedge. "We can formulate a plan of action over dinner."

We arrived at the Grange as the sun was setting light to a spinney on the far horizon and a gibbous moon was rising in the east, as insubstantial at this early hour as a paper doily; later, when we set off for Hopton Wood, it would cast an even stronger light to guide our way.

Over a dinner of jugged hare and baked potatoes, accompanied by two bottles of Carnegie's excellent claret, we discussed the forthcoming expedition.

"It is essential that we take the cameras in order to have an objective record of what we might find," Vaughan said. "Our subjective senses cannot be relied upon in times of stress, even if there are three of us to corroborate each other's story."

"I'll pack supplies," Carnegie said. "Coffee and brandy, as well as bed rolls. There is no need for us to go without."

"How far from the actual clearing do you think we should place ourselves?" I asked. "Considering what happened to the animals..."

Vaughan turned to Carnegie. "How far away were you when the blast rendered you unconscious?"

"On the very edge of the clearing itself."

"It's very difficult to judge," Vaughan said. "Perhaps it would be wise to put the solidity of a tree trunk between ourselves and the clearing, so that when – or rather if – the light appears, we will be afforded some measure of protection."

I nodded. "That sounds like a sensible idea."

Carnegie looked across the room at the grandfather clock. It was nine-thirty. "It's high time we were setting out, gentlemen."

While he filled three haversacks with provisions and bed rolls, Vaughan and I fetched cameras and tripods from the room next to my bed-chamber. Ten minutes later we pulled on our overcoats and left the Grange. We followed the tracks we had made earlier that day, which now showed as dark streaks leading uphill through the moonlit snow-field. Speaking for myself, I was more than a little light-headed from the wine I had consumed at dinner, and at the prospect of what might lie ahead. At one point, as we trekked up the incline, burdened down with cameras and tripods, I could not help but laugh out loud.

Beside me Vaughan said, "What amuses you, Jonathon?"

"It's just occurred to me what we are doing," I said. "If I'd told myself, a week ago, that I'd be toiling up a snow-covered hillside in order to photograph some mysterious light in an ancient forest... I don't think I would have believed a word!"

"We might," Carnegie declared portentously, "be on the verge of a momentous discovery."

"Or then again," Vaughan put in, "we might be embarking upon a proverbial wild goose chase."

Panting, Carnegie enquired, "You don't doubt that I did see something in the woods eight days ago?"

"Oh, I don't doubt that you saw something, Carnegie. But I rather think that that something might turn out to have a simple and rational explanation."

Like this, with much good-humoured banter and speculation back and forth, we made our way towards the wood and, one hour later, reached the tree-line.

We paused to catch our breath and consume coffee fortified with brandy. By the light of a paraffin lamp, Carnegie consulted his fob watch. "Eleven-fifteen," he said. "We ought to press on if we're to reach the clearing by midnight."

Carnegie led the way through the darkened wood. It was well that he had bethought himself to bring along the lamp, for the moon shone only intermittently through the cover of the trees. The orange flame flared up ahead, sending grotesque shadows dancing lively gavottes all about us. I brought up the rear, behind Vaughan's substantial form, and I must admit to experiencing a spine-tingling frisson at the thought of the expanse of dark forest that lay in my wake.

We took the fork in the path, climbed uphill aways, and five minutes later gained the clearing.

It possessed a magical quality that it had lacked earlier in the day, for the pewter light of the full moon gilded its every detail like a stage set. I stood upon its perimeter, reluctant, now that the time had arrived, to set foot within its mysterious precincts. Carnegie had no such qualms. He looked at his watch and declared, "Ten minutes to midnight. We'd better look sharp."

Together we set up the three cameras on their tripods, spaced equidistantly so as to form the points of a triangle, and Carnegie primed mechanical devices to activate the cameras at intervals.

As we went about the clearing, I paused to note the effect of the place upon my skin. Sure enough, the hairs on the back of my hands were bristling, and I was aware of a certain heat alien to the ambient coldness of the rest of the wood.

Not soon enough for me we had the cameras set up, and retreated from the clearing. Vaughan marched back along the path and paused perhaps five yards away.

"This looks as good a place as any." He indicated a fallen tree trunk, which would provide some measure of cover. We positioned ourselves behind the mossy log and spread out the bed rolls, Carnegie breaking out the coffee and the brandy bottle. From where I sat, I had a clear view of the moon-lit clearing, the three cameras standing there like incongruous interlopers upon this sylvan scene.

From time to time Carnegie dragged his deerstalker from his balding head and mopped his brow, when not nervously consulting his fob watch. Vaughan proceeded to fill the bowl of his pipe and set the aromatic blend alight. Soon he was puffing away, as if ensconced in an armchair in the domestic comfort of his front parlour.

I, for my part, was overcome with an intense nervousness. It was all I could do to stop myself from cowering behind the log.

An eerie calm and silence pervaded. Our measured breathing provided the only sound. The minutes seemed to take an age to pass.

At last Carnegie broke the silence, startling me. "It's ten past twelve," he announced, peering at his watch.

"Perhaps," Vaughan whispered, "last week's was the final *son et lumière*?"

"I must admit," I whispered in return, "that I cannot bring myself to feel much disappointment."

"Are you sure that the light manifested itself at midnight precisely on the previous occasions?" Vaughan asked.

"To the best of my knowledge, a matter of minutes either way," Carnegie said.

Another five minutes elapsed, and I experienced a perverse sense of anti-climax – contrasting with my earlier fear – that our vigil would come to nothing. I knew that, in the cold light of day, I would rue the fact that we had missed out on witnessing something extraordinary.

I glanced back at the clearing, and at that precise moment it happened.

The light exploded from nowhere – or, rather, it expanded from a point that seemed to hang in mid-air six feet above the clearing. One second all was stillness and moonlight, and the next a great coruscating membrane of lapis lazuli light filled my vision. In a fraction of a second it expanded into a vast oval perhaps twenty feet high and half as much across, and with it came a blast of heated air that singed my face. Carnegie shouted aloud as his deerstalker was snatched from his head and blown into the undergrowth. Vaughan gazed ahead in slack-jawed surprise, and I too gawped in wonderment at the thing in the clearing.

"Oh, my God..." Carnegie whispered to himself.

I felt an excited grip on my elbow: it was Vaughan, his face washed in the electric glow.

Together, transfixed, we could do nothing but gape at the great swirling oval of sapphire brilliance that hung in the air before us.

Only then did I become aware, by degrees, of the low droning sound which accompanied the light: it was the almost sub-audible note of an electric generator, an effect felt more in the diaphragm of the torso than in that of the middle ear. It seemed to throb to a steady rhythm which, I noted, had its counterpart in the steady pulsing brightness of the light itself.

Carnegie was on his feet now. As I glanced at him, he stretched out his arm and pointed. "Look!" he cried.

"Christ Almighty," Vaughan breathed.

I was struck dumb as I beheld that which had provoked the cries of my friends.

There was no doubting it: I could discern a series of shapes moving behind the membrane of the light. Tall, humanoid figures passed back and forth, like the grotesque, elongated caricatures in an Indonesian shadow play. They were fleeting, and faint, but indubitably present – perhaps as many as four distinct figures moving with mysterious and ill-defined purpose behind the illumination.

Then, before I could stop him, Carnegie had stepped over the log and was approaching the light.

"Get back here, man!" Vaughan cried, transfixed, like myself, by either fear or fascination.

Carnegie entered the clearing, dragging the deerstalker from his head and clutching it before him. In an effect at once terrifying and comic, I saw the little hair that he possessed stand upright in the strange energy field created by the supernal oval.

He was moving ever closer, his right arm raised as if to shield his face from the intense heat.

"Carnegie!" I yelled, and then forced myself from the paralysis that had pinned me to the spot.

I vaulted the log and sprinted forward. The energy belting from the light was intense. I felt my hair stand upright, and the heat burn my exposed face. I raised an arm to protect myself and staggered forward. Behind the light, I fancied that I saw the singular figures pause in their business and turn to peer through at us. I reached Carnegie and grabbed at his arm; he resisted me, shrugged off my hand.

"Don't you see!" he yelled, beside himself in some transport of ecstasy. "Don't you understand, Langham? They represent all that is powerful, all that is knowledgeable! If only I could join them!"

With a strength that seemed super-human, he pushed me off again and strode on. His absurd brandy glass physique was silhouetted against the light as he sought to leave this place for good. Behind me, Vaughan called at the top of his lungs and dived forward. He caught Carnegie just as he was about to step into – or maybe even *through* – the field of light, and I have no doubt that Vaughan's timely intervention saved Carnegie from an unknown fate.

At that second, as Vaughan wrestled his friend to the ground in front of me and we tumbled over, the light collapsed with a great inrushing roar of air, diminished to a tiny point no larger than a mayfly, and then popped out of existence.

A profound stillness obtained in the clearing, a silence that rang deafeningly in the aftermath of so much expended energy. We held each other for what seemed like a long time, for all the world like the benighted survivors of some catastrophic shipwreck.

What followed, the events of the next hour or two, are unclear in my mind. In a daze we left the clearing and somehow made it across the snow-covered downs to the Grange. We collapsed exhausted in the library and sought resuscitation in copious drafts of wine.

"The light," Carnegie said. "I almost..."

"Be still," I counselled, forcing wine past his lips. His face was red and raw from the heat of the light, and Vaughan and I took turns in bathing his exposed flesh with wet towels.

"I saw figures behind the light, moving figures!" he cried. "Tell me I'm not dreaming, man!"

Vaughan said, "We saw them, too. There can be no denying that."

I shook my head. "But what were they, Vaughan? What on Earth did we experience back there?"

Vaughan smiled to himself. "What on Earth, indeed. Or what not on Earth..."

"There were intelligences behind the light," I went on. "We cannot deny that. It was no mere natural phenomenon, such as we speculated before."

"But what *was* the light?" Carnegie asked.

"Perhaps," Vaughan offered, "it was a portal between worlds, between this dimension and the next, and the figures we saw were the dwellers in that mysterious realm."

My head swirled; I had the urge to laugh and cry at the same time. "What in God's name have we stumbled upon!"

"What indeed," Vaughan said quietly.

Carnegie stirred himself. "Next week... in eight days from now, the process will repeat itself, perhaps. Promise me that you'll return! We must investigate this further!"

Vaughan glanced my way, then nodded to Carnegie. "We'll be here, rest assured on that score, old friend. We'll be here."

It was almost dawn before we talked ourselves into exhaustion and retired to our rooms, and midday when we awoke and gathered in the library for a late breakfast. Once again we went over the events of the night before, and made plans to return within the week.

We resolved to keep our discovery to ourselves, and at two o'clock Vaughan and I left Carnegie – scarred and battered from his encounter with the inexplicable, but otherwise unbowed – and arrived in the capital as darkness was falling.

My life in London, the cares and concerns which had weighed so heavily upon my thoughts just two days ago, now seemed distant and unreal, the stuff of another life entirely.

CHAPTER FIVE

Kallithéa, July, 1999

LANGHAM DID NOT take up Caroline's invitation to call round and see her until three days after the exhibition. Had she dropped in and accused him of staying away, he would have claimed pressure of work, made some excuse about the novel not going too well. In fact it was progressing at a steady thousand words a day. What prevented him from calling on her was fear.

He found himself attracted to Caroline Platt; she was a lovely woman, warm, friendly and intelligent. There was something about her that was deeply humane, and it came out in the essence of her paintings. He could not look at the still life of oranges on his wall without seeing in their colour and vibrancy something of her life-force.

He was attracted to her, and it frightened him. He had been so long without a lover, had adapted himself very well to his solitary lifestyle, and while his heart craved her company, his head counselled caution.

Since the exhibition, his head and heart had battled, and on the third day his heart won. He completed his thousand words by midday and decided to call on Caroline and invite her to take lunch with him at Georgiou's taverna.

He set off along the track to her villa, pausing to stare out across the sea. A tiny fishing boat puttered away from the island, reduced to the size of a child's toy in the blue vastness. The sun was at its height and hottest, beating down with a relentless dry heat that smote the skin with something like a physical blow. In the shade of his vine-covered patio, he had been spared the sun's intensity; out here he was aware of its force. It was a good day for sitting in the shade with a simple meal and a glass of retsina.

Caroline was not at home, and he had looked forward to her company so much that he felt deflated. He knocked on the front door, and on receiving no reply stepped from the path and peered in through the big plate glass window that overlooked the pine-clad hillside and the sea.

The lounge was comfortable and homely, lived in rather than exhibiting the stark functionality of so many modern rooms, which looked like set-pieces for interior design magazines. He saw a big, battered sofa, woven rugs, bookshelves...

He squinted. On one of the selves he made out a hardback copy of every one of his novels. The sight should have gratified him, perhaps, but instead – something of his habitual paranoia resurfacing – he felt vaguely threatened.

He moved from the villa and continued along the track, feeling guilty for having pried.

Caroline had mentioned reading one or two of his books, but never the fact that she had every one of them. She had obviously built up the collection over time, which begged the question: why she decided to buy the villa next door to his own?

Perhaps she had heard of his legendary reclusiveness, and resolved to write a feature on the man... He was convinced now that she was a *bona fide* painter, but that did not exclude the possibility that she also wrote as a side-line.

He cursed the treacherous course of his thoughts, but, once in his head, they could not be dismissed.

By the time he reached Sarakina, he knew what he should do.

Instead of taking his table in the shade, he entered the taverna and slipped into the telephone kiosk at the back of the room. It was small and cramped, and reminded him of a confessional booth. He phoned the local operator and asked for an international line, and five minutes later dialled the London number of his agent.

In a day or two, he would know if Caroline was indeed who she said she was.

"Daniel!" Pryce exclaimed, as he did on the few occasions that Langham phoned. "This is a pleasant surprise. You're not in London, by any chance?"

"What do you think?"

"Somehow I thought it unlikely. How is tropical Kallithéa?"

"Well, it isn't tropical, for a start. But otherwise it's as beautiful as ever. I'm ringing to ask a favour."

"Ask away."

"I need some information on a painter."

"Now, if you were connected to the Internet..."

"Sod the Internet. Have you got a pen?"

"I've a keyboard, will that do?"

"I want to know about a painter called Caroline Platt. She's had exhibitions in London, and a gallery on Great Portland Street handles her work. What I really want to know is if she writes. Features. Essays. Even books."

"Got it. You want copies if I can get them?"

Why not? "Whatever you can get hold of."

"Why the interest, Daniel?"

He made up some story about admiring her painting and wanting to know more. "I'll ring back same time tomorrow, if that's okay?"

"Fine by me," Pryce said. "And how's the latest coming along?"

"It'll be on your desk in December, Pryce."

He rang off and remained seated, feeling guilty at what he had done, as if the kiosk were truly a confessional and he had withheld a sin from the priest.

He took his table beneath the awning and ordered lamb with butter beans basted in olive oil and tomatoes, with a big chunk of white bread.

He ate slowly, considering Caroline Platt. If she turned out to be another hack after his story, then his disappointment would be colossal. She had taken him in, made him believe that her interest in him, her friendliness, had been genuine – not prompted by the need to muck-rake for profit.

And yet, if she turned out to be what she said she was, and her friendship genuine... then that eventuality was almost as troubling. He was not prepared to admit anyone into his life: it was doomed to failure, tragedy and regret. He took out his note-book and wrote: *The process of living seems to me to be nothing but a gradual accretion of sadness*. The line would find its way into the mouth of one of his characters, sooner or later.

He had given occasional thought to the fat Englishman over the past few days, since seeing him at the exhibition. The fact that he was researching a biography on him surfaced in his mind from time to time like a recurrent headache.

It came back to him now, in a rush, because approaching the taverna from along the waterfront was the overweight hack himself.

Langham watched him with a mixture of loathing and trepidation. There was something obnoxious about every aspect of the man. Even the way he walked managed to annoy. He slumped along, marinating in his own sweat, weighed down by his hold-all which hung from his shoulder and gave him a decided list to starboard.

Langham slipped a hand into his pocket and rubbed the smooth surface of the mereth.

The man reached the taverna and stood beside a table, placing his hold-all on a chair but making no effort to seat himself. He did not acknowledge Langham, but gestured to Georgiou and ordered a beer. As Langham watched, the man rooted through his hold-all and pulled out a book – Langham's *In Khartoum*, which he had been reading a week ago.

He then surprised Langham by approaching him and holding out the book. "Daniel Langham? I wonder if you'd sign this for me?"

His manner was abrupt, peremptory, but his tone more educated than Langham had supposed it would be. He took the book and leafed through it. The man supplied a cheap biro, slick with his sweat.

Seen at close quarters, Langham noticed how the man oozed perspiration. It popped from every pore and trickled, soaking the collar of his white shirt and creating dark patches beneath the arms of his beige polyester suit.

"Who is it to?"

"Just the signature will do fine."

Langham looked up. "I like to know the name of the person I'm talking to."

"Then call me Nick."

Langham scribbled his signature in the front of the book, taking his time, while the man waited, mopping his brow.

He passed the book back to the man and said, "I understand you intend to write my biography?"

The man – Langham could not bring himself to think of him as Nick – pulled out a chair at Langham's table and seated himself with one arm on the table-top and the other resting on his knee. Langham wondered if the performance was designed to intimidate.

"I'd like to talk to you about that."

"I also understand that I've given you permission, which is news to me."

The man maintained a blank expression. It was as if he had decided, long ago, that he should give nothing away facially. Instead, he used body language to communicate: now he leaned forward, threatening, like a Gestapo interrogator.

"That was a necessary white lie," he said.

"You won't find out much about me from people on the island," Langham said. "Or anywhere else, for that matter."

The man placed his finger-tips together and contemplated them. "That's what I'm discovering, Mr Langham. You're something of an enigma."

"I'm a forty year-old middle-class English writer who enjoys his privacy," he said. "Like most people. End of story."

The man regarded him. There was something nerveless about his stare, and unsettling. "Oh, I think you're a little more interesting than that, actually."

Langham took a sip of wine to calm his nerves. He smiled. "Well, you're welcome to dig, but I don't think you'll find anyone to help you."

"The discoveries I've made so far have been less through talking to people," he said, "than by analysing your books. Did you know that there are certain textual similarities between your work and that of other writers?"

Langham fought to maintain an outward air of calm, while inside he was rattled. He smiled again, aware that it must appear forced. "'Certain textual similarities' is a rather long-winded way of hinting at plagiarism, isn't it?"

The man stood, picked up the book, and moved across to where he'd left his bag. His beer had arrived, and he remained standing while he chugged it down. Then he returned to Langham's table. He deployed his movements in a way that was, Langham thought, calculated to annoy.

"Whatever you might like to call it, Mr Langham, I'd like to talk to you about it at length. Would this afternoon at your villa be convenient?"

"It would not. I'm very busy at the moment."

The man considered his fingers. His repulsive nails were tiny and embedded in the surrounding flesh. "The thing is, Mr Langham, if I were to do a feature on you for the *Mail*, the editor would rather I use the term 'plagiarism' than 'certain textual similarities'."

A hand reached into Langham's chest and squeezed.

The man said, "Which afternoon would be convenient for you?"

"I'll be working every day for the next week. Perhaps some time after that."

The man nodded and stood. "I'll be in touch." He retrieved his hold-all and moved from the taverna, slouching along the waterfront and disappearing behind a line of buildings. Langham wondered if, out of sight, he was rubbing his hands at his little victory, or if such lavish gestures were not part of his repertoire. Perhaps he would be smiling quietly to himself.

He drained his wine and ordered another. He could not finish the little of his meal that remained, and his hand, as it took up the refilled glass, was shaking.

He returned to his villa and sat on the sofa overlooking the sea, contemplating what the journalist had said and wondering how much he might have discovered. If the unearthing of 'certain textual similarities' was all he had come up with, then Langham could rest easy.

The danger was that he might have used the textual similarities as a starting point and come up with much, much more.

Later that afternoon he concentrated on his work, then cooked himself a meal and retired early. He slept badly, the little sleep that he did manage inhabited by menacing spectres from the past.

In the morning his writing went slowly; every line seemed forced and unoriginal and he cursed the bastard Englishman for having such an effect on his work. By twelve he'd completed his four page quota, with a small sense of achievement at having done so against the odds, and then set off for the village to phone his agent.

He was dreading the thought of encountering the journalist again, but there was no sign of him as he entered the taverna and slipped into the phone booth.

Five minutes later he was through to London.

He was aware of his thudding heart. Let her be what she claims to be, he thought. Dear God, he could not go through all the pain again.

"Pryce, did you turn up anything on the artist?"

"Daniel, just a sec. How's things? You'll be delighted to know that it's pouring down at this end." Langham heard the distant rattle of a keyboard. Then, "Ah... here it is.

"I've got a bit of biographical information, in case you wanted it. Born 1960 in Harrogate, Yorkshire. Attended–"

"I know all that from an exhibition pamphlet I picked up."

"Did you also know that she's divorced, and that her husband was an alcoholic who beat her up? I bet that wasn't in the pamphlet."

"No. No, you're right," Langham said, at once shocked, and relieved that this information tended to corroborate Caroline's story. "Look, did you find out if she's written any books, articles?"

"Nothing," Pryce said. "No books, articles, critical theory. She was interviewed in the *Guardian* a couple of years ago, and in a northern arts magazine around the same time. But that's about it."

"Any idea if she might have written under a pseudonym?"

"I checked that," Pryce said, "but came up with nothing."

They chatted for a further minute or two, and then Langham hung up.

He sat at his table in the shade and ordered lunch in an expansive mood. Let the fat journalist do his worst – at least Caroline Platt was the genuine article. He looked forward to their next meeting.

He managed to finish his lunch this time without being accosted. Later, taking the path through the pines, he considered what his agent had told him about Caroline's abusive, alcoholic husband. He wondered if that might account for the melancholy he sometimes encountered behind her eyes.

He stopped by her villa again and knocked on the door. There was no reply, and he wondered if she was in her studio.

He moved around the house and approached the outbuilding. The door was open and he paused beside it, hoping to catch a glimpse of the artist at work.

There was no sign of Caroline within. He was about to close the door when he saw the canvas. It was at the far side of the studio, placed on an easel – evidently a work in progress. He stepped into the studio and approached the easel.

What struck him about the painting was its complete antithesis to every other one he had seen by Caroline Platt. Where the others were bright and optimistic, full of life, this one was dark and foreboding. It showed a big, darkened room in tones of blue and black, and, just discernible in one corner, the shadowy figure of a cowering girl or woman. The suggestion of loneliness, fear and despair was shocking.

He moved from the easel and regarded other works racked against the wall; many were similar to those he'd seen in the exhibition, but occasionally he came across darker, more despairing pictures: a storm scene with a lost figure in the mid-ground; a long, grim street with a little girl in silhouette at the far end; an almost wholly black canvas with the image of a women, falling.

He wondered if she had painted these in reaction to the abuse she had suffered at the hands of her husband; if these were her way of coming to terms, years later, with a period of her life she had been unable or unwilling to commit to canvas at the time?

He left the studio and hurried to his villa. He made himself a coffee and settled down to go though the pages he had written that morning. He preferred this afternoon shift. The first draft was always fraught with the fear that he would not achieve what he intended; the rewrite was an opportunity to improve, cut and tighten up, with none of the difficulty of original creation.

At six he finished work, then made a few notes about tomorrow morning's scene. He was about to slip the manuscript book into the drawer of the table on the patio, and then considered the journalist. He carried the book into the villa and locked it in the top drawer of his desk, instead.

He poured himself a beer, and was just about to prepare his evening meal when he heard a tap at the open door, and a second later a voice call out, "Hello in there... Daniel, are you home?"

"In the kitchen. Come in."

She appeared in the doorway and leaned against the jamb, smiling in at him. She looked, he thought, tired and drawn; her face was pale, her eyes sunken. Had she just recovered from her migraine, and dragged herself out of bed after three days?

He hoped she hadn't noticed his reaction.

"Caroline. Were you at home? I stopped by..."

"I just got back," she said. "I had to fly to London. Last minute thing. Business. Just got back, and to be honest I'm jaded. London really takes it out of me."

"What a host I am! Sit down."

He pulled out a kitchen chair and she sat down.

"Can I get you a drink?"

"I'd love one, Daniel."

He poured her a juice with ice cubes and set it beside her on the table. "Look," he said, on inspiration. "I'm just about to cook. Why don't you join me?"

"You wouldn't mind? I'm not interrupting?"

"Work's done for the day. This is the time I unwind. Leisurely meal, a beer on the sofa while watching the sun go down, the stars come out..."

"Sounds like a perfect evening."

"I'm afraid I'm no *cordon bleu* chef, but I'm international – I do a decent Spanish omelette and Greek salad."

"Lovely. Is there anything I can do?"

"Just sit there and talk to me. This doesn't take five minutes."

They chatted while he cooked; smalltalk, life in London, her business trip, the exhibition. He wanted to ask her about the dark paintings he had seen in her studio, but judged that this was not the time.

"Enough of me," she said. "What of life on the island while I've been away? Anything scandalous to report?"

"On Kallithéa?" he laughed. "And as if I'd notice!"

"No more encounters with your journalist friend?"

"Yesterday," he said. "I was having lunch and he came up and asked me to sign one of my books. He asked for an interview."

"And I hope you told him where to stick his interview?"

Langham nodded, feigning concentration on the tricky process of sliding the completed omelette from the pan and onto a plate. "There we are. Shall we eat outside?"

She helped him carry the things through to the patio table, the journalist forgotten. They ate and chatted while the sun slipped down the sky, and Langham contrasted this meal with the thousands of others he'd taken alone over the years.

"I called round today. Your studio was open. I couldn't help notice the painting on the easel. The girl in the room."

She nodded. "And? What did you think?"

"To be honest, I found it quite shocking. In contrast to your other work... Well, the work I've seen at the exhibition seems to symbolise the person I know. Those other, darker paintings..."

"You saw the others?"

He felt his face heat up. "I hope you don't mind. I couldn't help looking."

"Not at all. I'm flattered that you're interested."

"They're very dark pieces, very pessimistic."

She shrugged. "We all have our dark, hidden places, Daniel. Our secrets."

He nodded. "Yes, I suppose we do."

"It helps, being creative. You can explore these things, work them out."

"What do they symbolise? Or can't you talk about that?"

"No, that's okay. Well... my husband, the landscape gardener I told you about... It wasn't exactly a match made in heaven, and unfortunately it took me ten years to work that out."

And she told him her story, the marriage, the alcoholism, the abuse... and he listened with a deepening respect for this strange and powerful woman, respect and admiration for how she had survived and prospered.

They finished the meal and he poured her another orange juice. He suggested they sit on the sofa and watch the embers of the sun on the horizon. They sat side by side and talked while the sun disappeared and the stars came out, twinkling, above the darkening ocean.

"Did I tell you, Mr Langham, that I own first editions of every one of your novels?"

He looked at her, relieved at her admission. "A serious collector."

"A serious reader. I discovered your first novel just after I left my husband. You can't imagine what a good companion a great book is in times like that. I read your first three books one after the other, and they helped. They possessed a reality, the characters were suffering so much... I know it sounds corny, but I felt as if I wasn't alone."

"Thank you," he said. He paused, then went on, "When you came to Kallithéa, was it because...?"

"Because I knew you lived here and wanted to meet you?" She shook her head. "No, not at all. The biographical bits on the backs of your books don't give that much away. Born in '59 and lives in Greece, and that's it. So when I came house hunting and found the villa – and then learned that my neighbour would be the famous novelist... well, I had to have the place."

"And when you met me you were disappointed." He smiled. "Readers assume that writers will be intellectual, conversationally brilliant. But it doesn't work like that. Writing's something you do over a long time, and you make many mistakes and wrong-turnings. In real life I'm pretty slow on the uptake and know nothing of the real world."

Caroline laughed. "But you're a good person, Daniel. That's what I expected from the author who wrote the books. Or rather, that's what I hoped."

They were silent for a time. Her hand lay on the cushion between them, and more than anything Langham wanted to reach out and cover it with his.

"I asked you this before, but you didn't want to tell me," she said now. "And if you still don't want to talk about it, then that's fine. But... your books seem so full of pain, love affairs that never work, lonely men... They must reflect your life, Daniel."

So he told her, in fair trade for the story of her failed marriage, something of his own life, but altered, the details changed, out of necessity. It was the essential truth, a reasonable account of the pain he'd suffered, but rendered with the legerdemain of a novelist.

He told her about Sam, and how she had inadvertently taken her own life, about Tara and the other failed affairs in between.

"My God," she said, "you're only forty, and you've experienced so much! No wonder you hide yourself away these days."

He changed the subject, pointing at the stars. "Orion," he said. "Isn't it beautiful?"

She looked at him. "You have a thing about the stars, don't you?"

He smiled. "I think they represent hope," he said.

They continued talking long into the warm night.

CHAPTER SIX

London, February, 1935

LOOKING BACK ON the events from the remove of a year, I am amazed that I can recall the time with such clarity, as if it occurred just a week ago.

In the days following the incident at Hopton Wood, I tried to ease myself back into the routine of my writing life in London. I took up the notes of my latest novel, and the few pages I had managed so far, intending to continue from where I had left off. However, the event I had witnessed, or rather the implications of that event, would not allow me to concentrate on the process of creating fiction. In order to write I needed a clear mind, my thoughts unsullied by extraneous influences or emotions. And, to be perfectly honest, compared to what I had witnessed in Hopton Wood, the fictitious incidents of my lacklustre novel paled into insignificance.

I lay the book aside and began a long, descriptive piece covering the events of that night in Hopton Wood, which I have used extensively when making this more detailed account.

The last person in the world I wished to meet was Carla, and fearing that she might decide to call at the flat, I spent long hours walking around London, visiting galleries and cafés and the occasional public house. I seemed, in those days immediately after Hopton Wood, to exist at a remove from my fellow man. The world continued on its merry way – with the unrest in Spain and the Nazi threat filling the news – but I was no longer a passenger. The knowledge of what had happened that night in the Chiltern hills set me apart from the rest of the human race; I was privy to intelligence so fantastic that, if it were to be made public, then no doubt the entire history of the planet would be affected. I had a secret that made the cares and concerns of everyone around me seem trivial and of no account. It was a secret at once liberating and terribly isolating; yet it had the effect, naturally enough, of making me feel closer to the men with whom I had shared the experience. I counted the days to the weekend, when I would once again accompany Edward Vaughan to Cranley Grange.

On the day my father was due to return from Kent, I phoned him at home. As ever, Mrs Johnson answered. She informed me, without being able to keep herself from weeping, that Mr Harold had been taken into hospital that morning.

Her words thrust an icy fist into my chest. I sat down quickly and asked for whatever news she might have.

She knew very little, save that my father collapsed while in Kent, and that a local GP had advised a period of hospitalisation. He was in a private clinic off Harley Street. I took down the address, called a taxi, and fifteen minutes later was riding north through the grey and crowded streets of London.

I think I secretly feared that the medic's diagnosis had been in error, and instead of having weeks or even a month or two to live, my father had in fact days. I half expected to find him paralysed in bed and staring death in the face.

Instead, he was sitting in an armchair beside the bed, jotting down notes on a writing pad as if he had all the time in the world ahead of him. I noticed, lying face down on the bed beside him, a copy of *Summer in Kallithéa*. I was moved beyond words to think that, in the little time he had left, he was re-reading my books.

"Jonathon! I was hoping to be out of this damned place before you got wind of what'd happened."

Although infirm and pale, he seemed in good spirits.

"What happened? Mrs Johnson said you collapsed at Donaldson's."

"Something of nothing. Sudden blackout. Nothing to worry about. Sit down, on the bed. There you go."

I sat as instructed, trying not to smile. There was something at once idiotically brave, and at the same time heart-breakingly tragic, in his refusal to let the sentence of death affect his demeanour.

"Now look here, I've been making a few calculations..." He passed me a sheet of paper filled with columns and figures in his neat, copperplate handwriting. I smiled to myself; he was forever making calculations.

I scanned the columns and shook my head. They made not the slightest sense to me. My father harrumphed; it seemed to be his one gripe with me that I had not inherited his aptitude for figures.

At the foot of the page, impressed upon the paper in bold numerals, was the figure: £250,000.

"I've been going though my assets, Jonathon. Calculating what I'm worth. The solicitor's coming down tomorrow to draw up a new will." He leaned forward and tapped the page. "That's what you stand to inherit, after tax."

I knew then that he wanted what he considered best for me, but he was a man of limited imagination: he desired to be kind, and could not see the cruelty of making his bequest known to me.

"I don't know what to say," I murmured. How could I intimate to him the pain I felt then, staring down at a sum of money that was at once gross and dangerously liberating?

I wanted to tell him that the money meant nothing, that I would rather have him survive: but even to hint at this would be to evince a sympathy he did not want and would be unable to accept.

He tapped my knee. "Say nothing. What did you expect, that I'd leave it to a dog's home? Money will buy you time, Jonathon – time to write more. By the way–" he gestured towards the book on the bed, "–re-reading your *Kallithéa*. Tremendously enjoyable. How's the latest coming along?"

Tears filled my eyes, and my throat constricted. My father was my most uncritical reader; when I put pen to paper, I could do no wrong.

"It's coming along very well," I said, then made the excuse that I needed the lavatory and made my escape.

As I returned to my father's private room, I sought out a doctor and introduced myself. He showed me into his oak-panelled office, sat me down, and told me with a soft-voiced honesty, which I appreciated, that my father had in his estimation approximately six weeks left to live.

After a silence, I managed, "Have you told him?"

"He's demanded the truth all along, Mr Langham. Your father calls a spade a spade."

I smiled at this. "Will he be in pain when... I mean–"

"I assure you that, with the aid of modern drugs, his passing will be quite painless."

When I returned to my father's room, he was sitting bolt upright in his chair with my novel open on his lap. I stayed for an hour, wanting to tell him about the phenomenon in Hopton Wood, but unable to do so. My father was a severely pragmatic man, and I could not bring myself to attempt to subvert a lifetime of scepticism at the eleventh hour.

As I was about to leave, with the promise that I would visit him again the following day, he laid a hand on my arm to detain me. "About Carla," he said. "I think she's the right girl for you, Jonathon. Do the proper thing and marry her, you hear me?"

I smiled, gripped his hand and said goodbye.

I left the hospital and wandered the streets in a daze, heading vaguely south. I took a 'bus from Trafalgar Square and arrived home just before four, as twilight was bringing in yet another freezing winter night. I sat alone before the fire, stared at the dancing flames, and wondered what was keeping me in London. I had moved to the capital from Kent five years ago, upon the sale of my first novel, thinking that a young writer needed to be close to the centre of the publishing world. But the city frequently dispirited me, with its press of anonymous people, its filth and noise. After experiencing the Chilterns with Carnegie and Vaughan, something within me hankered after the beauty and simplicity of country life.

The telephone rang, and without thinking I picked up the receiver.

"Jonathon."

"Carla," I said, sounding less than enthusiastic.

"Where the hell have you been, Jonathon?" She sounded almost hysterical.

"What do you mean?" I answered vaguely.

"You disappeared without saying anything on Thursday. On Friday I 'phoned. You either weren't in or didn't answer, so I called around and you weren't at home. I've been 'phoning every day."

"I had to leave London. On business."

"Without telling me?"

I let the silence stretch. "After how things have been going between us lately, I didn't think you'd be much bothered."

"'Much bothered'? What do you mean by that?"

I said nothing.

"Jonathon? Jonathon, I'm coming round."

"Don't waste–" But she had already hung up.

I sat in silence and stared at the fire. I had not bothered to switch on the light, and the flames provided the only illumination. I realised that I hadn't eaten since breakfast, and then just as swiftly realised that I was not that hungry. I felt sick to my stomach and had no appetite.

I considered Carla and the idea of life without her, the freedom from routine and the liberating opportunity of being able to meet other women, women perhaps more suitable... And yet, as these thoughts occurred to me, like a drowning man I relived excerpts from my past with Carla, the good times we'd had, the intimacies we'd shared – the emotional connections which made our relationship unique and irreplaceable.

A knock sounded at the door, and I ignored it. I closed my eyes and willed her to go away. It was a measure of my cowardice and immaturity that I could not bring myself to tell her that I wished our affair to end.

The knocking continued, and she began calling my name. She sounded frantic.

In rage I stormed to the door and snatched it open. At the sight of her there, almost cowering on the doorstep, something within me relented.

I stood back and allowed her to enter. She hurried past and entered the lounge, reaching out for the fire as she had done on so many occasions before.

"It's dark in here, Jonathon. Why haven't you switched on the light?"

I switched on the light.

I could see, from her blurred mascara, that she'd been crying.

We were standing at opposite ends of the room, opponents in some ill-defined contest of the soul.

She laughed, but she was on the verge of tears. "You're tanned, Jonathon."

I looked in the mirror. Sure enough, my face was tanned a deep, unaccustomed bronze.

"Where did you say you've been, the South of France?"

"Hampshire. I was walking. The sun reflecting off the snow..." How could I tell her the truth, that an otherworldly light had burned my face?

"Why didn't you tell me you were going away? I was worried sick."

"I didn't think you'd care in the slightest."

The silence stretched. At last she said, "What's happening between us, Jonathon?"

"I was wondering the same thing. I thought that perhaps you'd be able to tell me."

She shook her head. "What do you mean? I thought everything was going so well... Why didn't you say something?"

"Do you mean on Thursday night, when you were throwing yourself over that creep Ticehurst?"

She narrowed her eyes and shook her head ever so slightly. "Is that it? Thursday night? I was having a good time. Al and I are friends."

"It looked like you were more than just good friends to me."

She regarded me for long seconds. "That's the one thing that I really cannot abide in you, Jonathon. Your insane, childish jealousy."

"Is that the only thing? I thought you'd be keeping a list."

"Jonathon, what have I done? This is insane. Everything was going so well. Please tell me what I've done wrong!"

I sighed, though really I wanted to bury my head in my hands and weep. "It isn't just you," I said. "It's not your fault. We're... we're just two different people, with very little in common, different friends. It isn't working."

"I thought you liked my friends? We both love the theatre." There was a note of desperation or disbelief in her tone which skewered me with guilt.

"I can't abide your friends, the crowd we were with on Thursday night. It's a society of mutual sycophants. I've yet to meet a friend of yours who comes over as genuine. They're all playing parts." I stopped myself before I twisted the knife and admitted that the only reason I claimed to have liked the theatre in the first place was because of her.

She looked stricken. "We needn't see them. We could go out together, see your friends."

I felt my throat constrict. I had not wanted her to plead like this. I had hoped that she might read between the lines, admit to me that our affair had not been working for her, too. In short, I had selfishly hoped that she might have made it easy for me.

Only later did I wonder how I might have felt, then, if she had casually accepted or suggested our parting: would I have experienced the egotistical pain of rejection?

She stared at me. “You’ve met someone else, haven’t you?”

“There’s no one else. Honestly.”

She stared at me, then said, “I don’t know whether to be thankful. At least if there was another woman... that would be a reason.”

“Carla, it isn’t working. I’m holding you back. If a couple doesn’t like each other’s social circle... You have your friends, people you’re comfortable with.” I realised I was gabbling, trying to find the words to make her accept that it was over.

Tears filmed her eyes. “It isn’t the physical side of things, is it?”

“That’s wonderful. But it isn’t everything.”

She seemed to deflate. “I can’t believe this. I can’t believe this is happening. I thought everything was so good.”

I almost said, “I’m sorry,” but that would have been crass, and also untruthful.

“We’ve been together a year, Jonathon. It seems impossible that it can end just like that. We have so much to talk about.” She opened her eyes wide and stared at me. “We can meet, can’t we? Talk things over?”

I nodded. “If that’s what you’d like.”

She almost shouted, “Wouldn’t you like that? Or would you rather not see me again at all?”

“No. No... there’s no reason why we can’t still be friends.”

She shook her head, slowly, watching me with a gaze I chose to interpret as accusing. “Friends? What an awful, empty word that is after all we’ve shared together.”

“Carla, I didn’t mean to hurt you. This isn’t easy for me, you know?”

From somewhere in her repertoire of stock expressions, she employed a cruel smile. “Do you know something, Jonathon? You all say that, every damned man I’ve ever known.”

“Would you rather we went on as we have been? Me becoming ever more dissatisfied, resenting you because you aren’t the person I wanted you to be?”

"We could have talked things through, Jonathon. If only I'd known how you were feeling, then maybe I could have done something."

"It's past that," I said.

She stared at me, then hurried from the room. I followed her. She opened the door and paused on the top step, her back to me. Then she turned.

"Let's meet again," she said. "I don't want this to be the last time I see you."

She came into my arms, like a thousand times before, and it seemed so right, she fitted so perfectly, that as I held her then I wondered why the exquisite physicality of our affair could not be matched by a similar union of temperament or soul.

She pulled away, then kissed me quickly on the cheek and hurried down the steps. I watched her stride along the street and turn the corner, a sensation of emptiness and desolation expanding within my chest.

I returned inside, switched off the light and sat before the fire. Why was it, now, that all my earlier reasons to end the affair with Carla seemed so empty and baseless? The prospect of freedom was a shallow concept when I felt so alone; the thought of tolerating her friends seemed a small price to pay for the joy of her company, the delight of her physicality which I would never again experience. Had she returned to me at that minute, I am sure I would have swept her into my arms and begged for her forgiveness.

I sat for hours in the light of the fire, the room dark around me. At that moment, with the thought of my father alone in his hospital room, and my affair with Carla at an end, I had never felt the future to be so bleak: even the wonders I had experienced in Hopton Wood did nothing to alleviate the simple human emotions of grief and loneliness I was undergoing.

I slept badly that night, even at one point dreaming of Carla. I awoke in a sweat in the early hours, remembering the times

I had woken with her beside me and stared at her face as she slept, unaware of my gaze.

I rose late, bathed, and decided to walk into the city in order to while away an hour or so. As I strode through Chelsea I passed a public house where Carla and I and the theatre crowd had met once following a show. I saw a small Greek restaurant that we had favoured in the early days of our courtship. It seemed that many such familiar places crouched in ambush all over the city, waiting to leapt out and remind me of all that I had lost.

I tried to look ahead, consider the possibility of other liaisons; but the simple fact was that she had been the centre of my existence for so long that it was well nigh impossible to imagine meeting another woman as real and alive as Carla.

I considered visiting my father, but the coward in me shied away from that encounter. I hurried across the river to Battersea through the busy rush-hour streets. I wanted nothing more than to be away from London, heading with Vaughan towards the Chilterns and Hopton Wood. Friday could not come soon enough, and it was still only Wednesday. The prospect of having to endure a cold winter Thursday in London filled me with despair.

I retired early to bed, and by some miracle sleep came early and was uninterrupted. I did dream – visions of coruscating blue light, and fleeting, surreal images of Carla, and my bed-ridden father – but woke reasonably refreshed at nine.

I forced myself to eat breakfast, bacon sandwiches and strong tea. I sat at my desk for the rest of the morning and read through my notes detailing the strange occurrences at Hopton Wood.

I decided to spend the remainder of the day at the British Library, and attempt some research into the phenomena of blue lights and haunted ancient forests and the like – though I very much doubted whether I would turn up much information on the subject.

I was about to set off when there was a knock at the door. Overcoat in hand, I pulled open the door and stared at Carla, standing on the top step.

I indicated my coat. "I was just about to go out."

My response might sound heartless, but the fact was that the sight of Carla standing there, beautiful in the bright winter sunlight, filled me with pain. It was all I could do not to reach out and pull her into my arms.

But I told myself that I had to be strong; that my decision to leave Carla would ultimately be for the best, for the both of us.

"In that case I won't keep you for long," she said in a small voice. She wore a long, ankle-length coat and a red bonnet-affair as close fitting as a swimming cap. Her face was pale, drawn.

She met my eyes briefly. "Are you going to let me in?"

I stepped back. She side-stepped past me and walked into the lounge. For once she could not warm herself before the fire, as I had neglected to build it that morning.

Instead she stood before the empty hearth and regarded me.

"Why didn't you tell me, Jonathon?"

I was non-plussed, at first thinking that she had somehow found out about the events in Hopton Wood. Before I realised the improbability of this, she went on. "I called your father last night. I spoke with his housekeeper. She told me about... about his illness. Of course I went to see him."

I found myself murmuring, "He'd like that."

"I wanted to ask him about you, if anything was troubling you."

"Isn't the fact that my father is dying enough to trouble anyone?"

She shook her head. "I don't think it's the reason for you finishing with me."

"Of course it wasn't."

"Then what was?"

I sighed. "Need we go through all that again?" I made to put on my coat, hoping that she would take the hint.

"Why didn't you tell me that Harold was ill?"

"To be honest, it didn't seem appropriate. How could I simply slip into the conversation the fact that my father was dying?"

"You could have... I don't know, phoned, or even written."

"I'm sorry. I didn't think it such a grievous omission."

She stared at me from across the room. "It was awfully thoughtless, Jonathon."

I shrugged, attempting nonchalance at the charge. A thought occurred to me. "You didn't tell him? About us, I mean?"

Her eyes widened in a kind of flinch that I could think her so crass. "Of course not! How could I have told a dying man... He told me that he wants us to get married."

I laughed, though in fact I felt closer to tears. "He told me that, too."

The silence stretched. "About yesterday – you weren't yourself, Jonathon. Something is wrong, isn't it? Whatever it is, you know you can share it with me."

"Carla..."

"A year is a long time, Jonathon. We've shared so much. I don't want it to end like this."

"What do you mean?"

She stared at me, an intensity in her gaze that I found disconcerting. Her lips trembled; if she was acting, it was a prize-wining performance. "I love you, Jonathon. I think I only realised quite how much I loved you when I left here yesterday. I went through hell... You can't imagine. Last night's performance. To be honest I don't know how I managed to get through it."

"I'm sorry."

"Why... why can't we try again? I can change. We won't see my friends as much. We could go away for a while, a short holiday. I just want things to be perfect between us, as they were in the early days."

My heart seemed to expand in my chest, as if it were bursting. I was aware that I was standing at a crossroads, and whatever decision I made, whichever road I decided to take, would be momentous and possibly regrettable.

I wanted to be strong, and turn my back and walk out of the flat, and out of her life forever. But weakness kept me there, a weakness and insecurity at the core of my being which I told myself was compassion; how, I reasoned, could I hurt her so much yet again?

Impulsively, she moved towards the bedroom. I was aware of my heart, thudding suddenly.

She left the bedroom door ajar, and I could make out her shadow on the floor as she moved. I could discern very clearly what she was doing, and a part of me wanted nothing else but to flee, while another part experienced the visceral tug of lust and affection that some people call love.

As I moved towards the bedroom, I thought of all the wonderful times we had shared over the year – the tiny shared intimacies that seemed magnified and made all the more important because they might never occur again. It was within my power, I realised, to make them happen... and the weight of responsibility, not only for one person's happiness but for two, brought tears to my eyes.

I stood in the doorway. Her clothes were scattered on the floor. She lay in bed, the sheets kicked back, her hands above her head. Her face was turned away from me, and I received the impression that she was holding her breath, and at the same time murmuring a silent prayer.

The thought occurred to me that I was unworthy of her heartache, that she would in time be better off without someone whose inexperience filled him with jealous rage and insecurity.

I walked around the bed and sat down. My hand trembled as I reached out and stroked her cheek. Her face was so pale, made even paler by her jet black bangs. When I pulled her to me and our lips collided, I was surprised anew at the weight of her, her warmth and sheer humanity.

I came late to love, and as mysterious as the baffling psychology of attraction was the renewed wonder, every time I held Carla, that the physicality of something that I had feared for so long, the giving of oneself and taking from another in the act of sexual intimacy, could be so perfect and so right.

We made love in silence, and in the same quality of needful silence lay in each other's arms for what seemed like hours, while outside the world went on its way and a fall of snow commenced to coat the streets.

Later still, Carla said, "I didn't tell you: the play's been closed. Poor attendances. Bad reviews. It's the final night tonight."

"I'm sorry," I said. I could hardly tell her that it came as no surprise.

"There's an end of run party tonight, or rather a wake." She pulled a pretty grimace. "I can't get out of it, Jonathon."

"Don't worry about it. I have to visit my father, anyway."

She stroked my chest. "What are you doing this weekend?"

I sighed. "I'm going over to Cranley Grange again, staying with the editor I mentioned, Carnegie. He wants me to do a series of stories for the *Scribe*... we'll be discussing the details over the weekend."

"Good for you, Jonathon. Tell me all about it when you get back, okay?"

"I'll phone as soon as I'm in London," I said.

Later I threw together a late lunch and we chatted of nothing in particular – the exchange of smalltalk familiar and pleasant – until Carla had to leave for the matinee performance of *Lost Horizons*.

We parted on the top step of my flat with a quick kiss and a hug, and as I watched her walk quickly down the street and turn the corner, I was filled with joy at our reunion and at the same time a subtle sense of despair.

That night I visited my father. He was home from hospital and sitting up in bed, grey of face but paradoxically full of life. A nurse was on hand to administer the array of pills he had been prescribed, and with Mrs Johnson in attendance I could be reassured that he would be well cared for while I was away. Nevertheless, I felt guilty.

My father waved away my apologies. “These things can’t be avoided, Jonathon. Business is business, after all.”

We played chess for a couple of hours, but I could see that the effort of concentration was taking its toll: he made a couple of elementary errors, which I purposefully did not take advantage of, and I managed to play out a stalemate.

I noticed that he had proceeded no further with my novel. From time to time he lost track of what he was talking about, and on occasion nodded off, and then came awake with a guilty start.

Before I left, I asked him if Carla had visited.

“Came yesterday. We had a good old heart to heart. Fine girl.”

I considered my next words. It had occurred to me only moments before. “Did you tell her about the will?” I asked, hating myself for doing so.

He frowned, considering. “I do believe I did. Mentioned the fact that you’d both be able to settle down pretty soonish...”

I promised I’d drop by as soon as I got back, and took my leave. In the taxi back to Battersea, I considered what my father had told me, and Carla’s appearance at my flat that morning.

The insidious suspicions were starting again, and we had been back together less than a day. I thought of the party Carla would be attending now, along with Ticehurst and the rest of the crowd, and I could not help an involuntary and painful pang of jealousy.

It was midnight by the time I reached home, and I slept badly. The only comfort I experienced was the thought of the weekend away in the country, and what secrets Hopton Wood might yet divulge.

CHAPTER SEVEN

Kallithéa, July, 1999

FOUR DAYS HAD elapsed since their last meeting, and for much of the time Langham had been unable to push thoughts of Caroline Platt from his head.

The tyranny of biology, the reclusive misanthrope in him said as he stared into the bathroom mirror on the morning of the fourth day. It was unnatural for man to live without woman, and vice-versa, and after more than ten years of celibacy his body was making its needs known. If she were to leave the island tomorrow, he told himself, he would be upset for a week, and then slip back into his old routine as if she had never interrupted it.

Nevertheless, after completing his thousand words that morning, he donned his sun hat and took the path through the pines trees to her villa.

She was in her studio, working.

He paused at the door and watched her.

She had her back to him, and was oblivious of his presence. She moved from side to side, swaying, her brush moving in broad, rapid strokes across the top of the canvas.

It was another dark painting, he could see, a nighttime scene with two figures staring up at the stars. They looked lost. He wanted to tell her that the stars were things of beauty, but who was he to gainsay her vision?

She stopped and turned, as if sensing him there.

He knocked on the door. "I'm interrupting. Sorry."

"Not at all. Please, come in. I've finished for the day." She stood back. "There, what do you think? It needs work, but it's almost done."

The figures were dwarfed by the immensity of the heavens. He shook his head. "I don't know. It could be so optimistic, but somehow it isn't. Is that how you feel?"

"At times," she admitted.

"Now?"

She smiled at him. "Not at this exact second, no," she said in a tone which suggested she wanted to drop the subject.

"Actually, I came round to see if you'd had lunch yet. I thought we might stroll into the village, have something at Georgiou's."

She beamed at him. "That sounds like just the thing after a burst of creativity," she said. "Come into the house while I change into something clean."

He followed her into the villa and stood in the lounge, admiring her collection of books. She moved into the adjacent bedroom and changed her paint-smeared t-shirt. She had left the door open, and when he glanced through she was pulling a clean shirt over her head; he saw her large, rather sagging breasts, and protuberant belly, and the sight struck him as both fecund and beautiful. He looked away.

Photographs lined the mantelshelf: Caroline and two boys in most of them; the boys were toddlers in some of the pictures, teenagers in others. In all of them Caroline looked radiant and happy. There were no photographs of her ex-husband.

"There we are." She emerged from the bedroom, smiling. "I feel respectable again. And hungry. I've never actually dined at the taverna. Do you recommend it?" They left the house and made their way down the track.

"I've eaten there practically every day for the past ten years."

She looked at him. "Even at Christmas?"

"Even at Christmas."

"You've no family, relatives?"

"Not one."

"Friends you could spend the holiday with?"

"My friends are scattered all over the place. I suspect that none of them celebrate Christmas, either."

"Georgiou must be pleased with your custom."

"After the first six months," Langham said, "he cut my bill by a third, and it's only gone up once in ten years. I leave generous tips, though."

They arrived at the taverna and Langham made for his table. "Not here?" Caroline said, indicating a table beside the water.

He hesitated, and joined her. "This is strange," he said, sitting opposite from her. "I get a whole new perspective. I usually sit at the table by the door."

"My God, Daniel, you are a creature of habit." She laughed. "I thought writers liked variety, change."

"I had enough of that in my twenties," he said. "The squid is excellent."

They ate, and chatted – and Caroline interrupted a story about her New York exhibition with, "God! I clean forgot all about it!"

"What?" he asked, alarmed.

"Guess who came calling last night?"

"I've no idea–" he stopped. "Not the journalist?"

"He appeared at the front door around eight and started firing off questions about you. I told him: sorry, you were a friend, and I don't discuss the personal details of friends with complete strangers. He was damned persistent, Daniel." She gave a theatrical shiver. "There's something detestable about the man."

"That's what I thought, too. I'm glad it's not just me. Have you noticed how his face is always expressionless – yet he moves his body in deliberate poses and stances as if to compensate?"

She was nodding. "You're right. He just stared, but stanchioned his arm against the door frame and leaned in at me."

Langham shrugged. "Journalistic trick of the trade," he suggested.

"Daniel... he asked a strange question."

He nodded, trying not to show his concern. "What?"

"Well, he asked a lot of questions, how long I'd known you, had I met your friends, what I thought of you as a person. Then he asked me if I'd ever read any novels by Christopher Cartwright." She shook her head. "And, Daniel, he told me to tell you that he'd asked me that. What did he mean?"

Langham felt his stomach turn. He shook his head, feigning ignorance. "I can't imagine."

"I asked who he was, and he told me he was called Nicholas Forbes. He said he was writing your biography."

"At least now I know the full name of my enemy."

"He's staying at rooms over Yannis's post office," she said, pointing across the waterfront. "He said that if I had any information, I'd know where to find him. I think I shut the door in his face around then."

"Well done," Langham said absently. "That explains why he's managed to catch me here a couple of times. He can see the taverna from his room."

"Speak," Caroline said now in low tones, "of the devil. Here he comes. My God, he looks as if the heat's crucifying him!"

Langham felt a hollowness in his chest at the prospect of the imminent encounter. He wanted to turn in his seat and watch Forbes' approach; he felt at a disadvantage with his back to the man.

At last the journalist hove into sight and deposited his burdensome hold-all – why did he carry the damned thing about, like Sisyphus? – on a nearby table. He ignored Langham and Caroline, but lifted a chair by placing one finger beneath an upper cross-piece and carried it over to within three yards of where they sat.

He positioned the chair meticulously in the aisle between tables, sat down and stared at his obscene fingernails sunk into the puddings of his stubby fingers.

He looked up. "I'd like to ask you a number of questions, Mr Langham," he said.

Langham was aware that he'd broken out in a sweat which almost matched Forbes' for profusion. He drained his wine. Caroline was watching him.

Why did the bastard have to spoil such a wonderful meal, he thought.

"I'd like to know if I'm correct in a few small but very important details." Forbes produced his spiral-bound note-book and a biro, leaning forward to open the note-book on his ample lap and ready his pen.

"I was wondering if I had your Asian itinerary in '90 right," Forbes said. "Would you mind going through it with me?"

"I don't see–" Langham began.

Forbes continued, regardless. "You landed in Bangkok in February and stayed there for three months, before moving to Koh Chang, where you remained for just two weeks. Then you crossed into Laos..." He went on: Vientiane, Luang Prabang, then into Vietnam, and from there to China. He gave the duration of stay in each of these places, and to the best of Langham's recollection he was correct.

It was a *tour de force* of meticulous research designed, he knew, to frighten him: to let Langham know that he had traced his every move.

"Well, Mr Langham, is that substantially correct?"

Langham said, "Your research is better than my memory."

Forbes looked up. His face held no expression whatever. "The only thing is, Mr Langham, that before '90 I have no record of the movements of Daniel Langham. It's almost as if you didn't exist before '90, and then miraculously sprang into existence."

Langham signalled to Georgiou for a second glass of retsina. He smiled across the table at Caroline, who was watching Forbes with undisguised distaste, as if she had discovered a slug in her salad.

"I assure you, Mr Forbes, that I did exist before '90."

The journalist shot his cuffs in another of his declarative, theatrical gestures, leaned forward and placed his elbows precisely on his kneecaps. "Perhaps," he said, "you used a pseudonym, a *nom de plume*, another name?"

"I do know what a pseudonym is, thank you. But I assure you that I was and always have been Daniel Langham." His voice caught, and he took a quick swallow of wine.

Forbes nodded. He replaced his note-book in the breast pocket of his polyester suit.

"Well, I shall have to go away and do my research a little more thoroughly," he said. "Oh, and may I ask how the latest novel is progressing?"

"As well as can be expected, under the circumstances."

"And have you scheduled a time for our little chat about the other matter, perhaps?"

"Not yet. I'll be busy for another week."

Forbes nodded his understanding and stood up. He replaced the chair and picked up his hold-all. "I'll be in touch, Mr Langham." He nodded to Caroline and struggled off along the waterfront.

Langham mopped his brow and took another long drink. "Daniel," Caroline said, leaning forward and touching his arm. "What was he talking about, 'the other matter'?"

Langham said, "He wanted to talk about my ideas."

"I don't like him one bit," she said. "He gives me the creeps. And that thing about there being no record of you before 1990. What was he on about?"

Langham shook his head. "I'm as mystified as you. But he had my Asian trip down pat."

"He's disturbing," Caroline said. "He wants something, Daniel. I don't know what, but I don't believe he just wants to do your life."

Sick to his stomach, Langham merely nodded.

They finished the meal and strolled along the waterfront. Langham felt relieved when they were no longer in view of Forbes' room above the post office. They talked of other things, but Langham's thoughts were a million miles away.

They walked around the village and back up the track, and outside Caroline's villa he tentatively asked if she would care to dine at his place tonight.

She touched his arm. "That's sweet, really it is. But I've had this low-level migraine for days now, and I really should get an early night. Another time?"

"Of course. Fine..."

He walked home, more than a little unsettled by Forbes' attention, and disappointed at Caroline's refusal.

She was out when he called the following day, and the day after that when she came to the door she looked so pale and drawn that his first impulse was to ask if he should call a doctor. She insisted that she was okay – another migraine attack, but she had strong pills to counter the worst of the effects, except they wiped her out...

He didn't see her for another three days, and was wondering whether he should call round again, at the risk of making a nuisance of himself, when she turned up at his villa, bearing a tureen of lamb casserole.

"I hope you haven't started cooking, Daniel. I owe you a meal."

"I was just washing some new potatoes. We could have those with the casserole."

She sat at the kitchen table while he put the potatoes on. He poured her an orange juice and himself a glass of wine. He felt surprised at the degree of his elation at seeing her again. Without her, the world seemed a gloomier place.

"Do you mind if I take a look at your study, Daniel? I'm fascinated by where people work."

"You're welcome to look," he said. "But actually I work on the patio. I just use the study in winter, and then mainly to read. Through here."

He led her along the passage and opened the door. She stepped inside and looked around. It was a pretty conventional study, a few big, comfortable armchairs, a writing desk with an ancient, battered typewriter sitting upon it, a few shelves crammed with books. He had written in here for a few months ten years ago, before deciding that he preferred the atmosphere of the patio. He didn't even type his manuscripts up now, but paid a woman in Xanthos to do it on a word processor.

Caroline was kneeling to examine a bookcase. "You like science-fiction?"

"Some of it. The more character-oriented novels."

"I see you have a lot of Edward Vaughan."

"You've read him?" he said, surprised.

Caroline see-sawed her hand. "One or two of his books."

He knelt beside her and slipped a Vaughan hardback from the case, the book dusty and foxed. He opened it to the dedication page and read: To Jonathon Langham, Fellow Traveller. He read the first line: *The Interspatial ships were massing on the cusp of Vark space, charging their ion drives for the final assault on the fourth quadrant.* He smiled and replaced the book beside the other uniform editions.

"My God," Caroline said. "An art book." She pulled out a big, glossy Thames and Hudson hardback. "Ralph Wellard. You never told me you liked his work."

"Look," he said, turning a few pages.

She read, "'Dedicated To Jonathon, Christopher, and Daniel.'"

She looked at him. "You knew the great Ralph Wellard?"

"He was a friend of my grandfather," he said. "I met him a few times way back."

"What was he like? I've heard stories. I've read he was reclusive, but had a loyal coterie of close friends."

"He was a very patriarchal, wise man. Softly-spoken, humane, extremely knowledgeable about art and literature and music. Something of a polymath."

"How did your grandfather know him?"

"They were great friends back in the sixties," he said.

"And was he reclusive?"

"He guarded his privacy, and hated the intrusion of the press. But I wouldn't call him reclusive." He smiled. "I wouldn't particularly call myself reclusive, but I've heard it said about me."

She was flipping through the book, stilling the pages with her elegant fingers to better examine a print that caught her attention.

She looked at him. "Does anyone really know what happened to him, Daniel?"

"It remains a mystery to this day."

"Some people say that he staged his own disappearance, so that he could start a new life somewhere, anonymously. Do you think that's true?"

"His boat was found drifting off the coast of Naples, deserted. The police assumed he'd fallen overboard and drowned. You never know, he might have staged it. He might be living in secrecy somewhere as we speak..."

"He'd be... how old now?"

"Oh..." Langham inflated his cheeks. "I never was any good at figures. When I met him in the seventies, he'd be around fifty. So he'd be knocking on for eighty now."

"I wonder why anyone would stage their own disappearance?" she mused to herself.

Langham stood. "Hungry? The potatoes will be done."

They returned to the kitchen and carried the food outside to the patio. They ate and watched the sun go down, and Langham opened another bottle of wine and felt himself become steadily more inebriated.

Caroline talked about her art, and then art in general, and Langham listened, captivated both by the woman and by her words.

He watched her while she spoke; she had a delicate, precise way of moving her hands to emphasise her words, her exquisite fingers as graceful as those of a Balinese dancer.

He considered how someone who you would not think overly attractive becomes, when you get to know the person, strangely alluring and captivating. Caroline was short, a little squat, but all Langham beheld when he looked at her was her essential human beauty. He wanted to reach out and crush her in his embrace.

Later he walked her home, and they faced each other outside her villa. He reached out and drew her to him, and they kissed. She pulled away, not aggressively, but in such a way that told him she did not want to follow where he was leading her. "Daniel..."

"I'm sorry."

"No, it's not you. It's me. I'm sorry." She seemed confused, a little embarrassed, and would not look him in the eye.

She squeezed his hand in farewell. "Thank you for a lovely night, Daniel. I'll see you later."

He watched her hurry into the villa, and then turned and walked back up the track. He sat on the sofa for a long time, staring into the night sky and considering the scene outside her villa.

He should have held back, he thought, not risked offending her like that. It was perfectly understandable that she might feel a reluctance to get involved again after what she'd gone though with her husband, even if that had been ten years ago.

God only knew, scars took a long, long time to heal.

CHAPTER EIGHT

Cranley Grange, February, 1935

I MET EDWARD Vaughan outside Kings Cross station at two, and we drove from London through a heavy fall of snow that made the roads treacherous and the going painfully slow.

The back seat of his Austin was loaded with a large timber box which he told me was a home-made Morse machine, with which he hoped to communicate with the beings beyond the blue light. While Vaughan drove, I read a treatise he had penned on the history of the human race, condensed into a little under ten thousand words. As might be expected from a writer of Vaughan's distinction, it was a masterpiece of succinct information. He told me that he hoped to launch the missive, protected by a tin box or some such, through the portal when we next witnessed its opening.

It was almost six o'clock by the time we reached Cranley Grange. For the last hour our progress through the narrow, snow-bound lanes had been slowed even further by the rapidly deepening twilight.

The library, with Jasper Carnegie roasting his brandy glass physique before the flames, was a welcome greeting as we staggered through the French windows with our baggage and the Morse machine.

"Gentlemen!" Carnegie cried at the sight of us. He poured two stiff measures of brandy and thrust them our way. He was already the worse for drink, rapidly questioning us as to the hardship of our journey and demanding a weather report.

"The snow is coming down without pause," Vaughan told him. "Some of the smaller roads are impassable. An hour later and we might have had to stay the night in Aylesbury."

"And miss the midnight show!" Carnegie said.

"If," Vaughan reminded him, "the creatures of the light decide to favour us tonight."

"Have faith, my friend!" Carnegie laughed, in his finest Micawber-fashion. "Charles and I thought ahead and transported the cameras, bedding and provisions across to the wood this morning, before the worse of the snow came down."

"Charles is here?" I asked. I had not seen Carnegie's younger brother for almost ten years. We had been friends at Cambridge, though I had always found Charles, if pleasant enough, somewhat reserved: he was as unlike his older brother as it was possible to be, in both physical aspect and psychological make-up. Whereas Jasper Carnegie was short to the point of absurdity, Charles was as tall as a grenadier, and wore his handsome good looks with a certain degree of flinching diffidence.

Charles had studied medicine at Cambridge, and upon graduating had worked in a hospital in Greece for a few years, before moving to India and working as a surgeon in a military hospital in Bombay.

"He's upstairs, changing for dinner," Carnegie said now. "He'll be down to join us presently." He glanced at his fob watch. "Almost seven," he reported. "I suggest we clean up, have dinner, and then draw up a plan of action."

He showed us to our respective rooms, and while I washed and changed I considered the night's imminent vigil. After the familiarity of London life, the everyday ordinariness of domestic routine, I still found the juxtaposition of this and the fantastic a little hard to believe: it was almost as if at any second I might wake up and discover the incidents at Hopton Wood to have been a dream – or more likely some collective hallucination or illusion. Had I alone witnessed the blue light, then I would surely have doubted not only my senses but my sanity.

When I returned to the library, Jasper and Vaughan were still dressing for dinner – the table was laid for what looked like a sumptuous feast – and a tall figure stood with his back to the fire.

"Charles!" I said. "Good to see you, man! It must be ten years or more!"

"A decade almost to the month, Jonathon. You haven't changed a bit."

Would that I could have said the same of my friend. As he proffered his hand with characteristic diffidence, I saw that ten years, or else the depredations of the subcontinent, had wrought substantial changes upon his person. I recalled him as tall and slim, but now he was stooped and thin to the point of emaciation. His face was lean, his cheeks sucked in to reveal the bones beneath, and his once fine head of hair was receding.

I could not hide my shocked expression.

"Malaria," he informed me. "And just a month ago a brush with dysentery. A while in England should do the trick."

"When did you arrive back?"

"Flew in stages from Bombay," he said. "The last leg from Paris to London yesterday. I received Jasper's cable last month, and frankly didn't know what to believe." He hesitated, then said, "I must confess to being a little concerned about him."

He poured a sherry and passed it to me. "Go on," I said.

"On the few occasions I've seen Jasper over the past few years, he's always appeared the model of sobriety, quiet and somewhat staid. Imagine my surprise when I met him yesterday. He seemed hyperactive, possessed of an illimitable nervous energy. And he seems never to be without a drink."

"What we saw in the woods would drive a saint–" I began.

Charles was plucking at his Adam's apple *pizzicato* fashion. "It isn't this so much as the content of his conversation that has me worried," he said.

I leaned forward. "Just what seems to be his problem?" I asked.

"He has already surmised that the light represents some kind of portal or doorway which might conceivably lead to another realm. He seems to think that this other place represents an improvement upon our own reality. He believes that because these beings possess the ability to manufacture the blue portal, then somehow their world is therefore more advanced not only technologically, but culturally and morally too."

"I can see that his thesis might not hold water," I said. "But I'm not sure that I would worry too much about it, if I were you."

"I wouldn't worry at all," Charles went on, "if that were the extent of his rantings."

I felt the sudden chill of unease grip me. "What's he been saying?"

Charles strode to the window, where he stood and stared out at the flurry of snow still cascading though the pitch black night. He turned to me.

"This is between you and me, Jonathon," he said. "But my brother plans to somehow attempt to transfer himself from this world to the other realm via the blue light. I gather that he attempted some such action last week."

I nodded. "But for the intervention of Vaughan, he would have walked into the light and likely fried himself in the process. The heat coming off the interface was terrific."

"So you perceive the grounds for my concern, Jonathon? If he attempts the same tonight, and we fail to..."

"I'll have a word with Vaughan. Together we'll devise some plan of restraint."

We were interrupted by the arrival of Jasper and Vaughan, and the latter was telling the former about his Morse machine. It stood beside the dining table, a mysterious wooden device of lenses and small electric bulbs.

Jasper introduced his brother to the novelist. As we took our places at the table I realised that, after having starved myself for the past couple of days, I had an appetite for two.

"I was just explaining the workings of the Morse machine," Vaughan said, helping himself to slices of roast beef. I followed suit, adding potatoes and parsnips. "We seemed to have arrived independently at the notion that the blue light is some kind of portal between realms, and that communication between the realms is not only advisable but imperative."

I glanced at Charles. "Just so long as it is carried out at a safe distance," I said.

Jasper was opening a portfolio beside his chair and drawing from it a series of large photographs.

He passed these around the table. "They're of much greater clarity and detail than the first lot," he said. "Though I take no claim for that."

The photographs showed the great explosion of light, rendered white upon these prints, and in three or four pictures the vague outlines of what were unmistakably tall, humanoid shapes.

"These figures," I told Charles between mouthfuls, "were much more clearly defined when seen with the naked eye. They seem almost abstract here. In reality they were frighteningly real."

"I'll vouch for that," Vaughan said. "The photographs quite fail to capture the otherworldly quality of the phenomenon, as you will hopefully observe tonight, Charles."

"I'm anticipating the experience with somewhat mixed emotions," Charles said, glancing my way.

"I'm sure that we have nothing to fear, gentleman," Jasper said. "Surely if the beings beyond the light harboured hostile intentions, then they would have acted before now?"

Vaughan pushed away his plate and considered his empty pipe. He glanced around at us, and there was an air about him of the expert being asked to propound. "I feel," he said, "that we cannot second-guess the motivations of creatures entirely unknown to us. I think that to imbue human rationality to beings manifestly not human might prove to be a grave mistake. My advice would be to assume nothing until we have sufficient proof for an hypothesis."

This set the agenda of the debate for the next hour, with Charles and myself chipping in with our own comments from time to time.

We had consumed during the course of the meal perhaps more wine than was advisable, and at ten o'clock Jasper announced, somewhat drunkenly, that we had better think about setting forth.

We donned stout boots, thick overcoats and headgear, and paused before the French window to peer at the blizzard still raging outside. Jasper and Charles equipped themselves with a paraffin lamp apiece, and Vaughan and I carried the Morse machine between us.

With Jasper leading the way and Charles bringing up the rear, we left the Grange and proceeded slowly up the snow-covered incline. It was well that the Carnegies had thought to transport the cameras and provisions to the clearing earlier that day, for I would have resented having to shoulder more of a burden than the Morse machine. The snow was a foot deep in places, far too thick to stride through with ease, and consequently every step was a labour.

With Jasper way ahead, I thought it an opportune time to apprise Vaughan of Charles' fears.

Vaughan heard me out and nodded, his craggy visage illuminated by the light of his glowing pipe. "After what happened the last time, I thought we'd better keep an eye on him," he said. "Between the three of us we should be able to forestall any mad dash he might choose to make."

"I can fully understand his being dissatisfied with this world," I said, "but to trust one's future to the blue light on the off-chance that it might lead to a better one..." I shook my head. "Has the man taken leave of his senses?"

Almost an hour later we came to the edge of Hopton Wood and paused beneath the shelter of a beech tree in order to regain our breath. In the light of the paraffin lamp, Jasper Carnegie's round face was animated. "Do you feel on the cusp of destiny, my friends?"

Vaughan glanced at me. "I trust that our hopes won't be dashed tonight," he said. "We're banking on the beings manifesting the light once more. But what if, for some reason, they decide that they've seen enough of this world?"

"To tell the truth," I said, "I would be unable to say whether I'd feel relief or disappointment."

"If we were never to see the light again," said Vaughan, "then I for one would be disappointed. To have the miraculous appear almost within one's grasp, only to have it cruelly snatched away..."

"You are being unduly pessimistic, gentlemen," Jasper said. "I feel that tonight a breakthrough will be made. Perhaps the appearance of the blue light thus far has been but a prelude, a rehearsal as it were for the actual opening of the... what did you call it, Vaughan, the trans-dimensional interface?"

Charles stared at his brother. "You think that tonight the beings you saw might actually step through?" He sounded fearful of the prospect.

Jasper laughed. "The wonderful thing is," he said, "that we don't really know what will happen!"

We moved further into the wood. The going was considerably easier now that we had left the snow behind, and we made good time. Ahead, Carnegie's paraffin lamp swung back and forth and sent magical shadows racing this way and that through the contorted shapes of the trees. I was filled with anticipation, and not a little fear. I could not help but hear again Vaughan's warning that we could not second-guess the motivations of creatures unknown to us.

We arrived at the fork in the path, and shortly after that the clearing itself. There was no moon to illuminate the arena tonight and the orange glow of our lamps cast it in an altogether more ruddy and eldritch aspect. It was as if I were seeing the clearing for the first time, and thus I noticed stunted trees that I had missed before, as well as the curious absence of ground cover.

The trio of tripod-mounted cameras stood gazing into the centre of the clearing like mute spectators. Jasper dashed from one to the other, fussily checking and rechecking his calibrations. At last he was satisfied, and returned to where Vaughan and I were setting up the Morse machine. It consisted of a box on legs, with a lens at the front and a lid that hinged and allowed access to its interior. Vaughan was adjusting something within, by the light of a paraffin lamp which I held high. Five minutes later he was finished, and we retreated from the clearing and settled ourselves behind the fallen log.

Jasper distributed brandy-laced coffee, and I huddled in my bed-roll and warmed my hands on the brew.

"Have you remembered your missive to the beings?" I enquired of Vaughan.

From the deep pocket of his great coat he extracted a Jacob's Cream Cracker tin, which he opened to reveal a scroll of quarto, weighted with a sizeable stone. "At the first available opportunity," he said, "I shall attempt communication with the creatures."

"And perhaps next week," I said with levity, "we might receive a reply contained in just as singular a casing."

"Fifteen minutes to midnight," Jasper reported, squinting at his fob watch. "All quiet so far."

Vaughan and I had positioned ourselves on either side of Carnegie, in case he might attempt another rash move towards the light. As Jasper gave the time signal Vaughan winked at me, reminding me to be vigilant.

Midnight came and went. Jasper was unbowed. "Don't be downhearted, gentlemen. Remember last week: it was almost a quarter past the hour when the portal appeared."

As minute after minute elapsed, I willed the light to appear, for something to happen. I think we all did, and the tension in the air, along with our nascent disappointment, was almost palpable.

Twelve-thirty came and went, and I settled deeper into my bed-roll. Charles began talking of his time in India, telling Vaughan of his experiences of working as a medic for the Raj.

His voice lulling me, I slipped into sleep. I awoke a little later; Jasper informed me that it was one o'clock. Vaughan and Charles were still conversing, evidently about the portal.

"But if it does manifest itself," Charles was saying, "and we do somehow establish communication with the beings, then how should we proceed? Have you considered the protocol of the situation? I mean, should we make our finding public? Whom should we tell?"

Vaughan stared at him, his face grim in the light of the lamps. "We should keep the findings to ourselves until such time as we can discern the motivations of the beings," he said. "I would be loath to tell the world and his wife immediately."

"I was thinking more in terms of informing the relevant government body," Charles said.

"I rather think," Vaughan replied, "That his Majesty's Government has yet to set up a department for trans-dimensional affairs! And anyway, what if these beings are innocent and peace-loving? Surely you'd be the last one to advocate our government getting wind of the portal? By God, they'd be through in no time and subjugating the natives there just as in India..."

I dozed again, only to be woken by a hand shaking my shoulder. "What?" I cried, sitting upright. Vaughan too had been dozing, and looked as startled as I.

Charles said, "It's almost three, gentlemen. I've been trying to persuade Jasper that we ought to beat a retreat. What do you think?"

"I'm happy to remain till dawn," I said. "Perhaps the creatures are running late."

Vaughan nodded. "I haven't come this far to give up so easily."

"That settles it, then," Jasper Carnegie said. "We stay."

Five minutes later he was pouring more coffee when, suddenly, we were startled by a brilliant flash of sapphire light, and a sudden raging gale of intense heat. I turned and saw the portal expand and hang in the air, accompanied as before by an almost inaudible thrumming sound that vibrated within my chest.

"My God!" I said.

Charles stared in slack-jawed wonder, unable to bring himself to exclaim aloud.

His brother, for his part, was struggling to his feet. Vaughan and I did likewise, and each held him by a shoulder. He seemed totally oblivious of our restraining grip, being more intent on the pulsing portal not thirty feet before us.

"It's come again!" he cried. "I'd almost given up all hope!"

It was even more magnificent in reality than the image I retained of it in my memory. It seemed larger than I recalled. I had thought the oval on the first occasion to be in the region of twenty feet high and half again across; now it stood perhaps thirty feet high, its lower ellipse beginning in the air at the height of a man, and its topmost curve as tall as the treetops. It pulsed and shimmered with the same effulgent lapis lazuli light as before, but was it this time more intense? Perhaps my thwarted anticipation invested it with greater properties, now that it had actually deigned to show itself.

One thing was for sure: none of us had ever perceived its like, and we stood agape like children as it radiated before us.

Jasper strained against our grip, his eyes almost popping to take in the details. "I see no shadow-beings this time," he observed.

Vaughan said, "They did not show themselves immediately on the first occasion, as far as I recall."

I stared at my friends. In the electric wash of the portal's light, their faces were transformed, thrown into stark shadow, their expressions of mingled fear and wonder seemingly exaggerated as if by the pen of some phantasmagorical caricaturist. No doubt my expression was likewise distorted; certainly, I was hardly in control of myself. My heart beat wildly, fit to burst, and my limbs were taken by a violent trembling that I could not quell.

Charles, until that second standing beside us behind the fallen tree, at that moment climbed over the trunk and stared in astonishment. At first I thought that, like his brother on the first occasion, he too was being drawn by some hypnotic compulsion towards the portal; but my fear was quashed as he halted, then looked back at us and shook his head in wonder.

Jasper struggled to join his brother, but we held him back. "Easy!" Vaughan counselled. "You will gain nothing from getting too close!"

Jasper made some half-strangulated noise in protesting reply, but did not increase his struggle. Still, Vaughan and I were gainfully employed in keeping him at a safe distance.

I noticed that the cameras were clicking away, and that Vaughan's Morse machine was projecting its series of coded messages. I wondered what the beings behind the light – if indeed there were any beings there tonight – made of the code, or of the staring cameras, or if indeed they were aware of our own shadowy presence among the trees.

"There!" Charles cried, pointing. "Did you see...?"

Indeed I had; within the light, but fleetingly, I had observed a shape: it was tall, its limbs monstrously elongated like some attenuated creation by Giacometti. It appeared briefly at the periphery of the oval interface, face on, for all the world as if it were staring out at us and our world. Then, just as quickly as it appeared, it retreated off-stage again, frustrating us.

We were not disappointed for long, however; a minute later not one but three humanoid shapes showed themselves. They seemed to float across the face of the portal, two tall figures and a third, this one perhaps half the other's height. The tall creatures' arms appeared longer than they should have, gangling tentacles reaching almost to their knees.

"Charles!" Vaughan cried, startling me. "Here!"

Charles spun around, and, on realising what Vaughan intended, joined us behind the fallen tree. He held his brother's arm while Vaughan, relieved of custodial duty, drew the biscuit box from his greatcoat.

I watched, my heart racing, as Vaughan approached the trans-dimensional interface.

I realised then, and it struck me again later, that this must rank as one of the most primitive, not to say absurd, attempts at communication in the history of our race. There was something at once wonderfully courageous, and at the same time pathetically optimistic, in the sight of a man with a biscuit tin endeavouring to effect inter-species dialogue with beings in control of technology at which we could only marvel.

Vaughan was approaching the interface by painful degrees, one arm raised to cover his face, the other drawn back in order to launch the biscuit tin. At last he could approach no further, the energy of the portal beating him back, and he chose this instant to hurl the tin towards the blue light.

I watched the slow arc of its trajectory against the pulsing glow, and it seemed to take an age to arrive at its destination.

And then, of a sudden, it made contact with the membrane and, instead of passing through as we had hoped, it seemed to hang for long impossible seconds in the light before bursting into sudden and voracious flame.

"And to think," I murmured to Charles, "that that might have been Jasper's fate!"

Between us, Jasper seemed not to have noticed my words. He was straining forward, seemingly oblivious to the fate of the biscuit tin.

Vaughan beat a quick retreat and joined us behind the trunk. His face was red raw from the heat of the interface, and the reek of singed hair hung about his person. "So much for that little idea," he muttered. "Let's hope the Morse machine effects better results."

Perhaps Charles and I had relaxed our grip on Jasper, assuming that even he would not now venture forth towards the interface, having witnessed the fate of the biscuit tin. If so, then we assumed in error. No sooner had Jasper perceived a lessening of our grip, than he pulled himself free.

I have no real notion of what his intentions might have been as he staggered across the clearing towards the portal, the shadow of his plump person thrown back towards us in elongated exaggeration.

Before we could shout aloud in warning, much less move ourselves to effect a rescue, Jasper Carnegie was within feet of the light.

I am certain that his life was saved a second time – not by Vaughan on this occasion, but by pure happenstance. For whatever reason, the beings in control of the interface chose that precise second to effect a change in the nature of the membrane.

As we stared, convinced that we were about to see our friend reduced to ashes, the blue light vanished...

It did not, as on the other occasions, shrink to a point and pop from existence. This time the light disappeared but was replaced by something equally fabulous – if not more so, to judge by subsequent events.

Just as it seemed that Jasper Carnegie was about to take a flying leap into perdition, the blue light changed instantly and became a scene of midnight calm. Not only did the light cease, but also the heat and the low thrumming vibrato, and instead there came from the portal an absolute silence, then the waft of a warm wind freighted with some heavenly, otherworldly scent such as I had never experienced before.

Jasper, brought up short by the transformation, came to a comical halt and stared.

Vaughan and I, released from stasis, ran forward and wrestled Jasper to the ground. We caught him by surprise, and his opposition was minimal; we succeeded in hauling him from the clearing and back behind the fallen trunk, where we gathered ourselves and took stock of the situation.

As my eyes adjusted to the sable membrane of the interface, in contrast to the blinding blue of earlier, I saw with amazement that the portal now framed a scene, an otherworldly landscape, much as a picture frame encloses a canvas: but no earthly canvas had ever depicted such a scene as this!

"Oh, my God..." Vaughan breathed in awe.

"What is it?" Charles said.

"Perhaps," I ventured, "the blue light was just a precursor to this, a stage through which the process had to pass before the true other world was revealed."

For through the portal we made out what could only have been another world. It was in darkness, but as we stared we gradually discerned a string of lights around what might have been a bay, for the lights were duplicated with a ripple effect on the surface of the water. Around the shore stood dwellings, but dwellings the like of which we had never seen before. They were bulbous and squat, like wasp's nests, with circular lighted windows positioned centrally upon their protuberant walls.

"Perhaps," Vaughan speculated, "this is some far future vision."

I pointed, my hand trembling as I did so. "If this is the future of our planet," I said, "then how do you account for those?"

For riding high in the sky of this tranquil scene were two large moons, one quite orange and the other crimson.

"Perhaps," I said, "now that the heat is no more, we might take a closer look?"

We glanced at each other, desire fighting with trepidation as we considered the advisability of a closer inspection.

Jasper was the first to speak. "I can see no harm in doing so," he said, "so long as we stay together. We might even chance a step through to the other side."

"Let's merely take a look, first," Vaughan cautioned.

"I'll second that," said Charles.

We released Jasper and moved cautiously from behind the log, walking four abreast towards the magically transformed interface.

We slowed as we neared the alien scene. The warm wind was stronger here, and with it the fragrant scent; it reminded me of honeysuckle, but with an undertone of spice.

I heard a sound: the gentle lapping of water, and the distant calling of what might have been an animal.

Vaughan placed a restraining hand on my arm as I ventured near. "The interface was opened for a purpose," he said. "Perhaps in order for beings to pass from the other side."

"I see no one abroad," Charles said. "There's no sign at all of the earlier figures."

We were perhaps five yards from the portal now, and edging closer like children playing dare with the waves of the ocean. I expected the strange beings to appear at any second and accost us.

Odd to relate, but although we were cautious, I was surprised at how we had accommodated ourselves to the fact of the wonder before us. Perhaps it was because, from the very start, the manifestation of the marvellous had been an incremental thing. We had become inured to the fantastic by degrees, so that now even this privileged glimpse of another realm failed to faze us.

The closer we came to the portal, the wider our view of the strange land became. By the light of the double moons I made out a range of hills to the right, dotted with lights that I took to be dwellings. I wondered what manner of being might inhabit this place.

Jasper Carnegie was closest to the portal. He stood on tip-toe and peered over its lower lip, which hung at the height of his head. "I see the ground," he reported. "Some kind of dark, coarse sand."

I joined him and looked over the lip. What appeared to be a beach shelved down to the water; on the black sand sprouted many-headed silver blooms, which glowed in the light of the moons.

More than anything I wanted to suggest that we climb through for a closer investigation, but at the same time a more cautious part of me recalled Vaughan's words. The portal had been opened for a purpose...

"Look," Vaughan said. "There, in the sky."

We looked up. Something passed before the double moons, some kind of small flying machine. As we watched, it turned and headed towards the bay. It was like a plane without wings, a graceful tear-drop shape that moved with alarming speed. Indeed, hardly had I observed this than I realised that it was heading directly for the portal.

It swooped low over the bay, skimming the surface, and at speed approached the interface. Charles gave a cry and dived to pull his brother out of the way, lest he be decapitated by the hurtling craft.

I ducked along with Vaughan, but not before witnessing yet another remarkable sight. Along the beach, two tall, attenuated figures appeared from the darkness and ran towards the portal.

Seconds later, with an eerie drone, the tear-drop craft flashed overhead and into our world. It side-swiped the trunk of the first tree in its path, caromed off a second and gouged a great furrow in the undergrowth mere feet from the log behind which my friends and I had earlier taken refuge.

No sooner had it come to rest than a segment of its upper integument flipped open and a being struggled out, no doubt dazed from its crashlanding.

I had no time to register the appearance of this creature before I made out sounds behind me and, on turning, saw the appearance of the two tall creatures above the lip of the portal. I felt rough hands grab me, and thought for a second that a third member of their party had waylaid me, until I heard Vaughan hiss into my ear, "Hide yourself, man!" and so saying he pulled me to the ground and dragged me to where Jasper and Charles were cowering beneath the great hovering ellipse of the portal.

From this relative sanctuary, we watched the drama enact itself before us.

The being from the craft had managed to jump free and hide behind the fallen tree trunk: it was an ugly little brute, a dwarfish manikin with a great domed head, no neck worth mentioning, and a thick torso. No sooner had I made this inventory than it disappeared from sight, evidently attempting to conceal itself from the two elongated beings in pursuit.

For here they came now, swarming over the lip of the portal and landing – mere feet from where we cowered – with a sinuous, lizard-like agility. It was all I could do not to shout aloud in terror, for if the first manikin had possessed all the hallmarks of ugliness, then these creatures were a match and more besides.

Their legs were long and thin, but bent as if in readiness to spring: they reminded me of the legs of lizards, scaled and oleaginous – as was the rest of their anatomy. They stepped forward, and walked with a cautious, bobbing gait, heads flicking this way and that. They carried what I assumed were weapons, silver, stylised things like futuristic rifles. Their headpieces were encased in globular helmets, so that it was impossible to make out their faces, but if the rest of their bodies were any indication, then I imagined the elongated jaws and snouts of the saurian genus.

By some method of detection unknown to me, the leading saurian aimed its weapon at the fallen trunk and fired.

A beam of white light sprang from the nozzle of the weapon and made short work of the trunk, which vanished in a blinding glow. I caught a quick glimpse of the stunted being as it rolled from its now non-existent cover and took refuge behind its flying machine.

Another white beam sprang forth, this time from the dwarfish manikin. It connected with the leading lizard, which hardly had time to issue a guttural cry before it vanished in an inferno of blinding light.

Its mate ran to the edge of the clearing and fired again, and I heard a cry from behind the flying machine as its erstwhile pilot received a hit – but not before loosing an almost simultaneous beam of light which found its target: the second saurian flashed before us and vanished in an instant, and seconds later I made out the charcoal reek of cooked flesh pervading the air of the clearing.

All was still, quiet, in the aftermath of the extraordinary battle played out before our disbelieving eyes.

I was lying on the ground, face down, with Vaughan and Charles beside me, and Jasper to my rear. My pulse was racing and I was trembling with fear and exhilaration. My mouth was so dry that words would not come, and my mind was in a whirl as it sought to explain the nature of the events we had witnessed.

Jasper was the first to move. Slowly he crawled forward, past us and beneath the lip of the portal. He stood cautiously and looked around him. He walked towards where the first lizard-like beast had met its end, and bent to inspect what little remained, a mere scattering of ashes upon the ground.

As I watched him, I made out a movement beyond the clearing. I opened my mouth to call a warning, but no words came. As I stared, pointing, I saw the stunted manikin crawl out from behind its tear-drop craft. It was on all fours, in evident distress, and hauled after it a weapon not dissimilar to the lizards' silver rifles.

It collapsed onto its stomach, facing us, then raised its rifle and aimed.

"Watch out!" Vaughan cried to Jasper, who stood oblivious to the danger he was in.

But the manikin did not intend Jasper as its target. It fired, aiming high, and above us the interface detonated with an explosion of blue light, then vanished.

We cowered with our arms about our heads as intense heat and sparks rained all around us.

Then a preternatural silence reigned, and only the dim light of the stars provided meagre illumination. Jasper fell to the ground and scrambled back to us.

"It still lives!" he hissed. "For all we know it might be a berserk mercenary bent on slaughter!"

"It would have wiped us out by now, if that were the case," Vaughan pointed out. "We were sitting ducks."

I noticed, not ten feet from where I lay, a paraffin lamp which had fallen and extinguished itself in the melée. Cautiously I crawled across to it, found matches in my pocket and set about providing a light.

My friends joined me and, huddling together within the orange glow of the lamp, we peered into the darkness in the direction of the injured manikin.

Presently my vision adjusted and I made out the small figure lying face down beside its craft.

Only then did I hear its cries. They were in a tongue wholly incomprehensible to the human ear, and yet heartrendingly pitiful. They sounded like the hopeless yowls of an injured animal, and yet with a sense of structure suggesting language.

"Eeee, ah orguk... Canak-ha."

Charles took my elbow in a vice-like grip. "What should we do, for pity's sake!"

Vaughan said, "Let us approach, but slowly. Raise our arms in the air, to signal that we mean no harm. Then we might get close enough to assess the degree of its injuries and determine whether it might be saved."

We nodded encouragement to each other, and yet each of us was reluctant to make the first move. After perhaps half a minute of vacillation, first Jasper and then Vaughan stepped forward and slowly approached the manikin. Charles and I followed cautiously, myself ready to flee at the first sign of hostile intent from the creature.

I stared at the manikin in the light of the lamp. It looked up, regarding us with great round, seemingly lidless, eyes.

It still held its rifle, and as we drew near the manikin moved. It lifted the weapon, and we froze, fully expecting to be reduced to ashes. Then the being flung the rifle with all its feeble strength into the undergrowth, and with that simple gesture signalled its lack of hostility.

We hurried forward. Jasper took the lamp and held it high while Vaughan and Charles with painstaking care examined the manikin, and then eased it onto its back.

Evidently the beam of light had not scored a direct hit – otherwise the being would have been annihilated like its opponents – but had caught the manikin a glancing blow. The flesh of its right hip and upper torso was a flash-burned mess, with pale spars of broken bones projecting through the wound.

Charles produced a pen-knife and proceeded to cut away, ever so gently, the creature's jerkin. "*Orguk... Vee-ha*," it mewled in pain.

I turned away, unable to watch any more. I was standing beside the tear-drop shaped craft, its open fuselage inviting inspection. I peered inside, noting many strange devices and implements fore and aft of what looked like a narrow sling or seat.

As I peered within, I happened to touch the skin of the craft, and to my surprise the entire thing rocked. I pushed it again. Sure enough, the craft was astonishingly light. And yet, as I stood back and stared at it, it looked as substantial as anything of its equivalent dimensions on Earth.

My friends were conferring. "I can do nothing for it out here," Charles was saying. "If we can get it back to the Grange without causing it greater trauma..."

"But if we try to carry it back," Vaughan said, glancing at the doctor, "do you think it will survive the journey?"

"It's our only hope," Charles said.

"One second," I said. "What if we replace the creature in the craft?"

Charles interrupted. "It's barely conscious. I doubt if it could control–"

"No need for that," I said. "We could carry the craft to the Grange."

"Carry it?" Jasper echoed.

"Look," I said, taking the vehicle in two hands and lifting it over my head.

"Good God!" Vaughan said. "Whatever next?"

I positioned the craft next to the alien. Charles knelt and attempted to gesture our intentions to the manikin. "*Hah ro*," it said, which we chose to interpret as assent.

Fortunately the being was as small and light as a child. With Vaughan taking its shoulders, and Charles its legs, while I hoisted the lamp aloft and Jasper held open the cover of the fuselage, we managed to transfer the manikin from the ground and into the sling of its craft with maximum care and minimum delay.

I recalled the creature's weapon, and gingerly retrieved it from the undergrowth and stowed it in the craft beside the manikin.

I took the nose of the vessel, Vaughan the rear. At a nod from my friend, I lifted, and proceeded to walk forwards with the ludicrously lightweight craft held at my back, Charles and Jasper bearing the lamps fore and aft.

Like this, carrying the creature in its craft as if it were some injured dignitary in a sedan-chair, we made our way through Hopton Wood.

The going was difficult, mindful as we were of making the ride for the manikin as smooth as possible. We proceeded slowly, choosing our steps with care; the dancing shadows cast by the lamps did not help: the path seemed like an obstacle course with hummocks and protruding roots I had failed to notice when walking unburdened. Nevertheless we walked for twenty minutes without mishap, and then at a call from Jasper slowly lowered the craft to the ground. Charles and his brother took up the burden, while Vaughan and I carried the lamps.

Twenty minutes later we emerged from the wood and paused before the snowfield that extended away from us, almost violet in the light of the stars. The Grange was a distant irregularity against the whiteness, the lighted French windows of the library promising warmth and comfort at journey's end.

Again Vaughan and I took up the burden. We stepped forward, but the depth of the snow impeded a smooth ride for our injured guest. We lurched about like drunken men, the craft rocking perilously to and fro.

"Halt!" Vaughan cried. "I have a better idea. Lower the vehicle."

We did so, and it sat upon the snow like a sledge – which was precisely Vaughan's intention.

"Now, Charles and Jasper – you stand at the front and make sure it doesn't get away from us. Jonathon, we'll guide it from the rear."

In just such a fashion did we begin the journey down the gentle hillside. The craft skated over the snow like the finest toboggan, the ride far smoother now. We galumphed through the deep snow alongside, merely having to touch the vessel from time to time in order to keep it on course.

"I've been considering what we saw back there," I said at one point. "Have you any idea as to what took place?"

Vaughan peered at me over the curved top of the vehicle. "It might be explained in a number of ways," he said. "Perhaps what we saw was simply a case of cops and robbers, our friend here being the fugitive. Then again, the reptilian beasts might have been the antagonists, and the homunculus some unfortunate hero."

"Or perhaps," I said, quoting Vaughan himself, "it might be a mistake to impute human motivations to alien beings."

Vaughan laughed at this and called out, "Touché!"

I marvelled at the cavalier fashion with which we were discussing that which, in the cold light of day, we would come to see as momentous.

"And what about the portal?" Charles said over his shoulder. "What was happening when it was in its blue phase, and who or what were those shadow creatures we beheld?"

"Its blue phase," I replied, "was probably a process of generating sufficient energy to open the portal from its source point to its destination. As for the shadowy figures..."

"Perhaps they were the equivalent of engineers?" Jasper put in from up ahead.

"The big question," Vaughan said, "is where the deuce did the portal come from, or lead to, whichever you prefer?"

"The moons in the sky seemed to preclude a future planet Earth," I said.

"Then how about Mars?" Charles offered. "That planet has two moons."

"But one orange and the other red?" Vaughan said.

"It's a possibility we cannot discount," Jasper said. "Who would have thought of it, the red planet...?"

Like this, with much banter and speculation back and forth, we made the last leg of the journey towards the lighted library of the Grange.

Within ten minutes we were dragging the craft through the French windows and across the carpet. Charles opened up the cockpit and peered inside. "He appears to be unconscious," he reported, "which is not surprising. Will someone help me ease him from the craft and onto the chesterfield?"

I took the creature's shoulders, its thick flesh clammy and cold to my touch, and when Charles had a grip on its legs we carefully lifted the manikin from the vessel.

Seen in light of the open fire, its true difference to a human being was apparent. It was perhaps the height of a ten year old child, but thick of torso and limb; its flesh reminded me in hue of nothing so much as a potato fresh from the ground.

It was unconscious, and for some reason I found this reassuring. Its face was as ugly as the rest of its body, with no nose but a hideous vertical slit where a nose should be, and beneath this a much longer, horizontal slit which I took to be its mouth. Its eyes were not lidless, as I had formerly supposed, but covered with a thin, flickering membrane. I gained the impression that, conscious, the being would have presented an even more hideous aspect.

Charles began a quick inspection of the creature's injuries, then stood. "We'll need a plentiful supply of boiling water, Jasper. Jonathon, can you get me a clean sheet or two? Vaughan, you'll find my medical bag in my room – it should provide me with the basics I need to treat our patient." I had never seen Charles less hesitant than now, as he took on the authority of his profession and gave us our orders.

Five minutes later, his bidding done, we gathered again in the library and convened around the alien figure.

Charles injected the manikin with a small dose of morphine, then with swabs of alcohol cleaned the wound in its torso as best as he was able. "The danger of performing the wrong procedure upon an alien physiology is always present," he said. "I can but treat the creature as I would a human, and hope for the best."

He cut away flaps and shards of dead flesh from around the wound, so as to counter infection, then set about investigating the broken bones therein. I saw enough to assure me that the manikin's anatomy in no way resembled a human's: instead of ribs, it seemed to have broad plates of bone about its chest, like the slats of a barrel.

At last, unable to watch any longer for fear of emptying my stomach of its last meal, I made myself absent and poured a round of brandies for my friends.

The tear-drop craft caught my attention. I walked around the vehicle, marvelling that but hours ago it had been sailing through the skies of some far distant world. Quite how it might power itself was a mystery. I could see no propulsion unit or engine, inside or out. Inspecting the fuselage, I saw before the pilot's sling a smooth dashboard, for want of a better description, marked with studs and alien hieroglyphs.

I took from the craft the creature's weapon, perhaps thinking it might at some point be required. Then my eye fell upon the devices and instruments I had seen upon my first inspection of the vessel in the wood. They were arranged haphazardly to the front and rear of the sling, as if thrown in higgledy-piggledy at the last second before departure. I reached in and pulled out these oddments.

The first was what appeared to be a blue ovoid, the size of an ostrich's egg, and very lightweight. As to its purpose, I had no idea, other than it might be some kind of ornament. Next I produced a circular plinth about the size of a halved keg; this was girdled with silver spars, upon which was yet another array of spidery hieroglyphs. I reached in again, like a child at a lucky-dip stall, and pulled out a circular stone as black as obsidian attached to a length of shiny material, like ribbon. The last object from the fuselage was a silver container, not unlike a bread box, but with an opening at its front and a series of marked lines within that formed a grid.

I ranked these gee-gaws before the craft and studied them again one by one, but at the end of the process was no wiser as to their utility.

I finished my brandy and poured another round. Charles was working industriously upon the manikin. I saw a needle and thread being pressed into service, and a scalpel flash once or twice. For all its ugliness, I felt a sudden compassion for the dwarfish creature, in such a state of grievous injury and so far from home.

At last Charles stood back and dashed off his brandy. The creature lay upon its back, its body enwrapped in bandages. Naked but for tight undershorts and bulbous boots, it appeared as comical as it did pathetic.

"Well," Jasper enquired. "Do you think it'll pull through?"

Charles drew an armchair to the fire and collapsed into it. "Impossible to tell, quite impossible. If it were human, then I would put its chances at no greater than fifty-fifty. But who knows the tenacity and strength of creatures such as these? I've done the best I could with the resources available to me. We can but hope that infection doesn't set in."

"Perhaps," Jasper suggested, "if we could get it to hospital...?"

Charles shook his head. "There's not a hospital within twenty miles that could do more than this, and the trauma of transportation might see him off."

"And besides," Vaughan said, "how we might explain a creature of such singular aspect?"

I looked at him. "Do you think it wise to keep what happened to ourselves?"

Vaughan glanced around the group. "What do you think? The last time we spoke on this matter, the consensus was that we should consider what might eventuate before calling in the authorities, if at all. I think that to inform others of our discovery would be a grave mistake."

Jasper nodded. "I'm of the same opinion. The leaders of men befoul whatever they touch!"

Charles said, "But if these beings – either those allied to our friend here, or the reptilian characters – prove to harbour hostile intentions, then a recourse to the authorities might be the only option." He was plucking at his Adam's apple again.

I nodded. "We cannot entirely veto the option," I said.

"But until such time as we learn the intentions of the creatures one way or the other," Vaughan responded, "then I think we should say nothing to anyone." He looked around the group. "Agreed?"

One by one we gave assent, then fell silent as we regarded the patient.

Jasper slipped from the room, and I was heartened to see him return five minutes later bearing a tray of bread and cheese, a joint of beef and a jar of pickled onions. At the sight of the food, I realised how famished I was.

We pulled a sofa to the fire and fell to eating as our alien guest slept beside us – and only when writing this now, a year later, can I see what a strange tableau we would have presented to any prying eyes: four men partaking ravenously of bread and meat, a gargoyle asleep beside them on a chesterfield and, at the back of the room, a sleek, futuristic craft standing upon the carpet in a puddle of melted snow.

I stopped eating, a wedge of cheddar halted before my mouth, and stared across at Vaughan. A thought had occurred to me. "What if," I said, "the reptile creatures decide to pursue our friend further? After all, he did account for two of their kind."

Jasper looked up from his brandy. "It's an eventuality we cannot discount."

"We must assume that they can open the portal at will," I said. "In that case we might be in danger."

Vaughan was shaking his head. "There are too many imponderables in the equation to be sure of anything," he said. "For all we know the feud between the homunculus and the reptiles might have been a local affair, about which the operators of the portal care nothing. We just cannot be sure."

"Perhaps," I said, "the manikin destroyed the portal when he shot at it, rendering it useless?"

Vaughan nodded. "A possibility," he said.

But Jasper was on his feet. "To be on the safe side, gentlemen, I think we had better arm ourselves. If the portal was not destroyed, and the reptiles come a-hunting..." And so saying he dashed from the room and returned minutes later bearing four pistols and ammunition.

He distributed them amongst us, ignoring my protests that I'd never fired a gun in my life.

"And little good these pea-shooters would be against the reptile's light-beam weapons," Vaughan said good-naturedly.

"Better these than our bare fists," Jasper declared.

"What about the creature's own light-beam weapon," I said, gesturing across the room.

"Good idea," Jasper said. "In the hands of the manikin it was certainly effective."

He opened another bottle of brandy, and we settled in for a night of conversation while beside us our alien patient slept in silence.

Towards dawn I could stay awake no longer, and slipped into a doze. By some miracle, considering the events of the night, I did not dream. It was midday when I awoke, stretched out on a settee; Vaughan was dozing in a nearby armchair, his leonine mane somewhat dishevelled. Of Jasper there was no sign; Charles, for his part, was attending to the manikin's injuries.

He looked up when he saw that I was awake. "Jonathon, if you could lend a hand for a minute."

I assisted him in the process of cutting away the old dressing and discarding it on the fire. As Charles peeled away the last of the lint from the wound, I saw his expression change to one of incredulity.

"What's wrong?" I asked.

"Look," he said, gesturing at the wound with a pair of tweezers. "I've never known such a rapid process of healing."

Indeed, where before the wound had been red raw and bloody, now a great deal of it was scabbed over. The broken bones, or plates, were entirely covered with what looked like a new growth of skin.

Vaughan awoke and joined us, peering down at the manikin as Charles detailed the specifics of the recovery. "In a human, this sort of progress might be expected after a week or more of intensive care. I do believe that the bony plates around his chest have knitted. This is most remarkable."

He re-dressed the wound and the manikin slept on with hardly a murmur.

A little later, Jasper appeared with a trolley bearing the makings of a fine breakfast, bacon and devilled kidneys, scrambled eggs and fresh brown bread.

"Cook thinks I've taken leave of my senses," he reported. "She usually serves breakfast in the dining room, but I insisted. I've given her a few days off, told her that we're going away for the week." He gazed at the injured creature on the chesterfield and shook his head. "Heavens knows how she might react if she clapped eyes on our friend here."

Over breakfast we discussed what might become of the manikin, should he survive his injuries.

"In that eventuality," Charles said, "and at his present rate of progress, I see no reason why he might not fully recover. Then we might have to inform the authorities of our discovery."

Vaughan frowned. "The poor devil will become a circus freak," he said. "Either that, or the government will impound him and subject him to a series of medical experiments."

"Perhaps," Jasper said, "if he does pull through, then we should attempt to ascertain how he desires to proceed?"

I considered the events of the night before. "It is possible," I said at last, "that he intended expressly to come here. I mean, the portal was opened upon our world, and the manikin in his carriage made a bee-line for the interface. Perhaps he has an errand here?"

"An errand," Jasper said, "that the reptiles were intent on him not achieving."

We contemplated that possibility for a while.

Our silence was interrupted by a sound from the manikin himself. He groaned, then gave vent to a soft, sibilant hiss.

We gathered around the chesterfield and watched as he regained consciousness. His membranous eye-lids fluttered open to reveal large, protuberant eyes: they were jet black, without any white at all, but with a vertical amber slit at the centre of each. His gaze was disconcerting, to say the least – all the more so for the fact that he did not once blink as he turned his head slowly on the cushion to regard us one by one.

His lipless slot of a mouth opened minimally. "*Goksan, nesah... Raksa.*" The words came with an obvious effort, and with long seconds between each sibilant pronouncement.

He fell silent, his mouth slot turning down as if in pain.

Charles reached out tentatively, took the creature's stubby fingers in his, and squeezed.

The manikin responded. As we stared, we saw his plump, dun digits tighten around Charles' hand. "We're doing all we can for you, old chap," he said. "Our medical methods might be primitive by your own standards, but you seem to possess a remarkable constitution that more than makes up for the lack."

The manikin lifted its free hand and pointed, feebly. I followed the direction of its trembling finger. "The craft," I said.

His hand fell back to the chesterfield, as if the effort of pointing had exhausted him.

"I wonder if he wants to be returned to his vessel?" Vaughan said. He moved into the line of the manikin's sight, and pointed first to the manikin, and then to the craft. He repeated the signal, then mimed carrying the manikin over to the craft and laying him in the sling.

Vaughan returned and knelt beside the chesterfield. The manikin regarded him. "*Tah*," it said. Once again it lifted a finger and pointed across the room.

A thought occurred to me. "Perhaps it doesn't mean the craft," I said, "but the devices I took from it last night."

I hurried across the room and knelt beside the ranked objects. I pointed to each one in turn, giving the manikin time to respond.

I indicated first the blue egg, to which the manikin said, "*Tah.*" Negative.

I pointed to the plinth-like object and received the same response.

Next I held up the obsidian medal on the silver thong. "*Vee!*" said the manikin, with emphasis. "*Vee, vee!*"

"It appears that our friend desires this, for some reason," I said, returning to the chesterfield with the medallion.

I passed it to the manikin. With anticipation, we looked on as the being attempted to slip the medallion around its neck. It gave up, its feeble strength unequal to the task.

Charles leaned forward and took the medallion; he parted the silver thong and looped it over the manikin's bulbous head, arranging the obsidian disc on the creature's chest.

As we watched, wondering what might happen next, the manikin reached up and touched the disc.

The obsidian medallion glowed suddenly a deep, lustrous crimson hue, for all the world like a hot coal.

And then the manikin spoke, its sibilant words coming with obvious difficulty as it fought against the pain. *"Hakan rahn, ochan kundra. Cahn tahgek."*

We looked at each other and shook our heads. Charles said, "I'm sorry, we cannot understand..."

He stopped, then, for a sound had issued from the glowing medallion around the manikin's neck. We each of us stood back in amazement as a voice came from the direction of the disc.

"Feel... no... alarm. Peaceful... I." The words came one by one, with much static in between, but perfectly comprehensible.

"A translation device!" Vaughan cried. "Good God, what next!"

More words came from the device. "Thank... you... I..." There was more static, and then, "Your... help... need."

Vaughan looked at us. "I wonder if the device can translate our words?" He knelt beside the chesterfield and leaning forward spoke into the medallion. "Who are you? From where do you come?"

Seconds later the disc translated, *"Jhen-nu... mah... Yekan... Tak... Duhn... Kur... gur."*

The manikin's eyes closed briefly, the membranes falling and flickering, as if the effort of communication was causing him pain.

Slowly, he spoke. *"Jhekan tah kahr Kathan..."* he began, and continued for a minute, before exhaustion claimed him and he fell silent.

The medallion translated, and I will report the essence of his communiqué without the interruptions and static.

"I am Kathan, from the fourth quadrant of the spiral arm, a planet my people call Theera."

I stared at Jasper, who was mopping his balding head and staring in wonder at our incapacitated guest. "The stars..." he murmured to himself. Charles was pacing back and forth before the fire, his fingers at his Adam's apple.

Of course, the possibility that the manikin might have hailed from beyond the precincts of our solar system had always been one explanation, but to have corroboration of the possibility from the lips of the traveller himself – or rather from his fantastical translation device – set me to contemplating the astounding fact of teeming life across the galaxy.

A minute later Kathan opened his eyes again and regarded us. Vaughan nodded that we had understood. He said into the medallion, "You came from the stars to our planet, but for what reason?"

He stopped to allow the device to translate his question, and a minute later it spoke in Kathan's language.

The manikin looked at us as he took in Vaughan's question. His thin eye-lids fluttered, a sure sign that he was failing. Feebly he began, *"Kirnah, ongkar. Tak la dekken na..."*

We waited, impatiently, for the device to render the translation.

A minute later it came. "Short explanation: I was fleeing evil authorities. I had to escape. My people effected my jump from the fourth quadrant. I came here because it was distant, and in time I will move on again."

My head whirled with a hundred questions. There was so much I wished to know about the universe beyond our planet, and about Kathan's flight in particular. Why was he fleeing the evil authorities? What had he done to provoke their wrath? Who were his people?

Kathan tried to speak again, but the effort was beyond him. He attempted to raise his hand, to point towards his craft, but never completed the gesture. His hand fell and his eyes closed, and his breathing became even.

Charles examined his alien charge. "We've tired him out," he said. "The fact that he was even conscious while in such a condition..." He shook his head. "Oh, the wonders that are out there!"

"We have so much to ask Kathan when he is able to respond," Vaughan said. "I would like to know more of the political situation of the galaxy out there... And, my God, consider all the technological innovations of which we know nothing!"

"Think of all the wondrous worlds out there!" Jasper cried, and I saw tears filming his eyes as he contemplated the thought.

"The main thing we need to know," Charles said, "just as soon as Kathan is fit enough to speak again, and not before, is what are his intentions. He said he wished to move on again from here, but will this entail another trip through... what did he call it?... the jump gate?"

I shook my head. "Perhaps his carriage will take him the rest of the way through space?" I surmised.

Vaughan was chuckling quietly to himself. "The fourth quadrant of the galaxy!" he said. "And we thought that he might have hailed from Mars! How parochial can you get!"

For the rest of the afternoon we sat while Kathan slipped in and out of consciousness. Jasper stoked the fire and opened a bottle of claret. Outside, a new fall of snow was obliterating the tracks we had scored down the hillside while transporting Kathan to safety.

After having my head filled with visions of galactic intrigue, great civilisations on far-flung planets, I considered my life in London, Carla and my father. How would I be able to go about my everyday life now, in light of what I had learned today? Would the knowledge help me overcome the petty concerns that make so much of life a trial, the mundane cares and worries that we all allow to get us down? Would I be better able to ignore Carla's maddening exhibitionism, and my petty jealousy, by considering the fact that humankind was but one intelligence spread about the vast galaxy? Would I be able to come to some acceptance of my father's imminent death when placed in the context of the many billions of similar deaths across the broad face of the universe?

The idea was fine, but the practicality hard to foresee. I was human, after all, and affected by the trivial concerns of my psyche. I would go on as I always had and, who knows, in time I might come to wonder if the events of the winter of '35 had been nothing more than a particularly vivid waking dream.

"A penny for them, Jonathon?" Vaughan said.

"Oh... I was just day-dreaming, considering what we've discovered here. I wondered if life would ever be the same again–" I smiled "–then I realised that of course life would go on just as before."

Vaughan considered my words. "It will be different," he said. "Oh, we'll still be slaves to the same old routines of habit and thought – but from time to time we will reflect on the singular fact of our discovery, and that surely will subtly change us as people, perhaps make us more reflective, less impulsive – less enamoured of the materialistic designs of modern life. Or am I being hopelessly romantic?"

I smiled. "Of course, if our discovery was made known to the world at large, and we were one day allowed into the fraternity of the star-faring races out there, then what a wondrous day that would be!"

Jasper said, "That would certainly change things, for sure! Shake up a few stuffed shirts in parliament for a start!"

"But do you think that the star-faring races would welcome the human race?" Vaughan asked. "We're hardly civilised at present. Hardly a year goes by without a war somewhere on the planet. And technologically we're a backwards species, compared to what we've seen of the other races... And another question: we're talking of being allowed to join the fraternity of the galaxy, but have you wondered why we haven't been asked already? These star-creatures know of us, of course. Perhaps they consider us but infants, who have yet to grow and mature before being admitted as equals to any co-fraternity of star-dwellers?"

We contemplated his words for a time, and then I said, "You've been writing about just such futures for years." I looked at my friend. He stood before the blazing fire with his hands deep in the pockets of his tweed jacket, his burning pipe clenched at right angles in his determined jaw.

I felt a sudden and abiding respect for the novelist then, the visionary who had shunned the medium of popular realism for the more daring and neglected form of the scientific romance. I went on, "Now that reality has caught up with your fictional visions, do you feel vindicated? Do you feel that you have vanquished the mundane critics who call your work far-fetched?"

He laughed at this. "Jonathon, I think that the answer is no – because, you see, I always knew in my heart that what I was writing about contained the truth: that, one day, visions more or less fantastical than mine would come to pass, that when the hide-bound critics were dead and gone to dust, humankind would embark upon an age little dreamed of by the majority. Now that I know the future is already out there, and waiting for us..." He shook his head, "...I find that exciting beyond words."

A little later we gathered around the chesterfield while Charles removed the dressing from Kathan's wound.

He shook his head in wonder. "I've never quite seen the like," he murmured.

The burn was almost wholly scabbed over now, and the flesh on the perimeter of the wound seemed almost like new.

Charles applied new dressings, and we were about to begin dinner when Kathan's membranous eye-lids fluttered open and his jet eyes regarded us.

We gathered around again, and Vaughan knelt before the recumbent alien. "If you are up to it, we have more questions."

He waited for the medallion to translate his inquiry, then Kathan spoke. A minute later the medallion relayed his words.

"I am much improved. I will do my best to answer your questions."

Vaughan looked at us. I murmured, "We need to know if we are safe, or if the reptiles might come through the jump gate in search of him."

He bent and relayed the question. A minute later the obsidian medallion translated Kathan's reply, "I think we are safe. My people are doing all they can to scramble my trail."

"Did you destroy the portal when you fired upon it?" I asked.

Presently the reply came, "With luck, yes. But I cannot be sure."

Jasper leaned forward. "The portal opened on two previous occasions, to my knowledge. Were you attempting to reach here then?"

"Affirmative. The engineers were sympathetic to our cause – but our enemies moved to halt my transit."

Vaughan said, "Your enemies? The reptiles creatures, I take it? Why are you fleeing them?"

We waited, watching Kathan's expressionless face as he replied. The medallion spoke, "The reptiles, as you call them, are known as the Vark. They are the dominant species in the galaxy. They are an evil, rapacious race, and rule without mercy. We oppose their regime, and will fight to the death to bring about its downfall. Rest assured, we are fighting for the freedom of the oppressed."

"How many races are abroad in the galaxy?" Vaughan asked. "And how many planets are habitable?"

The reply came. "There are more than fifty star-faring races," Kathan told us, "and over two hundred known planet-bound civilisations that have yet to join the council."

I stared at my friends. "More than two hundred and fifty different species of intelligent being," I said. I imagined the galaxy teeming with all manner of life, all types of bizarre and quixotic civilisations.

Vaughan said to the glowing medallion, "And we humans, I take it, are one of the two hundred races you call planet-bound?"

Kathan, having heard the question, gestured with his right hand – a quick flutter that conveyed no meaning to us. A minute later the medallion spoke. "That is so. You will be listed as Sentient-Technological Grade III."

"And what exactly does that mean?" Vaughan asked.

"It means," the translator said after a while, "that you are not sufficiently developed, culturally, to be allowed on the council, although it is but a matter of time before you are... advanced enough for contact to be established."

Kathan's eye-lids fluttered and his breathing grew ragged. "He is tiring," Charles said. "Perhaps he has answered enough."

"One more question," Vaughan said, and turned to the alien being. "Would it be advisable for our authorities, our governments, to know of the galactic situation?"

Kathan heard the question and attempted to sit up; he appeared distressed. His words came in gasps, and in due course the medallion relayed his reply.

"It would be ill-advised for your leaders to know! Such knowledge would only cause unrest, which would start hostilities among your people and set back the course of your progress. The council will contact you in the fullness of time, when you are deemed sufficiently ready. Until then, it must be your secret."

Charles knelt beside the alien. "Would you like water, a little food?"

The medallion duly replied. "Water only..."

Charles fetched a glass of water and held it to Kathan's hyphen-like mouth. The alien drank thirstily, and Charles fetched a second glass. After finishing this one, Kathan lay back on the cushions, as if the effort had exhausted him, and his eye-lids fluttered shut.

We took the opportunity to consume the stew that Jasper and Vaughan had made, a simple but satisfying broth of beef and vegetables.

We had almost finished the meal when a cry from the chesterfield brought us to our feet.

"Vee okan-gah... shanath ay rahk!" Kathan exclaimed, and we gathered around, anxious for the medallion to do its work. Kathan seemed agitated; his eye-lids were blinking rapidly, his hands trembling. I wondered if the apparent healthy state of his wound belied some more fundamental internal injury, which Charles had been unable to repair.

Then the medallion set my mind at ease on that score. "Please, come. Bring the shanath to me!"

Jasper knelt and took the manikin's hand. "What is the shanath?" he asked. "Can you point?"

The medallion translated. Feebly, Kathan lifted a stubby hand and pointed a finger towards the devices ranged before the star-carriage. I hurried over to them and indicated the blue egg.

"Tah!" Kathan cried. Negative.

I pointed next to the circular plinth-like implement, and Kathan dropped his hand. *"Vee,"* he said. I carried the device across to the chesterfield as my friends looked on, as intrigued as I.

Kathan sat up very slowly, taking considerable care not to cause himself undue pain. Charles rushed forward and packed cushions behind his back. Soon the manikin was sitting upright and staring at the shanath.

He spoke, and his medallion translated: "Please check the shanath for damage."

I inspected the plinth, lifting it and turning it this way and that, not at all sure what I was looking for.

The rim of the circular device had been dented, no doubt during the star-carriage's crashlanding. A number of the hieroglyphs were buckled and hard to make out.

Kathan spoke again and we had to wait, agonisingly, for the

translation. "The damage might affect its efficacy," he said. "If so, then all is lost."

"What is it? I asked. "What does it do?"

In due course the medallion relayed his reply. "It is a miniature hathan," he said. "It annihilates space and time."

I stared at him, alarmed. Vaughan stepped forward. "It is dangerous?" he asked.

"Not at all," came Kathan's eventual answer. He pointed. "Please, place it over there, where there is space."

I moved the shanath from where it stood on the rug before the fire and positioned it, as instructed, in the middle of the room.

I looked at Kathan expectantly. "Now what?" I said.

He spoke, and his medallion translated. "Touch the green light upon the upper surface of the shanath, and then stand well back."

Cautiously I approached the device, reached out and touched the green light, and then ducked away like someone lighting a firework.

I rejoined my friends before the fire, and waited. Nothing happened; evidently, this firework was a dud.

Then, just as I was about to quiz Kathan, a blue light sprang from the surface of the shanath with a great crack and fizz of electricity. The whole room was filled with a static charge, and I stared at my friends with a mixture of alarm and amusement. Their hair was standing on end, as was mine. The only person in the room spared this indignity was Kathan, who possessed no hair.

I looked back at the shanath and saw that a tall blue oval – identical in everything but size to the trans-dimensional interface we had witnessed in the clearing – now hung above the plinth. It coruscated with dazzling brilliance, and caused us to cover our eyes. Unlike its larger counterpart, however, this one generated only a modicum of heat.

"A miniature jump gate," Vaughan exclaimed.

Kathan spoke. The medallion glowed. "I have presumed upon your hospitality long enough. It is time I was leaving you."

"You're going?" Jasper cried. "But you said that the Vark were unlikely to follow you. Surely you could stay until you are sufficiently healed? You will only do yourself untold damage if you take flight now. Please, remain here as our guest for a day or two."

Charles said, "It would be wise if you rested a little longer."

Kathan looked at each one of us, his gaze lingering. "I must be away from here. I have business to conduct. Again, I thank you."

Vaughan said, "One thing. Why did you not use this jump gate from the fourth quadrant instead of going through the larger portal and have the Vark follow you?"

At length Kathan replied, and the medallion translated. "This gate jumps only small distances – tens of light years at a time. The larger, industrial gate can jump thousands of light years. Of course, it was a risk using the larger gate, but I wanted to jump into a sector of the galaxy where the Vark did not hold sway."

"And now?" I asked, marvelling that ten light years should be termed a 'small distance'. "Where are you going now?"

"Now, I intend to make a random jump to the nearest civilised, star-faring planet, and proceed like this to a world where I hope to rendezvous with fellow opponents of the Vark. There I will plan my next move."

Vaughan said, "We wish you good luck, and a safe journey."

Kathan pointed to the shanath. "There is a series of symbols about the base. If you would press them in a certain sequence..."

Jasper stepped forward. "Allow me." He approached the blue light cautiously, and then knelt at the base of the device. He regarded the hieroglyphs and turned to Kathan. "Precisely which ones?" he asked.

"Tuh!" Kathan said, which the medallion translated as, "Damn!"

"Do you have a writing implement?" the alien went on.

Jasper produced a pen from his breast pocket, along with a sheet of paper. He carried them over to the chesterfield and sat down beside the alien.

Kathan took the pen awkwardly, evidently unused to such a primitive implement. He rested the paper upon his lap and proceeded to draw, with painstaking care, a series of twenty complex symbols.

He spoke, and presently we heard, "This is the code that commands the jump gate to locate the most suitable inhabited planet in the locality."

He passed the code to Jasper, who took the sheet of quarto with reverence and paced over to the shanath.

He knelt, studied the symbols on the base of the plinth for a time, and then proceeded to tap the code into the command console.

Instantly the blue light rippled and seconds later a magical scene appeared from within the oval portal. We approached and stared in wonder. The oval framed a vista of weird alien beauty, at once familiar and at the same time unlike anything I had ever seen before. A plane of what might have been grass stretched away from the jump gate, but it was grass the colour of blood, and dotted about the plane were what I took to be trees, but silver trees with branches that more resembled knife-blades. In the distance, on the far horizon, I made out what might have been a city: a series of diaphanous constructions like domiciles blown from glass, backed by a range of towering purple mountains.

But as we watched, the scene flickered, the effect very much like a reflection seen in water, shimmering and breaking up. One second the alien panorama seemed as solid as the view through the French windows, and the next it was shattered into rippled fragments. Then it vanished altogether, to be replaced by the blue field.

It came again, and then disappeared, phasing in and out of visibility on a regular cycle. "I cannot risk jumping with the gate in this state of disequilibrium," Kathan said. "I might end up pitched into the hostile vacuum of interstellar space."

"Can you do anything to stabilise the image?" Vaughan asked.

"I am no technician," Kathan replied. "I can only wait, and hope that it stabilises long enough to allow me to jump. In the meantime, I must prepare myself."

"What do you need?" Jasper asked. "Your carriage?"

"It can go with me," he said. "It will take me to yonder city."

"And the other implements?" I said, indicating the blue egg and the thing that looked like a bread bin.

Kathan turned his sable eyes towards these devices, then looked at me. "I will take my weapon," he said. "The others you may keep. Perhaps, in time, they will serve a purpose."

"And what about the shanath itself," Vaughan said. "How will you continue your spatial jumps if the base remains here?"

I rather think that Kathan might have smiled at our technological naïvety, had he been capable of such a gesture. At last the medallion translated his reply. "The shanath duplicates its working end at its destination," he said.

We stared at the flickering portal, alternately showing the image of the bizarre alien panorama, and then the blank blue field.

Kathan gestured with a flung arm. "If you could manoeuvre my vessel towards the gate," he said.

I placed Kathan's rifle within the carriage, and then lifted it, amazed again at how light it was, and carried it over to the portal.

"The image comes in cycles," Kathan observed. "Note, there is a period of ten seconds in which the image of the destination planet is stable, then ten seconds of disturbance, and almost the same again when the transmission is lost and all that is seen is the blue generation field."

I nodded. "What of it?"

"I think," he replied at length, "that during the ten seconds of visual stability, it will be safe to effect the jump."

"But it would be madness to take the risk!" Vaughan said.

"I do not intend to risk anything," said the alien, "least of all my life." He looked at me. "If you could lift the car and insert it through the jump gate at the next period of equilibrium," he said, "then we shall see if my theory is correct."

With Vaughan, I lifted the star-carriage and approached the portal. We held it at its rear end, as if we were attempting to throw lumber onto a bonfire.

The alien scene broke up, rippled, and then vanished, to be replaced by the cobalt generation field. I counted ten seconds, and then the image of the alien vista materialised and solidified. "After three," I said. "One, two, three, now!"

We launched the car through the jump gate. There was a momentary ripple in the image as the vehicle passed through, and then we saw it skid across the blood-red grass and career to a halt not five yards distant.

"Kah rah!" Kathan said, and the medallion duly relayed, "It worked!"

He leaned forward, eyeing each one of us in turn. "Gentlemen," he said. "I have only my thanks to offer you. Farewell."

Vaughan said, "You have given us more than your thanks, my friend. You have granted us knowledge unique and marvellous, for which we will be eternally grateful." He stepped forward and took the alien's hand, followed by Charles who did the same, and then Jasper and I.

There was something at once comical and touching about the farewell scene, as we four gentlemen approached the dwarfish, semi-naked alien perched primly upon the chesterfield and soberly pumped his hand in a gesture to which he was obviously unaccustomed.

At length we stepped back. I thought that Kathan would attempt to stand upright, but he thought better of it.

"Perhaps," he said, "one of you gentlemen might...?"

Jasper darted forward, and his alacrity to assist the alien should have alerted me as to his motivations.

He eased his arms beneath Kathan's childlike body and lifted him gently from the chesterfield. Slowly Jasper, holding his burden like a prize, stepped towards the jump gate. As he passed me, I saw something, a light in his eyes as he stared, hypnotised, at the scene in the portal.

If I had stopped him at that moment, then the destinies of all four of us would have been altered forever and – who knows? – for the worse...

Jasper paused before the plinth. The gate showed the blue generation field; in a matter of seconds, the alien world would appear again. Jasper turned around and looked at each of us, and his gaze lingered on his brother, before he turned again and stared intently at the portal. Only then did the import of his farewell gaze hit me, and I realised what he intended.

I leaped forward, but too late. As soon as the portal cycled around again to the beautiful image of the alien world, Jasper Carnegie, holding Kathan in his arms, stepped through the portal from planet Earth and became the very first human being to set foot upon alien soil.

We cried out as one and approached the jump gate.

Carnegie, carrying Kathan, was striding through the red grass towards the star-carriage. As we watched, aghast, he lowered the alien into the vehicle's sling, turned and raised his hand in farewell.

At that second the image shimmered, rippled, and then vanished and Charles cried aloud with despair.

"All is not lost," I said. "The image will appear again."

"And then what?" Charles exclaimed.

I did not reply, but I knew what I would do when the portal opened again onto the strange alien world.

We stared at the blue generation field, and this time it seemed to remain longer than ten seconds. Then, as we were about to despair, it cleared – and we saw before us the vale of blood-red grass and the twisted blade trees. In the foreground was Jasper, standing beside the star-carriage and staring through the portal at us.

I lost no time, and jumped.

I have often thought about my actions then, the foolhardiness of what I did. In retrospect I can see what a risk I took, how momentous were my actions. In one bound I leaped through light years of space, I left one planet and landed upon the surface of another – but at the time, of course, it was as if I were merely jumping from one room into the next.

I landed in the grass and rolled. I was aware of two things almost at once: the incredible, raging heat of this planet – a massive red sun hung low in the sky to my right – and the increased gravity. It seemed, as I rose to my feet and gained my bearings, that the hands of a strongman were pressing down upon my shoulders.

I staggered forward, to where Jasper was staring at me in disbelief.

"Jasper!" I cried. "You must come back! You cannot leave everything!"

"I have nothing on Earth to keep me," he replied. "All my life I have craved adventure, and now I have the opportunity to fulfil that craving."

"But you don't belong out here," I protested. "Your home is on Earth."

"My home," he replied calmly, "is where I choose to make it." He looked past me, and stared. He pointed. "Look!"

I whirled around.

The jump gate hung in the air of the alien world, and the image within the oval frame of the portal shimmered as I stared. I could make out a familiar scene: the cosy environs of Jasper Carnegie's library, the ranked books and the glowing fire, and in the foreground, peering through the portal, the terrified faces of Vaughan and Charles, eddying like reflections upon a disturbed mill pond.

Then the image disappeared, to be replaced by the inhuman blue of the generation field. I cried out, and fear gripped my entrails.

I counted out the seconds. Each one seemed like an eternity. I turned again to Jasper. "Can nothing I say persuade you!" I said. "Think of your brother, your friends on Earth."

"I cannot forego this opportunity," Jasper replied. "And anyway, there is always the chance that I might return, one day."

I turned again to the portal. The blue field shimmered, and then the solid image of the earthly library established itself – but for only two or three seconds at the most, before the image shivered again.

I heard Vaughan's despairing cry, as if from a million miles away, "The image is breaking up! Its period of stability becoming ever shorter! You must both jump next time or forever be–"

And his words were snatched away as the blue field replaced the scene of the library.

I stepped up to the jump gate, positioning myself upon its very threshold, the increased gravity of this world making my every step a labour. The blue field seemed to last forever. I counted ten seconds, and a further ten, and I began to despair that I would ever return home.

Then, just as I had begun to give up all hope, the image of the library established itself, briefly, and I wasted not one second in diving through and into the arms of Vaughan and Charles Carnegie.

I whirled around in time to see the image ripple – it had lasted barely three seconds! – and then turn blue.

I was sweating, and my heart was racing fit to burst as I held Vaughan to me and looked around at the wonderful sanctuary of the library.

I turned and faced the portal. The blue field seemed to last for ever. At last it flickered, and briefly I made out the panorama of the alien world, and the incongruous figure of Jasper Carnegie staring through at us. As we watched, he raised his arm in valediction before the image wavered once again.

For the next five minutes we watched as the periods of equilibrium became less and less; soon, the alien world appeared for a second only – brief blips between long stretches where the field showed only blue. Then the image vanished altogether, and the connection between the worlds was no more.

Charles cried out loud and slumped into an armchair.

"Don't despair!" I said, and looked frantically around the room.

"What?" Vaughan asked.

"The paper on which Jasper noted down the hieroglyphic sequence," I said. "If we can find it–"

I stopped and stared at Vaughan, for he was shaking his head.

"I saw Jasper stuff the paper into his pocket," he said.

I approached the shanath, knelt and regarded the symbols upon its base. I looked up. "It cannot do any harm to try a random sequence," I said.

"You could try," Vaughan said, "but I doubt it would do much good, either. The chances of happening upon the right sequence must be astronomical." He stopped and grimaced as he realised his awful pun.

I knew that he was right, but nevertheless stabbed at twenty symbols in quick succession and stood back. Nothing happened, not even so much as a flicker in the blue field.

I tried again, to no avail, and yet a third time. As I stood back after this attempt, the blue field extinguished itself suddenly, and the room was once again illuminated by just the firelight and a reading lamp in the corner. I touched the green light upon the surface of the shanath, which had earlier activated the blue field, but this time nothing happened.

I stared at my friends, bereft.

Vaughan poured three stiff measures of brandy, and we drank in silence and gazed into the flames of the fire.

At last I roused myself to say, "When I spoke to Jasper, he said that more than anything he wanted to remain." I paused, then continued. "Also, Charles, he said that one day he might return."

He stared at me. He appeared to have aged ten years; his thin face was even leaner, his eyes sunken. "Did it really happen?" he said, more to himself. "Is my brother really out there?" He gestured in the vague direction of the heavens.

Vaughan shook his head in silent wonder. "He got his wish. He is among the stars. Who knows what great adventure he has embarked upon?"

We fell silent, each occupied with his own tumultuous thoughts.

Only then did it come to me that, however briefly, I too had stepped upon an alien world. Somewhere out there, beneath the light of another sun, light years away from Earth, I had breathed the atmosphere of another planet. I would never again be able to look up at the stars in the night sky without experiencing a sense of wonder and disbelief.

We remained in the library until the early hours and only then, with a sense of giving up, did we retire to our respective rooms. The following day we spent in silent vigil; again I attempted to activate the shanath, and prodded the hieroglyphs for hours without result. It seemed that whatever damage it had suffered in the crashlanding had finally rendered it inoperable. We also inspected the blue egg and the bread-box device, but could make no sense of either.

On the Monday morning Vaughan and I took our leave, promising Charles that we would be back the following weekend, and drove to London for the most part in silence and with heavy hearts.

In the event, I had to postpone my trip to the Grange that weekend. My father took a turn for the worse and was admitted to hospital on the Thursday, and I remained at his bedside over the course of the next few days. He rallied, but remained bedridden. I spoke to a doctor who said that my father's demise was only a matter of days away, now.

I rang Charles on the phone and explained the situation; he told me that he had found a post as GP in Aylesbury, so as to be at the Grange in the event of his brother's return. He had told the woman who cooked and cleaned for Jasper that his brother had had to leave the country on urgent business, and might be away for a year. He invited Vaughan and myself down to the Grange the following weekend, or whenever we could make it. We speculated then as to whether the Vark would attempt to trace Kathan, and it struck me as bizarre that we were discussing such galactic matters over the mundane implement of the telephone.

I spent most of the next few days at my father's bedside; we played chess, though his concentration wavered. He liked me to read aloud to him, especially from my own short stories, and this gave us both pleasure in his final days.

On one occasion, after a long day at the hospital, I met Carla for dinner in an expensive restaurant in Mayfair. I cannot recall what we ate, but I do recall that at one point Carla reached across the table and took my hand. "I'm sorry, Jonathon. I shouldn't have made you come out tonight."

She was, of course, referring to my father, which provoked a pang of guilt in me, for I had been lost in contemplation of Jasper Carnegie and his sojourn among the stars.

As we left the restaurant, I looked up to see that the sky, for once in London, was clear. I made out the massed array of stars, and stopped to stare up at them in wonder.

Carla held on to my arm. "What, Jonathon?" she said.

"Aren't they beautiful?" I said. And, "Just think, Carla, of all the life out there, all the inhabited planets, the amazing civilisations!"

"Sometimes, Jonathon," she said, tugging at my arm, "I wonder which planet you're on!"

I walked home that evening with Carla on my arm, my thoughts far away, considering the incredible events of the previous week and wondering what new marvels the future might hold in store for me.

CHAPTER NINE

Kallithéa, July, 1999

LANGHAM FINISHED WRITING at twelve, carried his manuscript book into the villa and locked it in the desk in his study.

He took his sun hat from its hook and set off for Sarakina. It had been three days since he had said goodbye to Caroline with a kiss that she had cut short; he had thought that two or three days would be a decent interval before he called again, though every day he'd hoped she might visit him. Now he would suggest lunch at Georgiou's, apologise for his forwardness the other evening, and fervently hope that he could see more of her. Hell, he was like a teenager suffering his first crush.

The villa was shuttered. He approached the front door and saw, blue-tacked to the stained wood, an envelope bearing his name.

He tore it open and quickly read the enclosed note.

Daniel, had to rush off to London at short notice. Business. Will be back in a week. See you then – Caroline.

The tone of the note seemed friendly enough, but even so he found himself wishing that she had found time to call on him personally and tell him of her trip. He continued along the track towards the village, contemplating an entire week without talking to Caroline Platt.

He ordered moussaka and salad and a glass of retsina, and sat in the shade and quietly ate. He considered Forbes, the English journalist, and looked across the waterfront to the post office, and above it the open window of the room where Forbes was staying. The window reflected an incendiary burst of sunlight, and it was impossible to see within the room. The thought that Forbes might be watching him at this very minute made him uneasy.

He hadn't heard from the man for three days, when Forbes had accosted him and detailed his movements in '90. More disturbing, though, had been Forbes' claim that, before '90, Langham had been untraceable. Well, there was a good reason for that, and let the fat Englishman try to discover it, if he could.

At two o'clock precisely, Langham paid Georgiou and walked home through the pines. He took his time, inhaling the scent of the trees and contemplating Caroline's return. He found himself wondering how their friendship might progress, looking into the future and seeing them together, which just a month ago he would have considered as absurd as it was unlikely.

The novel was going well. In a week, slightly less, the first draft would be finished. Its title was *Cairo*, and it would weigh in at around one hundred and fifty thousand words. He would get the manuscript typed up by Maria in Xanthos, and then begin the leisurely process of going through the typescript and cutting.

He was contemplating the scene he would be working on tomorrow when he stepped onto his patio and saw that he had a guest.

Someone was sitting on the sofa, staring out at the view. He could just see the top of the man's head, his disgusting ginger bristles.

The stuffed hold-all, deposited on the table, gave away the interloper's identity, and Langham felt a sudden rage at the intrusion.

He stopped directly behind the sofa so that, if the man wished to regard him, he would either have to stand or screw himself around in the seat. "Make yourself at home, why don't you?" he said. "I'd offer you a beer, but I'm out of them at the moment."

Forbes made not the slightest movement. He said, "Not to worry, Mr Langham. A glass of water will suffice."

"I didn't invite you here, Forbes."

"I think it's time we talked properly," Forbes said. "I arrived before you begin work at three. We have thirty minutes."

"What do you want?" Involuntarily, Langham reached into his pocket for the mereth.

"As I think I have mentioned," the man said without turning, "I would like to straighten out a few details here and there, settle a few outstanding matters."

"In that case, I suggest you get on with it. My time is valuable."

"If I could have that glass of water, please."

Langham paused, then went into the kitchen, selected the ugliest, most chipped mug from the draining board, and filled it without allowing the water to run cold.

When he returned to the patio, Langham saw that Forbes had taken the opportunity to move from the sofa. He was sitting at the table, his hold-all at his feet, and was staring out to sea.

Langham moved to the table and banged the mug down next to Forbes. Water sloshed. Forbes ignored him.

Still gazing out at the headland, Forbes said, "You've chosen yourself a beautiful little hideaway here, Mr Langham."

Langham, deciding to play Forbes at his own game, pulled a chair from the table and positioned it across the patio, so that a gap of roughly six feet divided the two men.

Suddenly Forbes turned and stared at him. He leaned forward, placing his hands on his knees, and Langham again saw the man's repulsive finger-nails, small and convex, like miniature television screens ensconced in dough.

"Why the need to hide yourself away like this? What have you got to keep secret?"

"Nothing," Langham replied shortly. "Nothing at all. I need privacy in order to write. I've never chased after publicity."

"In a way," Forbes said, regarding his fingers splayed across his fat knees, "the fact that your latest books have become best-sellers must have caused you no small amount of concern."

"I don't quite see what you're driving at."

"What are the sales figures of your books in total? Something like two million? That's quite an achievement. Your books are popular, and attract critical acclaim. But with popularity and acclaim comes scrutiny, does it not?"

"You're talking in riddles, Forbes. Like I said, my time is precious."

"I'll explain myself, in that case. As I mentioned the other day, I've noticed that there exist between your books and those of other authors, certain textual similarities."

His heart thumping, Langham watched as Forbes reached down and pulled his hold-all towards him. It was heavy, and scraped across the tiles. He reached into the bag with both hands and came out with a pile of books.

Langham saw, with a start of disappointment, the familiar covers of novels published in the thirties and forties, with quaint, sketched covers. All the books were by Jonathon Langham: fifteen novels and a collection of short stories.

All the novels were marked by torn strips of newspaper.

Next, Forbes reached into his bag and pulled out a dozen much fatter hardbacks – the collected works, to date, of Daniel Langham. These, too, were book-marked.

"I read the novels of your grandfather, Jonathon Langham, after reviewing your own books for my paper. I wondered if there would be any similarities: themes, settings, etc – I thought it would be an interesting literary exercise. I must admit that I didn't expect to discover quite what I did."

Forbes picked up a Jonathon Langham novel entitled *The Sacrifice of Fools*. He turned to a page marked with a torn strip of newspaper. "For instance, this passage. Let me read it out." He raised the book and glanced across at Langham.

"'There comes a time in life when the wise man will assess all that has gone before and adjust his circumstances accordingly; he will, if his wisdom is equal to the task, realise that his individuality is but a condition of prior experience, and attempt to discern those influences so as to be in control of his present and his future.'"

Forbes paused there. "Interesting, if a little overwritten." From the pile of Daniel Langham novels he selected *The Treachery of Time*.

He opened the book and began reading: "'Mallory realised that he had to take stock of all that had gone before and adjust his circumstances accordingly. He understood that his individuality was a condition of prior experience. It was his duty to discern those influences and so control his future.'" He stopped reading and stared at Langham. "Don't you agree that those two passage are remarkably similar, Mr Langham?"

Langham found his voice. "Are you accusing me of plagiarism?"

"I'm not accusing you of anything. But I am interested in your explanation."

Langham nodded. He told himself that he was in no danger from this scurrilous hack. "Of course I read my grandfather's work many years ago. I was in the habit of keeping an extensive commonplace book – I must have noted down the passage, and then inadvertently, years later, used it as my own."

Forbes nodded. "There are rather a lot of similarities between your novels and those of your grandfather," he commented. He tapped the pile of old novels before him, indicating the slips of paper bristling from the stack.

Langham gestured. "I read everything he wrote and made extensive notes," he said.

Forbes stood up suddenly and moved to the rail of the patio. He pulled a big white handkerchief from his jacket pocket and proceeded to swab his neck and face.

Langham noticed that the mug of water still stood, untouched, on the table.

"What happened to your grandfather?" Forbes asked, still mopping his sweat.

"I beg your pardon?" Langham asked, his pulse increasing.

"I said, Mr Langham, what happened to your grandfather?"

He was glad that Forbes was staring in the other direction and could not see how he had coloured. He almost snatched up the water and drank it down.

"What do you mean, *happened?*"

"It is true that Jonathon Langham disappeared sometime around 1948?"

"I was always given to understand that he left the country for South America," Langham said. "Nothing was ever heard of him again."

Forbes resumed his seat in a business-like manner. He pulled his spiral-bound note-book from his breast pocket and spent several long minutes consulting his tiny, crabbed handwriting.

He looked up. "Have you ever read the novels of an English writer very popular in the fifties, Mr Langham, a writer called Christopher Cartwright?"

Christ, but the bastard had done his homework. "I may have done, way back."

"But you can't remember them?"

"I don't recall every damned book I've ever read," he snapped.

Forbes nodded. He replaced his note-book, then leaned over the obstacle of his stomach and delved once again into his hold-all.

He produced half a dozen Christopher Cartwright hardbacks, all of them marked with slips of paper. No wonder Forbes laboured like a pack-horse under the weight of the bag, Langham thought; he had an entire damned library in there.

He felt his mouth go very dry.

"Last year I read all Cartwright's novels," Forbes said. "And lo and behold, I found an amazing coincidence. I discovered that Cartwright, too, borrowed rather freely from the works of your grandfather. Similar lines are used, though altered, themes repeated, even from time to time characters crop up in Cartwright's books that first appeared in Langham's. I checked again in your own books, and though I detected no straight liftings or borrowings, I noticed common themes and concerns, a penchant for faded colonial settings and third world venues."

"Many writers set novels in all of the above," Langham said. "What are you trying to prove?"

Forbes' sweat-soaked face remained expressionless. "Oh, I'm trying to prove nothing, Mr Langham. I'm merely very intrigued indeed at the connection between these three writers. If I wish to do your life, then I feel that I need to get to the bottom of the mystery."

"I think you'll be disappointed," Langham said. "There's no mystery at all. Writers are influenced by other writers, and pay homage in their books. I think you'll find that this is what happened here."

Forbes was staring at him. He slipped his note-book from his pocket again, consulted it, then looked up.

"Another mystery, Mr Langham, is what happened to Christopher Cartwright."

Langham smiled. "I'm afraid I can't be the slightest help on that matter."

"Are you familiar with Cartwright's story? He was a popular and critically respected author in the fifties, wrote novels set in South America and Africa. Media interest was intense. Who was this man? Even his publishers had never met him – not even his agent. He wrote a book a year from '49 to '60, and then nothing more. Nothing was heard from him ever again."

Forbes paused, then said, "Do you think the dates significant?"

"What do you mean?"

"In '48 your grandfather Jonathon disappears, and a year later the mysterious Christopher Cartwright appears as if from nowhere with his first novel."

"Have you ever heard of coincidence, Forbes?"

"But it's a very odd coincidence, especially as Cartwright's books have certain textual similarities in common with those of your grandfather." He leaned forward, elbows planted on knees, and stared at Langham. "Do you see what I'm driving at?"

"I don't, but no doubt you're going to tell me."

Forbes nodded. "It struck me as entirely possible that what might explain your grandfather's disappearance in '48, and the publication of Cartwright's first book a year later, is that Jonathon Langham and Christopher Cartwright were one and the same man."

Langham allowed the seconds to elapse. At last he said, "If that is so, then it's the first I've heard of it."

"And another intriguing thing," Forbes said, "is what happened to Cartwright after his disappearance in 1960? If indeed Cartwright was your grandfather, then is it possible that he staged a second disappearance and perhaps, who knows, emerged elsewhere and wrote other books?"

Langham looked at his watch. "It's after three, Mr Forbes, I really do have to start work."

Forbes nodded. "Far be it from me to keep a writer from his muse," he said. "I hope you'll give what I've said a little thought. Should you have any information you think I might find enlightening, I'll be around again to talk."

He replaced the books in his hold-all, stood and hoisted the crammed bag onto his shoulder. He nodded. "I'll be in touch."

Langham, remaining seated, watched Forbes as he negotiated the steps from the patio. The man turned and waved, and then disappeared from sight around the corner of the villa.

Langham moved to the sofa and sat down. He knew he would be unable to work this afternoon – he would attempt to clear his mind and make the necessary corrections to today's work later this evening. Forbes' investigation had rattled him.

The man knew more than was comfortable. He knew so much, in fact, that he seemed to be hinting at the truth. Perhaps it was time to move on again, he thought. Leave Kallithéa and assume another identity, start a new life somewhere far removed from here. The prospect appealed.

But Caroline, he thought? What of Caroline?

He slipped a hand into his trouser pocket and found himself rubbing the smooth surface of the warm, amber oval. If it were not for the reassurance of the mereth, he thought, he might even wonder if Forbes were a Vark...

CHAPTER TEN

London and Cranley Grange, March, 1935

On the second Tuesday of March 1935 I took a taxi up to Harley Street and climbed the stairs to the clinic for what seemed like the thousandth time. I was sure that I would remember every detail of the place for years to come: the iron-stoned steps, the white-painted mock Doric columns, the brass plate beside the big, maroon door. The sight of any one of these things now fills me with melancholy.

My father was sitting up in bed, my book open on his lap; he looked more like a patient convalescing than someone given only days to live.

He gestured to the novel. "Almost finished, Jonathon. Enjoying it tremendously. Can't think of a better way to–" He stopped, then, and not because he had lost the thread of his thoughts.

I pretended not to have heard him. "I saw Carla in a play last night," I said. "A hilarious farce." I talked him through it, beefing up the comic situations.

He tapped the cover of my novel. "I've been thinking, Jonathon. It must be wonderful."

I smiled. "What? Living in Greece?" The novel was about an expatriate writer living on a Greek island.

"No, you know what I mean. Doing what you do for a living. Writing."

"Well... it's lonely, badly paid, and you don't have holidays," I said.

He managed a laugh. "But you leave something to posterity. You're remembered. Your works live on."

"The greats live on. The rest of us are pulped."

He reached out and took my hand in a surprisingly strong grip. "Don't do yourself down, Jonathon. You're a good writer. You write about what's important. What's in here. I believe in the emotions you write about, because I know that you believe in them. Your work is tremendously affecting."

He had always said he enjoyed my work, but never quite so articulately, or so passionately. "That means a lot to me," I murmured.

He still had my hand in his. Now he gripped it tighter. "The terrible thing about dying, Jonathon, is not so much the knowledge that one day I won't be around to experience anything any more..."

He was staring at me, no hint of emotion in his expression. He had always avoided talking about his death, never even hinting at the subject. I was uneasy with this sudden candour, not knowing quite how to respond.

I said the first thing that came into my head. "I would have thought that... that would be the worst thing."

He smiled. "I've had a good life. I've experienced a lot. Oh, I might not have travelled, and I can't say I've had an adventurous life. But I've done what I've wanted to do. I have no real regrets."

I wanted to ask why he was not terrified by the prospect of death: surely the end of one's existence was the most terrifying notion imaginable?

I held my tongue.

"Then what?" I asked.

He squeezed my hand. "The most terrifying thing is the thought that I won't be remembered. That I'll be forgotten."

I hurried to reassure him on that score. "I'll remember you, and so will your friends."

He was shaking his head, sadly. "Of course you will, but for how long? Memory is a fragile thing. In time, memories fade. And when you pass on, who'll remember me then, and who'll remember you when your loved ones have grown and passed on, too? That's the terrible thing, Jonathon. Existence is so fleeting, and most of us leave no mark, only fading memories. Entire generations, millions of us, like fire-flies in the face of eternity."

His eloquence brought tears to my eyes.

He laughed. "But you, Jonathon, you're different." He knocked on the cover of the book, as if asking to be admitted. "You commit your life, what's important in your life – your thoughts and beliefs – to novels, and your books will be read when you're long gone and forgotten. You've achieved your own kind of immortality, and that's no small feat."

I wanted to tell him that we were all mortal, and the passing of one's thoughts from one generation to the next, and beyond, while commendable, was no compensation for an eternity of non-existence.

But he had obviously thought about his little speech, and I could hardly bring myself to counter it with cynicism. Later I realised that he was passing through what is known as the brightening, that period of increased vitality immediately preceding death, the sudden flaring of a spent candle before it finally fails.

I left him at five, with my book open on his lap, and thought of him and his words as I walked along a rain-soaked Harley Street and came to Oxford Street. I found a phone box and, on impulse, called Carla.

I knew she had an hour or two before she had to be at the theatre. I would ask if I could call around for a while; in the mood I was in, I might even try to sit through the play for a second time if it meant we could dine together afterwards.

The dial tone rang and rang, and I was about to replace the receiver when she answered.

"Oh, Jonathon."

"I've just been to see my father. Can I come round for an hour before you leave?"

She hesitated, then said, "Yes, of course. How long will you be?"

"I'll walk, so about twenty minutes."

"Very well. I'll see you then."

I replaced the receiver and looked out of the phone box. The rain, light a minute ago, was now lashing down and raising liquid crowns on the tarmac of the road. I would be soaked if I walked to Carla's, and I could imagine her expression if I entered dripping water all over her new hall carpet.

I hailed a taxi instead, and a minute later was heading through the twilight streets towards Belgravia.

My father's little speech about posterity had depressed me. Each one of us has an innate hankering after what we don't possess: the 'grass is greener' syndrome. To be told that one's achievements are what another finds desirable or commendable serves only to point up one's own dissatisfaction with one's lot.

By the time the taxi pulled into Carla's street, I was near to tears, and what I saw through the windscreen as we drove along the street did not improve my mood.

"Stop here!" I said, fifty yards from her flat.

I paid the fare and stepped out into the rain.

Another taxi was pulling out from before Carla's flat, and I had recognised the person who had hurried down the steps and ducked into the vehicle.

I walked steadily through the downpour, trying to assess my thoughts and feelings. Jealous rage, of course, but more: a feeling of vindication, and the notion that now I had reason enough to end it all, to draw a line beneath a relationship that had never truly worked but which I had held on to for reasons of insecurity and pride.

I climbed the steps to her ground floor flat and knocked on the door.

She answered almost immediately. "Jonathon. You're early. Just look at you. You're soaked!"

I pushed past her into the hall, then moved through to the lounge. The bedroom was adjacent. I crossed to the door and stared through. The bed showed no sign of having been slept in, or rather used – but then she knew that I was coming, and would have made it before I arrived.

I turned to see her watching me from the door.

There was a challenge in her stare.

"What was he doing here?" I asked.

She let out a sigh, as much to say that she was tired of this old game.

"Jonathon," she said, holding my gaze, "I don't have to answer for every minute of my life. I'll see who I want to see, when I want to see them, and neither you nor anyone else will stop me."

"It was Ticehurst, wasn't it?"

"Alastair and I are in a play together, or were you too drunk last night to notice? The director changed a scene today. There was no afternoon rehearsal scheduled, so Al came round here to go over the revised script." She pointed to an occasional table where, sure enough, a dog-eared playscript sat. "See?"

"Are you having an affair with him?"

"My God!" She looked away.

"Tell me. I want to know the truth. I can take it. I'd rather know for certain than wallow in a limbo of uncertainty."

"Good line!" she snapped. "Use it in the next novel!"

"Are you having an affair, for God's sake!"

She leaned forward, her fists balled before her. "No, I am not having an affair with Alastair Ticehurst! We're good friends, and have been for years, and we're both actors, and he's a good person despite what you might think – and I'm not going to have my life dictated to by someone who for some reason is eaten up by insane jealousy!" She was crying now, the words coming on a torrent of exasperated tears.

"Last night, you were holding his hand."

"He was holding *my* hand, for God's sake!"

"You looked like you were enjoying it!"

"I was drunk! We'd just had four curtain calls!"

"And before we left the bar... you even made me wait outside while no doubt you arranged this little rendezvous today!"

She could not hold back the tears. "Why are you doing this to me? You're making me ill! How many times have I told you, I love you and only you, and of course I have friends, and some of them happen to be men, and Al is a friend. But that's all there is to it. I love you, for God's sake!"

I shook my head. I wanted to believe her, but jealousy is insane, as she said, and jealousy does not believe in anything other than the thing that fuels it. In my case it was fuelled by inadequacy and immaturity, and there was nothing I could do, no matter how hard I tried, to see past the naïve rage that consumed me. Perhaps, deep down, all I wanted was to be freed from the chains of a complex relationship that I could no longer handle.

I pushed past her, through the door and along the hall.

"Jonathon, we need to talk!" She said, hurrying after me.

I turned on the threshold. "The only reason you say you love me," I said then with venom, "is because you want what my father's leaving me!"

She stared at me, stricken, and I knew that I should have held my tongue. My guilt began at that very instant.

She shook her head. "Jonathon..." she implored.

I ignored her. I strode from the house and down the steps, then turned along the street and walked though the rain without once looking back, and in retrospect I am not proud of myself, and can only cite immaturity as an extenuating factor, which is no excuse at all.

I walked all the way home, regardless of the rain, the exercise working as some kind of catharsis. I stripped off my soaking clothes, dried myself and changed, then made a fire and slept before it on the settee, unable to use the bed where, just the week before, Carla and I had made love.

I slept badly, and woke in the early hours only to experience that occasional existential dread which grips when the defences are down, when the mind is empty of all the everyday trivia that keeps our thoughts from dwelling on the brevity of our lives, the inevitability of our ends, and those of everyone we know and care about. At these times our souls are empty vessels, to be filled in the dark hours preceding dawn with the sour wine of mortality, the realisation that we are all of us doomed and that there is nothing we can do to avoid this terrible fact.

I sat up and turned on the light and tried to shake from my head these nihilistic thoughts of death and extinction. I paced the room, then made myself a pot of tea. In time, as stray small thoughts replaced the vacuum, I became sane again, and tried to settle down, albeit with the light left on and the fire prodded back into life.

I was dozing, later, when the phone rang.

It was a doctor from the clinic who informed me that my father had taken a turn for the worse, and suggested that I should come in.

It was the call I had been fearing for so long, and yet as I dressed and rang for a taxi I realised that I was not filled with dread, as I had expected I might be: it was almost a relief. I only hoped that his passing would be painless.

I recall little of the taxi ride through the quiet dawn streets of London: a few grey figures, hurrying to work, the occasional scarlet bus looming through the fog. My thoughts were strained and confused, alternating between the plight of my father, and my treatment of Carla.

And then I was climbing the familiar steps, and realising with relief that this would be the last time I would make the journey.

An unfamiliar nurse showed me to my father's room, and then withdrew. I approached diffidently, fearful then of what I should find.

He lay propped on three pillows, and he was either asleep or unconscious. I took his hand. I recall the shock that I felt then: his hand was cold, and I feared that he had died before my arrival, that he had slipped into oblivion alone.

But his fingers twitched in mine and I felt a sudden start of relief that I would be there to see him from this world.

A little later a doctor entered the room and whispered to me: a resume of my father's condition, what I might expect. I recall only that the doctor said my father was on a heavy dose of morphine, but that he was still conscious. He said something about his condition; that although the tumour itself was not causing him pain, its pressure upon certain centres of the brain was provoking phantom pains in different areas of his body. I asked how long he might remain like this, and he replied that it could be only a matter of hours.

I returned to the bed and squeezed my father's hand. His breath was uneven, ragged.

"Can you hear me?" I asked, leaning forward. I felt almost guilty, as if a passing nurse might reprimand me for harassing him.

I wanted some acknowledgement that he knew I was with him, that he was not alone.

I saw the book on the bedside table, my third novel. I picked it up and noted that a marker was positioned three pages from the end, and it was this simple fact, and not the sight of my father on his death bed, that brought tears to my eyes.

This was my first real experience of death. I was fourteen when my mother died, but my father had kept me away from the hospital during her final days: he felt, he told me later, that there were some things a young boy should not be made to endure. I recall that when he returned from the hospital with news of her passing, the entire episode had an extraordinary air of unreality; it was weeks before I fully understood the fact that I would never again see my mother, that her physical presence would no longer be a part of my life; that, now, she existed only in my memories.

I started as I felt his fingers tighten upon my hand.

He turned his head on the pillow; his eyes were open, and looking at me. He smiled. "Jonathon." A whisper was all he could manage.

I squeezed his hand, not wanting to break down and cry.

"Jonathon," he said, "I'm proud of you."

"I..." I began, wanting to talk to him, but at a loss quite what to say. "Are you in pain?"

He managed to shake his head. "No pain at all. Wonderful. Calm and peaceful. Will... will you do something for me?"

"What?" I tried to imagine what I might possibly do for him – and, when he told me, I realised that it was both perfect and right.

"Haven't finished your book. A few pages to go. Please, read them to me, Jonathon."

I took the book and opened it and gazed down at the words I had written more than two years before. Always when I re-read my published work I was struck at once with amazement at what I wrote, and then disappointment as I remembered what came next: it was a kind of *déjà vu* that did not allow me to gain the same enjoyment from my own novels as I did from those of other writers.

I read slowly; perhaps subconsciously I feared reaching the end of the book. I concluded the story of an isolated writer living in a remote Greek island, and how over the period of a long, hot summer he allowed his reserve and inhibitions to fall so that he might come to love a woman in need of his affection.

"Like all lonely men," I read, *"Maitland had feared living out his life without finding that which for want of a better word the romantics call true love..."*

From time to time I looked up; my father was watching me, his lips moving as he silently repeated the words to himself.

I arrived at the last line, and read, my throat burning, my eyes wet with unshed tears, *"They sat and stared out over the bay, at the constellations massed over the far headland, and it seemed to them that the stars were beckoning."*

I closed the book and took my father's hand.

He died one hour later; he had been squeezing my fingers for long minutes, the only indication, I interpreted, that he was either feeling pain or fearing the end – and then I heard a crackle or rattle in his breathing, and his fingers gave up their grip on mine. I was watching him all this time, but there was no facial indication that life had passed from him. I wondered at the exact instant he had died, whether with the mechanical failing of his body his thoughts had died too, or if perhaps his thoughts and memories had lingered, dwindling one by one.

I sat for a long time, holding his hand. It might have been hours; I have no idea. At last I was startled by the touch of a nurse's hand on my shoulder. I stood and left the room, and only later, in the street, did I realise that I was still clutching my father's copy of my novel.

I took a taxi through the grey and lifeless streets of London to Battersea, and the phone was summoning me as I arrived at the flat.

"We need to talk, Jonathon," Carla said.

"I hardly think this is the time–" I began.

"I don't want to lose you."

"You should have thought of that before carrying on with–" It was out before I could check myself.

"Please, we need to sort things out. There's been a terrible misunderstanding, Jonathon, please."

I said, surprising myself, "I'm going abroad next week. I'll be away for a few months. Working on the book." I paused, then went on, "I'm sorry. It wasn't working. You need to find someone more... more suited to you. I don't know what you see in me anyway."

"Isn't that for me to decide?"

"We're forever arguing."

"We can talk that through."

"Please, I need to..." I almost told her then about my father – but the last thing I wanted was her sympathy.

"Will you promise me that you'll call before you leave, Jonathon?"

I hesitated. "I promise," I lied, and replaced the receiver.

I brewed myself a tea and sat before the fire, staring into the flames and contemplating the future. I thought of the novel I was working on – or, rather, which I was not working on. Fortunately the deadline was not until the end of the year. I could complete the book in six months, if I did indeed leave England, found somewhere warm, peaceful and quiet, where I might concentrate for a while.

The phone rang, and I almost ignored it. I imagined it was Carla again.

I snatched up the receiver. "Yes?"

"There have been further developments," Vaughan informed me, and my heart began a laboured pounding. "Charles wants to see us at the Grange. Can you be ready in thirty minutes?"

"Of course."

"I'll pick you up from Battersea. See you then." He cut the connection.

"Edward," I began, wanting to question him about what these mysterious 'further developments' might entail – but he had replaced the receiver.

Intrigued, and glad of the diversion, I changed and packed an overnight bag for my stay at Cranley Grange.

Vaughan's Austin 16 rolled up half an hour later, and I hurried down the steps and slipped into the passenger seat.

"Well?" I asked. "What is it? What did Charles have to say?"

He glanced at me as he pulled from the kerb. "I didn't speak with him. He rang while I was out, unfortunately, and left a message with my housekeeper. She reported that Charles had simply said, 'developments at Cranley Grange'. That was the extent of it."

I stared out at the passing pedestrians on Oxford Street; they seemed a million miles away, their cares and concerns those of another species.

"What on earth might have happened?" I thought aloud. "Perhaps the Vark have indeed come in search of Kathan?"

"Then they would be unlucky in their search for the

homunculus," Vaughan said. "And there's precious little to implicate Charles in his escape." He stopped, biting his lip.

"What?" I said.

"Again," he said grimly, "I make assumptions based only upon what I know. What if the Vark have means whereby to trace or locate artefacts of technology not of this planet? By which I mean the defective shanath, the blue egg and the box-like device? In that case, Charles might indeed be in danger."

"Always assuming, of course, that the Vark thought to examine the Grange. They might have confined their search to Hopton Wood."

"All this is pure speculation, Jonathon. We'll find out more when we get there. But," he went on, "a thought did occur to me."

We were motoring from London now, with open fields on either side. The snow that had covered most of England for weeks was no more; it had given way, instead, to torrential rain storms. The heavens opened now, and it was all the feeble wipers could do to swipe a flood of water back and forth across the blurred windscreen.

"Go on," I said, eager to hear his speculations.

"Consider what Kathan told us about the shanath," he said. "It duplicates itself at its destination. Therefore, if Kathan or Jasper were to elect to come back to Earth, then all they need to do is select the planet's co-ordinates, if that is possible, and the shanath would duplicate itself on our planet. In effect, Jasper has the means to return home whenever he wishes."

"Always assuming, of course, that he has the Earth's co-ordinates."

I stared through the rain-smeared glass at the sodden countryside. Thunder and lightning had joined the storm, and a strong wind side-swiped the car: it felt as though we were aboard a small yacht on a storm-tossed ocean.

"We are assuming, too," Vaughan went on, "that the shanath can be used at will. But what devices do we use on Earth that come without the need to pay for them? I'll wager that the shanath's expenditure of energy is prodigious: it won't come cheaply, and as far as I know British pounds, shillings and pence are unlikely to be legal tender among the stars."

"But just think if he has returned," I said. "What wonders might he have brought back with him! And if a portal to the stars could be maintained..." My head reeled with the myriad possibilities.

"Recall what Kathan told us about the Galactic Council," Vaughan reminded me. "We're considered too primitive to contact and admit to the fraternity of star-faring races. I think it unlikely that any governing body would allow the free use of a jump gate linking our planet to the stars."

"But what a fanciful speculation," I said.

Just an hour or two ago I had been standing beside my father's death-bed, my thoughts anywhere but the stars – and now I was exchanging wild speculation with my friend. And yet it seemed perfectly natural that we should be doing so, for after all had not we alone, among everyone upon the face of the planet, witnessed more wonders in just weeks than most citizens were privy to in an entire lifetime?

Two hours after leaving London we arrived at Aylesbury, and Vaughan turned his car along the narrow lane bound for Fairweather Cranley. It seemed hard to believe that we had come this way for the first time just three weeks ago.

Thirty minutes later Cranley Grange came into view. Twilight was falling, along with the rain, and the Grange appeared dour and isolated set amid the hills and forests of the Chilterns.

Vaughan drove around the back of the house, and we climbed from the car and hurried through the downpour and into the familiar library.

Charles had a roaring fire built, and the claret breathing. He was standing before the hearth with a glass in hand, and he assured us that we would dine well tonight. He seemed heartier than on the occasion of our last meeting, and I wondered at the reason for his lightened spirits.

"Well, man," I said as I accepted a glass of claret. "What is it?"

I glanced across the room to where the shanath had stood, but it was no longer there.

Charles gestured towards a writing-desk in the corner of the room. "I thought it best to lock away the devices," he said, "in case the Vark came a-hunting."

"We can safely assume that they've left you unmolested?" Vaughan said.

Charles nodded. "I've seen neither hide nor hair of any beast answering their description."

"And the blue light?" I said.

"No sign of that either, though I must admit I've not looked too closely."

"Then out with it, man!" Vaughan demanded. "We didn't come all this way to play guessing games!"

Charles plucked at his Adam's apple, nodding to himself. I sat down on the chesterfield before the fire, and Vaughan accommodated himself within the padded comfort of an armchair.

Charles remained standing, glass in hand, as befits the teller of the tale we were eager to hear. "I was dining in this room last night," he said. "It was nine o'clock. I had had a long day in the surgery at Aylesbury, and I must admit that I had partaken of a glass or two of Jasper's claret. I was more than a little relaxed, and at first I assumed that what I'd heard was no more than something from one of those lucid dreams that sometimes visit one on the borderland of sleep. The sound was sufficiently loud, however, to wake me. I could have sworn that I heard my name called out."

I was sitting upon the edge of my seat. "And?"

"Only silence. I thought nothing of it, and decided to retire. I was about to leave the room when I heard it again."

"Someone calling your name?" Vaughan said.

"Very distinctly. I was awake, and relatively sober. I knew that my senses were not deceiving me."

"And the voice came from where?" I wanted to know.

"I was standing by the door, and the voice issued from behind me." He pointed towards the corner of the room, where the writing desk stood. "The voice said, 'Charles! Charles, are you there?' I turned in amazement, and not a little fear. Cautiously I approached the desk, and the voice came again, calling my name. And now I was certain – it was Jasper's voice, and no mistake."

I leaped up and strode over to the writing-desk. "May I?" I asked, indicating the sliding lid.

Charles nodded. "Be my guest."

I slid back the lid to reveal the shanath, the blue egg, and the device that put me in mind of a bread-box.

Charles was saying, "I approached the desk and opened the lid, and to my astonishment found that the blue egg was glowing."

Reverently, I took up the egg in both hands and carried it back to the fire. I sat with it before me, our eyes fixed upon its sky blue, ovoid perfection.

Charles said, "As I stared at it, my brother's voice came again, 'Charles, are you there?' I had overcome my surprise, and was about to reply, when the blue glow died and Jasper's voice came no more."

Vaughan was lighting his pipe, frowning as he did so. "So the egg is obviously some kind of wireless device between the stars," he said. "It sounds as though Jasper gave up when he thought you were not at home." He grunted a laugh. "I've done the same with the telephone! It seems that some devices, no matter how sophisticated, suffer similar inconveniences!"

Charles went on. "I carried the egg to my bed chamber, and slept with it on my bedside table, in case Jasper was wont to try again. Needless to say, he was not. However, knowing that my brother is a creature of habit, it occurred to me that he was more than likely to try communicating with me again at the same time, nine o'clock, tonight. Hence my summons to you earlier today. I thought you might be interested."

I smiled. "You thought right," I said, and glanced at my watch. "It's not yet seven."

"In that case we have more than ample time for dinner," Charles said. "Cook has prepared roast mutton."

We ate in the library, the blue egg taking pride of position in the middle of the table. The food was excellent, as was the wine, and by eight-thirty I was sated and a little tipsy, and excited at the possibility of Jasper Carnegie contacting us via the blue egg.

We sat back in our chairs and loosened our belts. Vaughan glanced at me. "You seem a little distracted, Jonathon," he said.

I was surprised at his observation, as I assumed that I had not allowed the events of London to cloud my manner.

"My father died this morning," I said.

Vaughan and Charles made sympathetic noises.

"It was expected. He'd been ill for some time." I refrained from telling them about my separation from Carla: how could I begin to elucidate the complexities of a failed love affair to people who had never even known the woman?

I drank my wine and considered my life in London of late, my shortcomings in the department of relationships. Carla had been my first true affair, discounting a chaste dalliance with a younger girl when I was in my mid-twenties, and the thought of my failure, of my inadequacy, filled me with a quiet despair.

I would devote myself to my writing, I declared to myself there and then – which is testament to my naïvety that I thought I might create worthwhile novels without experiencing the pain that is concomitant with meaningful, mature relationships.

Five minutes later, as I was yet again filling my glass, the blue egg gave off a great effulgent glow, lighting the entire room, and my thoughts returned to the immediate present.

I sat up and stared at the lambent egg, as did my friends.

Charles leaned forward. He licked his lips nervously. "Jasper, is that you?"

Seconds later a voice came through loud and clear, unmistakably that of Jasper Carnegie. "Charles? Are you there, Charles?"

"Jasper! You don't know how good it is to hear your voice at last!"

"And I yours, Charles. I tried to reach you yesterday, with no luck."

"I heard you, but too late. I thought you might try again. I summoned Vaughan and Langham to the Grange. They're with me as I speak."

"They are? Excellent!"

I leaned forward and addressed my words to the blue egg. "Jasper, are you well? It's been two weeks – you must have much to relate?"

"Two weeks? Is that all? It seems much longer. I have done much in that time, travelled far. The going has been far from easy..."

I stared around the table at my friends, hardly able to credit that we were conversing with someone light years distant. It was as if we were talking with him on a telephone line from the very next room.

The blue egg pulsed. "Tell me, have there been any further developments in Hopton Wood? The portal? Have by any chance the Vark shown themselves?"

"Not that we've noticed," Charles replied. "It's been all quiet here, Jasper."

"I'm relieved to hear that. As I've learned recently, the Vark are despicable beings. The pair pursuing Kathan were lone bounty hunters, and in all likelihood would not be missed."

Vaughan spoke. "But what of you, Jasper? We're eager to learn of your exploits among the stars. I've been thinking of nothing else since your departure."

We stared at the egg, and his reply could not come soon enough. "When the shanath closed down," Jasper said, "I travelled with Kathan to the transparent city, intending to board a transport ship off-planet."

Vaughan leaned forward and addressed the egg. "A ship? But you still had the shanath, presumably? Couldn't you have simply–?"

"As marvellous as the shanath is, it is also expensive to use. You have no idea of the cost of the short jump we made from Earth. Our flight is being funded by Kathan's political party in the fourth quadrant, and we can make only the occasional jump via the portal when we find ourselves upon worlds that have no connecting transport."

Vaughan was nodding. "We surmised as much on the drive from London."

Jasper went on, "However, when we arrived at the spaceport, we found the city in chaos. A Vark assault ship had visited the planet the day before, and wrought havoc. A thousand humanoids lay dead or dying in the streets. Kathan told me that this was common Vark practice, in order to subjugate a world. The lizards think nothing of laying waste to entire populations, as a warning. Then, when they come to occupy the planet, the citizens thereon know better than to rebel."

"You paint a bleak picture of the universe," Vaughan said, with sadness in his eyes.

"The picture that Kathan has painted over the past few days is bleaker still, my friend. The Vark rule three quarters of the inhabited galaxy with a brutal, blood-thirsty regime. They see all forms of life, whether sentient or not, as their inferior. As we moved through the city, I beheld ample evidence of this fact. My friends, the horrors I beheld visited upon those innocent people..."

He fell silent for a time; we stared at each other around the table, for once speechless to a man.

At last he went on, "Eventually we found the spaceport and negotiated passage off-planet aboard a slow freighter like a mammoth ocean liner, only ten times the size.

"During the voyage, Kathan took the time to tell me something about himself. His mission in this sector is to contact and liaise between cells and bands in opposition to the Vark, raising funds and publicising the many iniquities perpetrated upon innocent peoples. Kathan is attempting to stir opposition so that when the time comes, the advance of the Vark will not be unopposed."

"And your part in all this?" I asked.

"To be frank, I wondered this myself as I accompanied Kathan across the gulf of space. However, my friend has assured me that all hands are valuable in the fight against evil."

"And where are you now?" Charles asked.

"Two days ago the freighter set down on a mining world, the name of which I can hardly pronounce. So far, the Vark have yet to strike this planet. Kathan is doing his best to alert the government to the threat."

"I can only imagine what you're experiencing," Vaughan murmured, his gaze light years away.

Jasper laughed. "I have thought of you often, Vaughan. You would find this experience grist to the mill of your art, if dispiriting. I must admit that, as I stepped through the jump gate, I dreamed I might be entering a pacific, enlightened future realm."

"I sometimes wish that I had stepped through the shanath too," Vaughan said wistfully, "notwithstanding the horrors you describe."

Charles said, "But you are well in yourself, Jasper?"

There was a short delay, then: "Never better, Charles. Physically, I have never known such health. Which brings me to why I am speaking to you now."

"This is more than just a social call?" I said.

"A little more," Jasper replied. "I will call again tomorrow at the same time. By then I should know whether I can acquire the gift I have in mind."

"The gift?" Charles said, leaning forward and staring at the glowing blue egg.

"I wanted to talk to you today, Charles, in order that you might summon Vaughan and Langham to the Grange. I wanted you to be together when I send it through–"

"Jasper," Vaughan said, sounding exasperated, "you're talking in riddles! A gift? Send us something? Explain yourself!"

Jasper laughed. "Is the box-like device you took from Kathan's ship safe and sound?"

It stood upon the writing desk in the corner of the room.

Charles said, "We have it with us, Jasper."

"Excellent! Place it beside the egg tomorrow at this time, and with luck you will be in receipt of a marvel."

"Jasper!" Vaughan said.

Our friend among the stars laughed out loud. "I do not want to raise your hopes only to have them cruelly dashed," he said. "There is a chance that I might not be able to acquire this gift. It is not only expensive, but rare, and prohibited on planets such as Earth. But enough! It is late, gentlemen, and I must return to subterranean dwellings where Kathan and I are lodging during our stay on this dour world. Until tomorrow, my friends, I'll bid you good-day."

"Until tomorrow," Vaughan said.

Seconds later the blue glow ceased, and the communiqué from the stars was over for the evening.

We sat in silence for long seconds, each of us perhaps unable to believe what we had heard, dumbfounded as we were by the interstellar conversation.

Charles bethought himself to refill our glasses, which had remained empty and untouched for the duration of the dialogue. I took a deep draft, sat back and laughed aloud.

"I wonder what his gift might be?" Vaughan mused.

"Something that is expensive," Charles said, "and rare, and illegal on Earth? He called it a marvel..."

Vaughan strode to the writing desk and returned with the silver bread-box. It was perhaps two foot by two, and constructed of a thin, silver material that had the appearance of metal but the feel of bakelite. There seemed to be no working parts to it – its sides were too thin to contain machine components – and its only marking was the grid pattern upon its inner surface.

Vaughan turned the thing this way and that, and finally placed it on the table beside the blue egg.

"It is obviously some transportation device," he said. "A miniature jump portal, perhaps, for objects rather than people. I only hope that it is in full working order, unlike the shanath."

We retired to the fire and conversed until the early hours, each one of us too excited to even think of sleep. It was almost dawn by the time I made my way to my room, sedated by alcohol, though my mind was abuzz with wonder.

I awoke late in the morning and breakfasted in the library with Charles and Vaughan. That afternoon I told Charles I wished to take a hike in the countryside, and he had cook make me up a packed lunch. I set off from the Grange at two, heading up the hill towards Hopton Wood. The day was fine, though rain threatened; great bruise-blue thunderheads were massing like an armada in the west. I made it to the wood before the downpour began, and managed to follow the path to the clearing without losing my way.

The clearing, in my memory at least, had taken on epic proportions in the time since my last visit; it had been the venue for the most wondrous events I had ever witnessed, and I recalled it as a veritable arena. In reality it was much smaller, not at all a vast amphitheatre where opposing aliens had pitched a titanic battle, but a sequestered place barely twenty paces across, eerily still with a pregnant, pre-storm quietude.

I found the smudges that were all that remained of the vanquished Vark; they were barely distinguishable from the surrounding loam. The furrow ploughed by the crashlanding of Kathan's craft was still there, but already embroidered with fine green weed. I sat on the fallen log, eating my lunch and considering that fateful evening when Kathan arrived precipitously on Earth.

I thought of my father, then, and the marvels of the universe he had never lived to see. I felt a pang of guilt for not telling him my secret; surely, I thought, his last days might have been filled with wonder at the knowledge of the miracles that existed beyond the mundane remit of the only world we knew. But I told myself that I had done the right thing in keeping quiet; my father had been too much of a hard-headed realist to accept the fantastical nature of a reality revealed, like a magician's final flourish, at the very last act.

I finished the sandwiches and coffee and took my leave of the clearing, wandering through the wood and this time losing myself along the many pathways that wound around the moss-covered beech and elder. I came out in the village of Fairweather Cranley and took the lane back to the Grange through persistent rainfall, arriving later than I had planned, at seven. I just had time to bathe and change before Charles announced dinner in the library.

The blue egg stood on the table before us, and beside it the mysterious bread-box contraption. We chatted desultorily, our minds on Jasper's imminent communication.

After the meal Charles broke out a fresh bottle of brandy. "In celebration – a little premature, I grant you – of my brother's historic communiqué. To Jasper!"

We raised our glasses. "To Jasper!"

Nine o'clock came and went. Vaughan busied himself by stuffing the bowl of his pipe with Old Holborn and puffing away contemplatively. "Perhaps," he said, "he was unable to obtain the marvel of which he spoke. He did say that he might find it difficult, if you recall."

I was resigning myself to disappointment when, without warning, the egg glowed blue, startling us to various exclamations and cries of delight.

Charles leaned forward. "Jasper? Are you there? Can you hear me?"

"Loud and clear, Charles. Are the others there?"

"We're here," Vaughan and I called in unison.

"Excellent, gentlemen. I trust you've dined well – and I'll wager that you're partaking of claret or, dare I say, the brandy?"

"The latter," I said.

"I must admit to missing the odd snifter," Jasper said.

Vaughan leaned towards the blue egg and said, "How went it, Jasper?"

Jasper Carnegie laughed, like a parent indulging impatient children. "Better than expected. I rendezvoused with Kathan's courier, and we conducted business."

"A courier?" I echoed.

"A member of Kathan's race. At Kathan's instructions, he smuggled certain... devices, let's say... onto the planet."

"Dare I ask," Vaughan said, "precisely what these devices might be?"

"They are known, my friend, as Styrian serum pistols, and in a matter of seconds I will place them in the transmitter before me. These I will then attempt transfer to the receiver which I trust you have before you. Are you ready?"

"The receiver is sitting in the middle of the table," Charles said, glancing around at us. "We're ready."

"Then prepare yourselves," Jasper said.

I gripped the edge of the table. Charles leaned forward, staring at the receiver box. Vaughan leaned back, puffing his pipe and cocking an eyebrow somewhat sceptically.

Seconds later a piercing whistle filled the room, and the box before us glowed white. There was a miniature thunderclap, and the dazzling white glow vanished. The whistling ceased abruptly.

We stared. Sitting within the receiver box were three implements that resembled small automatic pistols, but of a green hue and of an attenuated, alien design.

"Have they arrived?" Jasper asked.

"They have," Charles said. "But what exactly are they?"

"Take them from the receiver," Jasper instructed. "There's one for each of you."

Charles took the pistols from the box and passed them to Vaughan and myself. Mine was extremely light, almost insubstantial, and fitted snugly into the palm of my hand.

I turned it this way and that. In the small butt of the pistol I noticed a transparent window, behind which seemed to be a red, syrupy substance. On the short barrel of the device were three coloured studs, white, red and black.

I glanced at my friends, who were examining their devices with a similar mystification.

"They're weapons, are they not?" Vaughan chanced at last.

Charles said, "Is that right, Jasper? They're weapons to use against the Vark?"

"Are you trying to tell us that we're in danger?" I asked.

Jasper Carnegie was chuckling to himself. "They are not to be used against the Vark," he said, "but upon yourselves."

We stared at each other, and then back at the pistols.

"Would you mind explaining–?" Vaughan began.

"Delighted to do so," Jasper said. "The Styrian injector contains a substance with a long name which I won't bother you with at this juncture. The substance contains a suspension of up to a hundred million microscopic machines."

"Machines!" Vaughan cried. "Is this some kind of joke?"

"No joke, I assure you, but the latest Styrian molecular technology."

"And just what," I said, "does this 'molecular technology' achieve?" I tried to consider the practicalities of a substance which contained a hundred million tiny machines, but my imagination was not up to the task.

"Please permit me a small digression," Jasper said, "by way of explanation. One week ago Kathan gave me just such a device. He said that it was in repayment for services rendered, for helping him evade the Vark and escape through the shanath. He said that its use by certain of the races of the explored universe – humans being one of them – was prohibited by the Vark. But he could not, as a compassionate, sentient being, deny me its benefits. He explained what it contained, and instructed me in its use. Thereupon I applied the pistol to my jugular vein and pressed first the white stud, then the red and the black. I felt an instant sharp pain in my neck, followed by a rush like that of blood to my head. There followed an hour of nausea, and then a period of extreme lethargy which lasted for about six hours. Thereafter I experienced an incredible feeling of well-being, which has been with me ever since."

I was aware of my pulse. "You injected yourself," I said slowly, "with a hundred million molecular machines?"

"Give or take," Jasper replied, "a few thousand or so."

Vaughan cleared his throat and leaned forward. He addressed the glowing egg. "And would you mind telling us, in your own time, quite why you did this?"

"Not at all, my friend. Each machine of the hundred million or so now circulating around my bloodstream is self-replicating; that is, they replace themselves with exact copies when they come to the end of their allotted lifespans, and are naturally flushed from the system. The exact function of the molecular machines is to facilitate the repair and maintenance of the physical structure of one's soma-form and metabolism, in effect combating the process of ageing, the onslaught of disease, viral and bacteriological, and the effect of externally wrought injuries, such as might result from accidents. The molecular machines are known by a phrase, roughly translatable into English as, Eternal Guardians."

He paused, and we stared at each other, and allowed the implication of what he had just told us to sink into our shocked senses.

"Did you say," Charles said, "that these machines fight disease, and repair the body after accidents?"

"In a nutshell, Charles, that is what I said."

Vaughan removed his pipe. I saw that his hand trembled as he laid the pipe upon the tablecloth and leaned towards the blue egg. "But in that case, Jasper, they might extend one's life for years." Jasper allowed the silence to stretch before saying, very quietly, "Not just for years, my friends, but for eternity."

"Are you trying to say," Charles began, "that, that–"

"I am saying, gentlemen, that if you apply the pistol to your jugular vein, or any other large vein or artery, and depress the studs in sequence, then you will effectively render yourselves immortal."

"I don't believe it!" Vaughan cried.

"Impossible!" said Charles.

I pushed my chair from the table and paced the room. I was trembling in every limb and was overcome with sickness. I realised that I was sweating, and tugged at my collar.

I returned to the table. "How can you be sure?" I began.

Jasper replied, "I have talked to people. I have read accounts of the Styrian research. The Styrians are a race opposed to the hegemony of the Vark, and wish to aid their allies with the immortality serum. Of course, the Vark are ruthless in their extirpation of any race, or individuals, who avail themselves of the Eternal Guardians."

I said, "Does that mean they can kill those who have taken the serum?"

"Unfortunately yes," Jasper said. "They have developed weapons which can annihilate even 'immortals'."

Vaughan asked, "And the Vark? Are they immortal?"

Jasper laughed. "The serum is effective only upon the metabolisms of humanoids. With it, we stand a fighting chance of defeating the Vark–"

"And you have–?" Charles began.

"Yesterday, as I said – and I can testify to its almost immediate life-giving properties. I exhort you, gentlemen, to lose no time and use the pistols upon yourselves. Also, I thought it a prerequisite of bestowing this gift that, in each device, there is sufficient serum to treat not only yourself, but one other person of your choosing, should you wish to do so." He fell silent. We stared at the pistols in our hands, and then at each other in wonderment.

"And now, gentlemen, I must say farewell. It might be some time before we speak again. Tomorrow Kathan and I take a ship into the Vark quadrant, and it would be unwise indeed to attempt communication with you when our enemy might intercept the signal."

"Jasper!" I said. "I don't know what to say. Mere thanks are not sufficient."

Jasper laughed. "How could I not bequeath you that which I have already enjoyed? Now do as I did, and administer the serum. Goodbye, my friends."

His voice faded and a second later, before we had time to respond, the blue egg lost its lustre.

I moved like a man in a daze and sat upon the chesterfield before the fire. I was undergoing hot and cold sweats, and my hand gripping the pistol was shaking as if with palsy.

I stared at my friends where they sat, immobile, around the table.

Vaughan said, "Wait, Jonathon! Don't use it yet... It would be foolhardy to rush into this. There are implications which we would be wise to discuss."

"I agree," Charles said. "We need to consider the ramifications of this before we go ahead, or not."

They joined me before the fire, the brandy forgotten, and we sat for a time in a profound silence – like, paradoxically, men handed down a death sentence, and not precisely the opposite.

"Elena..." Vaughan said at last.

I looked up. "Excuse me?"

Vaughan smiled sadly. "My wife, Elena. She died three years ago. If only I had possessed the serum then."

I stared at him. "My father..." I said to myself.

If Jasper had sent the serum a few days earlier, then my father would have lived; or if he could have hung on a little longer... I felt my throat tighten at the thought.

"My God," Charles said, more to himself. "Think of it, just think of it. If we do administer the serum, then everything changes. Our relationships with those with whom we fall in love... Consider: we cannot just administer the remaining serum to our next lover. What is the likelihood that that love will last the test of time?" He smiled bitterly to himself. "And then we will meet others, whom we will love perhaps even more, with the knowledge that that love will be doomed when they age and grow old and we remain forever young."

"Also," Vaughan said, "we will by necessity be forced to live a life of deceit and duplicity. How long will we be able to remain in one community before people begin to notice that we are not ageing? We'll be forced to move every so often, forever wandering the globe, leaving loved ones and friends and all we've come to hold dear..."

"But consider the alternative," I said. "Death, in thirty or forty or however many years. And an eternity of oblivion after that."

"Of which we will know nothing," Vaughan said, as if that were any consolation.

"I would rather experience an eternity of existence," I said, "even if it does entail ceaseless wandering, and doomed love. Imagine the possibilities, the experiences one would have, freed from the spectre of death. Vaughan, haven't you wanted to live to see whether your novelistic prophecies might come to pass, or other maybe even stranger futures that might arise instead?"

"There are benefits and drawbacks," Vaughan said, his gaze distant. "But to be granted eternal life while all around you millions are doomed to brief existences... Wouldn't the psychological pressure become too much?"

"Perhaps one would adapt," I said. "And if one did find a true love, with whom to share eternity..."

"Spoken like a true romantic," Charles said, "or a naïve dreamer."

I raised the serum pistol before me. I recalled the many times when I had awoken in the empty early hours of the night, beset with visions of oblivion. To be freed from the inevitability of death would, surely, compensate for all the drawbacks enumerated by Vaughan.

I looked at my friends. "We would not be tied to Earth, either. In time, when humankind is granted the status of a star-faring race, we too could go among the stars."

"Even before that," Charles mused, "if Jasper opens another shanath to Earth."

I shook my head. The possibilities offered by the serum were overwhelming, and I felt compelled to waste no time and press the pistol to my flesh at that very second.

"I have thought long enough," I said. "I appreciate all you've said, but to live without fear of death is worth all manner of hardship."

I found my jugular and placed the nozzle of the pistol against it. I located the studs, gazing across at my friends as they watched me with wide eyes. Vaughan opened his mouth to remonstrate, but too late.

One by one I depressed the studs.

A burning pain stung the flesh of my neck, and then I was taken in a dizzy rush as the serum entered my bloodstream and careered to my brain, bestowing an instant heady euphoria. I slumped back into the chesterfield and laughed aloud.

"Langham," Charles said. "How do you feel?"

"Light-headed best describes it," I reported. "A little drunk, and ecstatic!"

I watched Vaughan as he raised the pistol to his neck and, after a second's hesitation, pressed the studs. He slumped back into his chair, his eyes closed.

I looked across at Charles. "Well?" I said.

He was staring at the pistol in his hand, as if weighing the consequences of any action he might take.

I was overcome, then, with the nausea that Jasper had described. I felt dizzy and a little sick, as if at any second I might lose the contents of my stomach. I stretched out on the chesterfield and stared at the ceiling, sweating profusely. I did not see whether Charles had decided to administer the serum to himself, and cared little.

The nausea lasted about one hour and then I passed into a state of profound and languorous lethargy. My limbs seemed to weigh a ton, and yet at the same time it was as if I were floating above the chesterfield. I closed my eyes and drifted as if under the influence of a powerful anaesthetic.

I came awake later – how much later I was unsure, until I looked up at the carriage clock on the mantelshelf. It was seven in the morning. I had been unconscious for approximately nine hours.

I sat up, realising that I was still gripping the pistol that contained the one remaining dose of serum. I slipped it into my pocket and stood. Only then did it come to me that I felt not only invigorated but possessed by a sensation of fitness and well-being such as I had never known before. I felt as though every toxin had been flushed from my system, that every ache and pain had been eased; I felt, then, as I paced the room, possessed of energy and purpose.

Vaughan was slumped in his armchair, the pistol having fallen to his lap. An angry red weal stood out on his neck, where he had administered the serum. I crossed to Charles: he too was unconscious, stretched out upon the settee; he, too, had succumbed to the lure of eternal life and applied the pistol to his neck.

I paced the room, then, taken by the need to flee the confines of the library, fetched my overcoat and hurried through the French windows and up the hillside. Dawn was breaking, and it seemed to me the most beautiful sunrise I had ever witnessed: a myriad streamers of cerise and argent laminated the sky to the east. The air was still, and rent with birdsong; I heard the lowing of a distant dairy cow, the barking of a farm dog. The world was waking, and I was awaking with it.

I strode up the hillside and through the wood until I came to the clearing, and continued through it on a path I had never taken before. I was less interested in my destination than in the desire to exercise, to be part of the lightening world around me. At times I even ran, full of boundless energy and a feeling of unrestrained joy. It was a sensation I dimly recalled from youth: an open acceptance of the wonder of existence, of the million possibilities that lay ahead, untramelled by such obstacles as adult concerns and conventions. It was as if my mind were open, for the first time in years, to the wonder of reality that we all once felt but which, over time, the blinkers of routine and conformity work to hide from us. I was mentally liberated and physically, too: I walked for miles as the sun rose and the hours passed by in a rush. I had never felt healthier; my body was a perfect machine and my mind was open and alert.

At last I came to the lane above Cranley Grange, where just a few weeks ago Vaughan had stopped his car in order to take in the snow-bound view. I paused now on the crest of the rise, and stared down at the Grange before continuing on my way. I wanted to greet Vaughan and Charles on the first morning of our immortality, and share with them the joy of our renewed existence.

When I burst into the library, my friends appeared to have just awoken from their slumber; they were smiling, and stretching their invigorated limbs. I could tell by their expressions that they felt as reborn as I.

I hurried over to the table, snatched up the brandy and glasses and splashed out three generous measures.

We took a glass each and stood before the dying embers of the fire.

I raised my drink. "A toast," I said. "To the Kings of Eternity!"

My friends responded. "To the Kings of Eternity!" they cried.

PART TWO

A Trove of Stars

CHAPTER ELEVEN

Fairweather Cranley and London, 1936-1945

I AM WRITING this some ten years after the momentous day in 1935 when Jasper granted Charles Carnegie, Edward Vaughan and myself the gift of immortality. Much has happened since that day, and I will endeavour here to set down some record of the intervening years.

In 1936, soon after completing my account of events in Hopton Wood and the subsequent happenings, I decided that I had had enough of London life, and looked around for a quiet place in the country. My decision was prompted by two main factors: surrounded by so many people in the city, accosted by crowds whenever I ventured out, I was forever reminded that I was set apart from those around me by an accidental and arbitrary stroke of circumstance. Surrounded by people, I was in the paradoxical situation of being made to feel isolated and lonely. The sight of couples arm in arm on the street, dining together in restaurants, filled me with despair. I had two brief affairs in the years before the war, but neither of these were true meetings of minds, still less communions of the soul: the easy physical aspect of both liaisons served to point up the emotional lacunae that existed between me and both these women. I went out of my way to find in these people qualities that I might in time come to love, but failed: they seemed to me too caught up in the easy materialism of the time, interested in the shallow vogues of a contemporary culture I was coming to feel less and less a part of, and which in time I came to despise. For their part, they found me 'distant and remote' I was 'unable to commit emotionally', one woman said, and another found me, 'pathologically reserved'. They were probably right. How could I commit myself to people with whom I shared little understanding and who, in time, while I remained a constant thirty-five, would age and go the way of all flesh? I told myself that perhaps in time I might find someone with whom I would have something in common, and whom I might come to love... In time, and I had all the time in the world, after all.

The second reason I wanted to be away from London was that in the city I was forever haunted by reminders of Carla; the years seemed to do nothing to assuage the pain I experienced at our separation – pain not only at being without someone with whom I had shared a lot, but at the shallowness and cruelty of the person I had been back then in '35. So many venues in London filled me with a feeling of bitterness and guilt, and I had to get away.

During those pre-war years I spent most weekends with Charles Carnegie and Edward Vaughan at Cranley Grange. Our meetings began soon after Jasper transmitted the serum from the stars; once a week we would convene on Saturday evening and dine in the library with the blue egg taking pride of place on the table, in the hope that we might hear from the star traveller once again. Later, when we realised that in all likelihood we might never again speak to Jasper, the weekends became a meeting of friends who shared, aside from friendship, a unique secret. I came to rely on these gatherings, as I think did Vaughan and Charles. They were the only people in whose company I could completely relax; we shared, beside the bond of common experience, an even stronger bond of trust. Only with these men could I talk of my experiences and be sure that they understood; like me, they knew what it was to be set apart from the mass of humanity; like me, they knew what it was to crave emotional affection from people with whom, out of necessity, we could not share the whole truth.

It became our custom to embark upon long walks on Saturday or Sunday mornings, taking in Hopton Wood and the clearing and the village of Fairweather Cranley. On these rambles we would discuss the effects, both physical and psychological, of our condition. We each shared an improved fitness and well-being: we were never ill; the common cold, or worse, held no fear for us. Charles had even experimented upon himself to scientifically test the fact of our resistance to disease. He had introduced himself to a whole range of viruses and bacteria, to no ill effect. On one occasion he told us that he had injected himself with cancer cells, but other than a period during which he felt slightly under the weather, he suffered not in the slightest.

The psychological effect of being rendered immortal was more problematic, and much harder to define or detect. Vaughan and Charles seemed less effected than I, and admitted as much themselves. Vaughan continued his life as a respected and popular novelist, writing a book a year from his cottage in Kent; after the loss of his wife, he had no pressing desire for intimacy or even companionship, he told me. Friends in his village and in London, and our weekly company, satisfied his social needs. For his part, Charles too seemed satisfied with his lot: he worked as a family doctor in Aylesbury, had one or two friends in the town, and was engaged in an occasional liaison – his description – with a widowed woman ten years his senior.

"But don't you ever feel... I don't know... *excluded?*" I once asked as we strolled along the lane towards the public house in Fairweather Cranley. "The human race has its own agenda, and I have mine, and never the twain..."

Vaughan looked at me shrewdly. "I think your problem, Jonathon, is that you feel guilty."

I considered his words for a time. "You might be right," I said. "Why me? Everyone around me is slowly dying. That's always been the terrible tragedy of the human race, the single fact that touches all endeavour with poignancy: the ultimate futility of existence. Whatever we do, whatever great things we create, we die." I shook my head. "Now I'm freed from the fear of death, the fact of death... and I suppose you're right, I do feel guilty."

"Then put it into your novels, Jonathon," Vaughan advised. "Guilt is always a good device for generating emotional conflict."

I suspect his suggestion was meant only half-seriously, but I decided to take his advice. My next few books featured protagonists bowed down with guilty secrets, and for a time the process of writing such novels seemed to work as a catharsis.

It was during one of our weekend walks, while passing through Fairweather Cranley, that I noticed a cottage for sale just off the main street, and decided there and then to buy it. One month later I sold my father's house in London, which I'd moved into shortly after his death, and for the next few years lived the quiet writer's life in the country.

The situation was perfect; the countryside was idyllic, Cranley Grange and Charles were nearby, and I could make my weekly pilgrimage to the clearing in Hopton Wood, to which I felt obscurely drawn.

I enjoyed those few years in the village, away from the crowds of London: it seemed appropriate that I should spend my life in the area where my existence had been so radically and inexorably altered.

Then the war came and altered everything. I suppose it seems petty and small-minded to complain of one's safe and cosy existence being affected by something so cataclysmic as a world war, which devastated the lives of so many. Yet, if I am honest, that was my reaction to the outbreak of hostilities and the realisation that my life would not go on in the simple and satisfying fashion that it had been. I had lived a life of such solitude, untouched by the petty events of the outside world, that news of the war came, first, as a surprise, and then as an inconvenience.

As a supposed intellectual, I was dragooned into the War Office and set to work in the information department. I spent my war years writing propaganda pamphlets for overseas consumption, scripting cheap films with life-enhancing or patriotic content, and editing other writers' work, all of which I found relatively easy and often interesting. The only disadvantage was that I had by necessity to live in London. I rented a small place in Mayfair, commuted daily to the War Office, and spent my evenings and weekends working on my own novels and short stories: I sequestered myself in a world of my own manufacture, away from the good-time crowds and the greater mass of suffering humanity, which filled me with a disquieting sense of alienation and, if Vaughan was right, also guilt.

Our weekends at Cranley Grange were a thing of the past, put on hold until the safe old pre-war days could be resumed. I saw Vaughan perhaps twice a month; he too was working in London, in some hush-hush department involved in 'Intelligence' – a strange description which never really seemed to describe anything. We often met for a drink after office hours in the White Lion in Holborn, and it was there he arranged to meet me one Wednesday evening in the summer of '42. He told me that he had just that afternoon heard from Charles.

My immediate thought was that Jasper had established contact again via the blue egg, and I said as much as we sat down with our drinks.

Vaughan shook his head. "If only that were so," he said. "I would dearly love to know how our friend is faring."

Vaughan cut a distinguished and patrician figure; although forever fifty, but technically seven years older now, he had the kind of face, well-lined and with a mass of silver hair, that could pass for anything between fifty and seventy. He would be able to play the part for many years to come, without arousing the slightest suspicion.

"You might find this hard to believe, Jonathon, but Charles is being parachuted into Crete at some point in the not too distant future."

I said something along the lines that he had to be joking – but Vaughan was serious. "He came over to the office today and told me, but it's supposed to be top secret and all that, so mum's the word."

"Just a minute. Charles? Parachuted into Crete?"

The juxtaposed image of Charles the country doctor dangling from the end of a parachute was as surreal as it was absurd.

"Well, why not?" Vaughan said, smiling at my expression. "His Greek is fluent and the resistance movement is in need of medics. He volunteered a year or so ago, passed the medical with flying colours, of course, and will soon be seeing active service."

"I wonder..." I began.

Vaughan nodded, filling his pipe. "I was wondering the same thing." He looked around to ensure that we were not being overheard. "Last year I gave myself a nasty gash with the pruning shears, nearly cut off my finger." He held up the digit in question. "Two days later it was as right as rain."

"But how well will Charles' body repair itself if it's ripped apart by a hail of German bullets?" I said.

We were to find out the answer to this question the following year.

The war dragged on. My novels continued to sell. The reading public perhaps found my stories of small-town and country life, set in the halcyon pre-wars days, something of a comfort, though what the genteel patrons of the lending libraries made of my guilt-ridden protagonists I never found out. By '43 I had published twelve novels and a collection of stories, all from Hutchinson, and I was established as a safe, moderately popular author. Sometimes my books were even reviewed, but the praise always seemed to be faint and mildly damning. "Mr Langham paints the scene of village life with considerable skill, though perhaps his paint-box is becoming a little over-used."

One Friday in September '43 I left the office at five and walked home, through a London disrupted by a bombing raid the night before. I had heard that the Curzon on Shaftesbury Avenue had suffered a direct hit, and as that theatre was ever associated in my mind with Carla, it was perhaps natural that I should think of her as I strolled south to Mayfair. I was still visited by guilt that I had never contacted her after my father's death. Over the years I had meant to drop her a few lines, but like most good intentions this one too fell by the wayside. I sometimes saw her name on the billboards, and I often wondered how she might be faring.

Serendipity must have taken me by the shoulders then and steered me in the direction of the Odeon. I knew that she was starring in a recently released American film, but even so the sight of her, smiling out of a black and white still of the movie beside the cinema entrance, stopped me in my tracks.

I detected signs of ageing in the lines about her eyes, and something turned in my stomach. Carla was thirty-nine now, and wearing her beauty with a sophisticated air of mature glamour. Her dark hair was longer than when I knew her, but swept back to reveal the fine bones of her face.

I hurried on, wondering at the shallow fool I had been.

That evening, Edward Vaughan rang. "Jonathon, what are you doing tonight?"

"Nothing at all. Why?"

"I've just heard from Charles."

My heart surged at the mention of his name, thinking that perhaps Jasper had been in touch. Then I remembered that Vaughan had taken custody of the blue egg and the receiver before Charles had left for Crete.

"He's back in England?" I asked.

"Arrived last night. He wants to see us as soon as possible. The White Lion at eight."

"I'll be there." I rang off, only then wondering at the 'as soon as possible'. It sounded urgent.

I arrived fifteen minutes early, bought my usual pint of stout and secured the booth at the back of the bar, which Vaughan and I preferred for both comfort and security.

Vaughan arrived at seven on the dot and joined me with a double brandy. "Did Charles say why he wanted to see us?" I asked.

Vaughan began the ritual of slowly, contemplatively, filling his pipe. "He said no more than that he wanted to see us as soon as possible. But he did sound a little... perhaps agitated is the wrong word, but concerned."

"Thank God he survived Crete, anyway."

"Speak of the devil," Vaughan said, rising and signalling to Charles across the crowded bar.

Our friend pushed through the press and I took his hand. "Good to have you back. You're looking well." As indeed he was. Gone was the rather diffident Charles I recalled from the pre-war years. He had even filled out, and his hair had grown back to cover the bald patch high on his forehead. He was tanned, and appeared every inch the part of how I imagined a Greek resistance fighter might look.

Vaughan bought him a pint of bitter and we slipped back into the booth. "You're looking damned well," Vaughan said.

Charles stared from one of us to the other. "Very well," he said, "for a dead man."

My smile faltered, for I knew what he meant.

"Out with it," Vaughan said.

Charles was silent for a time, as if gathering his thoughts. "I'll get to the heart of it," he said. "There's a lot I want to tell you, but that can wait. The situation out there, the experiences... What I have to tell you concerns the three of us." He took a long drink of bitter.

I glanced at Vaughan, my pulse racing.

"I didn't see much fighting," Charles said. "I was mainly in the mountains, in a cave we'd set up to treat the wounded. The Germans had complete control of Crete, and all we could do was limit our action to the occasional sortie, sabotage. About three months ago, I was called out to treat a couple of our men too badly injured to be moved. It sometimes happened, and it was usually pretty safe as the fighting had moved on. For some reason, on this particular night we ran into trouble. A gun-carrier full of Germans found us and opened fire... I was hit in the chest."

He stopped, his eyes wide. His grip on his pint glass was so tight that his knuckles, despite his tan, were white. "I remember feeling the bullets thudding into my chest and thinking that this was it. My God, the fear..."

"But you volunteered," I said. "You knew the danger."

He was smiling. "In England, before I volunteered, I performed a few experiments."

"You told us about the viruses," I began.

"That was much earlier. These experiments were more... physical. I inflicted on myself increasingly severe injuries, attempting to assess the limit of the serum's ability to resurrect its host."

"And?" Vaughan asked.

"Before Crete, I never had the courage to go all the way. I came rather close, but I balked at slitting my wrists and seeing if the serum could heel the wound before I bled to death... However, I felt confident enough not to fear being badly injured when I volunteered. That did not lessen my fear when we were ambushed, and I received a round of bullets in the chest. One of our band of six survived and saw that I was dead, and left me where I was for burial later."

He shook his head, staring into his glass. "The next thing I remember is opening my eyes and watching the sun rise over the mountains, what must have been six hours later. I felt a pain in my chest, and I couldn't move, but I certainly didn't feel like I'd taken an entire round... At noon, half a dozen villagers came to collect the bodies for burial. They were surprised to find me alive – they'd been told that five dead resistance fighters awaited burial, and that meant five dead – no more, no less. The *andartes*, as the resistance are known, always retreat with their injured. By this time, I can only assume that my internal injuries had healed themselves. I still had the entry wounds, but even they were beginning to scab over."

"Just like Kathan's injuries, all those years ago," I said.

"Imagine Spiros' reaction when he saw me a day later. He was overjoyed, but disbelieving. If he hadn't been a true communist, he might have considered it a miracle. I kept my shirt fastened and feigned pain. He was never quite the same with me, after that."

"Physician, heal thyself," Vaughan murmured.

"So..." Charles concluded. "What happened is reassuring on one hand. We know we can survive usually fatal injuries. But that opens up a new risk I had never even considered."

Vaughan was nodding. "The danger of discovery."

Charles smiled, without much humour. "Can you imagine if the authorities got wind of what happened to us? They wouldn't be happy trying to find out why we're like this until they had us chopped up and stored in a hundred test tubes."

"Don't worry," I said, to add a note of levity to proceedings, "I always intended to be careful how badly I'm injured."

I bought another round, and the conversation turned to other topics. I asked my friends if they had any plans for what they might do after the war.

Vaughan took his pipe from his mouth. "I've been giving that question some thought," he said. "It's so easy to continue as one has been, but there is a whole world out there, boundless possibilities. I must in time give thought to moving on – it's something that all three of us need to consider."

Charles nodded. "I think I might survive another ten years in this guise," he said. "Any longer would be to invite suspicion from one's acquaintances. My plans for after the war... I don't know, I might return to India and explore the subcontinent. As to what I might do after that, I haven't given it much thought, I must admit. Nor exactly how I might go about effecting the change."

Vaughan pointed at him with the stem of his pipe. "I made contacts in the department," he said. "People who know people who can arrange these things. Passports, papers. That shouldn't prove too much of a problem."

"Have you considered when you might move on?" I asked Vaughan.

"The fortunate thing about being the age I was when I took the serum," he said, "is that I might quite easily pass for someone in his sixties. It will be some while yet before I move on. I have a few more novels in me yet, ideas and themes I wish to explore." He looked at me. "And yourself, Jonathon?"

"Immediately after the war, I intend to get out of London and return to Fairweather. Like you, I'll continue writing for a few more years, and then I might travel. My books so far have all been set in London and the country, with one exception. There's a lot more out there to write about. I want to experience the new."

Vaughan smiled. "The universe is so vast," he said, "and our understanding so small."

Last orders were called, and we continued the meeting at Vaughan's Holborn flat, our conversation fuelled by a bottle of excellent brandy. It was almost dawn when we said our farewells and parted, promising to meet regularly before Charles was posted abroad again.

In the event, he was shunted into a desk job at the Ministry of Defence, and during the last year of the war we recommenced our weekly meetings. Every Saturday night we would dine at Vaughan's flat, and drink a brandy or two to the fate of our errant friend.

As chance would have it, Charles was absent on the evening when Jasper Carnegie next chose to contact us. Vaughan and I had finished dinner and were seated before the fire, poring over a chess board. Charles had pressing matters to handle at the Ministry, and so Vaughan had suggested that we continue the informal tournament of games we had begun months earlier.

I was about to resign, having found myself in a hopeless position approaching the end game, when a strange blue light filled the room.

At first I was startled: it had been many years since we had beheld the light of the blue egg, and it was not until we heard Jasper's voice call out from the bureau in the corner of the room that I realised what was happening.

"Charles!" the disembodied voice said. "Charles, are you there? Vaughan, Langham? Can you hear me?"

We stared at each other across the board, like men in shock. Then Vaughan leapt to his feet and almost ran across the room and snatched up the blue egg.

He placed it among the scattered chessmen and leaned forward. "Jasper? We hear you loud and clear. I'm here with Jonathon."

"And Charles?" Jasper enquired.

"Working late," Vaughan said. "I'll contact him–" he was reaching for the phone when Jasper interrupted.

The blue egg pulsed, filling the room with its azure effulgence. "There's hardly time to say what I have to say. I have a minute, maybe two. The Vark are monitoring all our communications... You can tell Charles that I am fit and well, all things considered."

"We're delighted to hear that, old man," Vaughan said. "We've been more than a little worried."

"The last few years have been taxing, to say the least. More than once the Vark have almost had us, and only good fortune and tenacity won our escape."

"How goes the fight?" I asked.

"At the moment they have the upper hand. Their ruthlessness is truly terrible to behold. I have seen entire cities of a million innocent souls razed to the ground by weapons unimaginable to humankind. But the more peoples they dominate, the more determined and trenchant foes they find pitted against them. We will not give up the fight so easily. A veritable trove of stars is the spoils for the victor."

"Where are you now?" Vaughan asked.

We stared at the egg, awaiting Jasper's reply from the stars. "We are in space," he said, "and about to embark upon a flight to the galactic Core. We are transporting weapons and fighting machines for a world currently under Vark domination. Unfortunately, the enemy know of our mission, and are doing all within their power to prevent its success. It will be our most fearsome test so far. I contact you now, gentlemen, to say farewell lest I fail to survive the voyage." He paused, then went on, "But enough of me! How about yourselves? What news of the world do you have to tell me?"

We stared at each other, and I shook my head to indicate that we should not appraise Jasper of the fact that planet Earth was undergoing its very own fight against the forces of evil. Vaughan spoke, "We are well, Jasper. Jonathon and I are still writing."

"And Charles?"

"Ah... he is working in London, as a GP," Vaughan said. "We are all well, and contemplating the years ahead."

"I must interrupt," Jasper said. "I've had word that we should take our stations – we phase immediately into the interspatial realm. My friends, take care."

"Try to contact us again as soon as possible!" I cried.

The blue egg pulsed. "I shall do my best, my friends. Till then, farewell."

His voice faded, and the blue light went out, leaving Vaughan and I staring at each other across the chessboard as the glow of the fire flickered across our startled faces.

I took my leave of Vaughan in the early hours of the morning, and as I stepped from his porch and made my hurried way down the darkened streets towards Mayfair, I glanced up at the stars and considered my friend and his valorous exploits against the Vark.

Weeks passed, and then months, and the war at last came to an end. I lost no time in fleeing London and sequestering myself once again in my cottage in Fairweather Cranley. I wrote the novels I had told Vaughan and Charles I wished to write, very much like all the others I had penned over the years. I kept myself very much to myself, venturing into London every couple of months in order to meet Vaughan and Charles for a meal, and occasionally indulging in a couple of halves of stout in the village's one and only pub.

In '46, Charles suited action to his words and travelled to India. He left the blue egg with Vaughan and explored the length and breadth of the sub-continent. He kept in contact by frequent long and fascinating letters.

Three years after leaving London, in '48, perhaps spurred by Charles' wanderlust, I put the finishing touches to that year's novel in July and realised that I needed a change. There was a great danger, in the situation in which I found myself, of postponing all decisions until later. I had, after all, all the time in the world: why the hurry? But I was tired of writing the same old book over and over again, and though the quiet life of Fairweather Cranley suited me well enough, I craved a new location, somewhere quiet, preferably, but also warm and foreign. I had to overcome my inertia and actively seek out new horizons. And with new horizons, I hoped, would come new ways of seeing the world, new ways of writing about different characters in different situations.

Late in '48, my thoughts never far away from my friends on Earth, and Jasper Carnegie out there among the stars, I set sail for Argentina.

CHAPTER TWELVE

Kallithéa, July, 1999

THE DAY AFTER his meeting with Forbes, Langham walked into Sarakina and dined at Georgiou's taverna. As he ate, he thought about the journalist. Forbes was getting very close to Langham's secret – not that the hack would ever learn the truth, of course. But his claim that he was a plagiarist might prove troublesome.

He could always leave Kallithéa, start a new life somewhere...

He considered Caroline. She was still in London, and he missed her company, her lively conversation. How could he think of leaving Kallithéa, and Caroline too? He told himself that within weeks he would be over her, as he established the routines of his new, assumed existence – but a part of him did not want to get over her. A part of him looked forward to a life in which she was a central fixture, a companion upon whom he could unburden his cares and worries, the considerable secrets of his past. Someone, perhaps, whom he could love.

There was a burst of activity on the cobbled waterfront beside the taverna. A gaggle of school-children were boarding a rickety bus, and behind it a line of cars blared horns as if in some kind of celebration. He wondered what might be happening – not that it took very much to get Greeks out onto the streets.

He gestured Georgiou over and asked, in his fractured Greek, what was happening.

Georgiou laughed. "The Americans are filming in Xanthos. Everyone is going over to watch. Big name stars, actors and actresses. One minute!"

He hurried inside and emerged seconds later with the island's weekly newspaper. He folded it to the article about the making of a film, and prodded the grainy photograph of a famous American director.

Langham ordered a second glass of retsina and for the next five minutes worked hard at decoding the article. His understanding of written Greek was worse than his spoken Greek, but he could just about make sense of newspaper reports.

A film called *Summer and Winter* was being shot in Greece, and one of the locations was Kallithéa. The story was about how an English woman returns to Greece in old age to be reunited with a Greek lover she had fought alongside in the second world war. The part of the woman was being played by...

Langham stopped reading, and stared at the name. It was as if someone had dealt him a punch to the solar plexus. His vision misted and he felt nauseous.

The report went on to say that this was Carla DeFries' first film role in more than twenty-five years. The actress, who had turned ninety-five this year, had been tempted from retirement by the director, an old friend...

Langham laid the paper aside and stared out across the ocean, seeing nothing but old memories in his mind's eye.

If he went along to watch the filming, he told himself, and kept in the background so that she would not see him... There could be no harm in that. It would be a torture of sorts, but also a reminder, a reminder of the gift that he was forever in danger of taking for granted.

He paid Georgiou, crossed to the taxi office and ordered a cab to take him to Xanthos. Five minutes later he was bumping over the hills, cooling his face in the breeze that rushed in through the open window as he considered Carla DeFries. The last he'd heard of her had been back in the seventies when she had appeared in an English film set in France. In her sixties then, she had played the part of a grandmother, and Langham had been unable to bring himself to go and see the movie.

The filming of *Summer and Winter* was taking place in the town square. Langham alighted on one of the approach roads and wandered into the centre of town, accompanied by what seemed like the entire population of the island.

From the steps of the town hall he had a good view of the scene in the process of being shot. Amid the chaos of so much technical apparatus that he wondered how films were ever made – dolly-tracks, cameras like futuristic weapons, even lights, on a day like today! – two actresses were strolling through the deserted square, talking animatedly in the eye of the technical storm swirling around them.

Neither of the actresses was Carla DeFries. They were both young and blonde – playing the roles of American back-packers doing the islands. He searched through the production crew behind the cameras, but saw no sign of the great dame of British cinema, as he'd heard her called on more than one occasion.

He knew, then, that it had been a mistake to come. He decided to return, before he did see her: he would only feel like a voyeur, a ghoul feasting his eyes on a fate that befell others, and not himself.

He was about to turn and go when, inevitably, he saw her. She entered the scene from a building to the right of the square. He stared, pulse racing, as she walked, with a sprightliness amazing for her age, across the cobbles and began talking to the young women. She was thin, and upright, her blue-grey hair curled close to her head. Ninety-five, he thought, aware that his eyes were misting over with tears.

He found a taxi to take him home. For the duration of the journey he could not banish from his mind's eye the image of Carla as she had been in 1935. It was as if the sight of her in the square had released a flood of hitherto suppressed memories. He recalled their arguments, incurred by his naïve jealousy. He recalled, too, the times of intimacy he had shared with Carla. He saw her staring up at him from the pillow, blue eyes sparkling with genuine love, he realised now. He had been such a callow fool.

That afternoon he sat on the patio and made himself work. He corrected that morning's four pages and stopped writing at six, aware that the work, and the passage of hours, had helped to dull the pain.

He was about to make himself a meal – wishing that Caroline were here to join him – when he heard the sound of a motorbike approaching along the track from the village. His first reaction was outrage that the peace of the evening should be so violently disturbed: fortunately not many youngsters negotiated the rough track, preferring the metalled roads instead. The noise would be soon gone, anyway.

The roar increased, and then cut suddenly. He stepped to the edge of the patio and saw a leather-clad Greek youth holding the motorcycle steady while an old woman, head concealed in a huge helmet, climbed from the back. She pulled off the helmet, passed it to the rider, and looked around.

The years seemed to fall away, then. She still had the same amazingly blue eyes...

She saw him, and her mouth opened. She said something to the youth, who nodded.

Carla stepped forward over the rough path, staring at him. "I know you'll probably think this awfully rude of me," she said, "but I saw your photograph in a London paper a couple of months ago, and as I was on the island..." She stood below him now, staring up. "My word, you're the spitting image."

Langham was speechless; he knew it would be a mistake to let his emotions show, quite inexplicable to this old lady – but the fact was that he wanted to reach out and take her in his arms, and apologise.

"Excuse me?" he began.

"How rude of me!" she said. "I'm Carla DeFries, and I once knew your grandfather, Jonathon Langham. Well, I presume he was your grandfather!"

He smiled, nodded. "That's right."

She beamed, closed her eyes and lifted her face to the heavens. "When I saw the picture in the paper, I knew it had to be."

"Please..." He stepped back, gesturing for her to climb the steps and join him.

She did so with a gentility and grace in which he saw, like a vague memory, the much livelier movements of the young woman she had been, almost sixty-five years ago.

He pulled a chair from the table and she sat down. "Can I get you a drink? Coffee?"

"You don't happen to have any wine, young man?"

He smiled. "Daniel. I have some local stuff, not exactly vintage."

"When in Rome," she smiled, and her smile was still as enchanting.

He fetched two glasses and a bottle of retsina from the kitchen, his hands shaking as he lifted the glasses, and carried them out to the table.

He sat down and raised a glass.

She did the same. "To your good health, Daniel," she said.

"And to yours," he said, something catching in his throat.

"I hope you don't mind my intruding like this, barging in as if you didn't have a life of your own to lead? But I had to take the opportunity. You see, the photograph... It could have been Jonathon." She paused. "Did you know that your grandfather and I...?"

"He spoke of you often."

"He did? My word... It was so long ago. Sixty-five years! Did he tell you we were lovers, once?"

Langham nodded. "He often told me that he'd had an affair with the most beautiful woman in England."

Carla laughed, a wrinkled hand fluttering at her throat. "My word... He said that? The rascal!"

"He said he regretted how he parted with you. He always wanted to apologise." He smiled. "He said he was young and immature."

Carla reached out and touched the back of his hand. Her fingers were warm and very, very soft. "We were both young and immature! Do you know, I think I was his very first love. So of course he didn't know how to handle me – and I must admit that I was probably a bit of handful, then. I liked a good time, you see, and Jonathon was so very jealous! But we had some wonderful times together."

"He never forgot you," he murmured.

She smiled sadly. "I don't suppose he's still..." She waved. "Silly of me. I'm outliving everyone I ever knew. That's the problem of living for so long, Daniel, let me tell you. Everyone you once knew is no longer..."

He picked up the empty bottle suddenly, silencing her. "Excuse me. I'll get another."

And before she could protest, he hurried into the kitchen and leaned against the frame of the door, and he could not say whether his tears were for Carla DeFries or for himself.

He busied himself in the kitchen, arranging cake on a plate and opening another wine.

He returned to the patio, composed now, and offered her the Madeira and a refill.

"You shouldn't have," she protested mildly, taking a wedge of cake.

"My grandfather died in '75," he said. "He was healthy and happy to the end."

"He was? That's good to know. He was as old as the century, you know. He often reminded me of that. He joked that he'd never forget how old he was."

Langham smiled, remembering...

She went on, "I have all his books, every one of them. But he never published after '48, if I'm not mistaken."

"Not under his own name. He wrote a different kind of book in the fifties, under the name of Christopher Cartwright. He did well – became something of a best-seller."

"How wonderful for him. He always wanted to be a successful writer. I'm so pleased he achieved his ambition." She took a sip of wine. "Tell me, was he happy in love?"

He smiled. "I'm sure he was. He married when he was forty," he temporised, and went on quite involuntarily, "She was a lovely woman called Caroline, a painter. They were very happy, and had one son, my father."

"And you're a successful writer yourself? You obviously take after your grandfather. He'd be so proud." She shook her head again. "My word, looking at you, the years seem to fall away."

They drank, and she reminisced, and then told him about the filming of *Summer and Winter*. The sun was setting when she looked at the delicate gold watch on her fragile wrist and exclaimed, "Lord! And Stavros will be waiting! It's been so wonderful talking to you, Daniel."

"The pleasure was mine. It's not every day I get famous actresses dropping in for supper."

She laughed, stood and moved towards the steps. She paused. "Tell me, Daniel, is there a young woman in your life?"

He smiled. "I think there is," he said.

She nodded. "Like that, is it? Well, I wish you the best of luck. Treat her well, buy her flowers and chocolates. It always works."

He accompanied her out to the track. She turned to him.

"Well, thank you again, Daniel."

He reached out, and she was in his arms. They hugged, perhaps for longer than was normal, and she feigned breathlessness when he released her – ever the actress.

She fitted her helmet over her head, climbed carefully onto the back of the motorbike and lifted a hand in a brief wave.

Daniel watched the bike turn on the track and carry her away. He returned to the patio, picked up his glass and the wine, sat on the sofa and watched the stars come out.

He considered the Carla he had known, all those years ago, and the women he had loved since then, and could not stop himself from weeping.

At noon the following day, having finished his four pages, he made his way into the village for lunch.

At two o'clock he crossed to the post office. Yannis saw him coming and had the *poste restante* box on the counter as he entered. He checked for mail, but there was none for him today.

As he was about to leave, Yannis said, "Mr Langham... Your friend, the Englishman, this morning he said he must leave on urgent business. He said he had no time to say farewell to you."

Langham nodded. "Did he say where he was going, or when he might be back?"

Yannis shrugged. "He just paid for his room and took a taxi to Xanthos, Mr Langham."

He left the village and walked home, feeling as though a great weight had been lifted from his shoulders. Perhaps Forbes had given up on his quest, learned as much as he could, and decided there was no story in the reclusive novelist, after all.

Perhaps Langham's earlier thoughts about leaving Greece and starting a new life were premature. He passed Caroline's villa, but she was still away, and he looked ahead to her return with longing.

CHAPTER THIRTEEN

Tangier, 1963-1964

I AM WRITING this in Tangier in the month of October, 1964. Much has happened during my stay in the city; I have experienced love and tragedy in equal measure, and I feel that the only way I might come to terms with the events of the past year is to set them down in black and white, before I leave Morocco for ever.

In '63, after years of travelling from place to place around the world, I found myself in Tangier and decided to remain for a while. There was something about the city that appealed to me, that invited me to stay for longer than the usual month or two.

Since '48 I had spent six years in South America and a little longer in Africa. My usual routine was to find a town or a city whose atmosphere spoke to something within me. I preferred quiet, backwater places, towns which the modern world had touched once but then left behind; tropical or semi-tropical, well-composted, fetid and slightly run-down. I despised the trappings of the West, the advertising and the emphasis that the latest was the best, the corrupt ethos that image was everything.

In South America I enjoyed the cities of Santiago and Arica in Chile, Santa Cruz in Bolivia and Paraguay's lethargic capital Asuncion. I would spend a month or two in each place, making notes for novels and short stories, and then find some village well away from the bustle and commerce of town or city, preferably in the mountain climes of the Andes, and work on the first draft of a novel for three months or so.

These books were more ambitious than those I had written as Jonathon Langham. They were novels of ennui and angst set amid expatriate communities in countries whose temperatures, both political and meteorological, created cauldrons of conflict and insanity.

My first novel as Christopher Cartwright found a respectable publisher in London, and I mailed them a completed manuscript every year thereafter, with scant, usually fictitious, biographical information, and of course no author photograph. The books were reviewed favourably, often earning comparisons to the works of Graham Greene.

In the mid-fifties I moved to Africa and explored the sweltering hell-holes of the Congo, Cameroon and the Central African Republic. I continued writing a novel a year – the work giving my life a purpose it would otherwise have lacked. The ability to write was the only one I possessed; it was both a way of working out what I thought of the world, and coming to some small understanding of myself. The books increased in popularity over the years to the extent that their literary merit, along with the famed reclusiveness of their author, brought the Fleet Street hacks out to Africa in search of copy. They had little to go on; no photograph, no address, no contacts or friends in England. I employed an agent in London, but his cheques were always sent to me care of a *poste restante* address in whichever town I found myself at the time, and if they went missing, then I was little bothered. The money my father had left me in '35 had, through careful investment, grown considerably, and with my literary earnings throughout the fifties I once calculated that I was worth in the region of two million pounds. Not that money, or what money might purchase – other than the freedom to travel – much bothered me: I travelled light, my only constant possessions being my toiletry bag, a portable typewriter, and a notebook.

In the late fifties the enigma that was Christopher Cartwright, the best-selling author of *The Human Jungle* and *A Long Way from Timbuktu*, became too much for the feature editors of the Sunday papers. After speculation that Cartwright was the pseudonym of Greene or a number of other authors was quashed by my agent, the race to find the man who was Christopher Cartwright intensified. It seemed that my footsteps were forever dogged by persistent, perspiring Fleet Street hacks, eager for the slightest snippet of information concerning the elusive author. In Kinshasa in '59 the chase became too close for comfort, and in order to buy myself time I indulged in a game with the foreign correspondent of the *Telegraph*. I approached him in a bar with the story that I had travelled with Cartwright in '57; I even supplied him with a photograph of a hotel in Bamako I had taken years earlier for research purposes: seated at a table before the building was the figure of a slim, dark-haired Westerner, an acquaintance I said was the writer. I claimed that Cartwright had told me he intended to spend the next few years in Zanzibar.

While that unfortunate island was inundated with eager feature writers, I contacted Vaughan and changed my identity yet again.

Vaughan, Charles and I had continued to meet every year since '48. In the early fifties Vaughan lived in the south of France and, though going under the name of Kenneth Edmundson, continued publishing scientific romances, known now as science-fiction. We exchanged copies of our novels when we met, and I was amused to find that veiled references to the events at Cranley Grange and Hopton Wood occasionally featured in his books.

Charles Carnegie spent the fifties in India, working for the Red Cross as a doctor in Madras – I forget the name he used at the time. We kept in contact by means of letters, and every year in June or July we would arrange to meet for a week or two of reminiscences and catching up. As money or distance was no object to us, the venues throughout the fifties were as diverse as they were exotic. The Kings of Eternity met in Paris in '53, and Singapore in '54. In '55 we took a cruise of the Mediterranean for a month, and the following year trekked in the Himalayas.

1957 found us for a few weeks in Ulan Bator, Mongolia, and '58 in Anchorage.

In '59 we arranged to meet in London and go about the process of changing our identities yet again.

Vaughan kept a flat in Kensington, and it was here we were reunited in the June.

I would have been fifty-nine that year, Charles a year younger. Physically I appeared to be in my late thirties; travel in the tropics had made me lean and tanned, and something of my experiences over the past twenty-five years had etched itself into the lines of my face. My eyes, according to the occasional acquaintance, looked far older than the rest of me.

Charles had transformed himself over the years, from the rather thin, stooped figure I recalled from the thirties, to an upstanding, muscular mountaineer of a man. Vaughan, for his part, remained the tweed-clad, patriarchal man of letters. He looked to be in his fifties, while in fact he was almost seventy-five.

On the first night of our meeting in '59, I suggested a restaurant in Greek Street. We ordered a bottle of raki, and we toasted the Kings of Eternity with that noxious brew.

Conversation was continual and tremendously entertaining. We talked of our experiences since we had last met, the sights we had seen, the books we had written and read: from the personal and the specific, talk always turned to events in the world at large. Over the course of nearly twenty-five years, it was as if we had gained intellectually, as well as physically, from the serum. Our analysis was precise and perceptive, our conclusions often profound and radical. I lay no claim in this department – it was the company of my learned friends that promoted any originality of insight on my part.

But, most of all, I enjoyed these meetings because they brought me into contact with the only two human beings on the planet who understood what I had been through, and whom I could trust implicitly.

Loneliness, to a differing degree with each of us, was a constant problem. How was it possible to make friends when we knew that in time, ten years or fifteen or whatever, one would have to move on, leave behind the person one was, along with one's friends and acquaintances? Charles was only a little affected in this regard: he claimed never to have made great or lasting friendships – though he excluded us from this generalisation – and therefore he felt no qualms in leaving the friends and acquaintances he did make now: people moved on all the time, he said, and failed to keep contact. Vaughan was the same: he said he was so absorbed in his writing that he had no need for other friendships – the ones he shared with us, he said, sustained him.

I began to wonder, then, if my reluctance to make friends during my travels was less to do with qualms about giving them up, and more to do with some innate reserve: I did not want to make friends because I did not need them. I had the Kings of Eternity, after all, and they were sufficient to my needs.

"But what," I recall asking, somewhat drunk on the raki, "about affairs of the heart? Women. How do you both stand on that?"

"I think," Vaughan admitted, "that the serum caught me at a time when my libido had reached its nadir. I must admit that I seldom feel the urge."

I nodded. "Charles?"

"At the moment I'm engaged in a casual affair with a French nurse at the hospital where I work. There's no risk of marriage or attachment, and in time she'll grow restless and move on."

"But don't you want to find someone to share everything with? You don't crave love?"

Charles shook his head and smiled. "I recall a time at the Grange," he said. "Didn't I call you a romantic fool? Surely you don't still feel the same way?"

I considered my empty glass, then filled it up. "I'm caught between wanting more than anything to find someone, and being too afraid to try. Every affair I've had has ended in failure – through faults of my own in many cases. I want someone to share my life – to give me a different perspective on existence. Does that sound selfish, as if the only reason I want someone is so that I might benefit from a fresh insight into things? It isn't meant to be. I want to be less selfish: I want to share existence with someone."

"And share the serum, too?"

I swirled my drink, and finally nodded. "Eventually yes, when I find the right person."

Charles laughed. "But that's impossible, man! Forget about it now! Love never lasts – you're a fool if you think that if you do fall in love with someone you think worthy of the serum, then you would remain in love, together, for all eternity! You might as well save yourself the pain, go find some deserving stranger and bestow the gift on them!"

I shook my head. "I've got no illusions about remaining in love – everything ends. But if only I could find someone to trust, who I could depend on for years, even if our love did in time turn to mere friendship... I suppose that's what I want, in time."

"But you'll never find anyone, Jonathon," Vaughan said, "if you keep up this front of reserve. Take my advice and go out of your way to meet women. Embark on affairs, even if you get hurt in the process. Experience, Jonathon, is everything. You should not deny yourself the ultimate experience of intimacy or love merely because you fear hurting yourself or other people."

That summer, '59, I took on a new identity. My passport claimed that I was a man in his early forties named Daniel Sellings. I decided that I needed time away from the treadmill of producing novels for publication. I wrote, but for my own enjoyment and satisfaction, journal entries and long descriptive pieces. For three years I travelled around Europe, a continent I had stayed away from until then, and attempted to take Vaughan's advice: I frequented bars and clubs, and made myself talk to women – I even had two or three affairs.

But they failed. There was always something lacking, and I came to fear that it was some innate flaw within me. I would get to know someone for a month or two, appreciate her for who she was, but then would be unable to feel anything approaching love.

No doubt Vaughan would say that I had not tried hard or often enough, but I wondered if, because of my longevity, I was accreting a store of experience and insight that made me perceive most people as shallow and obsessed only with the materialistic. I lived in a society conditioned by the Pavlovian response to the market place, to the here-and-now cultural fashions that I was finding increasingly meaningless and banal.

Again, Vaughan would say that if I sought long enough, then I would find... and I knew he was right. But I was tired of the painful process of being rejected, and having to reject, that was inextricably bound up with the process of seeking.

Then I arrived in Tangier, on a ferry from Gibraltar, intending to stay for only two or three months.

I fell in love with the city almost immediately. I liked the contrast between the modernity of the old international zone and the age and tradition of its ancient quarter; it was different, in architecture and religion and social norms and customs, to anything I had experienced before. It was a city that lived on its own terms and did not kow-tow to the latest fashions or fads. You could be yourself in Tangier, and you were tolerated, and left alone.

Perhaps I was guilty of seeing the city through the eyes of a naïve stranger – perhaps Tangier's tolerance was nothing more than apathy. At any rate, I felt at home there from the start, and an intended stay of three months became as many years.

One month after my arrival I rented a spacious, airy apartment in the medina and set about exploring the city.

I liked the old part of town, its narrow alleys and cobbled streets, its market with a thousand stalls selling everything from great mounds of multi-coloured spices to artificial arms and legs. I could spend hours wandering around the medina, frequently getting lost only to turn a corner and recognise where I was once again.

Paradoxically, it was not to some ancient coffee shop in the kasbah that I was drawn, however, but to a relatively modern café on the Rue du Portugal. It was called Jerry's and run by a sixty year-old expatriate American – one of those disreputable but likeable rogues, dissolute and perhaps even immoral, who had lived for many years in Alexandria before relocating to Morocco. He could have been straight out of Durrell's *Quartet*.

I spent my afternoons sitting at a table at the back of the café, making notes and observing the young clientele. It was the men and woman who frequented Jerry's that were the draw for me. I say men and women, but they struck me more as boys and girls. They were the drop-outs from the strait-jacketed, bourgeois societies that Britain and America had become in the fifties and early sixties. They had had enough of the materialism of the West and were in Tangier *en passant* to all points East: Kathmandu and Delhi and Poona... I found myself identifying with their desire for freedom from capitalistic excess, but found myself at odds with their lax moral strictures: I was a child of the first decades of the century, after all, and, though I had experienced much, the concept of free love, while divine in essence, I thought potentially disastrous in practice.

I had been in Tangier six months when Vaughan called from Rome, where he now made his home. He had had word from Charles – Jasper had contacted him.

The Kings of Eternity – minus one – had met the year before in Oslo. Charles had cried off: he was living in an ashram in Calcutta, and could not interrupt his meditations. "It's something that each of us will go through in time," Vaughan had commented, "the need for spiritual enlightenment."

Now Vaughan told me that Charles had relayed the latest news from Jasper: he was aboard a rebel interstitial ship, and recently had undergone several 'prosthetic enhancements'.

Apparently, life in space demanded rather a lot of the fragile human frame. In order to pull his weight aboard the rebel ship, he consented to become 'modified'.

"But what of the fight against the Vark?" I asked of Vaughan.

According to Jasper, Vaughan reported, the fight went well. Perhaps, even, the tide had turned. The rebels were winning on many fronts. The Vark were sorely depleted, but still a tenacious foe. They had been pushed from the first quadrant, but they still controlled the third and half the second.

Vaughan reported that Kathan, the alien manikin we had saved all those years ago, was well and sent his regards.

Conversation turned to more Earthly matters. Vaughan had set up as an artist in Rome – he had even had a dalliance with an Italian woman – and he was enjoying life.

We made an arrangement to meet in Rome later that year, and rang off.

In the days that followed, I often contrasted Jasper's extra-solar existence with my own, and wondered who might be the happier, the more fulfilled. Surely fighting evil on a galactic scale, lost in the distracting process of survival, was preferable to whiling away one's time on a planet which was, for the most part, detestable?

Such was the course of my misanthropic thoughts following my conversation with Vaughan and the resumption of my solipsistic daily routines.

I spent more and more time at Jerry's Café, observing the Hippie children and sometimes even finding myself caught up in their conversations.

I must have presented a sight they were unable to weigh up. I was tanned and weather-beaten, and dressed casually, and yet I had the air about me of an English gentleman. Vaughan had described me, at our last meeting, as a cross between a jaded foreign correspondent and a washed-out public schoolmaster.

A month passed without incident. I kept my daily journal, even began a novel at one point, and then set it aside. It was about the Hippies I was observing, but I felt that I did not know them well enough to presume to write a novel on the subject.

A few weeks before I was due to meet Vaughan in Rome, I was in Jerry's Café when I noticed a young girl at a table in front of mine.

She was drawing in a big sketch book, her head bowed low. I could see, as I watched her, that the tip of her tongue showed at the corner of her mouth as she worked on the sketch with meticulous concentration.

She looked up from time to time, surreptitiously, and glanced at me: I feigned interest in my journal, obscurely excited that I was her subject.

I had seen her before in the café. She was a thin, pretty blonde girl, perhaps in her early twenties, garbed in bell-bottom jeans and a flimsy cheese-cloth top. She was always alone, which struck me as odd; the Hippies almost always went around in groups.

She glanced up again, saw me watching her and frowned.

I wondered why she was alone. The various groups that frequented Jerry's seemed to leave her to herself, as if they knew she did not want to be disturbed, and she never joined them when she finished her work. Instead she would quickly close her book and hurry out into the busy streets.

She seemed always flighty and nervous, and very shy. When Jerry wandered over with her coffee she would murmur her thanks to him but never establish eye contact.

I stood and walked past the kitchen to the toilet in the back alley, and on my way back I paused beside her table. I looked down and saw an excellent drawing of my head and shoulders.

"That's very good," I said.

Her face flicked my way, but she could not bring herself to look at me. "Not finished," she said, closed the book, gathered up her bag and hurried from the café.

She was there the following afternoon, at the same table. I concentrated on my journal. I did not make the mistake of staring at her or at the drawing in progress, but gave her time in which to finish it.

At one point she sat up straight, rubbing an ache from the small of her back, then tipped her head and regarded the sketch with the air of satisfaction.

"If it's finished," I said, "I'd like to buy it. If you sell your work, that is."

She stared at me. She had an elfin look, a fragile beauty. Her eyes were too big for her small face, and the effect was almost, but not quite, ugly.

"Tell you what," she said, and I detected a faint accent, maybe American, "buy me a meal and it's yours, okay?"

"That sounds as though I'm getting the best of the deal," I smiled. "Where would you like to go?" I suggested an expensive restaurant on the sea front.

"Here's fine. I'll have the falafel and salad, and a beer, if that's okay?"

I gave Jerry the order and watched her eat. She was obviously hungry.

I tried to engage her in conversation, but she was having none of it. She either nodded, her mouth full, or ignored me. Smiling, I desisted, but continued watching.

She finished quickly and wiped her mouth on the sleeve of her blouse. She ripped a page from the sketch book, stood and, on the way past my table, dropped the sketch with a breezy, "Thanks," and hurried from the café.

I did not see her for another three days. I sat at my table at my regular time, from three to five, and wrote, but the girl did not show up. I finished a short story about her, and wondered if I would ever see her again, and where she might be now. On a coach to Cairo, or a plane to Delhi, I surmised. I was disappointed. I found myself thinking about her, wanting to talk to her, wanting her to open up and tell me about her life.

On the third day she came into the café and scanned the clientele. She saw me and approached cautiously. She seemed nervous. She bumped her hip against the side of the table in an obsessive rhythmic routine that seemed a little mad.

"Say, you don't think you could buy me a coffee, do you?"

I looked up. I have never seen such fear or desperation in a face.

"Of course. Sit down. Have you brought your sketch book today?"

She slipped into the seat opposite mine and patted her shoulder bag. "In here. Never go far without my pad."

The coffee came and she gulped it down.

"Do you sell many drawings?" I asked.

"No one wants them," she said, and excused herself from replying further by taking another gulp of coffee.

"American?"

She looked up. "Everyone says that. Canadian." She finished the coffee.

"Would you like another?"

She stared at me, her alarmed eyes wide. "You can't buy me," she said. "I'm not that cheap."

Something in my appalled expression must have communicated itself to her. "I'm sorry," she said in a small voice. "It's just that, you know, so many people... There was this guy..." She shook her head, fell silent.

The coffee came. She drank this one more slowly. I said, not wanting to frighten her away, but curious, "What brings you to Tangier?"

She looked up. "You ask a lot of questions."

"I don't think I do," I said. "And anyway, aren't questions polite? They're an expression of interest, a legitimate part of stoking a conversation."

She laughed prettily into her fingers, like a child. "You talk like a writer," she said. "Are you a writer?"

"Very perceptive."

"And you're English, yeah?"

"Now you're asking all the questions."

She was silent, as if considering, and then said, "Actually, if you want to know, I left home because I dropped out of art school and got pregnant and had an abortion and I needed to get away. There, you know all about me, now." She looked up, something challenging in her eyes. "Thanks for the coffee," she said, and slipped from behind the table and hurried out.

She was back the next day, bumping her slim hip against the side of my table. She looked thin and ill, hugging stick arms across her flat chest, as if cold.

"Hiya, there," she said.

"Hi, yourself. Sit down."

She sat opposite me. Nervously, almost guiltily.

I said, "When was the last time you ate?"

She shrugged and looked away, avoiding my eyes.

"Listen, I have a suggestion to make. You're an artist, and a good one. I very much like the drawing you did of me. I have it hanging in my front room." I paused, watching her. She had her head bowed, and was nervously fingering a woven thread bracelet on her slim, child's wrist. "Can you do street scenes as well as portraits, buildings, things like that?"

She nodded without looking at me.

"How would you like a few commissions? Do me a sketch every day. Scenes in Tangier, people, whatever, and I'll buy you a meal. How does that sound?"

She said nothing, but reached her hand across the table, looking away. We shook. Her hand reminded me of a tiny bird, the bones thin and vulnerable, the flesh warm.

I bought her the first meal then, in lieu of the following day's sketch. She ate as though she were starving.

"I don't even know your name?" I said.

"Sam, Sam Devereaux."

"Samantha. That's a nice name."

She shot me a look. "Sam. Just Sam. My folks called me Samantha."

"Fine. Sam."

Through a mouthful of falafel, she said, "What do you write?"

"I wrote novels in the fifties. Now I please myself, keep a journal, make notes."

"Novels? Far out. That's cool. Can I read one?"

"I don't keep copies. You might find some in the secondhand bookshops in the medina."

"I'll look. What's your name?"

"I wrote under the name of Christopher Cartwright."

She nodded. "But that's not your real name, right?"

My real name? Jonathon Langham, Christopher Cartwright, Daniel Sellings. They had all at one time been my real names. "I'm Daniel Sellings," I said.

We met at three o'clock every afternoon, and she would present me with a newly-completed sketch: one day a street scene, the next the portrait of a stall-holder, and the day after that the Grand Mosque.

"What does it feel like to be a professional artist?" I asked her one day as I watched her eat.

"Good," she said. "What does it feel like to be a patron of the arts?"

I laughed. "I never thought of it like that."

She stopped eating and looked up at me. "Why're you doing all this?" she said. "Being kind to me?"

The way she said it, "Being kind to me?" made me want to reach out and take her in my arms. It was pathetic and childish and timorous, and suggested that no-one had ever been kind to her before, at least not for the right reasons.

"You're a good artist. You need feeding up." I shrugged. "I want lovely drawings for my walls. It's a good business relationship."

She wrinkled her nose. "Business relationship," she said. "That makes it sound so impersonal." And her eyes flickered away from my gaze as she said this.

Why was I being kind to her? For all the above reasons, of course... or at least it had started out that way. But there was something about her that brought out in me the urge to cherish and protect.

"How old are you?" I asked.

"Twenty in May. You?"

I was sixty-three that year – as old as my father was when he died. My passport said forty.

"Forty," I said.

She nodded. "I'm young enough to be your daughter," she said, and then quickly reached across the table and took my hand. "I didn't mean it like that. You don't seem old." She made a goofy I've-put-my-foot-in-it-again face.

I smiled. I didn't feel old, despite my years, just weary sometimes with the weight of experience.

One day, after passing me the sketch she had done that morning, and watching me with a pinched face to gauge my reaction, she said, "Hey, guess what?"

"What?" I asked. She was digging about in her shoulder bag.

She pulled out a creased paperback and presented it to me. *Eternal Safari* by Christopher Cartwright.

I opened the book and read a few words, recalling many times in the past when I had done the same with other books. I was disappointed; every scene seemed over-written, in need of condensing.

She was staring at me with big eyes. "I'm halfway through. Know something, I couldn't put it down. You're some writer, Daniel Sellings."

I took her hand across the table and told her of my travels in Central Africa, and before that in South America.

She was a child. The areas of her ignorance were vast, great uncharted territories waiting to be explored. But she was a willing explorer; she hung on my every word.

It seemed, in her company, that I was illimitably experienced and wise. I found myself thinking about her when I was not with her, which is always a fatal sign. I cared about her: as well as wanting to cherish and protect her, I found myself wanting to educate her, too.

Was that love? Who knows? I was not wise enough to say.

One day, after she had finished her meal and squeezed my hand and left, Jerry came to my table and sat down. He had never shown much inclination to chat before, and I was surprised now. "Dan," he said. "That kid. Wouldn't get involved if I were you."

My heart leapt into my throat. I smiled, trying to make light of it. "She seems harmless enough."

He made a gesture then that I had not seen before, but which I have seen often since. With his thumb he made a plunging motion into the vein of his left arm. "She's a junky," he said.

I was not accustomed to the word. I was confused, and a little frightened. "A what?"

"Never read Burroughs?"

I nearly said, "Edgar Rice?" but stopped myself.

Jerry sighed. "She's a drug addict. Heroin. Notice the track marks?"

"Sorry? Track marks?"

"Where the needle goes into her vein, scabs all the way up her left arm."

I shook my head, murmured something.

"She gets a monthly remittance from her folks back home, but it all goes on junk. That's why she never has any cash to buy food." He said all this with the world weariness of a man who had seen it all a hundred times before. "So be careful, okay, Dan? I just thought you'd better know, is all."

"Thanks," I murmured, and sat alone for an hour or two with a cold coffee and my thoughts.

The following afternoon she presented me with a wonderful sketch of a street in the Petit Socco.

I said, "What do you do when you leave here, Sam?"

"Go home. Read a little. Sleep. I've got to be up early to hit the streets, find a good subject for the sketches."

I was holding her left hand, my thumb a pestle in the mortar of her palm, rubbing. I could see a series of scabbed red marks on the inside of her arm.

When she left the café later that day, with a quick squeeze of my fingers and a wave, I followed her after an interval of twenty seconds and pursued her through the crowded streets. She was not that hard to follow: she was the only Western girl in sight, and her white blouse and faded jeans stood out among the hurly-burly of camel-coloured jelabas and dark business suits.

I followed her north through the medina, down mean and narrow side-streets and alleys, and watched her slip into a room on the ground-floor of an ancient three-storied building.

I stood outside, in a sweat of indecision, and wondered what to do next. Should I enter and confront her, or leave well alone and return home? As much as I was attracted to the girl, did I want to become involved in her tragic life?

I look back, now, and realise that I really had little choice in the matter.

Perhaps five minutes later I knocked on the door. There was no reply, which alarmed me. I knocked again, harder this time, and then pushed inside.

I was instantly repelled by the heat and the squalor of the hovel. A naked bulb illuminated a small square room. The only furnishing was a mattress in the corner.

Sam lay unconscious on the mattress, the accoutrements of her addiction scattered about her. I saw a small Bunsen burner, a tablespoon, a twist of silver foil, and on the bed beside her a hypodermic syringe.

I moved across the room and sat down on the mattress. I reached out and touched her cheek, swept her hair back from her forehead.

What struck me then was how anyone with a finite span of years ahead of them could risk death in such a manner. Was life so terrible that they had to seek the balm of ecstasy, irrespective of the risk?

I looked about the room. But for a pile of clothes on the floor, and her shoulder bag, which contained her sketch-pad and pens, she seemed to possess nothing else. I slipped my hand beneath the mattress and found a cheese-cloth bag containing her passport and two Canadian ten dollar notes.

I opened the passport. Her picture showed a smiling, fuller-faced girl. Samantha Elizabeth Devereaux, born in 1944, Ontario.

I placed the passport and the dollars in her shoulder bag, then slipped out and hailed a taxi. I returned to the room, picked her up – she was frighteningly light – and carried her out to the waiting cab. I lay her on the back seat, to the alarm of the driver, and returned to her room, looking for some means to lock the door. There was no lock, which I supposed hardly mattered as there was nothing within the room worth stealing.

Five minutes later I was carrying her over the threshold of my apartment – aware of the irony of the marital ritual – and into the spare room. I arranged her on the bed and placed her shoulder bag on the table beside it. I fetched a chair from the front room and positioned it beside the bed, then sat down to keep watch over her until she awoke.

Fearful that she might have died, from time to time I checked her pulse. It fluttered like some living thing, a butterfly, trapped beneath the pale skin of her neck.

At nine o'clock I visited the bathroom, and when I returned she was awake. She lay on her back, blinking up at the ceiling. I stood in the doorway, leaning against the frame, and watched her; I was conscious of not getting too close, afraid of her reaction.

She stared at me with her oversized eyes. "How did I get here?"

"I brought you."

"Why?"

"Because... you can't live where you were living."

"It was okay."

"It wasn't okay. It stank. It was filthy. There wasn't even any running water–"

"There was a communal shower around the corner."

I stared at her.

"You know?" she said. "You saw the stuff, didn't you?"

I nodded.

She made to climb from the bed. "I need to go back."

"Sam, this is insane. You can't go back there."

She avoided my eyes. "For the stuff, okay? I need the stuff."

"And then come back here. I have my own room. You can have this one for as long as you like."

She looked up at me then, her eyes widening. "You don't mind about the stuff you saw?"

"We'll talk about that later."

She stood, rubbing her eyes with both fists, just like the kid she was. She grabbed her bag and side-stepped past me without a glance, then moved down the hallway to the front door. I didn't turn to watch her go. The door snapped shut behind her.

I moved to the lounge and poured myself a wine and sat and waited.

I was old enough to be her grandfather, I told myself, and anyway the attraction was not sexual. I cared about her because she was so young and naïve, and the world was an awful place. I could look after her, ensure that she prospered, encourage her... I often look back and wonder if the person I was then understood, in his heart of hearts, that he was trying to deny what he knew to be a simple fact.

An hour passed.

I feared that she would not return. More, that I would never see her again. She would go back to her hovel and get her *stuff*, as she called it, then move out and never go back to Jerry's Café. She would be just another young casualty abroad in the world.

Perhaps two hours after she left, I heard a small knock on the front door. I remained where I was, waiting. The door opened, and a minute later she appeared around the doorway to the lounge, leaning against the jamb, her eyes downcast.

Her voice was hardly a whisper. "I nearly didn't come," she said. "I nearly just upped and quit the city, got on the first train to Marrakech."

"I'm glad you didn't," I said.

"I was frightened. Frightened to leave and frightened to stay."

"Sam, you have nothing to fear from me."

She stared at me. "Who are you, what do you want from me?"

I gestured to the armchair across the coffee table. "Sit down. I'll pour you a wine."

She moved into the room like a timorous kitten, sat down. I poured her a wine. The large glass almost eclipsed her face as she held it in both hands, tipped and drank.

"I don't want anything from you, apart perhaps from conversation, and friendship. In return I want to help you."

She laughed at that – she spluttered a laugh that was almost a cry. "How can you help me?" she asked.

I was honest. "I don't know. Perhaps all I can do is help you to help yourself." Before she could say anything, I went on, "Why did you start taking that stuff?"

She was silent for a long time, staring at her fingers as they worried the hem of her cheese-cloth blouse. "It was in Canada, just after I failed art school. This guy, he left me when I found I was pregnant, and my father paid for the abortion. I didn't want one, but you see at the time I wasn't in a fit state." She looked up and smiled at me through her tears, her forefinger describing a whirlwind beside her temple. "They had me put away in a psychiatric ward and I had the abortion, and when I came out I wanted to destroy myself, and drugs seemed like the most painless way to do that. That was a year ago. Some friends were going to Europe. I wanted to get away from Canada, so I went with them." She shrugged. "We split up in Spain and I found myself here." She smiled at me. "Heroin is cheaper here than in Canada, anyway."

I smiled. "So you can kill yourself on the cheap," I said.

Silence. Her fingers worked. She stared down, did not look up, and only after a minute did I realise that her slight frame was shaking with constricted sobs.

"I don't–" she said, "–I don't want–" and she was shaking her head, plucking at the hem of her blouse, "–I don't want to die!"

She rushed over to me and curled in my lap, her face against my chest, her tears soaking the material of my shirt.

I held my hands in the air, staring at the open palms, then lowered them and placed them on her back and tried to comfort her.

It had been a long time since I had last held a woman in my arms, and I was terrified.

Every day Sam would leave her room at eight, spend all day sketching the city streets, and meet me at Jerry's for a late lunch; then she would leave, and return to the apartment, and when I got back at five she would be sprawled unconscious on her bed.

I'd prepare an evening meal and around nine we'd dine together like father and daughter, and we'd talk.

This continued for almost a month.

I talked to people. I read books and wrote letters to experts in the field of addiction. I learned that heroin was hard to give up, and that trying to do so could kill the addict. I also learned that there were clinics in Europe which specialised in the treatment of the addiction.

When I felt sure of what I should say, and what I should do, and that I would not frighten her away, I mentioned the subject of a cure.

It was a warm autumn night and we were sitting on the balcony overlooking the architectural melee of the medina and the broad blue sweep of the Strait of Gibraltar beyond. Sam was dazed from her last injection, a little drunk with wine.

"There's a clinic just outside Rome," I told her. "They specialise in treating heroin addicts. As it happens I'm flying to

Rome in a few days, on business, and while I'm there I'll book you a room. If, that is, that's okay with you?"

She cast her glance down, at her lap. "How much will it cost?"

"That doesn't matter. It's not important."

She was silent for a long time. "Why are you doing this, Daniel? I don't deserve this. I've done nothing, I'm not special–"

"It's a simple arrangement," I said. "You're addicted to a substance that might kill you. You want off it. There is a way you can kick it. It costs, and I have the money to pay, and I'll gladly do so if it will save your life. I don't see the problem with any of that, do you?"

"But what I want to know, Daniel, is *why?* Why are you doing this for me?"

"Do you want me to tell you that I love you, Sam?"

She looked away. "I don't know."

"For a long time," I said, "longer than you think, I've been looking for something. Someone. Someone who deserves what I can give them. And I've come to realise that it doesn't really matter if I'm not loved in return. Respect and affection and tenderness is enough."

I wanted to tell her that to expect love, to demand it, is the ultimate in selfishness; I had lived long enough to know that we cannot expect what people cannot give, and that we should be grateful for what they can. I said nothing like that, of course; I could not find the words, nor assume that she would understand.

I fell silent. She was watching me, smiling, and I smiled in return. "You're a special person, Daniel. I don't really know who or what you are. I've never met anyone quite like you. Thank you."

"So I'll go ahead and book a place in the clinic?"

Lips pursed, she nodded, and came into my arms.

That night, as we lay in bed together, I held her close while she slept.

On the evening before I flew to Rome to meet Vaughan, I watched Sam as she slept next to me on the bed. It was hot. The fan turned, lifting stray strands of blonde hair from her forehead.

Quietly I unlocked the drawer of the bedside cabinet and withdrew the serum pistol.

I placed it against her carotid artery and held it there for what seemed like an age.

Should I, could I, bestow upon her life everlasting without first telling her? It would be one answer to her problem, and ensure that her addiction would not be fatal.

What we had would not last, I knew. She was young; I could not expect her to love me now, nor in the future. I wondered, then, the gun in my hand, if by granting her immortal life my gift was not so much an act of altruism but selfishness, a calculated means of tying her to me for ever more?

I returned the serum pistol to the drawer and locked it. There would be time later, once she was cured, to talk about the future.

Instead, I kissed the soft flesh of her neck where the pistol had rested, and in the morning said goodbye and took a taxi to the airport.

I cut short my stay with Vaughan; instead of a week, I remained just three days. I explained the situation, and Vaughan smiled to himself and said that he hoped I would find happiness. I visited the Vincenzi clinic just outside Rome and booked a course of treatment. It would last for six months and would cost almost ten thousand US dollars, a small price to pay for Sam's life.

On the last day of my stay with Vaughan, I attended an exhibition of his oils in a prestigious Rome gallery. He was going by the name of Ralph Wellard, and had made quite a name for himself in European art circles. He even looked the part, sporting open-toed sandals, white slacks, and a casual shirt – only the absence of a beret prevented his being identified as a fully paid-up member of the bohemian set.

He was escorted by a beautiful raven-haired women called Gina, and I thought they made a perfect couple.

I asked him whether he would tell Gina about the serum. He paused, then said, "I honestly don't know, Jonathon. And I've been thinking about it for months..."

I flew back to Tangier in high spirits. Sam and I were due in Rome in three days; I had rented a small villa next to the clinic so that I might visit her daily and monitor her progress. I thought ahead, extrapolated from the passion we had shared, and built castles of love in the air.

There was a letter pinned to the door of my apartment, and my stomach turned when I caught sight of it.

It could only be from Sam, and I wondered what excuse she might have found to leave me.

It was not from Sam. The single sheet of folded note paper was signed by the local Commissioner of police and requested my presence at the police headquarters as soon as I returned.

I opened the door and called Sam's name. I moved from room to room, but there was no sign of her. No sign, either – and this worried me even more – of her shoulder bag or sketch pad.

I took a taxi across town to the police headquarters, and eventually was shown into the office of Abdul Touzoni, Commissioner of police. He was a tiny man, with a minuscule clipped moustache and scrupulously clean finger-nails.

His manner was impeccable, his etiquette in dealing with the unpleasant matter exemplary. He sat me down and asked me if I would care for a coffee. I did not. He said that he understood that Samantha Elizabeth Devereaux had been living with me at my apartment. I agreed that she was. He said, "And I also understand that she was an addict of heroin."

It was then that I noticed the small black box on the table. He had attempted to conceal it behind a framed photograph of his wife and son, but nevertheless I saw it and knew, then, why I was here.

I heard what he said next, but the words seemed to come from very, very far away.

"I'm so very sorry, Mr Sellings, but Miss Devereaux passed away due to an overdose of heroin on the 24th of June. She was found by your cleaner the following day."

I tried to work out when the 24th had been. I was, I think, a little insane, then. I told myself that it was not too late. Sam had died three days ago... If I could take possession of her body, then the serum would be able to repair her. I had seen what it had done for Kathan. It was not too late. It could bring Sam back to life...

But I knew, of course, even as I was telling myself this, I knew.

The Commissioner, using both hands, removed the box from behind the photograph of his family and gently, respectfully, pushed Sam's ashes across the table towards me.

CHAPTER FOURTEEN

Kallithéa, July, 1999

At noon, Daniel Langham left his villa and followed the path through the pines. Cicadas rasped. The heat of the sun was merciless. Through the pines he could see the ocean, scintillating like silver lamé made liquid.

To his joy, he saw that the shutters of Caroline's villa were open, signifying her return. He quickened his pace, smiling at the irony of the situation: he who only a while ago had shunned the world, claimed to need no human contact and involvement, was hurrying to meet someone who in such a short time had become so unaccountably close to him.

There was an envelope blue-tacked to the front door, with a message scrawled across the front of it: *Daniel – come in.*

He stepped inside, calling, "Caroline?"

"In here."

He followed the sound of her voice. She was in the lounge, lying on a settee with a blanket drawn up to her chin. Langham stopped in the doorway, shocked at how terrible she looked. Her hair was dishevelled, her face thin and white.

"My God, Caroline."

"Come and sit down. Talk to me."

He hurried across to the settee and pulled up a chair. He took her hand. It seemed thin, insubstantial.

"Have you been eating?"

"A little?"

"When did you get back?"

"Late last night, on the last ferry. I would have called round, but it was almost midnight, and to be honest I felt rotten."

He noticed, on the floor by the settee, three bottles of pills and a glass of water. "Migraine?" he asked.

She nodded. "I lied. I didn't want to worry you. I said I was going to London on business, but I went to a clinic. They specialise in treating severe migraines. They gave me these..." She indicated the pills. "They said it might be a few days before I'm up and about."

"When did you last eat?"

"I had some toast for breakfast."

"My God, you need more in you than toast. Look, I'll make some soup."

"Daniel, please. Don't bother."

"It's no bother. I'll join you, if that's okay? It'll make a change from Georgiou's."

"They'll wonder where you are."

"Probably send someone up looking for me, thinking I've dropped dead."

Caroline winced. "Daniel, don't say that."

He squeezed her hand. "I'll fix that soup."

"You'll find everything in the kitchen."

He set the lentil soup to boil, then fixed a pot of tea and carried it into the lounge.

Caroline was sitting up, smiling at him. She was wearing a black t-shirt which hung on her. She seemed to have shed weight since the last time they'd met.

She patted the cushion beside her. "Here. Tell me what's been happening around here in my absence."

He sat down and took her hand. "Well, Forbes has scarpered."

"That's good news."

"I must admit it's a relief," he said. "I just hope he hasn't just taken a break, lulling me into a false sense of security."

He fetched the soup from the kitchen and they ate it on the settee. "Mmm, that's good," she said.

"How do you feel?"

"Up and down. I can be fine for a few hours, and then the pain starts again. It's like someone banging on the inside of my head, and the nausea..." She flapped her hand in a *you-don't-want-to-know* gesture.

They chatted about nothing in particular for an hour; the book she was reading, his novel, the news back home.

By the time they had finished the soup, he had come to a decision.

"I've been thinking," he said. "You can't stay here alone. You can hardly fend for yourself. If all you eat is toast in my absence..."

Her eyes seemed to sparkle. "Are you planning to move in?"

He shook his head. "I have a spare room at my place. I have a full larder, unlike your scant kitchen, and I can cook for you until you're up and about again."

"Daniel, really..."

"I insist. It'll be a holiday. You can lie on the sofa all day, eat, and regain your strength."

"But your writing!"

"I don't think you'll make that much noise," he said. "And anyway I only work for three hours a day, and a bit of correction in the afternoon. I'm not taking no for an answer."

She was shaking her head, less in refusal than with exasperated amusement. "Daniel, I don't know what to say."

"Say nothing. Just tell me where a bag is, and what you need."

"That's easy. My bag's in the hall, and it's packed already. They washed everything for me at the clinic."

"So what are we waiting for? Let's go. We can spend a quiet afternoon on the sofa. I might even read you the opening of the novel."

"You would? I'd like that. What luxury."

He was shocked at how frail she was as he walked her from the lounge and into the hall, where he collected her bag. She leaned on his arm all the way from the villa and up the track, taking small steps and having to pause for breath from time to time.

He installed her on the sofa and fetched a blanket – she complained of feeling cold, even though in the heat of the day he was sweating.

He poured her an orange juice, and a wine for himself, and joined her on the sofa.

"Do you know something, Daniel? I day-dreamed about this view while I was in London. It was grey and overcast and miserable. Just thinking about Kallithéa made me feel better."

"I must admit that I've missed our chats. Every time I passed your villa on the way to Georgiou's, I found myself wishing you were with me, challenging my brash assumptions, making me think."

"You do think!"

"But being alone for so long, it leads to lazy thinking. I've never had anyone to challenge me. Then you come along, a breath of fresh air."

She was looking away, out to sea. "You gave in, didn't you, after Sam and the others? You just gave in and shut yourself off from the world?" She shook her head, still not looking at him. "But you're a wise man. Didn't you see that that would only lead to more pain?"

How to explain, without telling her everything? "When I came here," he said, "I wasn't wise. I was hurt. I wasn't thinking, I was running. Like a wounded animal. At the time, I didn't want company, everything it entailed. I wanted to shut myself away and lick my wounds and write."

She smiled at him, then looked away quickly. "Perhaps you were right to do what you did. You wrote some great books. You survived, recovered."

He hesitated. "And now I'm ready to live again," he said, and immediately regretted it. It sounded importuning, even pathetic, as if he were asking for her sympathy, and more.

She closed her eyes, laid her head back against the cushion. "I'm tired."

"I'll show you your room later."

"Mmm..."

He corrected that morning's work while she slept on the sofa, and at six he moved to the kitchen and prepared a tomato salad with fresh mackerel. She was awake when he next looked out.

She rubbed her eyes and stretched.

"How do you feel?"

"Much better. Rested. What time is it?"

"Almost seven. Hungry?"

She laid her head to one side and frowned. "I am, actually. It must be the Greek air. I have an appetite."

"Mackerel salad with a special Langham dressing," he announced. "Hope you like mackerel?"

"Love it," she said, standing unsteadily.

He was ready to catch her. "You're still weak, Caroline."

"I thought I'd move to the table." She gave a little laugh at her feebleness as he lowered her to the sofa again.

"That's okay, we'll dine here and watch the sun go down. What could be better?"

He told her about his novel while they ate, outlining the story of Sam in Africa.

At one point she asked, "Isn't it painful, reliving the past? I mean, writing about someone you loved, and who..."

"I couldn't have written the book immediately. I had to come to terms with what happened. Then... I don't know. It might seem crass, using someone as a character like that, but I felt I owed it to her memory, and also, to be honest, it helped me. It was a cathartic exercise."

"She must have been a lovely person."

He thought back all those years. "She was an innocent, scarred by terrible events," he said, and left it at that.

The sun set and the stars came out, pricking the immensity of the sky above the ocean. He pointed to the constellations of Lyra and Pegasus. He took her hand and they sat for a time in companionable silence.

He considered how to start talking about their relationship; every gambit he thought of seemed crass. At last he simply said, "Do you ever consider the future, Caroline?"

"Never!"

Her vehemence surprised him. "Never? You never look ahead, plan things? Wonder where you'll be in ten years, or where you hope you'll be?"

She gazed up at the stars. "Never, Daniel."

"I do, all the time. I suppose it's a part of who I am."

She squeezed his hand. "So, where do you see yourself ten years from now?"

Something seemed to stick in his throat. "It's not so much *where* I see myself," he began. "I rarely think of where I'll be. In a way that doesn't matter much to me any more. I've come to realise that most places are pretty much alike. It's the state of mind you're in that matters."

He glanced at her. She had closed her eyes. He went on. "So... the state of mind I'd like to be in in ten years from now? Content," he said. "I'd like to be content, happy with what I was and who I was with." He did not mean to do it, but his hand tightened on hers.

She had opened her eyes, staring straight ahead. Her lips were pursed, compressed, as if she were thinking furiously.

"Caroline, I came to realise something while you were away... Sometimes, you only realise the value of someone when you no longer have them around. You suddenly realise how much they mean to you." He laughed. "God, when I saw that your shutters were open and I realised you were back... I was like a teenager, my heart was banging." He squeezed her hand again.

He glanced at her. She had shut her eyes again, and he could see that tears were squeezing from beneath her lids and rolling down her cheeks.

"Caroline?"

She shook her head, her lips tight. She pulled her hand away from his, quickly, and pressed her knuckle to her lips, shoulders lifting in quick, tight, constricted sobs.

"Caroline, I'm sorry if what I said..."

She was shaking her head. "I can't..." she began.

"I understand. These things take time to get over. What you went through with your husband must have been appalling. I understand that. I just want you to know how I feel, and that perhaps in time, if you feel the same..."

She turned her face to him. Her eyes were huge and blurred by tears, her mouth open in agony. "I can't do this to you, Daniel. After everything you've been through."

"Caroline–"

"I can't lie any more," she said. "Those times I was away, the other week and just now..."

Fear clutched him. "You were seeing someone?"

"No, you silly man!" she cried, half-amused, through her tears. "How could I possibly want anyone else, with you around?"

His heart gave a skip of joy, but delight was soon followed by fear and confusion.

She shook her head. "Oh, my God... This is so hard." She reached out and took his hand, staring at him. "I wasn't in a migraine clinic in London. I was undergoing chemotherapy. A couple of months ago, before we met, I was diagnosed with breast cancer. They thought they'd caught it early – they were optimistic. Then I met you, and do you know something, the meeting seemed somehow right."

He gripped her hand, experiencing such a surge of ambivalent emotion. Principally he shared her pain, an appreciation of her appalling fear – but beyond that, stirring deep within him, he experienced a nascent joy, a joy he wanted to share with her.

"Then I began feeling pretty bad, pains all over, aches, sudden, excruciating agony like you wouldn't believe. I made an appointment for another check up, and three days ago they told me..." She pressed her lips together.

He reached out and pulled her to him, and she was so light. She leaned against him with her head on his chest and sobbed. "I'm so frightened, Daniel. I'm so awfully bloody frightened!"

He patted her back, kissed her hair. He held her, as there was little else he could do. He was trying to think of the best way to break it to her, of telling her not to fear, that she could begin to think of the future again, that there was, indeed, hope.

He felt an exhilaration course through him, then, as he considered the fact that it was within his power to give her something that actually mattered. He could bestow upon Caroline Platt the gift of continued life, banish the dread at the prospect of all she had ever known and experienced being taken away from her, extinguished. He could give it all back to her, rekindle the flame.

She sniffed back the sobs and continued, "They... they told me it had spread. To my spine, lungs. They said that I have between three and six months."

He kissed the top of her head, and he was crying with her now.

How best to tell her, he wondered? She would never believe him. It was all too fantastic. She would think him cruel for suggesting such an incredible thing. He could let her read the journal he had kept over the years, of course, but that did not constitute proof in itself, or he could slice open his wrist and make her watch as it healed before her eyes, but that would be to resort to melodrama, and that was not part of his character.

Or, quite simply, when she was sleeping tonight, he could take the serum pistol from where he kept it locked in the drawer and, without telling her anything, apply it to her neck and let the tiny machines – the nano-machines, as they would be called now – do the work of saving her life.

She stirred on his lap. "Do you understand, Daniel?" she whispered. "I was so attracted to you, but I didn't want you to suffer all over again. I was weak. I should never have come back here. I was weak and terribly cruel. I thought of staying in London. You would have forgotten about me in time... But

I wanted you. I wanted you to hold me, just like this, because – I know it might sound stupid – but it does help to know that I'm loved."

He kissed her head. "Shh," he said, and almost whispered that in the morning it would all be okay.

She cried herself to sleep in his arms, and her sobs subsided and her breathing became even at last. He sat with her for a long time, regarding the night sky.

He recalled something they had talked about, on the quayside in Xanthos following her exhibition. They had discussed her painting, *Considering the Future,* and how for him it was optimistic because of what the stars symbolised. He had received the impression, then, that for her the painting held a different meaning, and now he knew that he was right. For Caroline, the stars represented night, and darkness, because for her the future *was* an unfathomable darkness towards which she was irrevocably heading.

He carried her into the villa, surprised at how light she was, and into his bedroom. He lay her gently on the bed and watched her sleep in the low glow of the bedside lamp. She seemed to be at peace.

He moved to his study and unlocked the drawer containing the serum pistol, and carried it back to the bedroom.

He sat beside her, reached out and swept the hair back from her pale neck. He could see the vein, raised in the lamp-light. He placed the pistol against her gently pulsing carotid, and paused.

He had almost gone ahead and bestowed eternal life on Sam, all those years ago, but something had stopped him then – just as now, on the cusp of saving Caroline's life, something stopped him again.

Even though he would be giving her the gift of immortality, it came to him that he could not do so without first consulting her; it would be somehow immoral to save her life without her having a say in the matter. She would choose to remain alive, he knew she would, but it would be her own choice, made in the full knowledge of all the wonderful and terrible implications that that choice entailed. To live was all very well, but life was pain and grief and much else besides, as he would make clear when he told her all about himself in the morning.

He replaced the pistol in the locked drawer, then returned to the bedroom and lay down on the bed beside Caroline, and took her in his arms.

CHAPTER FIFTEEN

Lower Cranley and Crete, 1975

In '64 I fled Tangier and what had happened to Sam and travelled the world. For nearly ten years I lost myself in the Far East, spending six months at a time in various quiet, sequestered places well off the beaten track. In the early years of that period I was unable to write, still less to commit myself to friendships, or relationships with women. I drifted, in both a physical and mental sense.

Every year I visited Charles in India and Vaughan in Rome; they were my saviours at that time – the only people who might come close to understanding what I was going through. They, however, had their own lives to lead; Charles had his meditation to occupy him, and Vaughan his art. After two weeks in their company, having unburdened myself of my anguish and relieved for having done so, I would move on with a feeling of renewed enthusiasm for life. In time I began to write again, long novels not meant for publication but to satisfy some craving for creativity deep within me.

After almost a decade of aimless wandering, I awoke one morning on an idyllic island in the Philippines and felt a strange compulsion to return home. In the summer of 1973 I flew to London, and then, the strange compulsion still drawing me onwards, took a train to Aylesbury and a taxi to Cranley Grange.

I walked around the house, peering in through the dusty windows at the library where, nearly forty years before, amazing events had played themselves out. From the Grange I walked to Hopton Wood, and relived that night long ago when the portal had opened briefly and Kathan had fled to Earth aboard his star-carriage.

I walked into Fairweather Cranley where, before the war, I had made my home. Little had changed in the village; my cottage was just as I had left it all those years ago, inhabited now by a retired couple in their seventies. I watched them pottering in the garden, bent and infirm with age, and realised with a sudden pang of sadness that they were as old as I.

I had another shock in store as I hurried away in search of a taxi to carry me to Aylesbury. In the street I passed a man in his eighties who, before the war, had been the landlord of the Fox and Hounds. The years had been kind to him, but even so had etched their lines deep in his face, and slowed his pace. He smiled and nodded as I passed, and for a fleeting second I thought I saw a light of recognition, and then confusion, in his ancient eyes.

I hurried on.

That weekend I decided to set up residence in the nearby village of Lower Cranley, two miles from Fairweather and just a mile from the Grange and Hopton Wood. A month later I bought a converted coach-house beside the pub and moved in. It was as if I had reached a time in my life when I needed quiet and tranquillity; something within me craved proximity with the area where, to all intents and purposes, I had been reborn.

I wrote novels for my own satisfaction, investing my emotional life in these invented scenarios. In time, a year or more, as if the process of fiction had worked as some form of cure or catharsis, I found myself venturing out more and more, making social contact and even establishing liaisons that I was loath to term friendships but which I knew could be called nothing else.

And then I met Tara.

After what had happened to Sam, I had vowed never to become romantically involved again, but the woman worked an invidious magic upon me. There are some things which seem entirely natural, ordained by that irresistible chemistry of pheromones and mental attraction, and that I should fall in love with Tara Sayang was one of them. I was powerless to resist.

I was sitting at my usual table in the corner of the bar, going through the recently completed manuscript and making last minute corrections and alterations, when I noticed the woman seated on a high stool at the bar.

She saw me looking at her, and smiled – and only then did I notice that she had a book in her hand. My surprise at seeing a diminutive, dark-skinned – and very attractive – woman in the public bar of the Fox and Hounds was compounded when I realised that the book she was holding was *A Tropical War* by none other than Christopher Cartwright.

She saw me looking and smiled, and soon we were chatting about the novel and the novelist's other books. She had read them all, and possessed, moreover, a keen insight into what they were about. It struck me as an amazing coincidence at the time – a coincidence which, only later, I would come to understand.

Tara was five feet tall and as slim as a reed, with a bone structure as delicate as some flighty tropical bird: slim wrists, long, articulated fingers, high cheek bones like arrowheads, a pointed chin. Her skin was a deep, rich *mocha*, and her eyes a lustrous brown.

She told me she was from the island of Vanuatu – formerly the New Hebrides – in the South Pacific, and I admitted that she was the very first Vanuatunian I had ever had the pleasure of meeting.

We talked for the next couple of hours. She was thirty-five, humorous and intelligent and friendly, and I wondered quite how I might tempt her to meet me again.

In the event, I simply asked if I might take her out for a meal, and to my amazement and delight she accepted.

We dined a few days later at a village pub on the outskirts of Aylesbury. She lived nearby, and told me she was writing a book on the town. I gathered that she was rather well off – she mentioned that her grandfather had bequeathed her an inheritance on the proviso that she leave her island and travel the world.

In 1970 she had found herself in Aylesbury, fallen in love with the town, and decided to stay for a while. She had researched the area's history over the next few years, and decided to write a book on the subject. I recall hoping, on the taxi ride back to my cottage, that it would be a rather long book, and that she was a slow writer.

We saw each other three times a week for the next couple of months, and I marvelled at how I could find another human being so constantly interesting. She made me think, for the first time in years, about someone other than myself; she gave me a different perspective on everything. This, I realised, was the very thing I had sought, unsuccessfully, from travel, a broadening and enriching of my personal experience. Quite what she received from me in return, I was not so sure.

We took to going on long walks at weekends. I showed her Hopton Wood and Cranley Grange, and told her of my friends Jasper and Charles Carnegie, and Edward Vaughan – or rather 'Ralph Wellard', the esteemed painter. She expressed an interest in meeting them one day.

More than anything I wanted our affair to become intimate; I felt that I had met someone to whom I could give myself wholeheartedly. But, at the same time, I was loath to escalate the terms of our relationship for fear of frightening her away.

I recall walking through Hopton Wood one radiant summer's evening. We came to the clearing and sat against a broad tree trunk, the very one where, forty years before, Vaughan and I had sat while Jasper Carnegie first told us about the blue portal.

"Jonathon, you're such a strange person. You seem... I don't know. You're only forty, and yet you seem much, much older."

"You mean," I said, "that I remind you of an old man?"

She laughed, and pushed me playfully. "No, not at all. It's just that you seem more experienced than most men I've met of your age."

I laughed. "I've packed a lot into the years."

"Tell me about Tangier," she said. I had mentioned the city in passing, and hinted of having experienced sadness there, but until now had been reluctant to broach the subject of Sam and what had occurred.

Now I told her everything and admitted that, until I had met Tara, I had been unable to consider the possibility of ever becoming close to another woman.

And what made her so different? Was it merely pheromones that attracted me to her; was it a meeting of minds? Why had my fear of commitment been banished by this diminutive South Sea naiad?

That night we returned to my house and, even before I could suggest dinner, she undressed me on the sofa in the lounge, then slipped and wriggled from her own clothes; we made love for what seemed like hours.

She moved in with me three days later, and the next few weeks were the happiest I had ever known.

One day, after walking through Hopton Wood and looking in on Cranley Grange to ensure that all was in order in Charles' prolonged absence, Tara took the photograph of myself, Vaughan, and Jasper from behind the clock on the mantelshelf. She stared at it for a long time, frowning.

"But why are you all dressed in such old fashioned clothes?" she asked.

I laughed, and made up some story about a 1930s party we had attended a few years ago.

She said, "Daniel, these men are important to you, aren't they?"

It was strange to hear my relationship with my friends described like that, and odd that it was so obvious to her. She was so perceptive that there was nothing I could keep hidden from her. Or almost nothing.

"I suppose because we've been friends for a long time. We understand each other. Often friendship, like love, can't be so easily analysed. It just happens."

She tapped a long fingernail against the picture, indicating Jasper. "And where is he now?"

I had a story prepared. "Jasper moved to America a few years ago and now works in a bank over there."

"And this person, Charles?"

"He lived in India for a time. Last year he moved to Crete. He's a doctor."

"And Ralph, Ralph is a painter, whose work I don't like."

I had one of 'Ralph Wellard's' abstract expressionist canvases hanging above the fire-place, much to Tara's irritation. It was one of the few things on which we did not see eye to eye.

"I'd like to meet your friends," she said.

I kissed her. "The next time Ralph's in London, we'll visit him, okay? But please don't say you hate his paintings."

"And Charles?"

I laughed, "If you really insist, we'll take a holiday in Crete this summer."

She laughed like a child and flung her arms around my neck. "That would be wonderful, Jonathon!"

One morning a few days later, while Tara was in the village on shopping errands, the phone rang. It was Vaughan.

"Edward," I said in surprise. "Where are you?"

"I flew into London yesterday, on business. Listen, Jonathon, I've just had a call from Charles."

"Good God. And?"

"Jasper communicated with him earlier today."

I was speechless. At last I managed, "Thank God he's alive!"

"He was brief, afraid he was being monitored by the Vark. He told Charles that he'd attempt to communicate again in a few days. He said he had urgent news."

"Did he say what?"

"He didn't have time. They spoke for barely twenty seconds, according to Charles. Anyway, he wants us to get over to Crete. Can you make it?"

"Of course."

"There are flights to Iraklion every day. The next leaves tomorrow at three. I've booked two tickets. I'll meet you in the morning at ten outside Waterloo station."

"I'll be there."

Twelve years, I thought. It had been twelve years since Jasper had last communicated with us. What marvels had he experienced in that time? And why had he contacted us now?

I wandered into the garden, where Tara was sitting in the sun. I told her that tomorrow I was flying to Crete to meet Ralph Wellard and Charles.

She sat up. "Perhaps I could join you later, no?"

"I'll arrange a flight. We'll make a long holiday of it, tour the island. How does that sound?"

She hugged me. "Can't wait."

I phoned London, spoke to a couple of flight operators, and booked a ticket for Tara on a flight leaving Gatwick for Iraklion in two days' time.

Later, after dinner, we sat in the garden and watched the sun set. I was looking forward to the trip with more than a little anticipation: it was hard to know what most excited me, the prospect of speaking with Jasper again after so long, or introducing Tara to my friends, and then holidaying in the sun.

The following morning I said goodbye to Tara, caught the train to London, and met Vaughan as arranged at ten. He was driving a hired Jaguar – a far cry from the Austin he'd owned in the thirties. Within seconds of greeting him and climbing into the passenger seat, he glanced across at me and, as shrewd as ever, said, "Well, aren't you going to tell me, Jonathon?"

"What?"

He smiled tolerantly around his pipe. "I don't know what," he said. "But you actually look happy for the first time in years."

So I told him about Tara as he drove, how we met and how things had developed. I told him that she was the most wonderful woman I had ever known.

"So it's love, is it?"

"Very much so," I admitted. "You'll meet her. She's flying out to join me tomorrow."

"You haven't–?" he began, glancing across at me.

I shook my head. "I wouldn't know how to go about it. But I must admit that it crossed my mind to tell her, break it to her gently, if that were possible. I was actually wondering what you'd think about it."

He considered for a while. "My advice, Jonathon, would be to give it time. You've known her what, a few months? Don't rush into it. See what happens in time – you've got plenty of it, after all."

I nodded. "You're right. I'll see how things turn out." "What you've got to remember, Jonathon, is that you have only one dose of the serum to give away." He shook his head. "It's an intolerable situation. How can one be sure that one's made the right decision in this matter? We'll have so much time to regret a wrong choice."

We took off from Heathrow at two, accompanied by a hundred holiday-makers and their riotous children. It was a brilliant summer's day, and I recall looking though the window at the fishing boats, made tiny by our altitude and the breadth of the amazingly blue English channel. I looked ahead to Crete, to the communiqué from Jasper, the holiday with Tara, and was content for the first time in what seemed like aeons.

As we flew high above southern Italy, the jagged coastline sharply defined in the azure Mediterranean, I said to Vaughan, "I really didn't think that we'd ever hear from Jasper again."

"I must admit that I had my doubts," he said. "Don't think me crass, but the fact that Jasper has survived also means that there's still the chance that some day he might open the shanath to Earth. We might actually be able to visit him among the stars."

I considered the idea. "You'd like that?"

He smiled. "Perhaps one day. And you?"

"Like you, perhaps one day. But not in the foreseeable future."

One hour later we landed in the small, dusty airport on the outskirts of the northern port of Iraklion. As I ducked from the plane and descended the steps, squinting against the incendiary dazzle of the Greek sun, the dry heat smote me with the impact of something physical.

We passed through a cursory customs inspection and stepped from the terminal building. Bored taxi drivers lounged against their cabs. At the sight of us, one of them hoisted a sign hand-written on brown cardboard bearing the name: Wellard.

"Nikos?" Vaughan said.

The Cretan smiled, a small, wiry, moustachioed Minotaur of a man. "Mr Wellard, Mr Langham. Welcome to Crete. In one hour you will be eating souvlaki and drinking retsina at Charles' favourite taverna. Come!"

He opened the rear door of the taxi with a theatrical flourish and we climbed inside.

We raced along the northern coast road and then turned inland, heading south through the hills. Nikos seemed to give scant attention to the sharp bends of the road, but negotiated them expertly while addressing us over his shoulder for much of the journey.

Charles lived in a big, stone-built villa on a hilltop overlooking the village of Mirthios. The taxi wound laboriously up little more than a goat track, deposited us outside the villa, and then reversed all the way back down, Nikos waving like a madman through the open window.

"Gentlemen! Greetings!"

Charles Carnegie leaned over the parapet of a vine-covered patio, staring out at the sunset. He had a full head of jet hair, flowing loose to his shoulders, and an intensity of gaze that seemed visionary.

I took his hand. "Charles. You look well."

"Never better! Greek life suits me. I love the people, the work I do in the village is fulfilling. I live for the day, my friends."

We sat on the patio overlooking the village that tumbled down the hillside. I stared across to the almost perfectly circular bay, and the procession of fishing boats chugging into harbour.

"Later we'll dine at a taverna in the village. First, let's have a drink to freshen the appetite."

He filled three small glasses with retsina and proposed a toast. "To my brother," he said.

"To Jasper!" we replied.

Charles refilled our glasses. "Imagine my surprise, just yesterday, when the blue egg began glowing and Jasper called my name. I keep the egg on a shelf in the front room, on the off chance that he should some day call. But I must admit that I had given up all hope of hearing from him again."

"We were discussing the very same thing," I said. "What did he say?"

"It was early. I was about to leave the house on my rounds when I saw the glow. Do you know, but at first I didn't realise what it was, and then I heard my name."

He took a draft of retsina. "Jasper had time only to say that he was fleeing the Vark. He said that he was aboard an interspatial ship, and racing through occupied space. His colleagues had managed to open a secure link, which was how he had contacted me. But he was worried lest the Vark interpret the signal and trace their ship. He was brief. He said he would attempt to open the link again in two days – and that he had urgent news. He also told me to ready the receiver. I was about to ask him what he might be sending us when the link was broken."

"It sounds as though he was in desperate straits," Vaughan said.

"At least he's alive," I said. "We have that to be thankful for."

"If he succeeds in opening the link, then tomorrow morning we might again hear from him. But come, let's eat. Dani's place serves damned fine food!"

We dined well that night on swordfish, and the whole village turned out to greet the doctor's friends. Drinks were pressed upon us, and it seemed impolite to refuse such hospitality. I was regaled by stories of Charles' expertise as a doctor. He was well-liked in the village, and, watching him across the table as he chatted in Greek to his friends, I found it hard to imagine that this was the same man who, before the war, had been so shy and self-effacing.

At some point in the early hours we wended our way back up the hillside to the chirrup of cicadas, the bright sweep of the Milky Way lighting the path.

I collapsed and slept in the front room on an old horsehair settee, and awoke at sunrise surprisingly fresh of mind and looking forward to what the day might bring.

I took a cold shower in an outside stall, and by the time I had finished, Charles was up and frying eggs and bacon in the kitchen.

He arranged a table on the patio, fetched the blue egg and the receiver and placed them upon it. We ate breakfast and drank fine coffee while the sun climbed and we anticipated the communiqué from the stars.

"Not quite the library at Cranley Grange," said Charles.

"But the view is hard to beat," I said.

The hour that marked precisely two days since Jasper's last call – nine o'clock – came and went. Charles made light of the fact. "There might be a hundred reasons he couldn't open the link on time," he said, but left unspoken was the possibility that one of those reasons was the Vark had apprehended the rebels' ship.

I poured more coffee and absently chewed on a wedge of fresh white bread. The sense of anticipation that hung over the table was almost palpable. It was agony to know that our wait was indefinite. For all we knew it might be another twelve years before Jasper managed to communicate again, if at all.

At ten o'clock, Charles jumped up suddenly and paced the patio. Finding its length too restricting, he hurried down the steps and strode back and forth outside. I left the table and sat side-saddle upon the patio wall, staring down the hillside to the bay. Perhaps, if ignored, the blue egg might transmit the communiqué all the sooner...

Urgent news, Jasper had said. I wondered what in his opinion might constitute urgent news. Surely it would be information that concerned the three of us on Earth – why else might Jasper gather us together? If it was news that concerned him alone, some progress report as it were, then surely he would not have described it as urgent. And, also, he wanted to send us something through the receiver. My curiosity was more than a little piqued.

At ten-thirty I gave up hope. Vaughan was pacing the patio, while down below Charles was seated upon a rock and staring out to sea.

I hurried down the steps and joined him.

He turned to me. "What if the Vark did intercept the signal," he said, "and at this very minute Jasper lies dead somewhere between the stars? The hell of it is not knowing."

"If only we had some way of opening the communications channel with him," I said.

The sun climbed, and with it the temperature. Cicadas scratched incessantly like a host of inept bouzouki players. I thought of Tara, who was due to arrive at Iraklion at two, and I hoped that Jasper would communicate before then.

I returned to the house and poured myself a glass of cool water. I was in the kitchen when I heard Vaughan shout out.

"My God! Charles! Jonathon! It's glowing."

I came close to choking on the water, set aside the glass and sprinted to the patio. Charles arrived at the same time and was staring at the egg. It pulsed out its effulgent azure light, illuminating the shaded patio.

"Charles," a voice said, and I did not immediately recognise it as Jasper's.

"We're here!" Charles cried. "Jasper, is that you?"

I sat down heavily, aware that I was sweating and a little faint.

"Charles, my friends," said the voice. "It is indeed I, though changed somewhat over the years. It is long since I have used the English language, and you must forgive me if I stumble somewhat."

"Are you well?" Charles asked. "Did you evade the Vark? What is your urgent message?"

"I am as well as can be expected, seeing as how we have been on the run for the past year. We have temporarily evaded the hunting party, but they are persistent, and no doubt will pick up our trail again."

"Are you still aboard the ship?"

"It is our home, and has been these past thirty-odd years. We are a band of six – four Theerans like Kathan, and a Qar. We are at the moment in a moon port, behind the protective shielding of a tiridium visor. With luck we will be safe until the Qar mind-powers the drive unit and we embark once again into the null-ether. Then we are fair game and the chase will be underway."

"Where are you heading?" Vaughan asked. "How goes the fight against the Vark?"

"We are transporting technology to a rebel planetary system, five thousand light years inward. The battle for the freedom of the galaxy goes well. Not to tempt fate, but we think we have the upper hand."

"And Kathan," I said. "Is he well?"

A silence greeted my question. The egg still glowed, so I was assured that the link had not been broken.

"Jasper?" I said.

"Six months ago, approximately, Kathan was captured by the Vark." Jasper's tone was flat. "Informants within the Vark hegemony have reported his condition. He was still alive, the last we heard, but had suffered much depredation. The Vark have perfected the terrible art of torture, and I dread to think what they might have done to my friend, in order to extract information."

We glanced at each other. I saw in my mind's eye the diminutive figure of Kathan, laid out upon the chesterfield at Cranley Grange.

"Compatriots of ours are attempting his rescue," Jasper reported. "He is a valued leader of the opposition, and we fear the information that he might be forced to divulge. To date he has given up little, but what he has said has proved costly."

He fell silent. It seems, looking back on these events at a remove of years, hard to believe that a trans-galactic battle raged between good and evil while we of Earth went about our business without care or concern. As we listened that morning to Jasper's pained report, however, it was the real world beyond the patio that seemed at once pale and inconsequential.

"It is what Kathan has divulged to the Vark," Jasper continued, "that made necessary this communiqué, and what we subsequently learned from our informant. Do you have the receiver ready, my friends?"

I glanced at the silver box sitting silently beside the glowing egg. "It is here," Charles said.

"Excellent. Make ready for delivery. It is on its way."

Seconds later the receiver glowed with a dazzling white light, and we sat back, covering our eyes from the glare.

The glow abated, and, when next we looked, six objects sat within the receiver. There were three devices that looked like weapons, and three small, oval objects which resembled nothing so much as golden tablets of soap.

"They've arrived safely," Vaughan said.

Charles leaned forward and hesitantly picked up one of the gun-like objects.

It was a device not unlike the serum gun he had transmitted all those years ago. It was jet black, sleek, and incredibly light. For a second I wondered if it was a new batch of the Styrian serum.

I reached into the transmitter and took out an oval object. It seemed to thrum in my hand, as if it were alive.

"My friends," Jasper said. "The pistols are called kree, not dissimilar to the light-beam device deployed by the Vark and Kathan in the clearing, but more powerful and effective. They work by means of pressure upon the green stud at the top of their butts."

"And the other things?" I asked.

"We know them as mereths," Jasper said. "You might be needing the kree and the mereths at some point in the future."

His words sent my pulse racing.

Vaughan leaned forward. "Explain yourself," he said.

"One of the things the Vark learned from Kathan," Jasper said, his voice grave, "was that I transmitted to you the Styrian immortality serum. As you know, Earth and its people are regarded as not advanced enough to join the fraternity. This disqualifies you from the benefit of the advanced technology. The fact that the three of you were in receipt of the serum is decreed by the Vark as a Grade One violation, punishable by death. I might also add that I, too, am under just such a sentence."

He paused there, and we looked at each other before returning our attention to the egg. We were like men in a trance as Jasper spoke again. "On behalf of Kathan, I am sorry. He must have been under intolerable extremes of pain to have divulged this information."

Speaking, I hope, for my friends, I said, "We understand. He cannot be blamed."

Vaughan leaned forward. "You sent us the pistols. You said we will need to protect ourselves..." He paused, his expression grim. "But from what?"

Jasper said, "From our informant we learned that the Vark despatched an assassin to track you down and carry out the death penalty."

Vaughan said, "But the Vark are easily recognisable. An assassin would have great difficulty in sneaking up on us unawares."

The silence from the egg was, I feared, ominous.

"Jasper? I said.

He spoke. "My friends, Vark assassins are a breed apart who can transform their shapes at will, and take on the characteristics of whichever race they go among. Beware! The assassin might even choose the form of an animal in order to track you down. But that is where the mereths come in."

I caressed the oval object. "What are they?" I asked.

"The mereths are detection devices developed by the Styrians in our fight against the oppressors. They detect a Vark at fifty metres, and set up an unpleasant, but silent, tingling sensation when you touch them. I suggest, my friends, that you keep them about your persons from now on."

The silence stretched, and at last Charles said, "Presumably, the Vark assassin will employ a shanath to transport itself to Earth?"

"This is more than likely, yes."

"How might it go about tracking us?" I asked. "Have the Vark some special technology that might detect us from the billions of other humans on the planet?"

"They know your old names only, and that at one point you were based at Cranley Grange – they know of you only what Kathan knew. As far as we are aware, the Vark have no technology that might distinguish you as immortal. The assassin will apprehend you as might any Earth-bound investigator, by means of simple detection."

I hefted the kree in my palm. "We appreciate the warning," I said.

"I wish I could have done more. I have attempted to gain access to a shanath, gentlemen, in order to whisk you away from Earth. However, the prohibitive cost of these devices... And also, to be perfectly honest, you would be at risk wherever you might be in the galaxy."

Charles leaned forward. "When will you next contact us?"

Jasper sighed. "I cannot be sure. Every channel I open increases the danger that we will be detected. It might not be for some time, much as I need the reassurance of your voices. The fight against the Vark is all important. The galaxy will not be free until the very last Vark-controlled planet is liberated."

"We wish you luck," Vaughan said.

"And now, my friends, I must close the link. In one hour the Qar will mind-push us through the ether. I must settle myself into the weapon's nacelle in the event of engagement with a Vark ship. Farewell, my friends, and good luck!"

The blue light faded quickly, leaving the patio in sudden shadow. A long silence predominated, which each of us was loath to break.

We held the light-beam weapons and considered what Jasper had told us.

"Well, gentlemen," Vaughan said at last. "Perhaps we should consider a plan of action?"

"The course of fate is never straight," Charles mused. "Just when I thought I'd found contentment, nemesis raises its ugly head."

"It'll certainly put pay to any complacency we might have slipped into as immortals," I said. "In fact, doesn't it once more add a frisson of excitement to existence – to know again that we are vulnerable?"

"I would rather," Vaughan commented, "be without the danger and suffer the hardship of complacency."

He slipped a kree into the pocket of his jacket, along with a mereth. "You heard what Jasper told us. The assassin might be able to assume whatever form it chooses, but it is limited in its detective capabilities. I think it imperative that we lose no time in changing identities, abandoning the lives we led and adopting new personas."

I nodded. "That makes sense. Charles, can you abandon your newly-found life here?"

Charles stared out beyond the patio, down to the dazzling sea. "There are other just as beautiful areas of Greece," he murmured to himself.

I looked at Vaughan. He smiled. "I'll move from Rome," he said. "I'll continue to paint, but I'll take care and cover my traces."

"And when we've established new identities," I said, "we can meet up again."

"Just so long as we are circumspect," Vaughan said. "The Kings of Eternity forever will be united."

Charles said, "And now? You will stay for one more day, at least? Or would that be to tempt fate?"

Vaughan smiled. "Shall we remain for another day, Jonathon?"

"Tara arrives at two," I said. "I'll bring her here for the night, and in the morning we'll begin a tour of the island."

After that... I thought of the life I had made for myself at Lower Cranley, which for safety's sake I would have to abandon when we returned to England.

I picked up my kree and slipped it into the inside pocket of my jacket. The mereth I concealed in my trouser pocket.

Charles stepped back into the house and returned a minute later with a bottle bound in straw. "Raki," he said. "When I fought with the resistance, we toasted future victories with a shot."

He poured three glasses, and we lifted them high.

"To the Kings of Eternity!" he said.

"To the Kings of Eternity!" Vaughan and I repeated.

That afternoon, Nikos drove me to the airport at Iraklion. Tara had said that she would make her own way to Mirthios – ever independent – but I wanted to surprise her.

The same line of taxis stood outside the low terminal building, and a gaggle of bored drivers lounged beside them as they awaited customers from the London flight. I made my way into the terminal building and stood before the great plate glass window overlooking the runway, along with a dozen other men and women awaiting friends and loved ones.

I saw the plane come in slowly from over the sea, bank and approach the runway. I thought of Tara, and the next few days on Crete. I put to the back of my mind the dire tidings Jasper had passed on earlier – beside the reality of the woman I loved, some alien assassin seemed an abstraction that had no place in my life.

I had seen the world through my eyes alone for too long now; I wanted to see the world as Tara saw it. I wanted to explore the island with her, and then beyond the island. There was no reason, with the funds I had amassed, why we could not explore the world for years to come.

At any rate, such were my fanciful thoughts as I watched the DC-10 taxi to a halt before the terminal building. Ground staff rolled out a flight of steps and a minute later the passengers began to disembark.

I looked for Tara's diminutive figure, my heart pounding at the thought of her in my arms. Perhaps forty people descended from the plane, and then two hostesses, a flight engineer, and a steward. I waited, obscurely worried. I was sure that I had checked every passenger as they alighted, and Tara had not been among them. Had she taken ill, and was still aboard the plane?

A minute later the pilot and co-pilot walked down the steps, and then cleaning staff climbed into the plane.

I moved to where I could see the passengers as they emerged through customs, but Tara was not there. I was sweating by now, despite the fans turning in the ceiling. She had the phone number of the taverna in Mirthios, and I had given her instructions to call the taverna in case of an emergency.

I approached the British Airways desk and asked if a Tara Sayang had been aboard the flight from London. The woman consulted a clip-board, running a red biro down a list of names. She looked up. "According to our records, sir, she boarded the flight. Are you sure she hasn't left the terminal?"

That, of course, was the obvious explanation. Hadn't she told me that she wanted to make her own way south? I had obviously not seen her leave the plane and board a taxi.

I returned to the taxi rank and told Nikos to take me back to Mirthios.

"The lady is not coming, Mr Langham?"

"I think she's already left," I said.

We drove along the coast road, then turned inland and climbed, a cooling breeze flapping in through the open front window. Again I anticipated meeting Tara, introducing her to my friends – if she had not met them already. I was curious as to what she would make of them.

We emerged through a cutting in the hills, and before us was laid out the southern coastline and the breathtaking sight of the shimmering blue Mediterranean. We turned off the main road and approached Mirthios along the winding lane, and then took the track up the hillside to Charles' villa.

Another taxi was drawing to a halt outside the building, and I assumed this to be Tara's. However, as I watched, a short man in a white suit climbed out and regarded the villa.

I said to Nikos, "This is fine. I'll get out here and walk." I paid him off and jumped from the car.

The man was walking towards the villa, and up the steps, and as I approached I knew where I had seen him before. The white suit was distinctive – I had seen him climbing down the steps of the DC-10 from London.

But what of Tara?

My heart commenced a fearful hammering.

I thought the man some harbinger of bad news from Tara, a representative of some hospital or legal firm or... My mind, at that moment, was not rational.

The man in the white suit walked up the steps, crossed the patio and entered the villa.

I hurried after him, frantic for some explanation.

Seconds later I heard the cry, and at the exact instant saw the blinding white flash that illuminated the villa like a nuclear explosion.

I sprinted towards the building and up the steps. I drew my kree and ran into the lounge. Vaughan was lying on the floor beside the settee, a great chunk of his torso burned away.

Charles was barricaded behind the settee, his kree pointing towards the open window.

"He came in and shot Edward!" Charles cried. "I returned fire – I don't think I hit him. He dived through the window. He might be anywhere by now." He was shaking, his voice high with fear.

I fought against the impulse to vomit. I ran across to Vaughan and inspected the damage. He was dead, technically – but the Vark had caught him only a glancing blow.

"It'll be back," I said. "One of us should hide, ambush it. Is there anywhere–?"

Charles pointed to a recessed hatch in the ceiling directly above the settee. "The loft."

"Get up there and wait," I said. "On no condition come down. Even if the Vark gets me, don't come down. It'll be back to finish off Edward sooner or later."

"And you?"

I saw movement through a window at the far end of the room: a flash of white suit behind an olive tree. I fell to the floor and crawled towards the patio. The Vark was circling the villa, attempting, I guessed, to enter via the patio again.

I stopped and hissed at Charles, "Into the loft!"

He obeyed, hauling down the retractable stairs, climbing up, and pulling the stairs after him.

I crawled out onto the patio, then into the kitchen. I stood, crouching, and ran towards the shuttered window. Through the crack between the shutters I sighted the gap between the olive trees where I judged the man in the white suit would emerge.

Seconds later I saw a flash of white suit. I pulled open the shutters and fired my kree. The glare almost blinded me, and the heat of the charge singed my day-old beard.

The beam of light lanced through the window and, more by great fortune than ballistic expertise, found its target. I heard a scream, and then the fire was returned. A blinding white javelin of light missed my head by inches and scorched the far wall: my lucky shot had only injured the Vark.

An injured assassin. Did that make it any more dangerous, like an injured bear? Very strange, the thoughts that pass through one's mind when under stress.

I was face down on the rough floorboards, frantically wondering what to do next. The Vark knew where I was. There was only one way out of the kitchen, apart from the window. I was reluctant to jump through the window, in case the Vark had it covered, and likewise the door. I checked the floor for a trap-door, but that would have been too convenient a means of escape.

A period of profound and very disturbing silence reigned. The only sound was the pulse in my ears.

Then I heard the voice, and I knew the voice.

"Jonathon!" Tara called. "Are you there, Jonathon?"

I wept, then, because I knew; all the clues that my brain had registered, but my conscious mind had refused to take in, came together, and I knew the truth.

To confirm it, to make my nightmare complete, I reached into my pocket and gripped the mereth. It gave off a painful vibration, and I withdrew my hand as if scalded.

"Jonathon!" So sweet! The woman I loved. I almost cried aloud that I was in the kitchen, that she could come for me. I was ready, ready to be taken, ready for oblivion if I were to be denied her love.

I heard footsteps on the stairs to the patio.

The human instinct for survival is fundamental and indomitable. I could so easily have given up then, having had the reason to go on ripped out of my life, but instead I dived through the window and landed with a thud on the ground. I rolled, fetching up behind a pile of logs. I righted myself and peered around the timber at the villa.

The Vark, now in the guise of Tara – tiny, innocent, loving Tara, was crossing the patio towards the lounge... and I knew what I had to do.

I could not rely on Charles to realise what was happening. If Tara entered the lounge and found Vaughan still in one piece...

I ran towards the patio and crept up the steps. She was there, before me, framed in the doorway to the lounge.

I was six feet away. I knelt, raised my kree and took aim.

My finger found the firing stud, but I could not bring myself to fire.

Something stopped me, something innate – the spirit within me, which had lavished love and affection on the woman I had known as Tara, which had built futures based on present happiness, rashly extrapolated years of bliss from just scant weeks of intimacy... How the heart is fooled!

But despite knowing what I knew, despite attempting to press the stud, I could not make my hand respond.

She took a step into the lounge. I saw her raise her weapon, to apply the *coup de grace* to my friend, and still I could not move.

She took another step into the lounge.

"Fire!" I cried to Charles, and Tara turned, her pistol jerking up to sight me, and I stared into her eyes and at that second hoped more than anything that she would fire and put an end to my suffering.

A blinding white pulse of light made me cry out loud.

For a second, Tara stood consumed in actinic fire, her diminutive naked outline searing itself into my consciousness. And as I watched, she changed. The tiny woman in the flame became a tortured, writhing Vark, a scaled screaming reptile squirming as it was cremated in the fire of Charles' kree. The dying assassin cycled through a dozen other personas, the man in the white suit, other alien beings, and then back to the image of Tara, and finally a Vark again, before it exploded and left only an afterimage of burning beauty on my retina, and ashes on the floor.

I slumped to the ground and wept, and for long minutes there was no movement at all, and only silence from within the villa.

Then I heard a sound, and Charles appeared in the doorway holding his kree, and stepped over the dark smear that was all that remained of Tara Sayang, or whatever she had called herself as a Vark.

"Edward..." Charles said.

He moved into the lounge. I followed, stepping over the ashes.

Vaughan lay on his back on the marble floor, a semi-circular burn wound extending from his lower ribs to hip. I knelt beside him. Already the wound was sealing; a diaphanous membrane, a slightly milky film, was coating the surface of his damaged flesh. His eyes were closed, his face expressionless in death. I reached out and felt for a pulse, but found none.

We lifted him onto the settee, and Charles fetched his medical bag. For the next couple of hours he attended to the wound, cleaning the surrounding flesh and cutting away dead tissue.

"I don't think this will help the healing process one little bit," Charles said, looking up at me briefly as he worked, "but it makes me feel useful."

"He'll survive?"

"I'm confident he'll pull through, but it might take time. I was pretty badly mangled back in '43, and the serum worked its magic."

Charles dressed the wound, and I returned to the patio. I found half a bottle of retsina and sat down with my feet lodged on the parapet and stared out at the silent, glimmering bay.

I could not erase from my memory all the small and trivial details of my time with Tara, the love I was sure we had shared. The reality of what she turned out to be in no way diminished the power of the emotions I had experienced then, or recollected now. I wondered at the enemy Jasper was fighting, the evil means they would use to gain what they thought was justice. I imagined a galaxy ruled by such creatures, and I was appalled by the prospect.

How might I be affected by the events of the evening? On a basic human level, disregarding the intellectual knowledge of what Tara turned out to be, I had experienced love for her, and that love could not be undone or denied. How could the experience not make me more cynical or suspicious in future?

I told myself that the circumstances in this instance were exceptional – that the betrayal of my emotion was not a human betrayal, but alien. For my sanity, for the sanctity of my humanity, I could not let it sour my relations with my fellow man. I smiled as I told myself this. It was all very well to be aware of this on some abstract intellectual level, but more difficult to determine how I might be affected psychologically.

A while later Charles called from the lounge. "Jonathon. In here."

I stood carefully, swaying a little. I had finished the retsina, and then helped myself to a bottle of raki. I moved to the lounge, scuffing the ashes, and slumped cross-legged on the floor before the settee.

"He's breathing," Charles said. "I detected a faint pulse a couple of minutes ago."

I reached out and took Vaughan's big, square hand in mine. It was warm, invested with life again.

Minutes later he opened his eyes and looked from me to Charles. "What happened?" he asked, a mere breath.

"The Vark attacked," Charles said. "It hit you. I fired before it could get in a second shot. Don't worry. We killed it."

"How did it find us?" Vaughan asked.

Charles looked at me. "It called your name," he said.

I found the words to say, "It was Tara... She always said that she wanted to meet you."

Vaughan's grip tightened on my hand.

Charles said, "My God, I'm sorry."

Vaughan said, "Jonathon, fetch the raki. I need a drink."

I looked at Charles. He smiled. "I don't think the recovery of this patient will be much retarded by alcohol."

I returned with the raki and poured three glasses. I held a glass to Vaughan's lips and raised my own. "To the Kings of Eternity," I said quietly, and we drank.

Vaughan made slow but steady progress over the course of the next few days. When he was fit enough to stand and walk, Charles rented a house fifty miles along the coast and we moved there for a month while Vaughan regained his strength.

In October we returned to England. While Vaughan remained in London and set about furnishing us with new identities – false passports, birth certificates, identity papers - Charles and I returned to the Grange. It had stood unoccupied since the Second World War, its windows shuttered and furniture covered in dust-sheets. Charles was putting the Grange up for sale, as I was the cottage. We had decided that it was too dangerous to maintain our links with the area, as the Vark were no doubt aware that we could be traced from Cranley Grange and the village.

I left the Grange and walked through Hopton Wood for the very last time. I came to Lower Cranley and the sight of it, the row of quaint cottages, the pub and the nearby church, brought back a slew of bitter memories.

I paused before the door of the coach-house, aware that I had to go through with this. I entered, and set about retrieving the few items I wished to save from my old life. Again and again I came across small reminders of Tara's presence: her toothbrush and cosmetics, a pair of shoes, a blouse... I bundled them all into boxes and left them outside beside the bins.

I made the rounds of the few acquaintances I had in the village, and told them that I was moving to Scotland for a while. I felt, oddly enough, guilty at telling this untruth. I walked back to the Grange with a few possessions in a rucksack, and the rest back at the coach-house boxed up in preparation for storage.

Charles and I returned to London to meet Vaughan and collect our new identities. Then I fled Europe and settled on the island of Antigua in the Caribbean. For years I rarely ventured abroad, and kept my own company. It was a quiet life, untroubled by the Vark.

THE ABOVE RECORD is an accurate account of what happened in Hopton Wood, Cranley Grange, and over the course of my life since. Perhaps my record has not quite caught the despair into which I was plunged from time to time, but it is so very difficult to write about despair, especially one's own.

The year is 1990, and the time has come, once again, for me to assume a new identity. I will meet Vaughan in London and take on another disguise. I feel the need to travel again; maybe Asia. I could call in and visit Charles at his monastic retreat in Bhutan, and from there head north.

And after that?

I like small islands – there is something about them both secure and microcosmic, the world in miniature – and I have been considering a new life somewhere in Greece. I might renew the writer's life again, but who can tell what the future might hold?

I might even take the name of Daniel Langham. I will keep the Christian name of Daniel – I liked the way Sam said it with her soft Canadian burr – and if a Vark assassin should come hunting for me, then so be it.

CHAPTER SIXTEEN

Kallithéa, July, 1999

LANGHAM AWOKE EARLY in the morning, pulled from sleep by the sunlight slanting in through the window. He lay and watched Caroline for a while, admiring her face as she slept as if she had not a care in the world. How different she would be when she awoke, and the realisation of her condition flooded into her stirring consciousness.

He slipped from bed and showered, and she was still sleeping when he returned. He fixed his usual breakfast of black tea, yoghurt and honey, and carried it out onto the patio. This was his favourite time of day, usually, as the sun warmed the air and he contemplated his novel, but today he could not concentrate for considering how he might go about telling Caroline that she need not despair.

She was still asleep thirty minutes later when he returned the dishes to the kitchen, so he took the opportunity to try and write. Much to his surprise, the words came. His subconscious produced its magic and the characters that existed nowhere but in his mind were made real through the medium of fiction.

He surfaced at twelve with a start of guilt, closed his manuscript book and hurried into the bedroom. Caroline was lying on her back, blinking up at the unfamiliar ceiling. She turned her head and gave him a dazzling smile when he entered the room.

"Wondered where I was for a minute then," she whispered. "Could you help me up?"

He assisted her upright, and before she could take a step he enfolded her in his arms and hugged her for a minute, as if to invest her with his strength.

She took small, pained steps to the bathroom, and he left her standing before the basin. "Something to eat?"

"Just an orange juice, and maybe a piece of toast. I'm not a breakfast person."

"Give me a shout when you've finished, okay?"

While she washed, Langham toasted a slice of bread and poured an orange juice. Something about the simple domestic task of preparing food for someone else struck him as tremendously gratifying, and he realised that this would be the first of many such occasions.

He carried the tray out to the patio, sat on the sofa and awaited her summons. It never came; instead, she appeared at the kitchen door, weak but smiling, and walked slowly towards him, gesturing him to sit down when he jumped to his feet to assist her.

"I'm not a complete invalid yet, Daniel."

She joined him on the sofa with a sigh of satisfaction. "Oh, it's beautiful," she said. "You're so lucky, waking to this every morning."

"How are you feeling?"

"Physically weak. Mentally, having stopped lying to you, not too bad."

He took her hand. "I understand why you said what you said. Don't let it worry you."

She smiled. "Do you know something, Daniel? The mornings aren't too bad, or the days, really. It's the nights. The darkness. When the sun goes down... I know it's supposed to be beautiful, but for me it's too... symbolic."

He said, "There speaks the painter."

And he knew, then, when he would divulge his secret. He would wait until the sun went down, and the stars appeared in the heavens, and only then would he tell her that he intended to save her life; it would restore her admiration of sunsets, and perhaps even give her, like him, an appreciation of the stars as symbols of hope.

She drank her juice, but could not eat.

"I wonder if you could do me a massive favour, Daniel?"

"Of course, anything."

"Next time, would you come to London with me? It's so lonely on my own. I know no-one. And to have you there... I know it'll be terrible for you, but–"

He silenced her by taking her fingers and applying gentle pressure. "Shh," he said. "I'll do anything you want."

She closed her eyes and rested her head on the cushion. "You don't know what a relief that is. I was really dreading the next trip."

"There's no need to think about it now," he said.

She was silent for a time, eyes open and staring at the sea. He wondered what she saw; did she see the ocean with a painterly eye, appreciate the aesthetics of its silver-scaled surface, its majestic breadth, or was the ocean a reminder of the many beauteous things she thought she would soon be denied?

"Do you know what I dread, Daniel?" she said in a small voice.

He wanted to tell her to be silent, to dread nothing. I am immortal, he wanted to tell her, and soon you will be, too – but the declaration seemed ludicrous and unbelievable in the harsh light of day.

"I dread," she said, "not being around to watch the boys grow into men. So much of our love for other people is an anticipation of our future with them, our hopes for how things might be. You... I want to see the publication of your next novel. I want to read it, and the one after that, and... and I really want to be able to love you. It seems so cruel – not for me, but for you. If I hadn't come along when I did–"

"If you hadn't come along, I'd still be the old miserable, misanthropic Daniel Langham. What you've given me is inestimable."

She smiled, seemingly close to sleep. "What a lovely, writerly word," she whispered. "Inestimable."

A while later he said, "I'll prepare lunch, okay? You've got to eat."

She nodded. "Okay. The mackerel was delightful. I don't suppose...?"

"There's some left, yes. With salad?"

She reached out suddenly as he made to rise and go to the kitchen. She clutched his hand. "You're a wonderful person, Daniel."

He prepared the salad, taking more care than he would were he making it for himself. That would go for his life in general, from now, he realised; everything he did would be invested with the fact that he was doing it for Caroline. Every word he wrote, every meal he prepared, every sight he saw and observation he made, would be made special by being shared with the woman he loved.

He carried lunch out on a big tray and placed it on the coffee table before her. He was gratified when she ate, and expressed enjoyment of the food.

"I honestly don't know how I might have coped on my own," she said, "and the thought of some hospital, and then a hospice..."

She was silent for a while, eating. Then she paused, staring at her salad. She replaced her fork on the plate. "I know you don't want to talk about this, but I'd rather get it over with now, when I'm able."

"Caroline..."

"No, please, Daniel. I'll say it now, so I don't have to make you hear it again. What I fear, near the end, is being alone. Promise me you'll be with me."

"I promise."

"And I don't want to be buried. Can't stand the idea of being locked in a box." She frowned. "And there's something else: my paintings. I want you to select a dozen, for yourself. And I want you to have *Contemplating the Future.*"

He would have said that he could not accept it, knowing that for Caroline it represented her fear – but the simple fact was that the painting might come to symbolise hope for her, very soon.

They continued eating in silence. After a while, Caroline said, "Daniel, are you calling in at the post office today?"

"I could, if you want me to."

"Only I'm expecting letters from the boys. If you could see if there's anything for me..."

"I need to check my own mail, too."

"I think I'll sleep this afternoon." She smiled at him. "I feel so tired. I've gone downhill so bloody fast!"

"Shh," he said, taking her hand.

After lunch, she did sleep. Langham watched her for a while, planning his afternoon. He would stroll into the village, check the mail, apologise to Georgiou for his absence two days running, and then return and prepare something for dinner. And, later, when the huge red sun plummeted into the ocean, he would produce his journal, and the serum pistol, and tell her the fantastic story of his life.

He moved from the sofa, collected his sun hat, and left the patio.

He passed Caroline's villa, and recalled meeting her just three weeks ago. Christos had dropped the crate outside the house, and she had been sitting upon it, contemplating how she might get it inside. If not for the lethargy of Christos the donkey man, he thought, I might never have met Caroline Platt.

He realised, then, that he was truly happy for the first time in... how long? He had been happy in Tangier for a brief while, with Sam, and then again in Lower Cranley with Tara. Was his happiness dependant upon having a women to love, he wondered? Whatever, he was happy: the future, the vast stretch of the future, beckoned him and Caroline, and the prospect filled him with joy.

When he reached the village and crossed the waterfront, Georgiou rushed out and shook his hand. "We were worried! Two days! I said to Maria, 'Never before has Mr Langham missed a single day. Never! And then two!' We thought you were ill. I was going to come up and check on you, but Maria, she says that you and the English lady..."

Langham smiled. "Caroline's ill. I'm looking after her for a day or two. She'll be fine."

"Say hello to the lady," Georgiou said, releasing his grip on Langham's hand and allowing him to continue.

Yannis had seen him coming and the old, worn teak box was out on the counter.

"Yassous, Mr Langham. We thought you were dead!"

Langham smiled. "Not yet, Yannis, but thanks for your concern."

He leafed through the envelopes, checking first the Ps for Caroline's post – she had none – and the Ls, on the off chance that there was something for him.

He stopped, heart thumping, when he saw the distinctive long, sky blue envelope distinguished by the florid hand of Edward Vaughan.

He ripped open the envelope and pulled out the single hand-written sheet. He read the message, not taking it in, and then began again, working to calm his breathing.

Dear Daniel,

I am writing again as you failed to acknowledge my first letter. In case you didn't receive it, I'll repeat here what I wrote: Charles and I will be arriving on Friday the 24th. Charles is flying in from India tomorrow (the 16th), when we will set sail. Jasper contacted me a week ago with much news. He is opening the shanath when we are all together, then he will tell us more.

By the way, the mereths no longer work – or, rather, the Vark have discovered a means of rendering them ineffective; so be warned, beware.

We'll see you on the jetty at Xanthos around one o'clock on the 24th, all being well.

Signed, Edward Vaughan.

PS, Jasper sends his regards – prepare yourself for revelations.

Langham tried to concentrate. He read the note a third time, and his stomach turned.

What 'first letter', he wondered?

He turned to the post master. "Yannis." He waved the blue envelope. "Was there another letter just like this one, a few days ago? Can you remember seeing a sky blue envelope?"

Yannis stared at Langham as if he'd taken leave of his senses. "Mr Langham," he said with infinite patience. "You came in and picked up the letter yourself, two, maybe three, days ago... You said it was an important letter from a good friend. Mr Langham, are you ill?"

His head throbbed. He leaned against the wall. He knew, of course: he knew what had happened, and he stifled a cry.

The mereth were no longer effective...

Forbes was a Vark!

He read the letter yet again. *Arriving on Friday the 24th... We'll see you on the jetty at Xanthos around one o'clock...*

"Yannis, what's the date today?"

The post master indicated a big digital calendar on the wall. Today was the 24th. Langham looked at his watch. It was one-thirty.

He ran from the post office. One of the village's three taxis was parked outside the barber's shop. The driver was in the process of extricating himself from behind the wheel and heading to the shop when Langham called out. "Taxi! Xanthos!" in his execrable Greek. "But first, up the track as far as you can go!"

He jumped into the back of the car and closed his eyes. He would be too late, of course. He would arrive to find that the Vark assassin had discharged its duty, killed Vaughan and Charles. At this very second, it might be returning to Sarakina to finish its tour of duty by eradicating him...

The taxi seemed to crawl across the waterfront. It edged so slowly up the track towards his villa that he was sure he could have run faster.

The driver braked, having reached as far as he was able. From here, the track narrowed and was impassable. "Wait here!" Langham cried, flinging a ten drachmae note at the startled driver and jumping out.

He ran the rest of the way up the track, arriving out of breath five minutes later. He hurried across the patio and into his study. He unlocked his desk. At the very back of the drawer, unused for years, was the kree. He pulled it from the drawer, slipped it into his pocket, and hurried from the villa.

As he was crossing the patio, he heard, "Daniel, is that you?"

He moved to the sofa. "Caroline, I'm just slipping into Xanthos on business. I won't be long, but I must go. See you soon."

"Daniel!" She reached over the back of the sofa and took his hand. "Promise you'll be back before sunset, okay?"

He squeezed her fingers. "I promise."

He leaned over and kissed her forehead, then ran from the patio.

Halfway down the track to the waiting taxi, a thought occurred to him. He pulled the kree from his pocket, took aim at a sapling beside the path, and fired.

A brilliant burst of incandescence, and the sapling was reduced to a pile of ashes.

He ran the rest of the way to the taxi. "Xanthos," he said. "Quickly!"

He sat back in the seat, exhausted, as the car reversed at speed down the track. Five minutes later they were racing along the high road over the hills to Xanthos.

He pulled Vaughan's letter from his jacket pocket and read it again. *Jasper sends his regards – prepare yourself for revelations.* Jasper would open the shanath when they were all together, and communicate his revelations...

It would all be for nothing if the Vark did its work.

The journey seemed to take for ever, even though they were driving at speed. They came to the highest point of the island, the ridge which afforded a spectacular three hundred and sixty degree view of the land falling away on every side. Ahead, far below, Xanthos came into view, a collection of white-painted buildings contrasting with the brilliant blue of the sea. Langham looked for Vaughan's motor launch, but the jetty where it might be moored was obscured by a tumble of white, sugar-cube buildings.

He willed Vaughan to be late. If the launch was not there when he arrived, then there was hope. He would pay a fisherman to take him out and with luck intercept Vaughan and Charles before they docked.

He nodded to himself, satisfied with the plan. Of course, it was dependent upon Vaughan's being late.

Then he had another, more worrying, thought.

What if Forbes... the Vark... had considered the very same thing? What if the alien assassin had taken a boat out to meet the launch?

He closed his eyes. Such speculation was futile. He could only wait and see what might eventuate in the next fifteen minutes, or however long the damned taxi took to reach Xanthos.

He considered his friends, and how under different circumstances he would have been overjoyed to be meeting them. For the past fifteen years Vaughan had made his home in Cairo, after abandoning his persona of Ralph Wellard, abstract expressionist. He had taken up the piano, with nothing like the success of his artistic career, and was content to play for hire in the many exclusive restaurants and hotel bars of his adopted city. Langham had last seen him five years ago, when he had visited Kallithéa aboard his luxury motor launch. He had seemed content with the life of an itinerant musician, but even then had been considering his next move.

Charles, for his part, still lived a devout existence in a monastery in Bhutan. Langham had not seen him for ten years.

Oh, to see his friends again under less hazardous circumstances! They would eat and drink and reminisce, consider the past and plan for the future. He would introduce them to Caroline...

He might still, if events turned out for the best.

But the Vark were fearsome enemies, and now the assassin had the upper hand. He knew where and when Vaughan and Charles would be arriving, and he had only to apprehend them under some suitable disguise.

They were motoring along the approach road when a terrible thought occurred to him. If, in the ensuing confrontation, the Vark did succeed in eliminating Vaughan, Charles and himself, then Caroline was doomed along with them. He told himself that he should have given her the serum before leaving in the taxi – but he had been in desperate need to get to Xanthos then, and how could he have explained in such haste, short of not explaining at all but forcing immortality upon her?

To ensure that Caroline had the choice, he would have to make sure that he survived; he would have to proceed with care, thinking through every move before he acted, putting himself in the mind of the enemy and second guessing the Vark's intentions... But how did one get inside the mind of an alien assassin?

Speculation was useless. He closed his eyes and tried to calm his thoughts. He slowed his breathing, settled himself. He slipped his hand around the kree in his pocket and gave thanks to Jasper for sending the weapons.

They drove into Xanthos, and Langham directed the driver along the road that gave on to the waterfront. Halfway down the street, he called out, "Stop here..."

Through the windscreen he could see the majestic shape of Vaughan's motor launch, moored alongside the jetty.

And, seated upon the foredeck, he made out three figures.

One of them was unmistakably Edward Vaughan, gone to fat over the years, and tanned, his mane of hair even longer now and silvered by the sun. Beside him was a tanned, shave-skulled figure garbed from head to foot in orange robes. It could only be Charles.

And seated to Charles' right...

Langham felt the blood drain from his face, and a hot fear gripped him. He stared across the waterfront at the three seated figures, drinking and laughing like old friends united – which, to all appearances, they were.

The third figure in the tableau was the perfect double of himself.

To see oneself as others see you... It was, he thought, an uncanny experience. The Vark impostor was wearing the same clothes that he, Langham, was wearing – the same clothes that he had worn, he realised, at his last encounter with Forbes: casual slacks, a white shirt, a pale blue jacket. The Vark appeared relaxed and at ease, tanned, his flaxen hair faded by ten years beneath the Mediterranean sun.

"Turn down the side-street," Langham instructed the driver, and a minute later he passed him a wad of drachmae notes – roughly double the fare – and slipped from the car. He ran back to the end of the street, past strolling tourists, and peered around the corner.

Vaughan, Charles, and the impostor remained seated in deck-chairs on the prow, facing west.

He ducked back around the corner and considered.

Was the Vark waiting for the first opportunity to get Vaughan and Charles alone and out of sight, before killing them? Would it suggest before long that they adjourn below-decks?

But why had it not simply killed them by now, assumed a new identity to evade arrest, and come in search of him?

The letter, of course.

Forbes had intercepted Vaughan's original letter to him. In it, Vaughan had mentioned Jasper's opening the shanath... The Vark had this information and was acting upon it.

If that were so, then it needed Vaughan and Charles alive until Jasper effected communication.

He told himself that he had time in which to act. The Vark would not kill his friends, just yet.

This time, when he peered around the corner, the three men were moving from the prow of the launch, strolling towards the stern of the vessel and the entrance to the cabins...

When they descended the steps and moved from view, Langham hurried down the street and across the road. It was the hottest time of day and there were few people about. He came to the jetty and paced along its sun-warped planks, aware that if Forbes were to look from the launch and see his approach... He banished the thought, concentrated on what he had to do next in order to save his friends.

He came to the boat. Through a brass-encircled porthole he saw movement within the launch: they were in the spacious lounge, then. He increased his pace, lest Forbes notice him, and quickly crossed the gangplank and stepped on deck. He moved to the stern of the vessel, as silently as possible. His hand reached into his jacket pocket and gripped the kree.

The lounge was situated at the prow of the boat. If they had closed the door behind them, then he would be able to move down the corridor without fear of being observed.

He came to the door that gave on to the passage-way, opened it slightly and peered through. The door to the lounge at the far end, perhaps twenty metres away, stood ajar. He judged that he would be able to approach without being seen, just so long as they decided to remain in the room as he approached.

He took deep breaths, steadying his nerves. He peered around the door again, and then stood and crept down the corridor. No matter how hard he tried to be silent, his footsteps seemed deafening.

Seconds later he was outside the door. Through the gap he could see the red carpet of the lounge, a sofa and chairs. He made out a strip of Vaughan's broad back, but saw nothing of the other two.

His heart pounded. To his right was another door, which he recalled gave access to the galley. If he heard movement towards the door, then he could always retreat into that room.

He moved closer to the lounge door and peered through. He could see Vaughan, addressing the others, "When we last spoke, he didn't inform me as to how the war against the Vark was progressing..."

Langham decided that it would be madness to burst into the room and fire before ascertaining the precise location of his doppelganger. Only when he knew where the Vark was standing would he move. He gripped his kree, aware of its lethal power. With luck, he would catch the Vark unawares, unprepared for the assault.

Then he heard the faithful reproduction of his own voice, deep and almost ponderously slow. "A beautiful vessel, my friend."

"Edward certainly knows how to look after himself," Charles said.

Langham judged that the Vark was standing to the left of Vaughan, and that Charles was between them. If he burst into the room now, then surely he could target the Vark and get off a shot before anyone could respond.

He prayed that neither Vaughan nor Charles had a weapon to hand. They would have no hesitation in firing at him, he thought, when he appeared wielding a kree. As far as they knew, the Langham in the lounge with them now was the genuine article.

Vaughan looked at his watch. "Twenty minutes," Langham heard him say. "I positioned the receiver in the centre of the floor so that Jasper can get a reading and locate the shanath a metre to its left. He's on a world called Kerrain, which orbits the star of Alnilam, the middle of the three stars in Orion's belt. To think that, in a little under twenty minutes, we will be standing beneath the light of another sun..."

Langham caught his breath. They were leaving Earth, joining Jasper among the stars. No wonder Vaughan had written and told him to prepare for a revelation!

And no wonder the Vark had not killed Vaughan and Charles earlier, when soon it would be able to account for Jasper, too.

He was about to push through the door when he saw movement beyond the gap. The Vark, his perfect double, moved past Vaughan and appeared in full view, standing side-on to Langham. The Vark was alone, no-one between it and the door, no-one nearby to get caught in the fire...

He knew that this was it. He had to act. He raised his kree. He counted to three, and then made his move.

He shouldered the door open and fired at the startled facsimile of himself.

He would look back, later, and wonder how something that should have been so simple could have gone so wrong.

The lance of light missed the Vark by inches, hitting the far wall and reducing it to a charred mess. The Vark dived to the floor and rolled, and Vaughan and Charles cried out loud in fear and startlement.

Before Langham could sight the Vark and fire again, he saw Charles draw his own kree and take aim at him.

The following sequence of events seemed to occur in slow motion, and he recalled them later as a series of terrifying freeze frame images.

Charles raised his kree and thumbed the fire stud, and at that second the Vark produced its own light-beam weapon and, turning towards Charles, fired. Charles exploded in an actinic detonation of light, blinding Langham and drawing a pained moan from Vaughan. For a long second, Charles' outline showed as a tortured, twisted silhouette, and then vanished.

The Vark fired again, this time at Langham, who rolled and eluded the light-beam. He came up against an armchair, raised his kree and fired just as the Vark was swinging around to fire for a third time.

Langham saw his beam hit the Vark – hit his mirror image – and illuminate the room with its sun-burst radiation. The

Vark screamed and convulsed within the fire, and it lost its hold on its Langham-persona. Langham saw the figure of Forbes appear, briefly, and then the Vark was itself, a bipedal saurian creature tortured and writhing in the annihilating fire. The entire sequence lasted perhaps five seconds, before the assassin winked out of existence and a ringing silence filled the room.

"The other..." Vaughan stammered, "The other Langham? A Vark?"

"It found me on the island, intercepted your first letter."

Vaughan slumped into a sitting position against the far wall, his tanned face ashen with horror. Langham gathered himself and stood.

He stared at the charcoal stain on the scorched carpet which was all the remained of Charles Carnegie.

"If I'd hit the Vark with my first shot..."

Vaughan shook his head. "You did all you could. Had you not intervened, then God knows what havoc the Vark would have wrought." He gestured, lifted his hand and pointed at the place where Charles had stood, just minutes ago. "He was telling me as we sailed here," Vaughan whispered, "that he was prepared for death. He said his meditations had made him realise that, even though he was immortal, death was natural and that he would die one day, as would we all."

Langham considered. "He came a long way, Vaughan. I've thought about dying, but I'm not ready yet. I have... there's so much to experience, so much to live for." He looked up, across at Vaughan. "Are you joining Jasper out there?"

"I've had enough of Earth," Vaughan said, "for the time being. I've done so much, experienced pretty much all there is to experience. I need something new. I was hoping to explore the galaxy with Charles and Jasper." He paused, smiling sadly. "And you? Will you be joining us?"

Langham smiled. "Who knows?" he said. "Maybe one day."

"But not today?"

"I've met someone, Edward. She means everything to me."

"You mean...?" Vaughan stared at him. "The serum?"

Langham nodded. "I'll ask her, of course, if she wants to become like us. I'll tell her everything. I think she'll join me. I know she's the one, the one with whom I want to share the dubious gift."

"You have only one choice, Langham," Vaughan said. "Eternity is a very long time."

Langham smiled. "We might not be together for ever," he said. "I know that love can't last that long. It would be selfish to hope it would. But of all the people I've ever known, she's the one who most deserves the opportunity of experiencing more than what we're normally allowed."

"She must be an incredible person," Vaughan said. "Maybe, one day, we will meet."

Langham looked across the room, to where the receiver sat upon the floor. "How long before...?" he asked.

Vaughan looked at his watch. "Jasper said he would open the jump gate at three o'clock our time," he said. "We're about a minute away."

They sat in silence for a minute, and then two. Langham was about to comment on Jasper's characteristic unpunctuality when the air of the room became charged, and a second later a blue glow appeared at head height, a fist-sized ball, which expanded with a breathtaking rush. It hung, an oval six feet high, in the air above the shanath's base.

Langham stood, and Vaughan with him, and together they approached the pulsing blue interface.

As they stared, the blue light cleared, and both men stood back involuntarily, dazzled for a second.

Langham squinted, and made out a strange garden scene, full of weird blooms and vines, with a house-like construct in the mid-ground, except the building had no walls and the garden extended into it.

Jasper Carnegie stood before the construct, staring through the portal at them – but a Jasper much altered from the man Langham had known all those years ago. The skin of his face and arms was iridescent, his face gaunt and attenuated, and yet something uniquely Jasper remained.

"Gentlemen!" he cried. "You cannot imagine my joy! Welcome to Kerrain, my home. A more beautiful world you will never experience. But quickly, I can maintain the link for minutes only, as the cost is prohibitively colossal. Please, step through."

Langham said, "I'm remaining on Earth, Jasper. Maybe in time, when I've tired of this world..."

"I will attempt to communicate more often," Jasper said, "now that the war is almost over."

Vaughan stepped forward. "You mean...?"

Jasper smiled, the iridescent swirls of his face shifting like rainbows in a kaleidoscope. "The Vark are defeated. They hold out on one or two planets, but they are routed. The galaxy is free at last, and peaceable once again. Slave worlds are no longer in thrall, and all across the face of the inhabited galaxy the many peoples of the many worlds can go abroad without fear. Truly, it is a wondrous age in which to experience the teeming universe!"

I thought of Kathan, who the last I heard was a prisoner of the Vark. "And Kathan?" I asked. "What of him?"

"You will be pleased to know that the rescue attempt was a complete success. The insurgency party penetrated the Vark stronghold and extricated the majority of him intact."

"The majority?" I said.

"He was enmeshed in a particularly bestial Vark implement of torture at the time," Jasper said.

"But he is fit and whole now?"

"Fit and whole and due to join me here within the week."

"Jasper," Vaughan said, "if only the news from this end were as sanguine."

Jasper Carnegie stepped forward and peered through the portal. "I see no sign of Charles."

"A Vark assassin found us," Langham said. "There was a brief fight. Without the weapons you sent us, we would be dead."

"And Charles?" Jasper said, resignation in his tone.

"I'm sorry," Vaughan said. "Charles did not survive."

Jasper nodded his attenuated head. "Another brave casualty in the war against oppression," he murmured. "You killed the Vark?"

Langham nodded.

"Thank you, gentlemen, for breaking it to me. I am cheered that you survived so that we might meet again and renew our friendship." He looked at Langham. "Are you sure I cannot tempt you with the wonders of this world?"

Langham smiled. "Not this time, Jasper. But I hope to join you, one day."

Vaughan turned to Langham. "I'll be in touch," he said, first shaking Langham by the hand, and then taking him in an embrace like the hug of a bear.

"Take care out there, Vaughan. My thoughts will be with you."

Vaughan stepped towards the jump gate, then turned. "Take the receiver with you, and the blue egg." He indicated the egg upon the sideboard. He smiled. "And the launch is yours, a parting gift."

"Farewell," Langham said.

"Oh, those days at Cranley Grange seem like an eternity away already!" Vaughan said, then stepped through the interface, passed from one world to another, with one short stride, and became a part of the strange alien garden.

Vaughan approached Jasper Carnegie and embraced his friend, and then both men faced the portal and lifted their hands.

"To the Kings of Eternity!" Langham said.

"To the Kings of Eternity!" Vaughan and Jasper replied from across the light years.

Langham waved, and seconds later the alien garden, and the two men with it, vanished as if they had never been.

CHAPTER SEVENTEEN

Kallithéa, July, 1999

He stepped from the taxi and walked up the track towards his villa. It was almost six, and the sun was falling through the pine trees to his left. He would keep his promise to Caroline and be back by sunset.

He passed her villa, and paused beside the place where, mere weeks ago, they had first met. He wept, then, whether at the good fortune that had brought her into his life, or at the thought that soon he would save her, or at Charles' death, he was unable to say. He felt possessed by a sensation at once joyous and sad, and quite inexplicable.

He continued up the track and came to his villa. He paused to stare at the whitewashed walls, its peaked terracotta tiled roof. Within was the woman he loved, with no knowledge at all of the surprise he had in store for her.

He stepped onto the patio and deposited the shanath, the blue egg, the kree gun and his mereth on the table. He looked around, and his heart almost missed a beat. Caroline was not seated upon the sofa. He entered the villa and called her name, then stepped back onto the patio and rushed to the railings. He peered over, irrationally, fearing what he might find. The cliff-face fell, sheer, to the sea far below.

"Daniel?"

He turned. She stood, framed in the doorway, wearing a baggy white t-shirt and faded jeans.

He hurried over to her and took her in his arms.

"Daniel! Where've you been? My God, your face is burned! What on earth have you been doing?"

He laughed. "It's a long story, Caroline. And you wouldn't believe it."

"Try me."

"After dinner, okay? When we're watching the sun set and the stars come out. How are you feeling?"

"So-so. I'm hungry, which I suppose is a good sign." She stopped, staring over his shoulder at the table. "What are those?"

He assisted her over to the table. "That's... well, we call it a blue egg; this a kree gun, this a mereth, and this a shanath. They're all part of the story."

She picked up the egg. "But it's beautiful, Daniel. Tell me what it is!"

"I can't. It has its place in the story I want to tell you. I can't tell you about it out of context."

She stared at him, head cocked, and then smiled. "I don't know what's going on, Daniel."

"I'm having a shower. Then I'll cook something. What would you like?"

"I don't know. Surprise me."

He showered, and then stood and stared at his reflection in the mirror. His forehead, where the Vark's light-beam had missed him by inches, was red raw.

He moved to the kitchen, poured himself a wine and Caroline an orange juice, and quickly prepared a salad with cold ham – he was impatient to tell Caroline the story.

They ate on the sofa and watched the sun go down, and Langham considered the miracle of all the sunsets on all the many planets of the galaxy. He drained his wine and poured another.

They finished the meal, and Caroline turned to him and said, "Okay, now out with it. The whole story, from beginning to end. No prevarication."

"One minute," he said. "The props."

He cleared away the dishes while she watched, amused. He moved into the villa and from the desk in his study took the serum pistol and the yellowing manuscript. He collected the blue egg, the kree gun, the mereth and the shanath from the table on the patio and carried everything over to the sofa.

He placed the shanath at one end of the coffee table, the blue egg next to it, followed by the kree gun, the mereth and the serum pistol, and last of all the manuscript.

"My God," Caroline said, "even more. What are they?"

"The Styrian serum pistol," he said, "and the manuscript."

She was shaking her head in bafflement, staring at the ranked objects. "They all sound like something from a science-fiction novel!"

He smiled. "I suppose they could be," he said, "but this novel actually happened."

He looked into the night sky, and he felt tears prickling his eyes. "Oh, my God," he said, pointing. "Look!"

She followed the direction of his forefinger. "Orion?" she said.

He stared at the central star of the hunter's belt, Alnilam, and tears rolled down his cheeks.

"Daniel?" she said, concerned.

He would tell her that he could save her, that he could bestow upon her the dubious gift of eternal life. It was a miracle, and conferred upon the subject wonderful experiences, but it was a gift not without terrible consequences. He would tell her that he would make her, like him, immortal, but that while she would be spared the depredations of time, others around her, friends and loved ones, would not. She would see her sons age and eventually die, and everyone she knew would grow decrepit and defunct likewise; she would watch societies rise and fall, whole epochs of history come and go; she would watch humankind destroy portions of itself in senseless wars, witness the ravages of plagues and famines... Unless, of course, they decided to flee this planet and journey among the stars and behold who knew what joys and tragedies out there also.

But he would tell her that he loved her, and that although their love might not last the test of eternity, their friendship would. He would ask her to trust him, and that whatever befell them over the millennia ahead, he would be there for her; she could rely on him now, and forever.

She leaned against him, hugging his arm like a frightened child. "The darkness," she said in a small voice, "the stars... I'm frightened, Daniel."

He placed an arm around her. "You have no reason to be," he murmured.

"I think I have."

He stroked her hair. "No reason at all, Caroline. You see, I can save you."

She looked at him, her eyes widening when she saw the tears coursing down his cheeks. "Daniel, how can you be so cruel?"

"Because it's true," he said. He pointed to Orion. "You are my Queen of Eternity, and the stars are my witness."

He passed her the manuscript. "This will explain the details," he went on, "but first I want to tell you the simple truth."

The middle star of Orion's belt twinkled, and Langham thought of Vaughan and Jasper beneath the light of the distant sun.

"Caroline," he said, "I am immortal. I will be one hundred years old next week."

She stared at him, her eyes wide, and opened her mouth to speak – but no words came.

He put his arm around her, and told her the story of his life, and above the glittering sea, all across the heavens, the massed and hopeful stars were beckoning.

ABOUT THE AUTHOR

Eric Brown's first short story was published in *Interzone* in 1987, and he sold his first novel, *Meridian Days*, in 1992. He has won the British Science Fiction Award twice for his short stories and has published forty books: SF novels, collections, books for teenagers and younger children, and he writes a monthly SF review column for the *Guardian*. His latest books include the novels *Guardians of the Phoenix* and *Engineman*, for Solaris Books.

He is married to the writer and mediaevalist Finn Sinclair and they have a daughter, Freya.

His website can be found at: www.ericbrown.co.uk